pendragon's heir

Pendragon's Heir

Books by Suzannah Rowntree

Non-Fiction

The Epic of Reformation: A Guide to the Faerie Queene

War Games: Classic Fiction for the Christian Life

Fiction

Pendragon's Heir

The Rakshasa's Bride: A Fairy Tale Retold

pen dra gon's heir

SUZANNAH ROWNTREE

Amica mitis, hic liber multos patronos habuit.
Sed, Schuyler, tu maximum fecisti.

Orkney

The Scots' Land

Britain

Lothian

Cambernic

+ Carlisle

Gore

Listinoise

+ Eboracum

Estrangore

+ Wigan

Norgales

Sorestan

Celidoine

Wales Powys

Logres

Cameliard

Lydaneg

Trinovant

Caerleon

+ Camelot

Magrance

Dumnonia

Lyonesse

Cornwall

Part I

The · choice · of · Worlds

I

Gloucestershire, AD 1900

Enter these enchanted woods,
You who dare.

Meredith

t began on the day of her eighteenth birthday. Blanche Pendragon woke that morning with Simon Corbin's note burning a hole in her awareness from where it lay under her pillow. She burrowed a hand under her head to touch the paper and lay there nibbling her lip in indecision until the clock downstairs struck half-six in a rich and muffled boom that echoed through the whole house. As the backwash of sound faded, Blanche slipped out of bed and began to dress. Half an hour later she stole out of the house by the back door and hurried between garden-beds and under blossom-laden fruit-trees to the gate between the orchard and the hills.

There was a young man leaning against the other side of the gate, looking out at the hills with folded arms. Blanche stopped walking. After all, shouldn't she have burned his note and refused to come? There was still time to slip back to the house, now, before he turned—

He turned and saw her and something that might have been a smile touched his thin secretive lips. All her misgivings faded away and she went up to the gate and put out her hand.

"Good morning, Mr Corbin. I'm sorry if I kept you waiting."

"Good morning, Blanche." Instead of shaking her hand, he bent over it with an oddly ceremonial gesture, and she felt the shiver of his breath across her skin. "Many happy returns of this happy day."

She pulled her hand back, hoping that the sudden pleasurable warmth in her cheeks was not too visible. "You wanted to see me?"

"Yes." He indicated a bag in the grass at his feet. "I am on my way to

1

Lydney to catch the London train, and I could not allow your birthday to pass without some token of my regard."

There. See? It was all perfectly proper and respectable. Blanche felt a little contemptuous of herself for the scruples that had haunted her since Kitty Walker passed his note to her yesterday afternoon.

Mr Corbin reached into the pocket of his coat and drew out a box, which he presented with a flourish. "Miss Pendragon."

She slipped off the lid and took out a little hourglass hanging on a silver pivot from a black ribbon, its belly full of twinkling black sand.

"Oh, it's beautiful!"

"You like it."

Her guardian, the antiquarian, who invested every colour, gemstone, beast, and planet with arcane and symbolic meaning, would likely give her a lecture on saturnine influences. Blanche decided not to care. "Yes, I do." She threw a wry smile up at Mr Corbin. "Sir Ector wouldn't."

He reached out and closed her hand over the box. "Then don't wear it where he will see it."

She couldn't do that; if her guardian didn't see the pendant, her lady's-companion Nerys would, and both of them would be hurt by her attempted deceit. Blanche smiled, trying to look daring and devil-may-care.

"Oh, I'm not afraid to wear it. And thank you. It was sweet of you to walk so far out of your way." She backed a few steps, signalling that it was time for him to move on and catch his train.

"Wait," he said, and leaned over the gate. "Miss Walker means to take a motor to Tintern Abbey next week. Won't you come?"

"Oh! I'd love to. When will it be?"

"Sunday."

Blanche's face fell. "Oh. *Perhaps* Sir Ector would let me go. But there will be church, and…"

The beginnings of a smile pulled at Mr Corbin's face. "Oh, the Galilean can spare you for a day, surely?"

She bit her lip to keep from smiling, and failed. He saw, and the amusement deepened in the corners of his mouth.

"Yet one day I shall convince you to become a Freethinker, too."

"Oh, I could never do that." But she did admire the casual way he carried it off, as if impiety was no great risk to a man of his worth. She backed another step. "Maybe Sir Ector will let me come. I'll ask. No, I'll beg." And with a laugh, she hurried away as quickly as she had come.

AT DINNER THAT EVENING, SIR ECTOR L'Espée was talking about the relief of Kimberly when he inevitably lost himself in historical minutiae and began lecturing on Roman cavalry. At last he paused between caltrops and stirrups to sip his wine and Nerys, from the other side of the table, said: "Blanche dear, I've never seen that before."

Blanche put her fingers up to the hourglass around her neck, and her heart sank a little. So there *would* be trouble. "It was a gift."

Sir Ector put down his wineglass, dabbed at his frost-white moustache, and leaned closer to see. "Someone has a morbid taste. Who was it?"

"It's from Simon Corbin."

"When did he call?" Nerys did not change her expression, or the mild tone of her voice, but Blanche thought she could sense reproof.

"I was walking this morning and met him going down to the train at Lydney. It wasn't improper in the *least*."

Nerys's eyebrow flickered up at Blanche's defensive tone, but she made no further comment. Only the air around her grew a little cooler. Blanche sensed that, too, and heaved a sigh at her plate, wishing Nerys could forget about being a chaperone, just for a moment.

Sir Ector said, "Have him come to dinner some day. I should like to meet your friend Simon Corbin."

Blanche poked at her food. "All right. I'll tell him next time."

Sir Ector looked at Nerys. Nerys looked at Blanche. "You know that your guardian would prefer to know your friends, Blanche. Especially such a close friend as Mr Corbin."

"I know it," said Blanche. She kept her voice sweet, but spoiled the effect by stabbing a potato. "He isn't such a close friend, anyway. I'll give the hourglass back if you don't like it."

Sir Ector blinked and said, "Give it back? Not if you really like it, Blanche."

She nodded and took another bite, not looking away from her food. After a moment's silence, Sir Ector's fork scraped his plate and she knew the discussion was over. But silence hung on them all, becoming more difficult to lift with every moment. Blanche felt a quiver of melancholy in the air and glanced opposite, to Nerys.

It was odd that her young companion, who went so quietly clad in grey with never one black hair out of place, who spoke so reluctantly and so rarely changed expression, should be so legible in her moods. It was also odd that nothing seemed bleaker than Nerys's melancholy, which might only be provoked by a birthday dinner gone sour, but held in itself all the tears shed since the beginning of the world. Blanche felt sorry for her petulance over the hourglass. She gathered all of her strength against the chill in the air and said with cumbersome gaiety:

"Why, Nerys, you look so thoughtful. Come, stop frowning like that. The wind will change, and where will you be then?" She leaned forward and whispered. "Remember what happened to the Queen when Prince Albert died—they say the wind changed at the funeral and she *never smiled again.*"

Nerys looked up gravely. "I'd not heard it." But there was a silver shimmer through the tone of her voice that hinted at laughter deep below the surface, and her shoulders went back a little, and the mood in the room lightened.

Blanche turned to Sir Ector. "Kitty Walker has asked me to go with some friends to see Tintern Abbey on Sunday, in the new motor-car."

"Sunday?" Sir Ector frowned.

"I know," Blanche said, "but Kitty's London friends are visiting, and I've never been riding in a motor before. And I haven't missed a service once this year."

"You might miss Evensong on Sunday, then. Perhaps Miss Walker can delay her excursion until after the morning service."

"I'll ask her." It was, she supposed, the most she could hope for. Still, it would be too bad to miss the jaunt and spoil the day for the sake of a few hours at church.

They finished dinner and went into the library, where Blanche made tea for Nerys and herself and coffee for Sir Ector. Nerys took a book into a corner, but Blanche stood in front of the fire to warm herself, leaving her saucer on the tray so that she could curl both hands around the teacup. Sir Ector sank into an armchair.

"Well!" he said in a comfortable murmur.

She turned and smiled, unsure whether he was about to make a birthday speech or relapse into another comfortable silence.

"Well," he repeated, "you're eighteen, Blanche."

The birthday speech it would be. "Yes. Not for another forty-two years will the word 'sweet' alliterate with my age."

He smiled as though he hadn't heard the joke, and she realised that a birthday speech was no time for banter. He'd laced his fingers together and was running each thumb in turn over the other.

"Blanche, I…there's something I've been putting off telling you. About your parents."

Her parents.

She'd never known them. She didn't even know their names. It was years now since she'd been curious.

Why had he waited until now?

Something hot fell onto her hand and Blanche looked down to see the tea in her cup rippling. She took a deep breath, replaced the cup on its saucer, and wiped her fingers before asking, "Is it very bad? The truth, I mean?"

"No, no." Sir Ector's voice died away. At last he looked at her under bushy brows, almost shyly, as if in fear of some rejection. "You may find it difficult to believe."

A quick, warm affection rose in her throat for him. "Tell me and see."

Sir Ector looked into the fire, fidgeting with something in his pocket.

"I have something for you," he said at last. "It was your mother's." And he drew out the thing in his pocket and held it up to her.

The ring Blanche took from him was antique silver, cabochon-set with a glimmering moonstone. Her mother's ring! Blanche folded it into her hand and held tightly to the only thing her parents had left her. There had never been anything else, not even a faded photograph or some old letters.

"I don't even know her name."

"Look inside."

There was a lamp on the mantelpiece and Blanche held the ring up to its pearly glow. Spidery engraved letters ran all round the inside of the band. " '*Guinevera casta vera.*' Guinevera?"

"Your mother."

Blanche twisted the ring onto her finger, thinking what a sentimental old-fashioned couple they must have been, rather like her guardian with his old gallantries and his Old French. She couldn't resist a chuckle. "What was my father's name? 'Arthur, King of the Britons'?"

Before the words crossed her lips, Blanche knew they were a mistake. Sir Ector dropped his head, and the shadows hid his face. When he rose, that shyly eager air was gone and he thrust his hands into his pockets with feigned briskness. "Well," he said, "that reminds me. I must work on my address to the Newport Antiquities Society."

Over in the corner, Nerys rustled to her feet.

"No, forgive me," Blanche begged, feeling inarticulately guilty, as if she had killed something small and helpless by accident. "I shouldn't have joked like that. Won't you tell me some more about them?"

Sir Ector smiled wistfully and kissed her forehead. "Soon, Blanche. When you're ready to hear. Goodnight."

"Goodnight." She went to the door and held it open for Nerys, who had the tea-tray. The lady's-companion passed and went down the hall, but Blanche lingered, looking back from the threshold. "Still—my father. Can't you tell me his name? Please? Now that I know Mother's?"

Sir Ector, riffling through the papers on his desk, stopped at the sound of her voice and leaned his hands on the oil-smooth wood. He didn't look up; only his shoulders lifted, then sank in a long slow sigh.

"No," he said, and to Blanche's ears, there was a bald honesty in his voice that allowed only one interpretation.

"Well, goodnight." Blanche, trying not to let mortification seep into her voice, closed the door, and went slowly down the dark corridor to the stairs. In her unlit room she looked again at the ring clenched in her hand, but now it was only a glint in the starlight. So it *was* very bad. A sense of revulsion gripped her stomach, contempt both for herself and for her mother. *Casta vera!*

She tossed the ring onto her dressing-table and began to undress. She was sitting at the table in her nightgown and peignoir, unpinning her hair, when a knock came on the door and Nerys entered.

Blanche glanced up and forced a smile. Nerys, without a word, picked up the hairbrush and began to work on Blanche's hair. It was no part of her duties, but Nerys was as patient with knots as with everything else, and Blanche leaned back with a little sigh. She stared at the two heads in the mirror, her own flame-haired, day-eyed; Nerys's moon-skinned, night-haired. After a moment she put her hands up to her throat and took off the little black hourglass.

She wondered why, since they so obviously distrusted Simon Corbin, Sir Ector and Nerys couldn't state their suspicions plainly. Was it because he was a Freethinker? At least, she thought with a twinge, a Freethinker would think no less of her for being ill-born.

She put the hourglass on the table next to the moonstone ring and said, "I like Mr Corbin, and I hoped you would like him too."

Nerys looked through the mirror at her with a glimmer of surprise, but then dropped her eyes back to Blanche's tawny-red hair.

Blanche spoke as patiently as she knew how. "What's the matter? Why do you not approve of him?"

Nerys shook her head. "I hardly know him well enough to approve or disapprove. I've only spoken to him once."

"I know he isn't conventional," Blanche said. "But he always speaks his mind and he doesn't let other people shame him into thinking differently."

"I think…" said Nerys.

She so rarely put the shifting transparency of her moods into words. "Go on," said Blanche, when the silence threatened to lengthen.

"I think it will take you a long time to know such a man. I cannot read him at all." She lifted worried eyes to Blanche.

"He is so full of news and events," Blanche said. "I like to hear about such things without getting tangled up in Roman cavalry tactics."

Nerys smiled before she could stop herself, and then tried to look disapproving. Blanche laughed at her. Nerys moved further up Blanche's hair, changing the subject.

"Are you going on errands with Emmeline tomorrow?"

"I did all my visiting today."

"Really? You went to see Mrs Jones, and the bricklayer's family?"

"No." Blanche picked up her mother's ring and fidgeted. "We met Kitty when we stopped in the street, and then we ran out of time to chatter Welsh with the parishioners."

It was, of course, unfair to say *we*, because it was no one's fault but hers that the time had run away, and no vicar's daughter could be more conscientious than Emmeline.

"Oh, Blanche. You know what Sir Ector says."

"I know." Blanche quoted. " 'A wise princess will not only feel sorrow when she sees people in affliction, but roll up her sleeves and help them as much as she can.' It's from that medieval book he gave me for my last birthday. I had to translate the whole thing from Middle French."

"You will be grateful for it one day," said Nerys, in a gentle tone that robbed the words of any possible sting.

Blanche grimaced. "I sometimes think that Sir Ector sees himself as some medieval lord, and me as a medieval princess. What will he ask me to do next? Intercede with him for the peasantry, as Christine de Pisan recommends, or learn siege warfare so that I can defend the house while he's away?"

"Both a good use of your time," said Nerys, with no hint of laughter. "When do you mean to visit Mrs Jones?"

"Christine said to send alms by a servant, and anonymously, 'by the example of monseigneur Saint Nicholas'." She shot an impudent grin at Nerys, and then admitted, "Emmeline will be busy tomorrow with the

Infants' Bible Study. We have agreed to go the day after, so you need not worry. In the meantime I shall be as medieval as I know how, and languish about like Burne-Jones's Briar Rose."

That night she dreamed about the King again.

She stood in a riverside meadow between greenwood and castle. Overhead the sun shone gilt in a sky like powdered lapis and struck golden sparks from the King's blood-red dragon banner.

For the hundredth time, she half-closed her eyes against the fiery colour of meadow flowers and silken pavilions. For the hundredth time a blinding glint from someone's mailed shoulder forced her to blink and turn her head to see the King.

In crown and heraldic red robes, bearded, belted, bear-like, he sat enthroned by an oak tree with two wolf-hounds at his feet. Youthful vigour lay couchant in his gigantic limbs and in his big veined hands, but his level look was grave and wise. There was a sheathed sword lying across his knees, and his fingers moved up and down the scabbard as though it could make music.

A harper sat at his right hand, mouth open in song. At something the minstrel said, graceful feminine heads swayed and laughed all around, and white hands clapped, scattering flashes of colour from undersleeve and lining. Yet no sound reached Blanche's ears. Unlike the vision, it had been lost long ago.

By the King on his left hand sat the Queen in a shower of silver-blonde hair that fell unbound to her hips. When she smiled it was to herself, secretly, as if to a jest only she heard. With the ladies round about she was tying may-thorn hoops, but then she looked up—this was Blanche's favourite part—and her mouth seemed to shape Blanche's name. In a turmoil of green robes she came forward, arms opening.

Blanche woke.

On most nights it was easy to turn over and go back to sleep, but tonight wakefulness caught and held. At last she slid out of bed and tiptoed to her dressing-table, feeling across it for her mother's ring. It slid onto her finger. She couldn't feel the spidery words against her skin, but she remembered them. *Guinevere*.

Guinevere was the name of a queen from legend. Like the one in the dream she had had since childhood.

Impossible thoughts wheeled through her mind.

In the next room, she heard Nerys moving, opening her wardrobe door…

For years, Nerys had woken her at midnight on her birthday, and they had stolen downstairs to have hot cocoa and cake by the kitchen fire. Blanche was much too old for midnight feasts now, of course. And it was a night too late. Still…they were both awake. And she wanted some company.

Blanche shrugged into her peignoir and went out into the hall. There was no answer to her tap at Nerys's door. Blanche hesitated, and nearly gave up and went back to bed. Then she remembered the creak of the wardrobe door. Perhaps she had knocked too softly. She twisted the handle, cracked the door ajar, and peeped in, whispering, "Nerys?"

There was light in the room. The curtains had been pulled back, and moonlight pooled on the floor. But the wardrobe door also sat ajar, and from it came a warm golden glow…

Nerys was nowhere to be seen.

Blanche assumed, yawning, that Nerys must have left a lamp burning in there. It seemed a dangerous thing to do, and she closed the door behind her and crossed the room to the wardrobe.

She opened the door and saw at once that there was no lamp. It was more like…

…more like *daylight*.

Blanche blinked at the light, and her heart skipped a little faster, but she was too curious to be frightened. Instead she ducked her head and stepped through the wardrobe door.

SHE EMERGED FROM A BIG WOODEN chest, up-ended so that its lid functioned like a door. Blanche glanced about her, and for a moment imagined that her childhood dream had come to life. A swift rush of gladness took her by the throat and almost knocked her to her knees. It was just like waking the morning after a nightmare to discover that one's worst fears had not, after all, come true. Then she shook herself, a little ashamed of the notion. Did she *want* to live in a picture-book? And her waking life was hardly a nightmare. She looked around again, with a more critical eye.

She stood in a pavilion, surrounded by the spicy smell of the woods on a warm spring morning full of light and birdsong. The pavilion itself was just like the ones in her dream, made of imperious saffron-coloured silk that rippled in the morning breeze. Sunlight filtered through the wall and drenched the pavilion's interior with rosy light.

It was like standing inside a jewel, and the pavilion's furniture was rich enough to do it justice. There was a couch, chairs, and a low table all made from carved and inlaid wood. On the table goblets and bread and apples and roasted meat were set out.

And still Nerys was nowhere to be seen.

Blanche stood without moving for a space, head bent to listen. Apart from the sighing of the breeze and the sound of birds, she could hear nothing. She was in a lonely place, then, and not (alas!) in the busy meadow of her dream.

Curious to see the place to which she had wandered, she began to move forward, lifting her eyes from the ground—and with a gasp, saw she was no longer alone. The flap of the tent was still falling without a whisper of sound behind a newcomer.

He was young and savage and dirty, reeking of horses, clad in skins. There was a knife almost as long as her forearm strapped to his calf, and he carried a pair of javelins with knapped-stone blades point-down in one hand.

He spoke.

"*Duw a rodo da ywch, arglwyddes.*"

Logres

—O mother
How can ye keep me tether'd to you?—Shame.
Man am I grown, a man's work must I do.
Follow the deer? Follow Christ, the King,
Live pure, speak true, right wrong, follow the King—
Else, wherefore born?

Tennyson

In the days when a man might travel from one end of Britain to the other without leaving the shade of the greenwood if he kept his word, let his sword rest lightly in its sheath, and watched for foes, when roads were hard to find and friends harder, and fire and steel the first necessities of life—long ago, deep in the hills of Wales, there lived a boy and his mother.

The boy's name was Perceval, and all the days he could remember he had run wild in the woods wearing deerskin and wolfpelts, knowing no enemies but wolves and wolf's-head outlaws, knowing no human company but that of his mother. But hers was enough. In her stories, in the long passages she had him memorise, and in the unknown languages in which she drilled him until he could speak and understand them with ease, lay a door to the outside world that had captured his imagination.

This could be ignored in the winter, when the world was dead and the cold and hunger bit so hard that survival took all their time and energy. But when each spring came and the sun gathered warmth and the whole forest woke into life, the call sounded more insistently to leave the hidden hills and go out into the world of men and deeds.

Last spring, for the first time, he had told his mother what he felt, for the need to be up and doing was too strong now to be ignored.

"I know I must stay and care for you, Mother," he finished, half

11

ashamed of the confession.

But she sat silently for a while and her answer, when it came, was the last thing he expected.

"Oh, Perceval, a falcon is born to hunt, and so are you. One day you will hunt indeed—but not yet."

"Why? Am I not ready?"

She looked at him sadly and said, "Give me a little longer."

That year his mother had barely given him a moment's rest. Odd requests sent him roaming far into the wilds or kept him scratching figures into the walls of their cave: the kindling of a lantern on a rocky western coast, a calculation of how the stars would stand at the vernal equinox. Old lessons, too, had to be repeated from beginning to end, and discussed in conversations that tested not only his grasp of the contents but also his fluency in the Latin, or Greek, or occasionally even Saxon or Irish to which his mother would change mid-speech.

This spring the call was back, biting harder than ever.

He had prowled far to the north on this particular morning, armed with the slender darts he made himself, when he saw the riders.

There were three of them, mailed and jingling. At their saddlebows hung vivid shields and iron helms; by their stirrups rode lances. In the dappled wood they made a bright splash of colour, and Perceval was pierced with the longing to ride with them to strange countries and stranger adventures.

On that impulse he stepped out into the road and hailed them.

The strangers reined in. Startled hands tightened on hilts and lances, but then relaxed at the sight of the boy in wolf-pelts. "Who calls?" asked the foremost, a dark man with a lean scarred face.

"First tell me who *you* are," said Perceval, so eager that his breath lagged behind his words. "Do you come from Heaven like the angels? Or are you fays from the other world?"

"Neither," was the answer. "We are not angels, though we serve the King of Heaven. Of the elves you, perhaps, may know more than we do."

"What are you, then?"

"Men. Knights who serve Arthur Pendragon the High King. I, Lancelot, hold these lands of him."

Perceval stood stock-still, thinking, for so long that the man went on with a smile: "Will you hold for me a corner of this wood? Then you may catechise whom you wish."

"No; only tell me this," said Perceval. "Where may I find your King? I should like to be a knight."

One of the men behind Lancelot coughed as though smothering a laugh, but Lancelot replied gravely. "I counsel you to go in search of him, sir, for it is the Pendragon's chief delight to grant such boons to bold men. Yet there are conditions. You must keep yourself either to gentle words or hard blows, and you must defend the weak and poor."

"I will do these things," said Perceval with a gesture of easy assurance, and the knight smiled again.

"Then travel east and a little south. When you come to broader lands there will be others to point the way."

Perceval lifted his darts in salute. "We will meet again," he said, and vanished into the forest.

THAT EVENING WHEN PERCEVAL CAME HOME his mother was sitting outside the cave, sewing in the last light of the sun. He exchanged greetings and dropped to a crouch beside her. Words had never come to him with difficulty, and he had had all afternoon to think the matter over.

"I went north today," he told her without preface, "and I met three knights who said they served the High King Arthur and the King of Heaven. And there is nothing else in the world I would rather do or be."

As she had the year before when he first told her his dreams, his mother sat in silence. Her needle went in and out of the patch on her old blue cloak many times before she answered, and the sadness was there in her voice again, but heavier. "Perceval, you must understand. It is not an easy life: full of wanderings, woundings, dangers, and death. In the end, always death."

"But those come to us and all mortals, Mother. Why! Would you discourage me, after all this time?"

For the length of a breath, her face was still and pale as stone. "To all mortals, yes. I know this is your calling, Perceval. But I cannot follow you when you go. If you go east, I must go west, and an end will come of me in Britain. Will you not stay another year?"

"No, Mother." He pointed to the chain about her neck. "I must follow my father's calling. You said it yourself on the night of the frost, when I speared the man from the hills."

"Then you have guessed," she said. "Yes. It was the Pendragon of Britain whom your father served, and loved better than a brother. And your father gave this to me before you were born." She lifted the chain over her head. From it hung a golden ring with a fire-red stone.

"Tell me why," he said, as he had when he was a little boy.

Her lips moved in a weary smile. "A knight will give a lady a ring from his hand and take a kiss from her lips, when he wishes to love her and serve her all his days," she recited, as she had when he was small. She pulled the ring from the chain and held it out to him. "This ring is the knight's who swore to serve me. Take it. One day you may find a lady to wear it."

Before the sun was up, Perceval kissed his mother goodbye. "Go to the King at Camelot," she told him. "Remember what I have taught you. Your father was among the mightiest of the knights of Logres."

"I will be a son worthy of him."

Perceval's mother looked up at him. Her grey eyes opened on him like fathomless wells of thought. Perceval found himself holding his breath dizzily to hear the echo of his words splashing into their depths.

"And you will be a son worthy of him," she said. Then he blinked, and she was his mother again; and she turned her head aside so that he could see only the white swell of her cheek, but heard her sigh: "Alas…"

He rode away in the rain on Llech, his little grey pony. His mother stood outside the cave watching him go; she waved once when he looked back. Then Perceval fixed his eyes on the forest ahead, and knew that the trees were clouding her from view, and he never saw her in the world again but once.

HE WOUND DOWN THROUGH THE WOODS and hills of Wales, sometimes walking and sometimes riding the clammy, muddy little pony he had taken for the journey. The rain drizzled steadily, dripped down his neck, and turned the pony's grey coat black. In the soggy valleys, Llech's hooves sank deep into the mire. It occurred to Perceval once that perhaps summer would be a pleasanter time for travel. But it never came into his mind to look back now, with the world and adventure ahead.

When he came to the River Usk, at the border of his world, he forded it, turned, and followed it south-east through the hills, pressing on as quickly as possible, up strange hill and down unknown dale until the land around him began to change. The hills fell gentler and lower, the trees thinned, and the river gathered strength and girth.

It was late on the second day, as the sun began to set, that he emerged from the forest and stared down one last long slope to a rolling plain, where the Usk turned and ran away south to the sea. Perceval stared at the scene in amazement. All his life he had lived in thickly-wooded hill-country. There were more hills and trees in the distance, but down in the plain lay short-cropped pastures with many sheep and cattle, the first farmland he had seen.

He rode down the hill, turning his head from side to side to drink in the view. Far away on the right, he glimpsed the sea and what might be more land beyond.

Perceval rode straight to the village, but was stopped by the sentry at the gate, who came running out of the little guard-house pulling on his helm. He squinted at Perceval and snapped, "What do you want here?"

"Your hospitality, fair sir," said Perceval. "I have travelled far today."

"Go on!" said the gate-warden. "You're one of those elvish folk from the hills. Steal a man's breath from his mouth if it weren't nailed down."

Perceval blinked in surprise. "I—"

"No," said the gate-warden. "Move on. We've trouble enough without your kind adding to it." He put his hands on his hips and planted himself in the gate, glowering.

"Certainly. Only tell me in which direction is Camelot."

"Straight east. Why are you riding there?"

"To be a knight," replied the wild boy, and faded into the dusk with his dirty pony before the man could gather breath to reply. Before night he had coaxed Llech to swim the river and was among the trees on the other side.

Perceval lit a fire, huddled into his pelts, and closed his eyes. He was hardened to the cold and wet and slept lightly, darts in hand. Long before dawn came, he toasted the last of his mother's bread over the reawakened fire and was on his way across the hills, straight for the rising sun. He camped near the Wye that evening, found a ford by which to cross in the morning, and kept on until he came to a high treeless ridge overlooking low wooded hills and the glimmer of water, and saw nestled within them green pastures studded with little farms and animals like ants. The distant lowlands looked sunny and warm, but up here on the ridge blew an icy wind that seemed to turn the sun cold.

There was one tree, an oak, not very old, but gnarled and disfigured. On it a brace of ravens sat complaining. If there had been a stone lying on the ground, Perceval would have tossed it at them.

He was distracted from his surroundings by Llech, who buried his head in the grass and began tearing up wads of it, roots and all. Perceval slid down from the pony's back, letting the halter trail on the ground. Llech moved off a pace or two. "Well, then," Perceval said to him. "Eat if you like, but I see a pool down the hill, and I am thirsty enough to swallow all of it."

He strode through the grass, then slid down the steep slope, taking care not to make a sound, for he was beginning to hunger for fresh meat. At the slope's foot he found a little, dark, deep mere, with strands of early-morning fog still clinging to its surface, very secret in the hills and the wood. But Perceval saw immediately that he was not alone. There on the other side of the lake, mirrored in its surface, stood a bright saffron-coloured pavilion still limp with morning dew.

Perceval went warily toward the strange structure. Trampled grass showed where horses and men had walked around the pavilion, but he could hear no sound of voice or harness. He lifted the tent flap and went in.

There was a gasp, and he was looking into the startled face of a tall and stately damsel, crowned with hair like flame.

BLANCHE WAS SURE, NOW, THAT SHE wasn't dreaming. Her heart was hammering too hard for this to be a dream.

The young savage spoke again in the shushing tone she used herself to calm a horse. *"Duw a rodo da ywch"*—but now suddenly the words made sense to her. It was Welsh. It was a greeting in Welsh. She knew Welsh because Sir Ector insisted that she practice it often when she went to visit poor folk in the village.

"Good morning," she said in the same language, and swallowed hard.

He looked at the food on the table by the couch. "I have travelled far, damsel, and am very hungry."

Blanche edged away from the table, closer to the wooden chest which led back into Nerys's bedroom. "Eat," she said with an imploring gesture.

He went to the table, dropped into a low crouch, and began to eat with great tearing bites, never taking his eyes from her face. Caught in that gaze she dared not turn and bolt into the wooden chest, so she stood motionless staring back at him. He was lean and brown, all bone and sinew. There were white scars and scabbed cuts on his bare arms and legs and the skin wrinkled like old leather at his knees and elbows. Above all that his face was incongruously young, so young that she began to fear him a little less. Then for the first time she really saw the look in his eyes, so frankly admiring that she turned her head away with an angry blush, and the taste of dread came back.

He ate half of the food exactly: one of the bannocks, one of the apples, and one of the collops of meat, wolfed down in less time than she thought possible. There were two cups on the table as well, and when he had finished everything else, he sniffed and tasted the wine. Immediately he spat it onto the grass.

"It has gone sour," he said, seeing her horrified look.

She shook her head at him, lest he suspect her of meaning him harm. "It's wine. It should taste like that."

He replaced the goblet on the table and rose to his feet, picking up the javelins again.

"I thank you for the food, damsel," he said, but he made no move to leave. Blanche tried to think of something to say, but before she could open her mouth he moved forward and caught her hand, even as she shied away. She smelled smoke and sweat and horse.

"Be not frightened," he said, very earnestly, pulling her back to face him. "I will serve you. I will give you a ring for this one."

She looked at him blankly, then glanced down at her hand.

The ring of Guinevere.

"It was my mother's," she murmured, but her mouth had gone dry and no sound came from her lips, and she was already reaching up with her free hand to pull off the jewel. Let him have it, if he would only leave her. And who was her mother, anyway?

He took the ring and dropped it into the pouch that hung from his belt, and produced another, gold with a blood-red stone, which he slid onto her hand where her mother's ring had been.

"I thank you, damsel." And he leaned forward and kissed her, very quickly but fiercely, on the mouth.

When he had kissed her he released her and fell back a step, looking doubtful, as if suddenly aware that he had trespassed some boundary. At that look Blanche's mind began to work again, and she found she was clenching her hands into fists by her sides.

"You had best run," she told him coldly. "My guardian is near, and if he finds you here he will kill you."

He fell back another few steps, said "Be well, damsel," and turning on his heel left as silently as he had come. Only the flap of the pavilion shivered to show that he had been.

Blanche stood rigid for as long as it took to count to a hundred before she sank onto the couch. Now that the boy had left, she began to shake. In vain she told herself that he had not hurt her, and (after another moment) that she did not think he would have. She threw her arms around herself in an absurdly literal attempt to pull herself together. And what of the country in the wardrobe? And what of the sun, shining in the night?

There was a rustling sound in the grass outside, and Blanche bolted to her feet. If it should be the boy again—

It was Nerys: hair loose, robed in blue, looking more like a queen than a lady's companion. But when she saw how Blanche was trembling, she came forward with quick compassion.

Blanche flew into her arms and gasped, "Oh, Nerys—I was looking for you, and there was a savage man, and—"

"Shh," Nerys said, as if she were a mother comforting a frightened child. "Nimue never—I didn't know of it until a moment ago."

Blanche pulled away when she realised that she had been clinging for safety to a woman whose head nearly fitted under her chin. In embarrassment she changed the subject. "Nerys, why is it morning here?"

Nerys sighed, a long slow breath of regret. Instead of answering, she said, "Blanche, you're very tired. Sleep."

"No," Blanche protested. She wrenched away from Nerys and staggered toward the pavilion door with some idea of retrieving her mother's ring, if she could. "He won't be far—"

The words thickened like syrup on her tongue, even as she pulled aside the flap of the pavilion. Outside, she saw a dark pool and a forest under a bleak ridge. She took another step forward, missed her footing, and fell...

When Blanche opened her eyes, she was curled into her own warm bed early on a frosty spring morning.

So it had all been a dream. She could even feel the cabochon-set ring on her finger; the threads of worry, pulled tight in her mind, came loose and drifted. She had woken from the nightmare, and it was not true after all.

She slid the ring off her finger and brought it out from under the covers. But it was not her mother's ring. Red-gold it shone in the grey dawn light, red-gold as the ring which the stranger in the pavilion had given her.

For if he live, that hath you done despite,
He shall you do due recompense again,
Or else his wrong with greater puissance maintain.

Spenser

It was a feast-day when Perceval came to the High King's city of Camelot, riding in an uneasy fog of thought, for he began to wonder if his mother might not have meant something different by her instructions about the ring. Once he had become a knight, he thought, he would go in quest of the damsel of the pavilion, and if he had done wrong, he might yet give her reason to forgive him.

Camelot castle stood on a hill in a low wide valley opening toward a plain on the south, a labyrinthine many-spired place melting into the noisy little town at its feet. A river came down out of the northern hills to moat the town and castle, the eastern bank of which was good black farmland, but the western bank was weaving forest.

Llech distrusted the bridge. He stepped onto it only after persuasion, and when he heard the hollow thud of his hooves on the wood he threw up his head and plunged into the crowded street, swerving around to face the echoes when he had reached safety. Perceval, accustomed to riding bareback, kept his seat easily and glanced about for the sentries. They stared, but made no move to challenge him. And no wonder! Turning Llech to continue up the street, Perceval saw farmers, beggars, knights, tumblers, jugglers, minstrels, kegs of ale, and the blazing colours of best clothes.

Someone called out, "Come and have a drink, stranger!" but Perceval replied, "Not I! I am going to the King."

His voice was almost swallowed by a ringing clatter on the bridge. Llech shied around again to see, and Perceval saw a knight in gilded armour upon a mighty horse like a thunderhead bearing down upon them. For a confused moment Perceval's pony planted his feet and balked. A voice grated out of the knight's helm, "Way, fellow," and the iron figure hefted the butt of his spear to sweep Perceval aside. In the nick of time Llech danced out of the way. With a rush the knight clattered past, up the hill toward the keep, leaving merrymakers tossed in his wake.

"Follow that oafish one," someone called to Perceval. "He's off to the King, no doubt."

Perceval heard and dug his heels into the pony's sides. Up the hill they cantered among the protests left in the knight's trail, and trotted beneath a massive carved door-lintel into a high-roofed hall rippling with bright banners. Here under soaring arches in the light of a hundred high windows stood a great round table in the midst of the hall, scores of men seated around it talking and eating and laughing. Perceval looked once, then again, and his stomach quaked as he realised that he was in the presence of the greatest warriors of the world, each one tried and tempered on the field of war.

Could he prove himself worthy to sit among them? For the space of a breath he was glad that none of them saw him come in. They were falling silent, staring at the gilded knight, who trotted between the round table and the long straight tables that flanked it on each side toward the King's seat at the head of the hall.

Here at the Table the King sat enthroned (pewter-grey hair the King had, and the marks of war on his hands, but piercing eyes that would be wise in judgement); the pale Queen stood beside him with an upraised goblet of silver and glass, and words dying away on her lips. The gilded knight swung down from his horse and strode toward them without a pause. "Who is this," he shouted, "who is this that stands at the head of the Round Table to pledge them all to truth and virtue, and is herself no better than a common stale?"

There was the rattle of a chair sliding across cobbles, a raking up of rushes, and a flash of light as a blade was drawn. One of the knights, on the far side of the table, was on his feet, moving—the King, more slowly, rose from his seat—the gilded knight snatched the cup from the Queen's hand even while he spoke.

And flung the wine in her face.

"A fig for the Table," the ruffian was shouting, with a laugh, over the uproar of shouts and falling chairs. Perceval saw the King say a soft word, and a lean grey shadow leaped from under his chair. The gilded knight vaulted to his horse as the hound sprang with bared teeth and straining red maw for his heels. Then the warhorse neighed and lashed out with a hoof. The dog scrabbled uselessly across the floor; another heartbeat, and the gilded knight was gone with the drumming of hooves.

Above it all the Queen of Britain stood still, wine dripping from her face, her mouth pressed shut in a white and wordless fury which swept impersonally across Perceval and all the people gathered in the hall before alighting on the King. Arthur turned to meet it and with a curiously practical gesture offered her a napkin. Then everyone was talking at once—the knights around the table, the ladies in the galleries above, the plain people at their low tables. But in the midst of the commotion, the man who had risen from his seat at the table when the strange knight first snatched the Queen's cup now sheathed his sword, stalked up the hall to the King and said, low and grinding: "Give me leave, lord, and I'll beat him like a dog."

It was the hawk-faced knight Perceval had met in the Welsh forest, the man called Lancelot. His words would have gone unmarked in the clamour but for the hush which fell upon the hall when he came to the King.

Every face was turned upon the knight Lancelot as he stood before the High King of Britain. The Queen bent her head and pressed the napkin to her eyes. Only the injured hound whimpered from the corner.

Crash! A knotted fist smacked the table, making the cups jump, and its owner—a stocky, bull-headed man—growled, "Sire! I'll go."

"Gawain!" said Lancelot. "Of your courtesy, this is my fight. Sire, give me the quest!"

Perceval knew that if he waited another moment his own chance would pass. He kicked Llech into a trot and rode to the head of the table, scattering attendants. "My lord king, a boon!"

The King had stood unmoved amid the outcry, but when Perceval spoke he turned his head and looked from the muddy pony to its skin-clad rider, and a gleam shone in his eye. "Speak, good fellow."

"My lord, send me to avenge this insult, and let me receive knighthood when I have proven myself."

"What!" A very tall man who, when the knight came, had leaned back and begun to crack nuts, laughed at Perceval. "Look at him! Darts and rabbit-skin armour! One look down that knight's spear and he'll run back to his pig-pen. Go away, boy, this is work for knights."

If Perceval had doubts about facing the enemy knight, he lost them now. "I came here to be knighted," he said loud enough for everyone to hear, "but I see I must have an iron pot to put my head in. Very good! I will ride after that knight and equip me with his spoils, and I will bring back the goblet to the Queen."

The man laughed again. But one of the damsels who had come to tend the Queen went to Perceval smiling.

"Sir Perceval, the flower of knighthood," she said. And she curtseyed to him.

The tall man jumped up, knocking his chair over behind him. "Spiteful imp! You live here a year, refusing to smile or speak, and now you smile at this puppy in the face of King Arthur and the Table Round, and call him the flower of knighthood?" Before Perceval could stop him, he had reached out and cuffed the girl's ear.

"Kay," said the King, quietly, but Perceval saw the man named Kay flinch at his tone like a dog coming to heel. "Will you prove the knights of the Table no better than their enemies? Be sure you will suffer for that." He turned to Perceval. "I grant your boon, boy. Follow that stranger. When you return bearing the cup, and wearing the armour, the knighthood is yours."

Perceval did not hear the murmur of protest that rose in the hall; he hissed in a breath through teeth clenched on the foretaste of victory. He had no words for thanks, but he bowed his head low to the mane of his pony. Before he turned, he spoke to the knight called Kay. "I also swear—when I return, you will pay for that blow." He set heels to Llech's sides and went out the gate and down the hill at a reckless canter.

Folk at the castle gate pointed north when he asked in a shout for directions, and Perceval and his pony went thundering up the road, the mount toiling gamely, the rider laughing and brandishing his darts.

PERCEVAL CAUGHT UP WITH THE THIEF of the goblet a league from Camelot on a slope running down into the forest. The knight was walking his horse, evidently not in dread of pursuit, and though he glanced behind when he first heard Llech's hooves, he paid no more attention to the pony or its rider until Perceval came within a spear's length and hallooed. "Turn around and face me, coward knight!"

Ahead, the knight yanked his horse around and gripped his lance. "Do you think to fight me?" he asked, laughter in his voice. "Which swine-shed did they raid to find you?"

"They keep wolves where I come from," Perceval said. "Why should I fear a sneaking dog? Be on your guard!"

The gilded knight gestured behind Perceval, where the road ran over the crest of the hill. "Run home, boy, and send one of those knights on the hill to fight me. I see the bars of Lancelot, and I did not dare this adventure to fight with such as you."

Perceval did not spare a glance over his shoulder, but he breathed slowly once to calm the fire in his belly. So if he died here today, the pale Queen had other avengers. And if he lived, his victory had witnesses. He took a dart, balancing it in his hand, choosing it with as much care as his next words. "Buckle to fight," he said. "If I allow it, you may yet live to boast of the day you met Perceval of Wales."

Within his helm, the knight snorted in derision.

"Besides, I go in need of arms, and I mean not to leave without yours."

"I should only dishonour my blade on you, boy."

"No fear of that," said Perceval, and grinned. "You have seen to that already."

The knight spurred his horse forward suddenly and swiped at Perceval's head with his spear-butt. Perceval ducked, and the blow fell on his left shoulder, momentarily numbing the arm. He forced a laugh.

"I only ever allowed my mother to beat me," he said, "and even she could hit harder than that!"

His enemy drew back up the hill, set his spear in rest, and came thundering down toward Perceval. The spear passed through empty air, for Perceval slid aside and down and clung to his dozing pony with just one arm and leg thrown athwart the back.

"Hah! You call yourself a knight!" he mocked, pulling himself upright. "First you go to spear an unarmed man, and then you run away down the hillside!"

The knight kicked his horse around and drew his sword, galloping back up the hill. Perceval waited for his chance. The distance between him and the knight closed to only a few yards before he lifted and flicked his arm. The dart flew true, striking home in the slit of the knight's visor.

The dead man toppled backward and fell to the ground at Llech's feet. With a snort, the pony awoke.

Perceval slipped to the ground, kicked the sword away from the body, yanked out his dart, and knelt to listen at the visor slit for breath. There was not a sound. Opening the knight's wallet, he found the Queen's cup and set it carefully in the grass by the road. Then he began to tap at the joints of the armour, and managed to slide off one of the knight's gauntlets. He glanced up the hill, wishing that the two knights on the crest would come and help him, but they had ridden after the dead man's horse.

Perceval unclasped the knight's belt and sword, and laid them in the road. He pulled off the wine-coloured surcoat and began searching for an opening in the mail. There was a leather lacing at the neck, where the helm was attached, and when he undid it and lifted the helm he saw the face of the man he had killed—his eyeball a bleeding mess, his pale, sweat-streaked face looking idiotically surprised. It was not the first time Perceval had killed a man, but it was the first time he had had to disarm a body. He thought of pulling the knight through the gorget, but the effort was obviously useless. He sat back, trying not to retch.

There was only one thing he could think of—fire. He scraped up a pile of tinder and took a flint from his pouch.

At that moment he heard the clatter of hooves and looked up to see the two knights who had followed him, Lancelot who bore red bars on a field of white, and the one named Gawain, whose sign was a five-pointed golden star.

"What are you doing now, boy?" asked the knight of the star.

"He is dead," said Perceval, working at the flint. "And I need his armour."

"And the fire?"

"Out of the iron, burn the tree," said Perceval, quoting a saying of his mother's.

Sir Gawain laughed. "There is no need to burn the man," he said, dismounting. "Let me show you."

He showed Perceval how to unlace the armour and draw it off, and with Sir Lancelot's help armed him, belted on the sword, and put shield and lance into his hands.

"Will you return to Camelot?" Sir Lancelot asked.

"Not today, sir," said Perceval. "Take the Queen's cup back to her. Tell her how I avenged the insult, and tell the chieftain of Britain how I bore his trust. But I will not go back myself until I have proved myself in a better fashion, with knightly weapons."

"You have proved yourself well enough," said Gawain. "If you will not come back to Camelot, let me knight you now."

So Sir Gawain knighted Perceval there on the road, and the two knights took the Queen's cup and left him. But Sir Perceval rode away into the forest, leading Llech with the bundle of skins and darts strapped to his back.

He rode north and west, choosing the loneliest paths, and at sunset he came to a castle on a green lawn beside a lake bathed in golden light. On the lawn an old grey-haired man stood watching a group of boys shooting with arrows at a mark. To him Perceval approached and said, "May I lie here tonight? I am weary, and have travelled far."

"Surely you may," said the old man, "and longer, if you will. What is your errand in this country?"

"I am a new-made knight," said Perceval. "But I have never used arms before, and so I am riding out to find some adventure on which to test them."

The old man laughed. "You had best stay awhile with me, and learn the use of them first," he said. "Come! It is long since I trained a knight, but I remember the old art well."

I was afeared of her face though she fair were,
And said, "Mercy, Madame, what is this to mean?"
Langland

lanche was still staring at the red-gold ring when she went downstairs to the dining-room and found Nerys making tea. The girl was wearing quiet grey and her raven hair was pinned up at the nape of her neck: surely, thought Blanche, the unearthly beauty that had been hers in the dream of the pavilion could not have shone from this meek shadow. The contrast was so strong and sudden that Blanche slid the ring back onto her finger, sure now that she had been mistaken and the ring had been red all along. She would say nothing.

At breakfast Sir Ector said "Good morning" absent-mindedly, and if he had noticed the change in the ring—or that she was wearing a ring at all—he did not say. After the meal, Blanche went upstairs to wrestle with the *Aeneid*. Sir Ector had insisted she learn Latin when she was small, and still expected her to construe a hundred lines or so every day, although he allowed her to choose her reading.

It was while fumbling with a particularly difficult line that Blanche's mind began to wander and she remembered the inscription that had been in the ring Sir Ector had given her last night. *Guinevere, chaste and true*. She tugged once at the gold ring before the awful truth hit her and she looked down at it again with her stomach quaking.

She could not have dreamed that talk in the library. She could not have dreamed the inscription, and if it was not on this ring, then this was a different ring and sometime during the night, in who knows what place or time, a ring had been taken from her finger and replaced.

She touched her mouth. Her breath shivered against cold fingers.

Slowly, Blanche drew the ring from her finger. She sat there a moment longer, holding the heavy jewel without looking at it. Then she turned it and saw—nothing. No words spidered within the band.

Blanche sat in her chair a moment longer, thinking. Then, quite calmly, she rose from the desk and went—her feet soundless as the dream of the meadow—downstairs to the library.

The door stood ajar. She lifted her hand and laid it on the door, but could not for a moment gather the courage to push it open.

Then she heard Nerys speaking in a soft and urgent staccato: "But the time is growing short. That was Nimue's message. Again, and more often, I hear a rumour on the night airs—"

"She isn't ready, Nerys."

Ready for what? Blanche strained her ears over the thump of her own heart and the muffled protests of conscience. Nerys said: "I know. But how long have we already waited?"

Sir Ector did not reply and for one brief moment Blanche heard the shushing murmur of Nerys's skirts. When she spoke again, it was in Welsh, and there was an odd cadence in her voice:

"Sir, I have not the wit nor craft to know what might be coming upon us, or from which quarter. But be sure that either it is coming, or it is already here. And this place will not shield us when it comes."

Blanche blinked at the dim-pale shadow of her hand spread out across the massy oak panels of the library door. What was coming?

Suddenly the door twitched away from under her hand. Light struck her in the face and she looked into Nerys's eyes with a guilty start.

Nerys said nothing and Blanche could detect no sign of contempt in her expression. But even a scolding would have been easier to bear than that level unblinking gaze. Blanche flushed painfully and stammered. "I—I—"

Sir Ector came to her rescue. "Blanche, my dear, come in."

Nerys moved aside. With another start Blanche remembered why she had come. She went forward to her guardian's desk, put the red-gold ring down on the blotter, and looked up at Sir Ector as if hoping that he would explain the change in such a way that she could go on believing that this safe corner of the world so shrouded in comfort was the waking, and that the adventure in the pavilion and the dread in Nerys's voice was the dream.

"What does it mean?" she said. "What am I unready for? What is coming?"

Sir Ector lifted his hand to his beard and tugged on it with an odd gesture of helplessness. He looked at Nerys.

"You tell her, damsel."

"Damsel," repeated Blanche, and her stomach grew a little colder.

Nerys took both Blanche's hands and led her to a chair. "Some wine," she said over her shoulder to Sir Ector. Then, with a sympathy that shone from every look and word like a lantern on a cold night, she said, "How long have we known each other, Blanche?"

Blanche swallowed. "Years. Always."

"And you know you can trust me."

She nodded.

"How old am I, Blanche?"

Sir Ector came with a glass of port. Already her mind was beginning to work again, but Blanche took a velvet-sweet sip before replying. "About my age, aren't you?"

"Do you remember how, years ago, I taught you to read? How old was I then?"

Blanche felt another stabbing chill. "You were already grown-up." She stared into her governess-companion's face. "Nerys. It's been fourteen years and you haven't aged."

"No." Nerys settled back on her footstool, her shoulders falling, her chin lifting. For a moment the veil rose: Blanche sensed a dignity so awful and majestic that she almost expected the footstool to splinter into diamond shards beneath its burden.

"I am ageless."

"I never noticed," said Blanche in a dry mouth.

Nerys shimmered in amusement. "No."

"How could I never have noticed? Is it magic?"

"It is natural. For me."

Under her eyes, the ageless woman folded back into herself and the glimpse of glory was gone. Blanche was glad, for under its weight she had felt too small for her own comfort. But once seen, the thing was not to be forgotten or brushed from mind. Blanche drank some more port and stared at the carpet. It was no use, she thought. She was in the dreamworld now.

She looked up tiredly and pointed to the ring on the blotter. "The ring. The boy. The pavilion. It was all real. ...My mother, Guinevere." She turned to Sir Ector. "I said—I said, 'Who was my father, Arthur, King of the Britons?' I was *joking*."

Sir Ector and Nerys looked at her, and their solemnity, like a wall of marble, threw her doubt back in her face.

Blanche gasped for breath.

"That's why you're an antiquary, Sir Ector. You're not fascinated by the ancients, you *are* an ancient. L'Espée. The Swordsman."

A smile hovered on his lips. "Keep going, Blanche. You're doing well."

She shook her head, drained of words, and covered her face with her hands. Sir Ector laid a comforting hand on her shoulder. Blanche snatched uselessly at her whirling thoughts for a moment before she remembered what she had overheard.

"Nerys. You said something was coming."

"Yes…" Once more, Nerys answered obliquely. "When you were born, eighteen years ago in Logres, the King sent Sir Ector to Broceliande."

Sir Ector said: "In that tangled forest, in an enchanted tower by a hawthorn bush, the magician Merlin slumbers until the end of the world. When the Lord Arthur was a boy Merlin counselled and guided him, but when the King became a man, Merlin departed and no mortal man has seen him since—although, perhaps, he is seen by the Lady of the Lake and her people." And the knight glanced at Nerys.

"I rode many days before I found the Lady Nimue, and when she heard my quest she agreed to take me to the tower. I saw not a stone of it. But when I asked, a voice came which I knew like my own brother's. 'Pendragon's heir is the life of Logres.' "

Nerys said: "Therefore the Lady my mistress knew that your life would be in danger."

Blanche stared at her. "Danger from whom?"

"From all those who hate Logres."

She shook her head helplessly. "I don't know what that is."

Sir Ector gestured. "The Pendragon is your father—it's the title borne by the High King of Britain. Arthur is the Pendragon by election and conquest and the divine will of the High King of all kings. His realm is Logres, of which Camelot is the capital."

"The Pendragon has many enemies," Nerys went on, "and his sister Morgan le Fay had already tried to destroy him. He is not a man to spend a thought on his own danger, but even he saw that you could not live safely in Logres. By the gates of my people you were carried across the gulf of worlds to another place, a world where the sorceress Morgan could not find you, a world where you—and the life of Logres—would be safe."

"But you said time was running out."

Sir Ector leaned against his desk, folding his arms. "Blanche, this is what we have been trying to prepare you for all these years. You do not belong in this world. One day you must return to Logres for good and take your rightful place."

"And it will be soon, Blanche," Nerys added.

It was too much to think about. Blanche got up and took the gold ring from the blotter. "Who was he, Nerys, the boy in the pavilion?"

"His name is Perceval of Wales. By the account of my mistress, Nimue, he was going to Camelot to be made a knight."

"That savage, a knight?"

"There were prophecies at *his* birth, too."

Blanche frowned at the implied rebuke and looked at the ring. He is still a savage, she thought. "Will I see him again?"

"It is likely."

"Good!" Blanche flashed. "Prophecies or not, I shall box his ears." She thrust the gold band onto her finger. Then, as quickly as the spark had flared, it died away and suddenly she was exhausted, almost fighting back tears. "Was there anything else I should know?"

Sir Ector shook his head. "A hundred things. We need not speak of them now."

Blanche nodded and went toward the door. On the threshold, she looked back and saw Sir Ector and Nerys still sitting where she had left them, staring into another time. She cleared her throat.

"Thank you for telling me the truth," she said very softly, and went away.

SHE WAS SITTING IN HER WINDOW-SEAT staring out at the rain when a tap sounded at the door and Nerys entered. She moved swiftly over to the window, concern in her voice.

"Will you weather this, Blanche?"

Blanche nodded.

Nerys glanced out the window at the colourless grey sky and sank onto the window-seat. "You will have questions, I imagine."

Blanche looked at her clasped hands and tightened her lips. There was a small hard knot of resentment under her breastbone, and it did not want to ask any questions, or learn any more about the place Nerys called Logres.

"How can you be sure," she ventured at last, "that Merlin was referring to me?"

Nerys's eyelash flickered. She glanced sidelong at Blanche, and Blanche knew that she had hit something, there.

Nerys said, "He spoke of the Pendragon's heir."

Blanche looked back down at her twined hands. "And I am the Pendragon's daughter? When I asked Sir Ector last night, he did not seem so sure." And she held her breath, almost afraid of what Nerys might say to that.

Her answer came quickly, lightly: "It's only talk, Blanche."

"So there's talk…It's about my mother and—that other knight. Lancelot, isn't it?"

Nerys sighed. "Gossip a thousand years old and more, in the French romances. Blanche, it's true that when you were born, every malicious tongue was clacking, but…"

"Nerys, you don't seem sure yourself."

A pause.

"And I am unsure, but for no good reason." Nerys rose to her feet and paced the room, eyebrows stitched together. "The Queen claimed you were true-born—"

"Claimed?"

"How should I know if the White Shadow of Cameliard was lying? I only know that no one believed her—save the King, of course—and sometimes, I thought she intended them not to. But only God knows why, for if the Queen had betrayed the King, it would be the ruin of Logres."

Blanche was silent for a while. Then she said:

"If I am not true-born then I need not return to Britain. And I will be safe, for my life will mean nothing to Logres or its enemies."

"Not return to Britain?" Nerys turned on her in blank surprise. "But it's your home."

"Is it?" Blanche looked around the cosy room that was her own. "I never saw it."

Nerys looked at her, shoulders slumping a little. "It is where your heritage lies. A patrimony for which men have killed and died, suffered exile and sorrow and counted the price little. …I thought you might have been less indifferent to it. Or can it be that you are afraid of these enemies?"

Blanche coloured under her gaze. "Of course not," she said. But it was impossible now to keep the resentment out of her voice, for she knew she was lying.

ON SUNDAY, BLANCHE WENT WITH KITTY Walker's party to Tintern in a sour mood that was only fretted by the idle and carefree chatter of the others. But it was better than being trapped in the house with Sir Ector and Nerys, she thought to herself, and besides, she wanted to see Mr Corbin.

She took her chance when they reached Tintern, lagging behind Kitty and the two others as if she took some deep interest in the empty roof and lonely arches of the ruined abbey. Mr Corbin, as a matter of course, remained with her, looming on her left hand like some gigantic but melancholy bird. His silent presence, and the peacefulness of the grass-floored abbey, made it easier to let go some of the tension she had hidden with difficulty in the motor-car.

"Do you think it is more beautiful ruined than it might have been whole?" Mr Corbin asked presently.

Blanche tilted back her head to admire the delicate tracery of the great west window. All the glass was gone, of course, but the lingering gracefulness of the blind stone outline made the breath catch in her throat.

"My guardian would like it whole," she said at last, with a bitter laugh. "I think he would prefer it if we all lived in castles."

"Ah," said Mr Corbin, "but think how chilly and dark that would be. Can't you imagine all the monks, like brown mice, shivering in here of a winter morning?" And he sang a bar or two of the *Te Deum* with an exaggerated vibrato.

Blanche tried to smile.

Laughter echoed from the walls as Kitty and her friends came tripping back to them. "Blanche," Kitty called, "we have seen it all, and we are going into the village to find a tea-shop. Are you coming?"

"I had rather stay a little longer," she told them, and they giggled knowingly as they went away.

She and Mr Corbin walked on, further into the abbey. She felt his eyes on her when they should have been on the ruin; she was not surprised when at last he said:

"You are quiet today, Miss Pendragon. Is anything troubling you?"

The mockery that lived in his eyes was gone for the moment, and Blanche let some of her distress show in her face.

"You would only laugh," she said helplessly.

"Try me."

Blanche shook her head. "You don't believe in things like this."

"Anything that worries you is real enough to concern me." He bent head and eyebrows to look into her face. "Look at me, Blanche. Can't you trust me?"

She searched his eyes in a wordless hush more intimate than speech. Before long she dropped her gaze to the grass beneath their feet. "My parents," she began at last.

His silence encouraged her to go on.

"All my life I thought they were dead. Now I find that they are alive, but so far away… I don't know what to do." She looked up, but he was still silent. "My guardian says I should go to them."

"They are a long way away?"

Blanche nodded, afraid to say anything more.

"And—you?"

"I suppose I must go…"

Mr Corbin smiled. "Miss Pendragon, how can I help you if you speak of *musts?*"

She looked up at him with quick hope. "What do you mean?"

Again the silence bore that odd secrecy, before he replied, "Whoever made a decision because of what *must* be done? Ask, rather, what you truly desire."

She looked into the sky and the sun was smiling. "A decision? You mean—I could say *no?*"

"Why not? If it is what you truly desire—on your own account."

Blanche gulped. But she was unsurprised by the thought, for it had been lurking at the back of her mind until liberated by Mr Corbin's words. Sudden tears rose in her throat and she blurted out:

"I can't go! I *can't!* It would kill me!"

She stared up at him, blinking back the tears. He took her arm with a swift gesture of comfort. "But this is melodrama, Blanche. How far away can they be? Paris? Milan?"

The mention of those two kindly cities struck her as a cruel joke. "Oh, if only!"

"India, then? But that isn't far. Not today. Haven't you read that capital book, by Mr Verne, wasn't it?"

"It isn't India," she said.

He frowned. "Surely not Australia?"

In the midst of her tragedy she couldn't help laughing. "No, indeed!"

But Mr Corbin remained serious. "You said I wouldn't believe you, Blanche. What aren't you telling me?"

"You would laugh…"

"I give you my word not to laugh. Tell me, Blanche. Better than keeping it all bottled up inside."

Blanche screwed her eyes shut. Then she said, "My mother is named Guinevere, and she is the one you are thinking of."

"THERE'S EVEN A PROPHECY," SHE FINISHED. "Pendragon's heir is the life of Logres. If I go back there, I'll be killed!" She glanced up at Mr Corbin's saturnine profile. "Oh, but you can't believe me. You don't believe in fairy-tales, do you?"

"I do not," he said. "But I know of science, and the strange properties of space and time. Why shouldn't this all be possible?"

Blanche gaped. "You mean you believe me?"

"Of course I do. You are not crazy, and why should you be lying?"

"You're *wonderful*," she cried. "Tell me, what should I do? This is my home—this time, this place. I don't want to leave."

Mr Corbin shrugged. "Your parents thought they were doing their best for you, sending you here. Who would willingly leave, having stood on the brink of the twentieth century and looked into a bright future where war and poverty might very well vanish, within fifteen years or so, before a peaceful brotherhood of humanity…? It is hard on you, having lived here, to go back to the Dark Ages." He glanced up at the abbey with a laugh. "Only just now I was speaking of the discomforts of such places."

"I shall probably have to live in something like it." Blanche felt tears crawling up her throat again. "Oh, what shall I do?"

Mr Corbin shook his head. "Miss Pendragon, you are not a child any-more. Nobody can advise you, least of all me. You must follow your own heart and judgement."

She looked at him in doubt. "I've always done what Sir Ector advised. Or Nerys. They always knew best. And I know they love me. How could I disappoint them?"

"But everyone makes mistakes," he said gently. "Especially with their children, I think; they are so full of their own hopes that they forget to let you have yours. Don't be afraid to know your own mind."

Blanche nodded, and let her gaze fall to her feet. "I will try. I will try to make the right choice."

"Miss—Blanche," said Mr Corbin, and stepped closer. She shivered with surprise as his cool fingers tipped her chin. She looked up, into his eyes, and smiled awkwardly; after the adventure of the pavilion, she felt shy even of Mr Corbin. But he returned the smile, and her discomfort smoothed away.

"The only wrong choice," he told her with gentle insistence, "would be to let someone else choose for you."

5

Nay, then,
Do what thou canst, I will not go to-day;
No, nor to-morrow, not till I please myself.
Shakespeare

It was a warm May evening not long after the excursion to Tintern, and Blanche sat on the hammock in the garden. She had been reading a Miss Austen novel, *Mansfield Park*, but even the charming Crawfords no longer distracted her thoughts, and she had flung the book down among the cushions. Instead she was tatting lace for a collar, her fingers scrambling wildly across the cotton. The sun, sinking into flaming clouds, would be gone soon and the bite of cold would send her indoors, to dinner and Nerys and polite conversation. Blanche tatted a little faster. She needed to *think*.

The shuttle, followed by its inky shadow, danced up and down above the cream-coloured lace and Blanche, staring through it, still saw the windows of Tintern. Since the trip she had not spoken to anyone about what she had learned from Nerys and Sir Ector in the library. If anything, she had tried to forget. But her time was running out. Her guardian would return in a day or two from the Newport Antiquities Society's monthly meeting, and when he spoke to her about it again—as he certainly would soon—she needed to have a decision.

But what decision? "Don't be afraid to know your own mind," Mr Corbin had said. Blanche felt like laughing. Know her own mind! It was easy for him to say it, but her mind fought knowing. Mr Corbin was right, of course: it was hard, it was *impossible* for her to leave this time willingly, with everything that she knew and loved. But Sir Ector and Nerys expected her to go—expected her to return to take up the life to which she

36

had been born and even, in a way, raised. How would she ever talk them into letting her stay? She stirred uncomfortably in her seat.

She heard a door close and looked across a lawn like green fire to see Nerys coming from the house to call her for dinner. The sun flared once and was swallowed up in a velvet bank of cloud. The light changed from gold to purple. Red bled across the horizon and Blanche, suddenly in shadow, rose from the hammock. Then she shivered in a breath of wind that scattered the perfume of roses and sent a dank, earthy scent fluttering around her.

She pulled her shawl closer. The wind raced across the lawn and tugged loose the strands of Nerys's hair. For a moment, apart from the leaves and grasses stirred by that chill breath, all motion ceased. Blanche saw her draw breath. Then the gust died and Nerys was hurrying across the lawn calling her name.

"Blanche—come quickly."

Blanche dug among the cushions for her book and thrust it with the tatting into her work-basket. As she fumbled with the catch, Nerys caught her arm. "Leave it," she panted. At the uneven note in her voice, Blanche turned and looked at her. Something of the immortal woman's glory had broken loose with the strands of hair, some hint of power hung about her, but her eyes were wide with what could only be called fear. Blanche dropped her work-basket.

Then Nerys's fingers gripped Blanche's arm convulsively, and her gaze slid past, into the shadows of the bushes beyond. Blanche turned to see. For a moment she saw nothing; then the shadows coalesced. There, just beyond the beeches from which the hammock hung, stood the statue of a man in armour, shield on arm, sword drawn.

Blanche felt the hair rise along the back of her neck. The weird light of dusk, the trembling of Nerys—*Nerys, trembling!*—and above all the mute, inexplicable figure reminded her of a childish nightmare. For one horrible moment she supposed that it must have been standing there watching her for hours. But it moved, and was an armoured man with a sword coming at them around the tree.

Blanche screamed before she could stop herself. Then Nerys snatched her hand and they were fleeing across the lawn to the house. Footsteps pounded behind them. Blanche did not dare to look over her shoulder. They reached the door and flung against it. Blanche grabbed blindly for the knob; then the door spilled them into the hall.

She looked back. Nerys was there, almost stumbling into her arms;

behind Nerys, the knight and the sword, only yards away and closing in. "Quickly—the wardrobe," Nerys said, slamming the door shut, and shooting the bolt.

At the foot of the stairs, in the middle of the house, stood a wardrobe which Blanche knew had nothing in it but coats and tennis-racquets, though it was always kept locked. Was it like Nerys's wardrobe upstairs? Would it take them to safety? She darted down the hall and tugged the handle. Then a heavy blow struck the back-door and shook the whole house. There was such implacable malice in the shivering air that Blanche nearly screamed again. Nerys pushed her aside, fumbling at a chain around her neck.

Voices and running feet came up the passage from the kitchen. One of the housemaids looked into the hall just as another violent crash shook the house. The bolt on the door was not a heavy one. Already the bar was bending and the wood of the door was splintering. But Nerys, poised with a key in her hand, said calmly to the maid:

"Tell Keats we shall be a few minutes late for dinner, will you, Lucy?"

Whether it was Nerys's cool manner, or some exertion of that veiled authority, Blanche never knew. The girl nodded and disappeared. Nerys fitted the key into the wardrobe lock and turned it. With a jerk, she pulled the door open a crack, and stood waiting.

"What are you doing?" Blanche gasped.

Nerys lifted a finger.

The next blow came accompanied by the sound of splitting wood. Then with one more crash the door burst off its hinges into the hall. Blanche drew a breath like a sob. The knight stepped over the threshold toward them, silhouetted against angry twilight. Nerys, pale and concentrated, whisked open the wardrobe door and swept Blanche inside.

Blanche stumbled into iron-grey rain slashing down from a clouded mid-afternoon sky. She stood in the stony courtyard of a castle, empty except for three posts standing erect by the wall and a man holding a sword. She blinked and gasped under the battering rain.

The man in the courtyard straightened and turned to her, sweeping rain and sweat from his eyes. Blanche, reeling toward him, looked into his face and saw recognition. The boy from the pavilion.

In that moment of terror she remembered that meeting only as something insignificant and long ago. She only saw his lean whiplike strength, the sword in his hand, and the eyes that had always been honest. "Please," she gasped, glancing past Nerys, behind her, to the low stable door she had somehow exited, "help."

As she said the word the door wrenched open and their pursuer came out into the rain. She had forgotten to speak Welsh, but her panic spoke for her. Perceval glanced from the terrified women to the knight—immense, armoured *cap-a-pie*, with a two-handed sword that made his own feel like a toy—and laughed, more from the unexpectedness of the thing than anything else.

"Stand behind me," he said to the flame-haired damsel, and as she and her attendant darted out of the way he raised his shield, lifted his sword to shoulder height, and crouched low.

The strange knight spoke, his voice echoing inside the iron helm. "Do you seek death, boy?"

Perceval grinned. "I've yanked his beard once or twice. I can do it again."

Something stirred beneath the massive iron plates of the knight's armour—something that may have been a shrug. Then the great sword lifted like the blade of a guillotine: two steps forward, and a rain of blows fell upon Perceval, who staggered back just too late and fell to one knee, lifting a smashed shield on a senseless arm to receive a new attack. Blanche gasped; at any moment she expected to see the boy crumple like blotting-paper. But then he lashed out at the knight's knee and somehow reeled to his feet out of the enemy's reach.

The two circled in the rain with quick, taut steps. Blanche and Nerys, clinging together, shuffled to stay behind the boy. The knight lunged; there was a flash of steel like lightning and the fierce shriek of metal. Perceval maneuvered again, and Blanche found that she and Nerys were standing before the stable door.

On the other side of Perceval the enemy knight had also seen this, and Blanche flinched again as he burst into deadly motion. But Nerys, tugging her arm with white fingers, hissed in her ear. "Now!"

Blanche resisted for a moment. "Can't we do something?" she groaned under the screech and crash of swords.

"We can run!"

Nerys pulled her toward the stable door. Blanche glanced back and what she saw remained frozen like a photograph in her mind long afterwards: two swords crossed in the air, and the planted feet and straining arms of both combatants. There was blood, mixed with rain, flowing down the boy's shield arm. Then she was in the hallway of her own home again, dripping rain from an afternoon far away. Nerys slammed the wardrobe door and locked it, and even the dim light which shone from the keyhole had vanished when she removed the key.

Nerys leaned back against the wardrobe, closed her eyes, and took a deep, trembling breath.

Blanche's legs buckled and she slid down the wall to the floor. She hugged her knees and breathed for a moment. "H-he can't come back?"

"Not at present."

"And the boy?" The boy in the pavilion, who had frightened her and robbed her. Again in her mind Blanche saw blood running down the young knight's shield arm and with dispassionate wonder realised that somewhere in the last few breathless seconds, she had forgiven him. "Will he live?"

Nerys opened her eyes, her voice matter-of-fact. "I cannot tell."

Blanche swallowed. "He'll be killed!"

"It's possible," said Nerys. "But not, I think, probable. The sons of Orkney are made of sterner stuff than the brigands of Gore."

AN AGE AWAY IN THE RAIN, Perceval heard the door slam behind him, and at that distracted moment his enemy disengaged. The next stroke caught the broken shield on his arm, scooped him aside, and flung him to the cobblestones. His enemy did not pursue the advantage, however. Instead he threw open the door of the stable and stood motionless, staring into the warm questioning eyes of horses.

In the sudden silence, there were shouts from within the castle and men-at-arms spilled into the courtyard.

The knight fell back a step and breathed out a curse, looking at Perceval.

"Do not doubt that this debt will be repaid with interest." And he strode into the stable.

BLANCHE SHOOK HER HEAD, A WAVE of dizzy tiredness sweeping over her. "Nerys, I don't understand. How did this happen?"

Nerys looked at her with quick compassion. "The thing we feared," she said. "She has found you at last: Morgan le Fay, the Queen of Gore."

"The sorceress? But who was the knight?"

"Did you not mark his shield?"

Blanche gave a barking laugh. "I did not!"

Nerys shook her head. "I forget that to you, a shield is not the same as a placard. He bore the Blue Boar, the device of Sir Odiar, the Queen's paramour and cutthroat."

PERCEVAL STRUGGLED TO HIS FEET AND reeled toward the stable door. Just as he reached it, a screaming neigh warned him to dive aside. Even so, the rush of horseflesh that broke open the door almost swept him away. All the horses of the castle spilled into the courtyard at once, and in the midst of them the knight of Gore, riding easily without saddle or bit, raced them across the courtyard, burst open the closing gate, trampled down the rising drawbridge, and was gone.

In the lull that followed a cool silence and numbness fell on Perceval. His knees gave way and he sank to the threshold of the stable, cradling his gashed shield arm. Dimly, in the background, he heard the roar of flames.

"AND THIS?" BLANCHE GESTURED TO THE wardrobe. "It goes back to Logres?"

"Yes." Nerys laid her hand on it. "When I knew that Sir Ector would be gone, I bound the key to the Castle Gornemant so that if there was need we could go to Sir Perceval. Not that I imagined we would need it." Her brows knitted. "How much does Morgan know? She could not have chosen a better moment for an attack. Did she know Sir Ector was away?"

A drip of ancient water ran down Blanche's neck, but the shiver tingling her spine felt more like fear. "What now?"

Nerys shook her head. "If the Queen of Gore has found you, the best I can do is hold the walls for a while. Sooner or later she will find her way back."

Blanche swallowed. "You mean that I'll be sent back to Logres."

"We knew the time was coming," Nerys reminded her.

In the sudden relief of escape, Blanche could no longer hold back the words.

"I don't want to leave. I don't want to live in that place. The very thought of it makes me feel sick. Nerys, I'm so sorry, but I just *can't*."

6

See ye not the narrow road
By yon lillie leven?
That's the road the righteous goes
And that's the road to heaven.
The Queen of Elfland's Nourice

n the silence after Blanche's words Nerys went down the hallway to the smashed door and stood silhouetted against the last
purple and yellow streaks of sunset, risen up on tiptoe with her
chin lifted as though sniffing or listening. At last she turned.
"Come with me."

She plunged out the door and Blanche ran to catch up with her. Outside,
a cold gale whipped through the trees, tumbling leaves and twigs across
the lawn toward the house. Already the rose-bushes by the hammock were
stripped of their petals. Beyond, in the orchard, the apple-trees creaked
and groaned: the blast almost seemed stronger here. It whipped hair into
her face and blinded her, and in that dizzy moment the gale seemed the
wind of an incredible speed, as though she was rushing through a tunnel
on the viewing-platform of a train. Then, unsettled and breathless, she
pushed her hair back and struggled after Nerys.

The gate at the end of the orchard was open, with a snapped latch
and one broken hinge. Nerys wrestled it upright and flung all her weight
against it.

"Help me," she called back. The wind snatched the words from her
mouth, but Blanche understood the sense, if not the purpose, and threw
herself against the gate. They strained in the teeth of the wind for a few
gasping seconds. Then the gate closed, and the wind was gone.

Nerys, catlike, smoothed hair and skirts before gesturing to the gate.

"Look at this. Brute force. A hole blown open between the worlds."

Blanche stared. "Is that where *he* got in?"

"Yes," said Nerys. "Feel it." She took Blanche's hand and held it to the broken latch of the gate where a cold jet of air still whistled through. "That woman has done damage to the very weft of the world. If you opened that gate and walked through, you would be in Logres. And if anyone there knows about this…"

"Morgan knows," Blanche whispered. "What are we going to do?"

Again Nerys looked at her with inexpressible sympathy. "It might frighten you to think of living in Logres, Blanche, but all our defences are thrown down in this world. Logres is the safest place for you now."

She turned back to the house, walking quickly, and continued.

"They won't think to look for you in Britain. We'll telegraph Sir Ector and tell the servants you've been called suddenly away. Pack light, for we haven't a moment to spare, and we may have far to travel. I don't know how far it is to Camelot from the Castle Gornemant."

To Camelot. Now. Already. Blanche, choking down her dismay, caught Nerys's arm. "But we'll come back, won't we?"

Nerys sighed and shook her head. "I know this is sudden, Blanche. Only believe me when I say that you are in deadly danger now, every moment, until we have you back in Camelot. Sir Ector and I can close up the house, mend the rift, and say goodbye to the neighbours. There is no point in exposing you to the danger of another journey."

Blanche felt helpless—a cold dull panic which she was beginning to recognise. "Mr Corbin," she said. "I want to say goodbye. Kitty, too, and Emmeline. I can't just disappear. How will you explain it to them if I do? They'll have to be told *something*."

Nerys stopped walking and looked at her. "Blanche," she said, and despite the gentleness of her words Blanche knew she was vexed, "do you really mean to put your friends above your own safety and the future of Logres?" A pause. "The decision does not rest with me, at any rate. Gather your things."

When Blanche came downstairs with her bag she found Nerys already waiting by the wardrobe, key in hand. She had thought of another objection.

"What if that knight is still on the other side? The one with the Blue Boar?"

"Odiar loves not the company of true and faithful men like Gornemant," Nerys said. "He will be fled or captured by now. Stand back."

But when she fitted the key to the lock and turned it, there was a sudden muted roar and the door fought like a wild thing against Nerys's hand. Through the narrow opening yellow flames shot out into the hallway, singing Nerys's hair and licking the wallpaper. She said "Ah," slammed the door shut, and turned the key again.

"*Heavens!*" Blanche cried, staring at the buckled and blistered door.

"The door is on fire," Nerys said. "And the key can only be linked to another door from the Logres side."

"We can't leave?" Blanche looked hopeful.

"We can and we must. We'll go out through the orchard."

"But Morgan is on the other side!"

Nerys went to the doorway again and sniffed the night air. "Such damage is not done in a chamber. She would have done it in the open. Also it is raining in Britain. If we take the horses, we may slip through without being seen and ride away without being caught."

"Are you positive it wouldn't be safer to stay here?"

"Waiting to be attacked at any moment? Or leading the hounds of Gore a merry chase around Gloucestershire?"

Blanche bit her lip. For all Mr Corbin's insistence that she make her own choices, it looked as if she would be forced into Logres, for refuge if nothing else.

"We must go on, and take the adventure that comes." Nerys went out the door toward the stable, and there was nothing to do but follow.

FLORENCE WAS BLANCHE'S HORSE, AN UNINTELLIGENT but sweet-tempered bay. Nerys, who did not have a horse of her own, had taken Sir Ector's, a retrained grey racer named Malaventure. The pair of them pricked their ears and swished their tails in the face of the wind between the worlds. Blanche fidgeted with the reins.

Nerys had already gone, taking with her a windfall apple. "If all is well, I'll throw the apple back through the gate, and you'll know it is safe to bring the horses. If not, *ride*."

Then she had stepped through the gate. The quick-falling dusk made it difficult to see what happened next. Only Blanche had blinked, and Nerys was gone.

Deep inside she was panicking again, fearing that the worst must have happened when the apple landed with a *plop* on the grass at her feet. Then, without a pause to let herself think, she clucked to the horses and plunged into the wind, dragging at their reins.

It was dark beyond the gate, and again she felt that sense of limitless speed. Soon the wind lashing her face had water in it, and as the rain grew heavier, the wind died away and under shadowy oaks Blanche looked down to see that she was standing in a circle of blackened stones. Hurriedly she stepped out of it, with low calm words for the skittish horses.

No one was to be seen. Away to the right the trees thinned and the towers of a castle could be glimpsed rising out of the clearing, black against the dark evening sky. At the sight, Blanche's scalp prickled and the blood hummed in her ears. She was engulfed, quite without expecting it, in a high and dauntless mood. Here she stood under weeping skies, she, Blanche Pendragon, who bore a name of legend. In that castle, all unaware, lay a witch-queen who desired her death, and echoing in the back of her mind she could still hear the fierce steel voices of swords, harsher and sweeter and wilder in her veins than any other sound on the green earth. And she had been caught and kissed by a brown boy from the woods, and he had paid for the pleasure in blood.

For one titanic heartbeat she felt as tall as the trees.

Then above her a shadow rose with a sound like the tearing of cloth and her heart leaped into her throat before she saw that it was only a black bird beating the air with sharp pinions. The trees bent down over her again, and it was night in Logres and very cold in the rain. Blanche ducked her head and turned up the collar of her jacket. Not until then did she see Nerys coming toward her through the trees from the direction of the castle with a finger lifted to her lips.

Nerys shoved Malaventure's hindquarters away from the stone circle on the ground. This she unmade, moving with an queer and wordless vehemence. One by one she tore the stones out of the turf and flung them like missiles into the undergrowth. She was finished in a matter of moments and straightened, catching her breath. Then she swung into the saddle and led the way south through the soft murmur of rain.

Neither spoke until the castle was out of earshot. At last Nerys said:

"A raven was watching us as we came through."

"Yes, I saw."

Nerys pushed hair out of her eyes. "You saw, but did you understand? Some of the ravens are *her* creatures. In any case she will be on our trail by morning."

No need to ask who *she* was. But in a country where legends walked, what could go wrong?

"If she waits until morning to follow us, we'll leave her far behind."

"Unless she left a guard," said Nerys. "When she sees that the stone ring was destroyed, she will know we used her passage."

"Then why did you destroy it?"

"The keys to the doors between the worlds are ours to use—I and my people," Nerys said. "But Morgan le Fay is a mortal, and has no right to them. She must use unnatural force. Magic which I will have nothing to do with and destroy when I find it."

"You and your people?"

"The Fair Folk."

"You mean—fairies. Immortals like you." Blanche glanced sidelong at her companion, her fancy kindling. "Are there many of you in Britain?"

"Two or three, perhaps."

"So few?"

"My people are not of Logres. They have no concern here."

"But you do?" Blanche was puzzled.

Nerys was quiet for a time before replying. "All mortals die," she said at last. "All take the broad road to Hell, or the narrow road to Heaven. But my people do not die while the world endures. Therefore they spend their time doing what pleases themselves. They have no stake in the struggle between Logres and darkness."

"And you?"

"I cannot tell," she said with a sigh. "In the lore of my people it is said that we are outside salvation. But within the last hundred years I have heard differently. It was a wandering saint who told me that even the bonny road to Elfland comes to a fork in the end. If only it were true! If only there were hope for us."

Far in the distance behind them, a horn blew, a sound so lovely in the moonlight that a chill ran down Blanche's spine. Then came the bell of hounds and the cold settled lead-heavy in her stomach.

Nerys stiffened in the saddle. "The dogs. She knows."

Blanche glanced back. It was full night, now, and the rain had stopped, leaving the moon swimming through cloud. Only a weak and fitful light filtered through the arching branches overhead. "We can ride faster, even in this dark."

"A little."

Nerys led them now slightly to the right and they pressed on into rough hill-country. Behind, at intervals, they heard the horn, and each time it drew closer. This slow cold hunt across the hills in fainting moonlight was worse even than the terror of the Blue Boar, Blanche thought, as they went down a rocky slope with the horses stumbling and slipping beneath them. And for one impious moment she wished to stand again in the shattered calm of the hallway at home with nowhere to run and the door splintering beneath the enemy's blows.

The moon was low in the sky when they stumbled into a bog between two towering hills.

Malaventure found ground on the other side of the slough, but Florence stuck fast, too weary to fight. Blanche dismounted and sank up to her knees in scummed water as cold as conceit. At that moment a breeze gusted from the north, carrying the noise of the hunt.

"Come *on*," Blanche begged. Florence wallowed and plunged, and Blanche lost her balance, stumbling into softer mud and deeper water. The cold gripped her thighs. She struggled back to higher ground with her skirt clinging to her legs, and began to rattle in the icy wind. Chill fingers ran down her cheeks as the tears spilled over.

Then Nerys was beside her carrying a scrubby bough from a dead bush on the bank, and Blanche was grateful for the dark that hid her cowardice.

"Shh, be calm," Nerys said to the horse. To Blanche she said, "We must throw down branches for her to step on."

Blanche scrubbed her woollen cuff across her eyes and splashed to the bank. She could hear the hounds crying. Were they already in view? She seized more twigs and branches and plunged back into the water. So Morgan wanted to kill her? Good. But she would not die whimpering.

Beyond all hope they extracted Florence from the bog, but the sound of the hunt was coming over the hill and the horses were stumbling with weariness.

"Mount again," said Nerys through the darkness. "They may yet lose our scent in the water."

They toiled on up the slope ahead, and had reached the rocky shoulder of the hill when the baying of hounds fell silent behind them. Blanche looked back and a gleam of moonlight showed dark shapes coursing to and fro on the far side of the slough.

"We've outfoxed them!" she said, and they turned the corner of the rocky outcrop and blundered into firelight.

The campfire under the rocks illuminated only one man, a wizened old creature with a beard that reached his knees. His mule lay in shelter, chewing stolidly, but the man himself stood leaning on his staff by the fire, watching the night.

At the sight Florence and Malaventure stopped of their own accord, their heads drooping, sensing, perhaps, the bewilderment of their riders. Blanche looked at Nerys and saw something like defeat in the line of her mouth. Her eyes prickled with tears again. What was this old man doing here, so far from any shelter?

The ancient shifted his weight and spoke.

"Nerys of the Folk," he said. "It's a cold night to be wandering in the wilds."

Nerys's voice was flat as she replied. "How do you know me?"

"And Blanchefleur, heir of Logres. Exalted company for my poor fireside."

In the distance, the musical cry of a hound announced to his fellows that the scent was found. Blanche saw Nerys's back pull tight and knew that she had heard.

"Tell us your name, since you're so free with ours," said the fay fiercely.

"My name? That is no secret," said the old man. "I am Naciens."

A pause—a long pause, while the hounds behind them gave tongue. At last Nerys spoke again. "Naciens of Carbonek? I know the name. What brings you here?"

"The witch of Gore is on your trail," Naciens said. "You will find the Castle of Carbonek in the valley beneath us. She will not."

"Carbonek!" The word came out like a gasp, raw with desire. Blanche stared. But then Nerys's hands gripped the reins tighter, and she was herself again. "I am taking the damsel Blanchefleur to safety, to Camelot. I cannot risk losing her in a place beyond space and time."

Naciens shrugged. "Ride to Camelot, then!"

The sound of hunting-horns floated mockingly up the hill. Blanche set her teeth and shivered in the wind. Nerys did not change expression.

"Camelot is seven days' ride from here, with fresh horses and on the right paths," said Naciens more gently. "If you ride alone, Morgan will certainly catch you. If it is safety you need, nowhere is safer than Carbonek."

Nerys said: "If I leave her at Carbonek, what hope have I of finding her again?"

Naciens stroked his beard in silence before replying. "Carbonek is not lost to those to whom it is given to find," he said at last. "Or do you think that I myself have brought you through these hills to our doorstep in the nick of time? Tell me, have you forgotten what is kept there?"

Nerys bowed her head. And then Blanche thought she must have gone mad, for in the hush, below the ever-louder baying of hounds, she sang.

I have fled from the wilderness fasting, with woe and unflagging travail,
I have sought for the light on the mountain, and skirted the devilish dale.
I have laid my mouth in the dust, and begged the Might to be kind,
I have come to the feast, and I famish. Now grant me the Holy Grail.

Blanche stirred like a sleeper waking. Naciens was speaking. "To you, it is granted."

7

But a lamp above a gate
Shone in solitary state,
O'er a desert drear and cold,
O'er a heap of ruins old,
O'er a scene most desolate.
Rossetti

Art thou, like Angels, only shown,
Then to our Grief for ever flown?
Heyrick

ne day Sir Perceval took his horse and arms, both the spoils of the gilded knight, and rode into the forest, aiming north and west into the deepest regions of Wales. Summer had slipped away since he first came to the castle of Gornemant to be trained in arms, and during that time he had worked harder than he had thought possible. Even the old earl had been pleased with his progress. All the same, when Perceval decided to leave, Gornemant had objections. His training was incomplete, his shield arm needed another fortnight to heal, and autumn was wearing on, and would slip into winter early this year.

Perceval listened to the earl with the reverence due to an elder and benefactor, but the next morning at sunrise he was in the stable saying goodbye to his old pony Llech and saddling his war-horse Rufus. He rode away into the wilds with the sharp clean air of autumn scouring his lungs with every breath. As he looked into the colourless sky, he stretched away all the stiffness of the last months, and quickened his horse into a trot between his knees. He brought the animal to an easy canter and hummed a few bars of the *Gloria*. It was too long since he had slept under the cold stars.

He rode toward the mountains. Down in the grey-and-green valleys at their roots, the hush before wintry storms lay thick on the landscape.

Days passed. In the woods there had been settlements, farms, travellers, and the odd chance of a joust. Now he was alone, his silent musings set to the rhythm of his horse's hooves. His food, cold stiff hardtack, dwindled and vanished at last, and he fasted on black icy streams. Had there been anything else to eat, he would have killed and roasted it, but he seemed to have left every living creature behind.

Where was he going? At first he had intended to find some adventure, but very little had come his way before he wandered into this waste. Now, although he could always have turned back, something kept him pressing forward, some sense that this stillness and desolation signified something, if the interpretation could only be found.

And in the meanwhile, peace settled upon his soul. For the first time since his journey to Camelot, he had the luxury of solitude. Nothing came between him and the quiet voices of the world.

The land changed around him. Every day it became more craggy and forbidding. Deep shadowed meres opened at his feet, sheer sunless sheets of rock barred his path, black clouds heavy with unshed snow loomed above him.

An evening came on stormy wings. The long twilight had begun at midday under frowning clouds that blocked the sun, but as the light began to fail altogether, a wind rose and began to clamour through the valley. Perceval hunched shivering into his armour. With a high-pitched whinny the wind flung the first snowflakes at him. He pulled on his helm for shelter, but the inside filmed over with water droplets at once.

Snow began to drift over the path, transmuting the landscape in bites and swallows from lead to silver. Perceval crested a low saddle, bending in the wind, looking in vain for shelter. Below and to the right, a desolate valley full of black stunted fir-trees ran away to the lowland. It looked kindlier than the mountainside, so he turned Rufus to pick his way down the slope.

Down in that valley the wind's bite blunted and the snow fell more gently. Perceval urged Rufus into a slow trot and followed the downhill course of a little black stream. Then the path took a sudden turn, and Perceval looked up and saw, in a cleft of the valley wall, a castle.

Like its surroundings, the castle was black and ruinous. All its outer walls had been shivered as if struck by lightning. Its gates lay in a twisted wreck, its battlements had fallen away like teeth in a battered mouth, and even the rooks' nests bristling from the walls seemed long deserted. The keep itself was seamed with cracks and the windows blind and black. Only one tower still remained standing, but in all its loneliness it was worth seeing, for a single light burned within it.

Perceval rode up into the keep, disturbing long-silent echoes. Although the place was utterly shattered, he saw no weeds growing in the cracked pavement. He passed through a courtyard into the great hall where, to his astonishment, he found light and warmth. A fire was smouldering on the hearth, and torches lit the wall behind the high table.

He could not see a soul.

Perceval dismounted softly. Rufus bent and nosed the floor before discovering a bundle of provender in a corner. Perceval leaned his shield and lance against the wall, pulled off helm and gauntlets, and went warily to warm himself. There must be someone about, but were they friends or enemies?

As he held out his hands to the coals he saw a little table nearby set with red and white chess-pieces, ready for a game. Perceval brushed the dust off a stool and sat down, stretching his feet toward the fire.

Presently he picked up one of the chessmen to look at it. When he had blown and rubbed the dust away, he found that it was an ivory knight with shiny black eyes which seemed to return his scrutiny. He replaced it on its square and sat listening to the darkness and the shadows. After a moment, he rose and went to look out of the hall into the snowy courtyard.

Nothing. Nobody. He went back to the chess-table and sat down. Outside, the wind whispered along the roof-tiles. For a moment he imagined that the whole hall was full of shadowy presences, moving and talking under ghostly torches, but then he blinked, and was back in the desolate ruin. Perceval shook himself and moved the white queen's pawn forward two squares.

He was still looking at the board when a red knight slid forward in response.

Perceval sat up and stared into the darkness, hands stealing to the hilt of his sword.

Not a breath stirred the air.

Slowly Perceval reached out again and moved another pawn. Instantly the red king's pawn moved forward.

Perceval moved again, and the red responded almost before his fingers had left his own piece. Six moves later, he was checkmated. Perceval stared in bemused displeasure, and set the board again.

Twice more the red chessmen bested him, so easily that at the third defeat Perceval lost his temper entirely and rose to his feet, drawing his sword. "Come out, wherever you are!" he shouted.

"You are—you are—you are," the castle mocked.

Perceval passed his hand around the table, hoping to catch some thread used to move the pieces. There was none. He went to sweep the red pieces from the table, but they stuck firm.

Machine, or magic? The firelight had burned very low, and suddenly Perceval thought he heard footsteps far away. The hair prickled on the back of his neck and he swung his sword up meaning to smash the set and then take his chances with whatever was coming. But before he could move the castle broke its silence.

"No! Don't touch the chessboard," someone called. He was facing her before she had finished speaking. The first thing he saw was a white glimmer in the shadows behind the great table. Then she came closer and he saw her hair in the dark, a crown of sulky red which, being pinned to the top of her head, gave her the illusion of lofty height. It was the damsel in the pavilion, the damsel in the rain.

"Oh, it's you," she said, stopping short.

For the fraction of a moment, Perceval felt like a small boy caught in mischief. Then in vexation he rebounded into something more than his usual nerve, shot his sword back into its sheath, and bowed with a flourish. "And still at your service, damsel."

"Oh, yes," she said with the same distant civility. "How is your arm, by the way?"

He had been unsure if she had seen his wound, and knowing that she had gave him a petty pleasure. "That? It was nothing, and is nearly mended. Tell me whom I have the honour of serving."

"My name is Blanchefleur, as they say here."

"I am Perceval, a knight of the Table," he told her, and the words alone lifted his chin and pulled his shoulders back. "And I crave your pardon for the wrong I did you in the pavilion."

Blanchefleur waved a cool and graceful hand, on which his mother's ring glinted. "You fought the Blue Boar for me. We are acquitted."

In her place, Perceval thought, he would have been angry, and this indifference perplexed him. "But I took your ring." He was wearing it on a thong around his neck these days, and pulled it over his head. "I am no robber of women. If it was given unwillingly, take it back."

She took it from him and stood doubtfully staring at the writing that ran around the inside of the band.

"What do the words say?"

Blanchefleur glanced up. "They speak of my mother." She held the ring out to him. "It was given willingly. Keep it."

He lifted his hand. "Not if it is precious to you."

"It isn't." The words were abrupt, and she paused. "I don't know my mother very well. Please take it."

Nothing loath, Perceval took the ring and grinned at her. "And serve you also?"

"Serve me?"

He quoted his mother. "When a knight wishes to serve a lady, he will give her a ring from his hand and a—well, never mind that part. But of all ladies in the world, I would most gladly serve you, damsel, and repair the injury I did you."

"I have said that we are acquitted."

"No," he said.

She frowned. "No?"

"No," he said again. "I fought the Blue Boar for you, but I am a knight. I am bound to do as much for anyone, high or low, old or young, man or woman."

She tilted her head and looked at him with new respect. "What would you give me in recompense, then?"

"I would do as I offered. I would bear your ring and serve you a year and a day, taking no other lady during that space."

She gave him an odd look, with a twist like a smile at the corner of her mouth. "That is your request?"

"That? No. That I will do regardless. But if you would grant a request, you will wear my token during that time."

At that her eyebrow quirked up as if she meant to mock at him, but then the smile broke through and she was blushing and trying not to laugh and shaking her head all at once. Perceval wondered what it was that made her both so delighted, and so ashamed of being delighted. Almost every knight he had ever heard of had *some* lady to serve. What he suggested was no uncommon thing.

"I am silenced," she said ruefully, when at last she recovered her poise. "Have your wish, and come and eat."

The table on the dais was bare of anything but dust. When Perceval had wiped two of the weathered old chairs and a segment of the board, they took their seats at the empty table, facing the unfriendly mirk of the hall.

"Tell me how you come to be here in the wilds alone," he said, brushing his hands on his armour.

"Alone! Can you not see them? Not even a shadow?"

Perceval remembered the moment in which he had almost seen the hall lighted and full of people. "If they are here, I cannot see them."

"But you are from this world," Blanchefleur said, and they looked at each other with twinned confusion before she shook her head and went on. "I cannot see them either. But Naciens says they are all around us."

Perceval grinned. "One of them is very good at chess, then."

Blanchefleur laughed, and became serious again before he could return to the question he had first put to her. "Naciens said you have come here for a purpose."

Perceval thought of the long hushed days in the mountains, and nodded. "I thought so. Tell me what to do."

"You must take the message back to Camelot of what you have seen."

"What have I seen?"

"It's coming. Wait."

He leaned back into his chair, stretching out his legs. "As long as you want. That is, if there will be food."

"Naciens said there would be."

Silence settled back onto the castle. Perceval scanned the hall and finally fixed his eyes, like Blanchefleur, on the doors at the end of the room. The fire on the hearth had revived a little, but now it began to fade into a dull red glow. Even so, it was a lifetime before he knew he had not imagined the light stealing into the blackness beyond the door.

The doorway grew lighter by slow degrees. Then Perceval discerned singing voices, coming like the light from far away and moving closer. It was like nothing he had ever heard before, even in the old earl's chapel on Sundays, and he straightened in his chair to listen. The three voices sang simultaneously, but each wove a different melody in and around the others, so that the whole became a bewilderingly complex tapestry of sound. Yet the themes shared perfect clarity and perfect co-inherence. At no point did one voice overwhelm the others; at no point did they become confused.

It was like listening to the universe in motion. Planets spinning on their appointed courses, the lives of men intersecting and parting, the unimaginable harmony of the human body itself in hierarchy and order, were all implied in the song, but something greater as well: the genius of the composer, which must surely approach the miraculous. Perceval closed his eyes and was lost in the weaving music.

He came back to the waking world to find that the music had stopped. The light beyond the door still grew stronger, until he was sure that it would blind him if it shone any brighter. Then at last, with a triumphant blast of wind, its source appeared like the sun on a clear morning.

There were three veiled damsels. The first held a spear that dripped blood (its dark redness as positive and blinding as the white light)—blood that vanished before it could reach the ground. The second held a golden platter, and the third a cup covered with a thin veil. It was from the Cup that the light shone.

They paced up the hall. Perceval knew what he was seeing. His mother had told the story of Joseph of Arimathea, who gave his tomb for our Lord, coming to Britain in his old age with three incomparable treasures: the spear which had pierced Christ's side, the platter that had borne the bread at the Last Supper, and above all the cup from which he had drunk, with which Joseph had caught his blood running down the Cross. The cup of cups, the Holy Grail.

There was a rustle at his elbow as the Grail drew closer. Blanchefleur had pushed back her chair and sunk to her knees, blinking like an owlet in the light. Perceval moved with her. The damsels were passing them now. He could feel the light wash over them, almost tangible, and smell perfumes and spices for which he had no name, although they smelled like all the good memories of his childhood.

Then the Grail passed out of the hall, the light faded, and they were alone in the dark. Only a little light came from the fire. Perceval stood slowly, stiffly; groped for the dead torches on the wall and, finding them, coaxed them to life at the coals. In their rekindled light he saw Blanchefleur sitting in her chair again, a huddled and somehow smaller figure, staring unseeingly before her.

The table bore food, now—everything he most liked to eat, from fresh plums to milky cheese. But the sight of it could not distract him from what they had seen, and one thought sparked like fire in the dry tinder of his imagination, and leaped through him all at once.

"Now surely," he said, "the Quest of the Grail is close: the time they speak of, when the Grail Knight comes to Camelot and the knights of the Table ride out in search of the grace it holds."

Slowly, as if returning across vast distances of thought, Blanchefleur turned to him. "Yes. That was the message."

"It is close." Perceval drew a breath through clenched teeth. "It is in my mind to go in search of it now."

"But the message—"

"They say it dwells in the castle of Carbonek—Carbonek, cut off from mortal lands. If the Grail is here, then Carbonek cannot be far away," and he was already striding down the hall to where he had left his arms and horse.

Blanchefleur pushed her chair back and came running down after him. "Perceval—" it was the first time she had used his name, and it sounded well, but he had no time to stop and listen to that music—"Perceval, you don't understand."

He pulled on his gloves and turned to her with his helm in his hands. "What? Do you know where it is? Is it near?"

She opened her mouth as if to speak, then caught herself, and shook her head. "You must go to Camelot first."

He pulled on his helm and fitted his shield to his arm. "Not before I have seen it again, just once."

"No! Wait and listen!" said Blanchefleur. But he swung into the saddle, laughing.

"I am coming back," he called. "I will bring you the Grail. Wait for me here."

"No, wait," she wailed again, but Perceval thrust the doors open and the wind swallowed her words. If she said anything else, it was lost in the clamouring echoes woken by his horse's hooves.

NOT UNTIL DAWN DID SIR PERCEVAL come fully to his senses. By then the snow had ceased, and the jubilant sun rose shining on dazzling whiteness striped by black trees. He sat looking at it in something close to despair. For the last hour he had believed that that glimmer on the horizon was the light he sought. When it finally broke above the trees he could no longer deceive himself.

Of course that castle was the Grail Castle. He had been in Carbonek herself. He had found the damsel of the pavilion again. He had seen the Grail, and he could have eaten from its provision. What had possessed him?

And what had he thrown away? Carbonek was cut off from the rest of Britain since Sir Balyn the Unlucky struck the Dolorous Stroke and maimed the Fisher King. No one found the road to Carbonek now, no one not watched over and guided by some gracious destiny.

Which he had flouted.

Was there still hope? He turned back to the west, and retraced his steps. For a few miles his trail was clear, but at last it vanished under last night's snow. The white-and-black of the forest held no clue. He pressed on while the sun rose higher, burning away the mist that lay in the valleys. Afternoon came, clear and bright. Then the day faded to evening and he knew he would not find Carbonek again.

Perceval reined in his horse and sat with bowed head, trying not to think how tired, hungry, and cold he was, or what a fool he had made of himself. Slowly the shadows grew deeper around him. More clouds were coming down from the North, piled up in gigantic purple and gold palaces, so that the sky looked like a window on Heaven.

Far above he heard a bird's scream, and looked up to see a hawk driving a dove across that sumptuous sky. The dove fluttered for the cover of trees, but the hawk folded its wings and dropped from higher air like a stone.

Perceval heard the soft *thud* of the two bodies meeting and saw crimson splash across the dove's breast. Three drops of blood chased each other down through the air and spattered on the snow, dark against dazzling white. Perceval stared at them and remembered Blanchefleur with her red hair and white tunic, the red stone of his mother's ring on her hand, and above all the drops of blood falling from the Spear at Carbonek.

While he sat musing, four knights came riding through the frosty air with a comfortable jingling of harness and with the breath steaming from their mouths as they talked and laughed. Sir Gawain was there with his cousin Sir Ywain, and Sir Kay, and King Arthur himself.

"Do you see that knight, sitting so listlessly staring at the snow?" said the King. "Do any of you know him?"

"His mount is familiar," said Sir Gawain, and chuckled. "He must be asleep, or witless, or deeply in love. He has not noticed us."

"Kay! Go and ask who he is," the King said.

"I'll stir him up, sire," said Sir Kay, and he came jogging up to Perceval and cried, "Sir! Ho, sir! Yonder is the Pendragon of Britain, and he wishes to know your name."

Perceval was aware of him, as if in a dream, and heard his voice, but not the words or the sense, and he did not lift his head or show any sign that he had understood. Sir Kay looked back to the King. "Hoy!" he suddenly shouted at Perceval.

Perceval, his eyes caught in the red and white and his mind in memory, still did not move, though he began to swim slowly to the surface of thought.

Kay waited a moment longer, and then lost his temper. "Answer me when I speak to you!" he said, and gave Perceval a clout on the head with his iron gauntlet.

Perceval came to himself then, boiling angry, reacting almost before he had a chance to think: swept up his spear-butt and with a satisfying *crack* returned the blow and laid Sir Kay senseless on the ground.

Then he looked up and saw the other three knights sitting there, watching. Laying his spear in rest he shouted, "Since it seems that nowadays a man must fight for a little peace and quiet, come on, all of you at once, if you wish!"

Gawain laughed, for he was fond of a bold speaker. "Sire," he said to the King, "surely that is the boy you sent on the adventure of the Queen's cup a while ago."

"Then go and give him my greetings," said King Arthur, "and perhaps now that he has beaten Sir Kay, he will let us pass in peace."

So Sir Gawain rode up to Perceval, his spear upright for peace, and said, "Sir knight, over there is the High King of Britain, who wishes to speak with you. As for this knight, this is Sir Kay, and he is not always as mannerly as he should be."

"I am glad to hear it is he," said Perceval, unhelming. "I warned him I would repay him the blow he gave to the maiden at Camelot."

"You charge a high interest," said Gawain, chuckling. He searched Perceval's face. "Your shield is blank, I see. What's your name and lineage, sir?"

"My name is Perceval, as I told you before," he said. "My mother's name was Ragnell and I do not know my father."

A look of delight danced in Gawain's eyes, and then he laughed, a long peal of pure joy, and turned back to King Arthur and Sir Ywain. "But I do, I think."

"Tell me!" Perceval urged, trotting his horse after. "Who was he?"

"My lord king," cried Gawain in the same delighted roar, "Here is my son, Sir Perceval."

The Holy Grail!—

...

What is it?
The phantom of a cup that comes and goes?
Tennyson

hen the echoes of Perceval's going faded away, Blanche
went back into the great hall of Carbonek and looked at
the feast on the high table. More for something to do than
because she felt particularly concerned about it, she divided
the food into two parts and put half of it out in the pas-
sageway near the entrance, where it would be preserved by the autumn
cold. Then she took her seat at the high table, but could not bring herself
to eat. She was not hungry, and she did not want to eat in the cold and
cavernous hall. She had seen it filled with light and music. She had sat
at table with a companion more substantial than any of the whispering
presences she half sensed in the shadows. Suddenly, and for the first time
since she had come to Carbonek, she felt lonely.

She carried the rest of the food into her own little room, one of the
few intact chambers in the castle. The room was dry and could be kept
clean, but it was never completely warm or light even with the fire burning
and her candle lit. Naciens had given her few necessities and no comforts:
plain food, a change of clothes, sleeping-furs, and a book. Then he had
gone off with his mule on some urgent errand, and Nerys had returned
to the house in Gloucestershire to meet Sir Ector and arrange their departure, and Blanche was left alone.

She had hardly noticed the solitude. She had been busy keeping house,
or making camp, or whatever her life in this little room could be called.
She had cooking, cleaning, and washing to do, and reading for when the

time dragged. Above anything else, she had a firm and anchoring certainty that she was safe.

It had come to her on the night they had been hunted by Morgan, when Nerys sang on the hillside above Carbonek. It could not, of course, be compared to what she had felt a month or two back in her guardian's house, before she learned of Logres or Guinevere or the Queen of Gore, before she had known any cause of dread. Now she had escaped dogs and the sword, she might with justice have feared a whole host of shapeless threats, and yet the battlements of Carbonek surrounded her like the walls of a warm house in a winter storm. Perhaps that was what fended off the loneliness.

She was reading by the fire in her room one dark afternoon a week after she and Perceval had seen the Holy Grail when she heard the sound of hooves in the hall. Was it Naciens, wandering back from another pilgrimage, or some other stranger? Blanche wrapped herself in a cloak, went very softly down echoing black corridors to the hall, and peeked through the doorway. There was Naciens, sure enough. As he pushed back his hood, drops of water in his long white beard twinkled as though it really was made of snow. Beside him, speaking quietly, there was a smaller, slighter figure holding a bay horse.

"Nerys!" Blanche called, and ran into the hall.

Nerys left off speaking to Naciens and turned with a smile to greet her.

"Are we leaving?" Blanche asked, as soon as courtesy allowed.

To her surprise, Nerys hesitated. She glanced at Naciens and said, "You understand that I can make no decisions on my own."

He bowed his head. Blanche looked from one to the other with curiosity.

"I thought you had come to take me to Camelot."

"I had," she said with a reassuring smile, and changed the subject.

They dined well from fresh store Naciens had brought in his saddlebags—a pair of moorhens and new brown flour which Blanche baked into cakes on the hearthstones in her room.

Nerys watched her with silent surprise. Blanche, glancing up, saw the look on her face and thought it better than any praise.

"Naciens showed me how to do this," she said.

"A month ago you couldn't even build a fire," Nerys said. "Now, you're cooking on one."

Blanche laughed. "It was rather dreary at first," she said. "But I learned to manage!"

She meant to ask what Nerys had been speaking to Naciens about, but was forestalled again. Dropping her voice almost to a whisper, Nerys said:

"Have you seen *it?*"

A week ago, Blanche might have been tempted to respond, "Seen what?" simply to assert herself as a free-thinker slow to believe extraordinary claims.

But she *had* seen it.

"Yes."

Nerys laughed, a little self-consciously, and tapped Blanche's cheek with her forefinger. "Yet you look no different."

"I am no different," the free-thinker wanted to say. Instead Blanche smiled and shook her head and gave the fowls another turn. Even if she had wanted to, she could not have put her experience into words, not yet.

Nerys's voice held years of longing. "Think of it, Blanche. The Holy Grail, here for the finding. Here for Logres. Naciens says the time is near."

"Yes."

"With the Grail,"—she was whispering now—"with the Grail, perhaps it can be done. A kingdom that shall never be destroyed…"

"Why, what are you talking about?"

Nerys quoted: "*Fiat voluntas tua, sicut in caelo et in terra.*"

"But how?"

"How?" Nerys looked at her. "Didn't you feel it?"

"How can I know what I felt?"

"That I cannot tell you."

"But what did you expect?"

Nerys said: "They say that those who see the Grail are changed in will, so that they will in communion with the Divine will. Do you see now what it might mean for the Grail to come to Logres?"

Blanche stood up slowly from the fire, wiping her hands against the woollen skirt of her riding-habit. "No," she said at last. "I felt nothing of that kind."

Some of the light faded out of Nerys's eyes. Blanche, seeing it die, felt a twinge of conscience. What had Nerys suffered in the last eighteen years of exile? She had given up home and friends and loyalties, fled across the worlds, served as guard and governess. …And now the time came to return home to all those things she loved, and Blanche, the only reason for her exile, neither understood nor cared for them. No wonder that when Nerys fell prey to melancholy, the very stars seemed to weep.

Blanche spoke bitterly. "It should have been you, not me."

At that moment Naciens, having seen to the comfort of their beasts, came back into the room. Supper, although more satisfying than anything Blanche had eaten since the night of the Grail, could not overcome the sour taste left in her mouth from her conversation with Nerys. Yet what else could she have said? She had felt none of what Nerys described. And from the way Perceval had left Carbonek, it seemed plain that neither had he.

After supper, Naciens and Nerys left; no doubt, Blanche thought, to finish the conversation she had interrupted earlier. She was left to clean away the dinner things and brood. Nerys had returned to Britain. What would happen now? Would there be a chance to go back to the house in Gloucestershire, or was she trapped in Logres forever?

Blanche put another log on the fire and huddled into her furs, planning the best way to tackle Nerys. But when the elfin woman returned to the little warm room, her first words swept away every difficulty.

"We are going back to Gloucestershire in the morning," Nerys said.

Blanche blinked at her, then lit up in a smile. "You really mean it, Nerys?"

"Yes, of course." Nerys laughed.

A reprieve. Another chance. "Oh, thank you!"

"Only briefly, mind you. The rift between the worlds is mended, but Logres is still the best place for you now. But you certainly cannot stay here in Carbonek—not like this." And she looked around the room with a shiver.

Blanche wondered what had happened to revive her spirits. As Nerys paced the room rubbing her hands and stamping her feet to work up some warmth, she seemed to shine like a lamp with happiness. But if there was a cause, she did not explain it, and at last she picked up the book Blanche had been reading that afternoon. "What's this?"

Blanche felt a little embarrassed to reply. After all, she was only reading it because Naciens had left her with nothing else. "The *City of God.*"

"Oh, yes. I read it eighty years ago. What do you think?"

"It's a good late example of Ciceronian rhetoric."

Nerys paused a moment, and again the light dimmed. "Yes, I suppose it is," she said, and after that, neither of them spoke until bedtime.

They left Carbonek early the next morning. Naciens rode his mule, and Blanchefleur perched on Florence's hindquarters behind Nerys. The snow which had fallen on the night Perceval came had long since melted and the starkness of the dead trees and shattered stones in the valley was unrelieved by snow or bud. Blanche, looking at the barren rocks from the castle gates, had felt that it was the most horrible place she had ever seen. But now she was struck not so much by the desolation as by the fact that the Grail dwelt here: so much light and richness in the unrelieved desert.

The sublime light and music came into her mind again. She understood, she thought, why Naciens should choose to live in this wilderness with the lost people of Carbonek—a people so very lost that they, and the relic they guarded, could not even be seen by visitors to the castle without a special grace. But then, she wondered, why the desolation, if the Grail was as marvellous as they said?

Naciens led them out of the trees, up a narrow path climbing the steep wall of the valley. In a little over an hour they dismounted in the place where they had first met him under the overhanging rock.

Whether it had been there all along, or whether the side of the hill had opened since last time, Blanche could not tell. But now there was a narrow cleft leading into darkness among the rocks.

Naciens said, "We are out of the Waste of Carbonek now. But I think, if you come this way again, you will find us."

Nerys held out her hand to Naciens. "Thanks, friend," she said. Then, to Blanche's discomfiture, she added, "Bless us before we go."

When this had been done, Nerys walked ahead of Blanche and Florence into the cleft in the hill. It became darker and darker as they went, until at last the blue thread of sky above vanished completely. The next moment they had all stepped out of the wardrobe in the hall of the house in Gloucestershire.

Nerys took Florence's reins and led her to the back door, now mended and replaced. When she opened it, Blanche saw that it was late evening, and the moon was shining.

She followed Nerys out onto the lawn. Here the air was mild, almost warm. The scent of roses and good rich earth rose around her. Somewhere in the orchard, a nightingale was singing.

Home, she thought, and drank in the air. But what brought them here? What had changed Nerys's mind?

Nerys was speaking to her, almost in a whisper. "Blanche, find Sir Ector and tell him we've returned. Don't let the servants see you."

Blanche turned back to the house. The curtains in Sir Ector's study were drawn, but warm yellow gaslight streamed through the crack down the centre. Moving slowly, soaking in the mild air and delicious scents of autumn, she went to the French windows of the study and scratched on the door.

The curtain twitched aside. A moment later she had been caught into her guardian's bear-hug.

IN THE END IT TOOK SOME finessing before Blanche could call herself really at home. A charade had to be performed for the servants' sake: Nerys rang the front-door bell so that Sir Ector could pretend to have received a telegram, and the next morning he drove out in the barouche on time to meet the train and returned with Blanche and Nerys both dressed crisply and correctly, as though they had been on holiday at the seaside instead of roughing it in Britain.

But Blanche had slept in her own bed again, and woken late in the morning in warm and blissful content. She might soon be compelled to return to Logres, but at least they would never take her back to Carbonek!

Or *would* she return to Logres? Again, Blanche remembered Mr Corbin's words—"How can I help you if you speak of *musts?*" She had followed Nerys to Logres last time unthinkingly, reluctantly, frightened into submission by the Blue Boar's attack. She promised herself it would not happen again. Before she condemned herself to Logres for good, she would try, if she might, to find a way out. Perhaps Mr Corbin would be able to suggest something. She would go to the village to find him as soon as possible; this afternoon, maybe, or tomorrow.

Yet the thought of going to Logres did not seem so unbearable as it had before. Even Carbonek might have been worse. And there was the twinge of conscience she had felt when, for a moment, she had seen through Nerys's eyes. For a moment she had sensed what the fay had had to give up, and it had occurred to her for the first time that it was possible to love Logres, even to feel homesick for it…

And not only Nerys, but Sir Ector had made that sacrifice. For her. The least she could do was make an effort to understand their love, if she could.

Thus, when Sir Ector had fetched her home in state, and Blanche had looked over her correspondence and enjoyed an unhurried lunch, she went down to the library to find a book.

Her guardian was there, apparently dealing with some correspondence of his own. Blanche's heart sank at the sight of blue legal paper. So he was still preparing to close up the house and return to Logres. She had hoped that, whatever Naciens had told Nerys, it had postponed that at least for the next few months.

Sir Ector looked up at her with a smile. "Hullo, Blanche. Looking for anything?"

It occurred to her to look for something about Logres—wasn't there a famous book, *Le Morte D'Arthur* or something? But all her pride rose up in arms at the suggestion. She had given away her mother's ring, not once but twice, and she had quenched every spark of curiosity about her parents, and if she was bending now it was only for the sake of Nerys and Sir Ector, no one else.

Her conscience jabbed her. She pacified it with a moment's quick bargaining, and said to her guardian, "When I was at Carbonek I began reading *The City of God*. I'd like to finish it."

Sir Ector twiddled his pen. "In the English translation, or original Latin?"

"Latin, please," she said. Latin would undoubtedly make Nerys happier. And it left her conscience with no right to complain.

Sir Ector pointed. "Third shelf from the floor." But when Blanche found what she was after, she lingered.

"Are we going back to Logres soon?" she asked.

"Yes." Sir Ector laid down his pen. "But not right away. Nerys and I have much to arrange."

"Then is there time for me to see my friends before we leave?"

"Of course, Blanche. See them whenever you like."

"I was thinking of having a dinner party. I'd invite Kitty Walker, and Emmeline Felton. And Mr Corbin."

Sir Ector pushed his spectacles further up his nose and nodded. "I don't see why not. Arrange it whenever you like."

"Thanks," Blanche said. Still she didn't move. "And thanks for everything else, sir."

"Pardon?" He was already shuffling through the blue paper again. "I know you must have been sorry to leave it all behind—Logres, I mean. Your home. You must have missed it dreadfully."

He looked up at her, blinked quickly two or three times and cleared his throat, and she knew he was deeply touched. "Yes. I do miss it."

"I don't love it like you do," she said, apologetically. "It seemed so cold and ugly."

"But you've only seen Carbonek!" said Sir Ector, with uncommon vehemence. "Nerys told me what a grim ruin it is now. But you should have seen it in the days before the Dolorous Stroke! The vale of Carbonek was full of song then! All the apples in Logres went down that river to the sea. And you've never seen Camelot in summer. Camelot, the garden-city of Logres, full of towers and trees. You've never seen the sun on the windows of Carlisle, or walked in the river-side meadows of Trinovant in the spring."

"I suppose I haven't," Blanche said. It was hard not to get carried away on the tide of his enthusiasm. She said mournfully, "But you have friends there, too."

"The best brothers-at-arms a man could wish for. The most gracious King—" and something seemed to go wrong with Sir Ector's voice.

"Would I belong to anyone there?" Blanche asked.

Sir Ector blinked.

"Nerys told me there's some doubt. About me being the true heir of Logres. What about that? What will I have to face, there in Logres?"

Sir Ector looked out the window, playing with the coins in his pockets. At last he stood and walked around his desk to Blanche. "Prepare yourself," he said simply. "It's not going to be easy, Blanche. If you want your father's legacy, you'll have to fight for it."

Blanche kept her eyes on the carpet. "What if he isn't my father?"

"If he doesn't doubt it, why should you?" Sir Ector raised her chin with one finger and kissed her on the forehead. "I raised him, Blanche, and I can tell you this as surely as if it came from his own lips: he won't desert you."

That was exactly what she was afraid of. She didn't say it out loud. "How much time do I have left at home?"

"It depends," he said, becoming more vague and more businesslike, all at once. "As a matter of fact, Nerys and I will need to go to Camelot to speak to the King before we know."

"To make sure that he really does want me?" she asked, just to be contrary.

"No, no, no, Blanche!" Sir Ector sighed. "When Nerys went to Carbonek to fetch you, Naciens the Hermit told her something which upset all our plans. He says they need you at Carbonek."

Carbonek. Ugly, funereal, holy Carbonek. "*What?*"

"Do you know what the Grail Maiden is?"

"I don't."

"The maiden guardian of the Holy Grail. She watches, and prays, and contends. Since the fall of Elaine, eighteen years ago, there has been no Grail Maiden. Naciens says that you have been chosen for the next."

g

And when he came to the Tearne Wadling,
The baron there co'ld he finde,
With a great weapon on his backe,
Standing stiffe and stronge.
The Marriage of Sir Gawain

I saw the Lady of the Lake last night, riding north," said the King.

They were camping on the hills of Powys, roasting venison and their faces over a campfire built high and blazing to fend off the nip of frost at their backs. For once the clouds had withdrawn, unveiling the bitter stars and ice-haloed moon.

Perceval had been remembering his first journey to Carbonek, and how hushed and lonely it was by contrast to this good fellowship. Then the King's words fell into a momentary silence, and they all stirred and took interest.

"A dream?" Sir Ywain asked.

"No, it was herself. She said she would meet me in Camelot by All Saints'."

"To what purpose?" There was a combative gleam in Sir Kay's eye.

The King sighed, as if picking up the thread of an argument long standing. "She has always shown us friendship, Kay."

"She is a fay," Kay reasoned. "She may not mean us harm, but she will do it sooner or later."

Sir Gawain, whetting his sword, looked up. "We know the Lady Nimue can be trusted."

"Why are you defending her? You know better than any of us what harm comes when Elves meddle with men, however good their intentions."

Silence fell, as breathless as the space between lightning and thunder.

Perceval saw the others slowly straightening to look at his father.

No thunder came. Instead Gawain said quietly, "Yes. I know it."

A pause. Ywain said, "Harm, Gawain? I should never have expected to hear *you* say so."

"Everything comes with a price."

"Then the price of an immortal love is too high for me," laughed Kay. "How long did you wander around Camelot looking like Saint Sebastian's ghost?"

At that they all laughed. But Gawain reached out to grasp Perceval's shoulder. "I meant something else. I did not even know I had a son until yesterday. I had both paid and profited more than I knew."

"What does that have to do with the fay?" Perceval asked, curious.

Gawain stared. "Did you not know? Your mother was one of Nimue's people."

Perceval searched his father's face, unsure whether he was joking. "A fay? Mother?" He glanced around the fire. Not even Sir Kay was laughing up his sleeve. "She never told me…"

"Never?"

Perceval shook his head. "I wonder why."

"Perhaps she was afraid you'd follow her." Gawain put his hand over his mouth; there were tears in his eyes. "She could have taken you, you know. To the west, to Avalon. You could have become one of them. Ageless. …Instead, she sent you to me."

Perceval grinned. "What, me go to Avalon? No fear of that. I wanted to be up and doing, sir father."

Gawain blinked, and smiled back at him. "Yes. You would think so. But it was no small sacrifice for your mother."

Perceval tried to imagine what it might be like to turn his back on the splendid war of the world and retreat to Avalon, the peaceable isle. He laughed at the thought and said, "But this explains why everyone feared her and called her a fay. Why did she leave you, if she loved you?"

"The price of marriage to a mortal. The laws of her people took her from me after seven years. Did you really never hear the story?"

"Never."

A faint smile crossed his face. "She left that for me, too. Well, she was one of the people of the Lake, and my aunt, the sorceress, loved her brother."

Perceval glanced at the King and Sir Ywain. "Morgan le Fay? Is she an Elf, too, then?"

Sir Ywain stirred. "My mother," he said slowly, for he was always reluctant to speak of her, "is no fay, although she calls herself that. She was the daughter of the Queen Igerne and her first husband, the Duke of Tintagel. Full sister to Morgawse, the Queen of Orkney, your grandmother. Half sister to the King. There is not a drop of real fay's blood in her veins. Go on, cousin."

Gawain said: "When Ragnell and her brother refused to sell Morgan the secrets of their people, she enchanted them both. The brother, Sir Gromer Somer Joure, she bound to her evil will in the fortress of Tarn Watheline. But Ragnell, Ragnell she changed into the loathliest creature you could imagine if your eyes had drunk their fill of Hell itself."

Perceval's scalp prickled. "Morgan was able to do all this? Christ guard us all."

"He does. But Ragnell and her brother were unbaptised then. For the Elves say they are beyond salvation." He turned to the King. "The next part is your story, sire."

Arthur smiled. "An inglorious one, I have always thought, compared to yours."

"I have known the King of Logres since we were boys together, and he has done nothing inglorious in all that time," said Gawain, inclining his head.

"No? But if I have done anything worthy of praise, it is only that I have gathered praiseworthy men around me."

"Only a mean man seeks the company of mean men, sire."

"You honour me, fair nephew. But today I claim no more than my right, which is to win the honour of honouring one who merits it. I will tell the tale."

That was a game they played between them, these warriors of the Table—if it could be called a game, when done with such sincere gravity. The name of it was courtesy. Perceval listened, but he did not yet dare to play it with them.

The King went on. "At Christmas that year I held court at Carlisle. When a maiden came and sought justice for the tyrant of Tarn Watheline, I determined to undertake the quest myself.

"Not until I rode onto the bridge of Tarn Watheline to challenge Sir Gromer Somer Joure did I discover that the damsel had betrayed me to my death. For she was one of my sister's maidens. When my horse's hooves struck the bridge, all my power left me, so that I could hardly sit upright in the saddle. Then I looked up, and saw the lord of Tarn

Watheline standing there, and he was a tall man, so that mounted as I was, our eyes were on a level."

"And I have always said that he grows taller each time you tell the tale, sire," said Sir Kay.

"That is why I keep you with me, good Kay," said the King without anger. "Nevertheless, as I sat upon the bridge of Tarn Watheline, I could not lift a finger, and I knew that I would be but a dead dog if I could not rescue myself. 'Think on your sins, O King,' he said.

" 'Think on your own,' I said. 'For your last days have come, and although I am at your mercy now, my justice shall certainly find you after my death. A hundred of the best knights of Logres sit feasting in Carlisle, and they know where I have gone and on what errand. If I do not return, they know my will.'

"That puzzled him. Then he said, 'A bargain.'

" 'Say on,' I said, for I was not so sure of myself as I seemed.

" 'I will give you a year and a day,' said the knight of Tarn Watheline. 'Answer this question: what is it that women desire above all things? If you can answer me this in a year and a day, you shall go free. But if you cannot answer, I will have your head, and the knights of Logres shall leave me in peace.'

" 'It is a bargain,' I said. And then the weakness left me, and I rode back to Carlisle alone, for my sister's damsel had stayed only long enough to jeer at me."

The King turned to Sir Gawain. "Now you shall tell the rest of it, Gawain, for it is your story."

Gawain nodded. "When the King told me of the bargain he had made to save his life, the task did not seem difficult. But at the end of a year and a day, when he and I had ridden the length and breadth of Britain, we had a thousand different answers from a thousand different women. Some wanted wealth, some wanted idleness, some wanted richer homes or nobler husbands. And we both knew that the true answer must be something else entirely. We were within a league of Tarn Watheline when we met *her*."

"She was foul beyond description," interjected Sir Kay. "One eye beneath her snout, and the other in the midst of her forehead. All clothed in scarlet, with yellow tusks gleaming in the last light of sunset. I saw her at the wedding."

Perceval shuddered. "This was Mother?"

"You should have seen *mine*, on the night of the new moon," said Sir

Ywain, eyes gleaming with unwonted laughter. "Go on, cousin."

"The loathly lady asked us our business, and although we felt that nothing could save Logres now, not even one more answer, we spoke her fair.

" 'I know this baron,' said the lady. 'And I know this riddle, and will tell you—for a price.'

" 'If it is one that may be paid with honour,' said our good King.

" 'That is for you to determine,' said the loathly lady. 'I wish to wed one of your knights, lord King.' Do you remember, sire?"

"I remember it well," said the King, poking the fire.

"So do I," Gawain said. "I remember a time of silence, and then I remember how slowly you turned your head and looked at me with a manner that seemed to say, 'Why, here's Gawain, a bachelor.' "

"And then I told you that if you loved me, you would not burden my conscience with such a sacrifice."

"I did not do it for you, sire." Gawain was deadly serious now. "Death comes to us and all mortals. I shall still lose you one day. But Logres! The only perfection under heaven would fall if I could not save you."

"Not perfection, Gawain. Not Logres. Not yet."

Perceval's father smiled. "Well. The loathly lady told us the answer to the riddle. When we came to Tarn Watheline, Sir Gromer Somer Joure was waiting for us. And we read all the answers we had gathered.

" 'All so much warm air,' said the knight. And he heaved up his mace.

"And the King said, 'Wait! As we came, we met a loathly lady all clad in scarlet, and she told us that the thing women desire above all other things is *their own will*.' "

("It is true," said Sir Kay. "And not only for women," said the King.)

"The knight of Tarn Watheline fell into a rage. 'It was my sister Ragnell who revealed this to you,' he said, but although he gnashed his teeth and called down curses upon her head, there was nothing he could do.

"So the King repaid his vow and was free, and I gained a wife. We married in the view of all at Carlisle, and there was no dancing and little piping at our wedding. Not even the children in the street had the heart for it. But when the sun went down and we were alone, she returned to her true form. And her beauty after the horror was like all the fires of heaven."

He spoke slowly, here, as if by drawing out the telling of it he could draw out the memory. "I thought I was dreaming. Or mad.

"But she said to me, 'You have broken half the curse. But I shall be fair only half the time. Choose whether I shall be fair by day, or fair by night.'

"I said, 'By day I must travail and fight, from one end of Britain to the other. Be fair by night, when I am there to see you.'

" 'But think!' she said. 'By day I must sit in bower, and brave the pity and horror of everyone who sees me. At least, at night, the darkness will cover me.'

"Then I yielded my desire to her choice. But she replied: 'There will be no choice. For those words have broken the spell entirely.'

"And we had seven years."

CLEAR NIGHT GAVE WAY TO CLEAR morning. The water in their bottles had frozen, and not until the sun rose high enough to touch it did the frost vanish from the grass. Sir Perceval, following his four companions in single file down the slope of a hill, closed his eyes, leaned back, and basked in warm sun. Then Rufus stopped and he opened his eyes to see that the others had reined in and were speaking.

"I have passed this way before, sire," Sir Ywain was saying, pointing to the towers of a castle rising through trees in the valley below. "This is the castle of Sir Breunis."

"I have heard of him," Sir Gawain said. "A robber of women and old men. It is his custom to stop travellers and demand ransom."

"Let us turn aside here, then," said the King.

The castle of Sir Breunis was a small keep in a green valley amidst unkempt farmland. Some scores of paces from the gate his shield hung from an oak-tree. Sir Gawain spotted it at once.

"Watch this," he said to Perceval. He trotted up to the shield, and dealt it a ringing blow with the butt-end of his spear.

"Gawain!" Sir Ywain protested over the echoes. "This man rifled my father's steward three months ago. I had sworn to myself the right of retribution."

"Wait, gentlemen," said the King. "We have an untried knight with us. Of your courtesy, let him fight."

Perceval looked his gratitude. But his spirit cooled when he glanced up at the sound of hooves and saw a gigantic knight emerging from the castle bearing the same sable shield that hung on the oak-tree. His voice boomed inside the helm.

"Well, well—I see the lion of Ywain, the pentacle of Gawain, and the dragon of Uther's son. Has Camelot emptied to fight me?"

"No," Perceval shouted back. "They have come to watch."

He felt rather than saw the four others move to the wayside, off the path, which seemed even lonelier without them at his back. But it was too late to complain. The enemy was already moving. He laid his spear in the fewter, breathed, "Jesu, defend me!" and clapped his spurs to Rufus's sides. The great horse gathered himself and leaped forward like a thunderbolt. Perceval's eyes narrowed on his target. He measured out fractions of seconds with crystal clarity and was conscious, despite the speed at which his enemy surged closer, that his own form was perfect and he could not fail to strike true.

With a bone-wrenching shock they met. The spear in Perceval's hand melted away into wooden shards. Rufus reeled and staggered. The landscape spun wildly and then the road reared up and slammed against him.

The double shock and the taste of dust were familiar enough from his training at the old earl's castle: he had been unhorsed. Perceval gritted his teeth, rolled, and staggered to his feet, drawing his sword. Through the slit of his helm he saw his four companions standing under the oak tree. Then Rufus, moving off the road in a daze. Perceval whirled, searching for his enemy. As he did so, something blocked the sunlight and he threw up his shield just in time to catch Sir Breunis's sword. Not until he had evaded the blow and retreated a step or two did he have the time to realise that the other knight, too, must have been unhorsed. Also he was wounded, with the blood already running down his sword-arm.

The sight flooded through Perceval's veins like new life, and sluiced away the shock, not to mention the embarrassment, of his fall. The combat had hardly begun, but victory was already within his grasp. He yelled, and rushed Sir Breunis with a storm of blows. The enemy guarded himself, but his wound made him sluggish, and he staggered back under Perceval's assault. Then he rallied, and Perceval felt some of that gigantic strength.

He danced back a few steps, hoping to weary the enemy knight by forcing him to follow. But Sir Breunis knew better than to waste his strength, and took the opportunity to breathe. Perceval rushed in again, lunging for the right shoulder, left unprotected by a drooping shield arm. What came next happened so fast that his eyes could barely follow: Sir Breunis parried his lunge with such a powerful stroke that Perceval spun under the impact, turning his unshielded right flank towards the enemy. At the same moment, Sir Breunis snatched a poniard with his left hand and aimed it for the underarm joint of Perceval's armour.

All this Perceval saw and understood in a fraction of time. The only question was whether he was too overextended to take the quick step back that would save him…no. He recovered and disengaged. The glittering blade no more than kissed his mail. All the enemy's attention was on the poniard, leaving his sluggish sword-arm still out of play through that flailing parry; he left himself, for a moment too long, unguarded. …Perceval laughed and lunged, every ounce of bone and muscle flung behind his sword's point, and thrust with tremendous force clean through his foe.

They stood face to face, panting through the bars of their helms. Sir Breunis lifted the poniard in his left hand and drove it at Perceval's extended arm. It was a futile gesture: the mail at that point, unlike the clumsy ring-stitched leather the brigand wore, was too fine-woven for the blade to find entrance. Perceval recovered his lunge. Sir Breunis staggered back off the blade and fell to the ground, clutching his wound.

Perceval stood, rasping in great breaths of air. Dimly he was aware of his father and the King coming toward him. Then he remembered what came next, drew his own poniard, and cut the laces of Sir Breunis's helm.

The bandit's face twisted with agony underneath his big black beard. Perceval held the poniard to his throat with trembling hands.

"Do you yield?" he asked.

Protests reached Perceval's humming ears, it seemed, from far away. "No! Kill him!" Sir Kay was saying.

"I yield, I yield," gasped Sir Breunis.

"If you let him live, more innocent travellers will suffer," said Sir Ywain.

Perceval looked down at the man's vice-ravaged face and shuddered. Sir Gawain was saying, "Better put an end to him, boy. Let justice be done."

The word reminded Perceval of the King. "Sire?" he croaked.

Arthur stepped over the wounded man and knelt on the other side, removing his helm. He glanced up at Perceval and said, too quietly for the others to hear, "Well done." Then he looked down at Sir Breunis.

"Do you wish to live?"

A nod.

"You know who I am," said the King. "Say my name."

Breunis grimaced and groaned and got it out. "Arthur Pendragon. High King."

"Then you know what charge is upon me. You have robbed and pillaged my people. You have robbed and pillaged *me*. If I do not avenge them, who will?"

The man was silent.

"Answer me. Tell me why I should spare you."

"They say that no one ever asked your mercy in vain…"

That was bold, perhaps bolder than Perceval himself would have been in such a case, and he half expected the King's anger to kindle.

But Arthur Pendragon nodded. "It is true. And it does not delight me to kill and maim, but neither do I give my mercy freely. The cost is your freedom. You must become my man. You must swear to abandon your pillage, restore their property to those you have robbed, and put your strength at the service of all oppressed ones, wherever you may meet them, for as long as your life is spared upon the earth. Will you so swear?"

"I swear it." The brigand began to sob, loud heaving cries. "I swear it. Let me live, O King."

Perceval, sickened by that abject plea for mercy, suddenly despised him, and the hand holding the poniard went ice-steady. But the King said:

"I give you your life, then, sir, what's left of it. See that you mend yourself and abandon this habitual thievery, for if I hear otherwise you will surely die."

He nodded to Perceval, who with a mixture of relief and disappointment shot his poniard back into the sheath and picked up his bloody sword. The King rose and turned to his knights.

"Sire," said Gawain with a note of reproach in his voice, "your mercy is too sublime for my understanding. This man is worthy of death."

"So too are we," said the King. "Have the castle thrown open and thoroughly searched."

Kay and Ywain went up the road to see to this, but Gawain held his ground. "We? How so? We are your majesty's instruments of justice. And your majesty's justice is the justice of Heaven."

"Fair nephew," said the King, "all this is true, I hope, especially that I am ruled by the justice of Heaven. And yet, Gawain, we are sinful men."

Perceval flopped to the ground and watched the King and Sir Gawain with a furrowed brow, wiping his sword on the grass by the wayside.

Gawain was saying, "We are sinful men, sire, but this man is beyond saving."

The King laughed. "God help me, Gawain, if you were ever to read the sin in my soul."

"I know you better than to think it might be found there, sire," said Gawain, with an oddly sweet smile lighting up his harsh face.

But the King's laughter had faded. He glanced at Sir Breunis, whose men had come from the castle to carry him in.

"Do not deceive yourself, Gawain. There are black places in the heart of every man."

Perceval thought of the disappointment he had felt when the King gave Sir Breunis his life, and was suddenly ashamed. As Sir Breunis's men lifted him onto a handcart, Perceval ran to him.

"You have taken as your lord the best man of the world," he said, gripping the sides of the cart on each side of the wounded knight's head. "You know it."

At first Breunis threw back his stare from a blank face. But then he dropped his gaze and grunted: "I know it."

"That makes us brothers." Perceval spoke slowly to let each word, with its weight of menace, sink in. "But if I find that you have deceived him, you will die by my hand. I swear it."

IO

Then they showed him the shield, of shining gules
With the pentangle pictured in pure gold hues.
Sir Gawain and the Green Knight

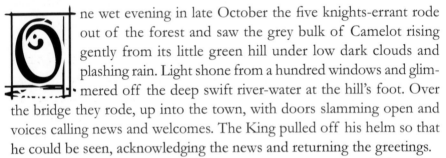ne wet evening in late October the five knights-errant rode
out of the forest and saw the grey bulk of Camelot rising
gently from its little green hill under low dark clouds and
plashing rain. Light shone from a hundred windows and glimmered off the deep swift river-water at the hill's foot. Over
the bridge they rode, up into the town, with doors slamming open and
voices calling news and welcomes. The King pulled off his helm so that
he could be seen, acknowledging the news and returning the greetings.

They had ridden hard all day to be back at sundown, and when they
reached the castle courtyard Perceval was glad to slide from his saddle,
hand the reins to a squire, and walk stiffly after the others into the keep.
Here they were met by a flock of maidens. Two of them took Perceval
by either hand and led him away without a word. He glanced back at the
others, almost in a panic, and saw them being spirited off likewise. From
the door into the Great Hall he heard the buzz of voices, saw the warm
blaze of candles, and smelled meats and spices that made his stomach
growl—but it was already too late to say anything, for he had been swept
into a dark passage, and could only blindly follow his maiden guides.

They brought him to a room on the east side of the castle, not large but
by far the most luxurious place he had yet seen, with clean rushes underfoot and thick bright tapestries to shut in the warmth. These were worked
with trees and grotesquely beautiful creatures he did not recognise, so
that for a moment he thought he stood in some foreign and oppressive
wood. The hearth was wisely built, drawing the smoke off the fire and

78

filling the room with heat. Perceval, accustomed to the crisp free air and endless halls of the forest, stood still in dumb amazement while the two maidens whisked off his armour. A third brought him a cup of heated and spiced wine, and then hot water and a flannel.

When they ushered him back to the Great Hall, Perceval hardly knew himself—clean and warm, clad in soft new wool under the fur-lined robe worn by knights in time of peace. Although they were inexpressible ease to his weary body, something about the warm furs, the scented heat of the fire, and the all-embracing tapestries had disquieted him, and when the maidens bore away his armour for cleaning and repairs, he had almost begged them to leave him his sword—then felt a little foolish when they silently returned it to him, and found a new belt, not clogged with mud and rain, for him to hang it from.

But with the heft of it at his hip he felt more of a man, and less of a house-cat, and better able to walk into the Great Hall, and the company of the knights of Logres.

He could not help remembering the last time he had been here, at the Feast of the Ascension with the hall in an uproar over the insult he had avenged. But here was a peaceful, almost a domestic scene: the Queen at the head of the Table plying the King with food, a hum of conversation from the ladies in the balcony, a louder chatter from the long tables where the squires and servants sat, and little knots of knights clustered among the empty spaces at the Round Table, deep in talk.

Perceval paused, uncertain, in the doorway—did he belong at the Table, or with the squires and wanderers? But then a foot fell on the rushes behind him and he turned to see Sir Gawain, who beckoned him to the Table.

"Gawain! About time!" said one of the knights, rising from his seat, and Perceval blinked at him, for the smile which flashed across his face seemed a duplicate of Gawain's. "Who have you brought with you?"

Gawain seemed to expand slightly. "Cast your eyes over the Table, lads, and see if there's a place for Sir Perceval...*mab* Gawain."

"What's that?" someone asked, and Perceval found himself surrounded by a curious ring of onlookers.

"Sir Perceval's seat is over by the Siege Perilous; the letters appeared at midday," said the knight who had spoken first. "What do you mean, *mab* Gawain? I've a grown nephew? Why was I not told?"

"I could not have known, myself," said Gawain. "Ragnell left without telling me."

"I thought she had gone to Avalon."

"Not until last spring."

"And you say you knew nothing about it?"

"Sir Gareth, we do not starve information out of our captives here." It was a lady's voice, cool and imperious. But when Perceval glanced at the Queen, he saw that she was laughing.

Sir Gawain laughed with her, and said to Perceval, "This is my brother, Gareth. Now come and eat. No, no, Caradoc, later. Gaheris, I'll see my new niece after I eat, or I may eat her. Perceval. Your siege."

Like all the others it was a big, square-hewn wooden chair, carved with leaves and acorns, and bearing letters on the back in gold: *Sir Perceval of Wales*. Gawain's own siege was next to him on the right. On the left was an empty seat with no words on it at all.

"What's this?" he asked, but Gawain was piling food onto his trencher and did not hear.

"This? This is the Siege Perilous. Never sit in it, as you value your life." Sir Gareth kicked away the seat on the other side of the Siege Perilous (it was labelled *Sir Bors*) and sat on the Table.

Perceval nodded, and leaned back for the serving-man to give him bread and a partridge. "I've heard of it. It is intended for the Grail Knight?"

"Yes. Anyone else who sits there—*fzzt*, he turns to flame and ash."

Perceval remembered the damsel Blanchefleur's message, which he had given to the King in the hills of Wales. "He will come soon."

Gareth nodded. "The King told us. When will it be?"

"I know nothing more, neither the day nor the hour." Perceval paused before biting into the meat. "It is strange to find an uncle. Are there more?"

"Two more," Gareth told him. "Gaheris is over there." He pointed. "Agravain is gone on some quest or another."

Perceval swallowed. "And your father?"

"King Lot of Orkney, dead many years. Mother—Queen Morgawse—rules now. Then there are the cousins. Ywain you know. He's the son of Uriens King of Gore."

"And of the Queen of Gore."

Gareth laughed softly. "Our sweet aunt Morgan. Yes. But Ywain is like his father. Mordred is like—Mordred is *not* like his father."

Gawain turned to them.

"Mordred," he said, frowning. "Have you seen him, brother?"

"Not for months." Gareth squinted across the Table and sighed with mock disappointment. "He must be alive somewhere. His siege still bears his name."

"Gareth!" said Gawain, but his reproachful voice shook with laughter. "What has he done to deserve that?"

"Nothing," returned Gareth. "Ah, Gawain, you are right. Mistrust is an ugly guest, and the only one not welcome among brothers." He turned to Perceval again. "Gaheris and I are married men, and can give you cousins of your own, but they are yet young to break spears."

Perceval was beginning to speak, but when the other knights fell silent and Sir Gareth slipped off the Table, he turned to see what had made them all stand up so straight.

It was the Queen. The back of his mind noticed that he, too, had stiffened as if to attention. Perceval had lived with the immortal beauty of his mother all his life, but even he was awed by Guinevere.

She set a silver and glass cup before him. "You sent this back and avenged the slight upon me," she told him. "The cup is yours now."

"I thank you, madam."

She smiled, and walked on. "Goodnight," she said in a louder voice. "Sleep well, and sleep safe. Ye are guards on the borders of darkness: look upon what you protect, and rest from your labours. Goodnight!" And she passed from the hall.

As November blew in, turning the forest to grey smoke, Perceval stayed at Camelot, for here he had the chance to continue his training under the eye of his father and other knights of the Table.

There was also an item of business that had to be finished before he could undertake another quest. Sir Gawain took him one afternoon to see Sir Bleoberis, the King's herald, about a device of his own. The knight was surprised to hear that Perceval had been using a blank shield. "Surely," he said, reaching down a folio stuffed with painted parchments, "you used *something* to signify your name and lineage."

"I had not the slightest idea of my name and lineage, sir," Perceval said cheerfully.

"Well. Look at these." Sir Bleoberis produced a parchment showing a white shield bearing red diagonals. "Argent, three bendlets gules. You know this one, of course."

Perceval squinted thoughtfully. "Oh, that is Sir Lancelot's shield."

"Right. And here—Argent, a dragon passant gules."

That was more familiar—the King's own shield, with its red dragon. "The Pendragon. What about Father? A red shield with a yellow star."

"Here it is," said Sir Bleoberis. "Gules, a pentacle *or*. But the question remains what bearings you should carry. I meant to show you this." He extracted a sheaf of parchments and spread them out.

Gawain leaned over to look. "Here are the Orkney arms." He pointed to a purple shield bearing a double-headed golden eagle. "Gareth, Gaheris, and Agravain bear variations of this."

"Why do you have something different?" Perceval asked.

From the look that fleeted across Sir Bleoberis's face, Perceval wondered if he had said something wrong. But Gawain bent his head and traced the pentacle with his forefinger, answering without heat. "The Endless Knot signifies the five virtues of knighthood. And these are generosity, fellowship, purity, courtesy, and compassion. I took it to remind me of them."

"Then there is nothing I had rather bear," said Perceval.

Sir Bleoberis picked up the parchment and pursed his lips. "We should have to differ it from your father's shield, to prevent confusion."

"Label it," Gawain said. "When I am dead, he can remove the label."

Sir Bleoberis took a new parchment and dipped his pen in ink. "Gules, a pentacle *or*, bearing a label of three points *or*. I will enter it in the rolls."

ON AN EVENING NOT LONG AFTER this, Perceval was on his way to Sir Gareth's rooms when Sir Kay passed him in the passage with a woman shrouded in a black cloak, glistening with rain. He caught a gleam of eyes from within the hood, and then the lady put her hand on Sir Kay's arm to stop him.

"Sir Perceval," she said. "Come with us to the King's solar."

Perceval wondered how she knew him and looked at Sir Kay half-expecting a reaction. But even Sir Kay dared not gainsay this lady. "If you think so, madam."

"I am sure of it," she said, and passed on.

Perceval waited only to send a page with a message to Sir Gareth, then followed Sir Kay and the stranger to the solar. This was a warm room on the south side of the castle, well-tapestried against the cold, where in his few leisure hours the King could often be found playing chess or hearing the news of knights-errant. He sat there now with the Queen by him and an assemblage of the older knights: Sir Gawain, Sir Lucan, Sir Bedivere, Sir Ywain, and Sir Kay.

In other words, a gathering of the King's council. Perceval bowed deep, wondering what he might have done to draw their attention. But then the lady he had met in the Great Hall turned from the fire, where she had been warming herself, and came to him with an outstretched hand.

"Sir Perceval," she said, "do you know me?"

She had laid aside her cloak and wore a robe sheened with silver threads like water. Her hair, tied into a long black braid, snaked almost to the floor. Her face—but when he looked at her face, he wanted to fall to his knees and grip the ground to know that it was still there, that he was not suddenly floating lost and anchorless in vast starry spheres.

With an effort he stiffened his knees and remembered when he had last sensed that overpowering immensity. This woman was a fay.

"The Lady of the Lake."

She smiled, and the stress of her regard lessened a degree. "Very good."

Gawain said: "Now that he is here, let us begin. You have yet to explain what he has to do with the King's daughter."

"A little, son of Lot. And more hereafter, if I see clearly. He has spoken of the errand given him at Carbonek Castle?"

"That the Grail Knight draws near? He has," said the King.

"And, sir knight,"—to Perceval—"do you remember the name of the damsel who gave you this message?"

"She said her name was Blanchefleur." His mouth went dry all of a sudden, and he gulped. "The King's daughter?"

No one heard his question. The King was speaking to the Lady of the Lake. "She is here, in Britain?"

"She was in Carbonek, and has returned to the other world now," said Nimue. "But I have seen her keepers and they say they must speak to us, Lord Arthur. She is no longer safe in hiding. Morgan has already been there."

"Then it is time for her to come home," said the King. "We have been too long without her company."

A slight frown wrinkled the Queen's brow.

"Remember the reason you sent her away," said Nimue.

"That she might be safe until the time comes to fulfil the prophecy," said the King. "Yes. But if Morgan has found her way to the other place, she will be safer here."

"Even Camelot has not always protected you, O King," Sir Ywain put in. "My mother has the cunning of a rat in a garderobe."

"And yet I am still alive," the King said.

"You face the danger for Logres's sake, sire," said the Queen, speaking for the first time. "But Blanchefleur is yet young for such burdens."

"Is she?" The King spoke gently, to make the words less harsh. "She can be no younger than Sir Perceval, here, whom I have seen adventure his life in combat. One day she must carry Logres. I only hope we have not kept her unburdened too long."

"There is another choice, besides Camelot," said the Lady of the Lake. "With safety, but also hardship, and a certain kind of danger."

The others in the room looked at her in surprise. "Say on," said Arthur.

Nimue said: "I was riding in the night through Torfaen when I met the Hermit of Carbonek, waiting for me at the Greyflood crossing. 'Tell the High King,' he said, 'that Sarras needs a maiden.'"

"Sarras!" Arthur put up a hand to smooth his beard over his chin. "And his meaning?"

"The maiden guardian of the Holy Grail," said Nimue. "They want Blanchefleur at Carbonek."

"Have you been there, lady? To Carbonek?"

"No." There was a hint of wistfulness in her voice. "The damsel Nerys has been."

"She and Sir Ector are right, then. I must speak to them. But who will guard Blanchefleur while they travel?"

Nimue said, "Send a knight you trust. Sir Perceval here has already fought Sir Odiar of Gore on her behalf."

"What?" Perceval, jerked so suddenly into the discussion, spoke without thinking. "Not me, I beg you."

"Why not?" asked Sir Gawain with knitted brows.

Perceval turned to the King. "Sire, I will do whatever you command, but I have offended the lady Blanchefleur. I did not know she was your daughter when I did it."

The King frowned. "When you did what?"

"I misunderstood my mother's directions, sire. I…"

"Well?"

Perceval looked around at the solemn knights, at his father, at the immortal queen of Avalon, and at Blanchefleur's august parents. "I kissed her," he mumbled, going red.

Sir Gawain's eyebrows reached for his hairline. A look of almost malicious pleasure crossed Sir Kay's face and he said, "Speak up, lad. I didn't hear you!"

The King looked at Nimue, who made some signal which Perceval just missed. Then Arthur turned to the Queen and said, "Lady wife, do you remember what the penalty is for kissing a king's daughter? Something lingering, with molten lead in it, I think."

"I thought it was burning alive," said the Queen.

"No, no, that's for adultery."—"It was certainly lingering."

"I have promised to serve her a year and a day to repay her," Perceval said, stoic on the surface, although inside he was hot with shame. "But I think she might prefer it if you sent someone else, sire."

The King looked at him for so long that Perceval felt himself reddening once more. At length he stroked his beard again and said with a smile which Perceval did not understand, "If you have promised to serve her, then you had best keep your word. What do you say, Gawain?"

"I will ensure you can trust him, sire."

"Oh, I have no doubts about that. I meant whether you approve of his serving the lady Blanchefleur."

"Oh, *that!*" said Gawain. "No, sire. I wholeheartedly approve." And he too smiled, all white teeth, like the wolfhound under the King's chair.

"Guard her well, then," said the King to Perceval. "Remember that the fate of Logres may rest on your faithfulness in this."

"Sire," said Perceval, "if mortal man can guard your daughter, I will."

With this the council broke up, but as he went out of the solar Perceval felt a hand on his arm and turned to see the Lady Nimue.

"There are things you should know about the place you are going," she said. "Where can we speak?"

But when Perceval had led her to his chamber, which as usual in Camelot did double duty as a sitting-room, she did not immediately begin to tell him of the other world where he would find the Lady Blanchefleur.

Instead she turned to him and said, "There is a thing it would be wise for you to know, son of Gawain."

Perceval bore up under the weight of her attention and said, "Say on."

"You are a newcomer to Camelot; indeed, to Logres," said Nimue. "Therefore you have not heard the stories about the birth of the damsel Blanchefleur."

"Stories?"

"For a time," the Lady said, looking at the ring on her finger, "it was whispered that the lady Queen loved Sir Lancelot."

The ring should have flattened to silver leaf between those adamant eyes and that stone-white hand. "No whisper ever reached my ears," he said.

"Spoken like the son of Gawain," and there was a mocking twist at the corner of her mouth. "But you have only come to Camelot today, true?"

Perceval said, "What is the point? You say this has something to do with the birth of the damsel Blanchefleur. Is she not the King's daughter? Is that what you mean?"

"Hush!" said Nimue, and her look hit him like a slap. "I mean to say nothing of the kind. Only that such was said once, before Sir Ector took her to the other world. Therefore, whatever lies in the damsel Blanchefleur's future at Camelot, I am sure that these stories will come to her ears. In that day, as in this, she may need a protector."

"But the King doesn't doubt she is his daughter. Does he?"

Nimue's eyes opened innocently, more like a mortal's, now, in their blank candour. "The King believes the Queen."

Perceval was suddenly angry with her. "You make him sound like a fool."

"Do I? I do not mean to. Whatever Arthur Pendragon is, he is no fool." She tilted her head. "Nor is the Queen. But even a very great man may have his blindnesses."

"Not him."

"Yes, even him. If there is a thing I have learned in all my endless years, it is that every man is blind in some direction."

"And you think the Queen is his?"

"I think he would be slow to think ill of her, and slower to think ill of Lancelot, and slowest of all to charge the most beloved knight of Logres with treason. Even if he cared nothing for the Queen, even if the brotherhood of the Table were not founded in his heart's blood, not even the Pendragon can afford to make an enemy of a man like Lancelot."

Perceval's mouth went dry. He went and picked up the Queen's silver-and-glass cup from the chest by his bed. "But Lancelot does love her, doesn't he? The day this was stolen, he claimed the quest as if by right."

"Yes," said Nimue.

Perceval turned the fragile vessel over and over. "And the Queen? What would happen to her?"

"You heard it yourself," said the Lady of Lake. "She would be burned alive."

II

If men should rise and return to the noise and time of the tourney,
The name and fame of the tabard, the tangle of gules and gold,
Would these things stand and suffice for the bourne of a backward journey,
A light on our days returning, as it was in the days of old?

Chesterton

ou really are leaving, then?" said Kitty Walker.

"I might *have* to." Blanche swished at the long lush grass with a stick, keeping her head bent. If she looked up, she would see the imperious autumn larches, sulphur fretted with black and grey, sitting in judgement on her sulky mood. "I'm sorry to hear that Mr Corbin has gone to London. I particularly wanted to see him."

Kitty said, "I'll be sure to give him your invitation when he comes back in the morning. Blanche! How shall I get on without you?"

"I expect you'll get on very well."

"Do you *want* to go? Oh, Blanche, and I was going to ask you to come to Paris with me next year."

Blanche sighed and reached for another clump of grass. "Of course I don't. But I haven't much choice. You'll come tomorrow night, won't you, and say goodbye?"

"For the dinner party? Of course I shall. But I refuse to say goodbye. Remember, it's my birthday party in a week. You must stay long enough for that, for everyone is coming down from London, and they will need *someone* brainy to talk to, or they will think us no better than Welshmen."

Blanche chivvied millipedes absent-mindedly. "If I'm still here, Kitty, I'll come to it. But I can't promise."

"Oh, *bella*," said Kitty, and hugged her. "Sir Ector has a heart of stone. Now I must run home before those clouds decide to rain again."

Blanche glanced through the larches at the sky. Red-and-gold needles sprang jubilantly into relief against the purple clouds. Blanche couldn't help smiling. "I had better do the same."

"Although *you* won't mind if it does rain." Kitty reached out and touched the thick woollen cloak Blanche had brought back with her from Carbonek. "I *must* have one of these, Blanche! It would hold off a downpour!"

Blanche laughed and wrapped the luxurious garment more closely around her. "I don't care to put it to the test. Goodbye!"

Kitty tripped back down the path to the village, and Blanche, walking with a long swinging step, passed on under the flaming larches. The afternoon darkened toward the slow twilight that comes on an overcast day, and the forest, which at first glowed in the gloom, lost its colour as the light faded.

Blanche came out from under the trees and began climbing the bald ridge behind the house. A wind sprang up and lashed at her hair with a scattering of idle raindrops. She put up her hood, toiled up the last few feet of slope, and stood on the ridge. Looking back, she saw a long streak of red-and-gold sky where the bank of cloud ended over the Welsh hills. East, down the slope at her feet, she saw the house nestled in its garden, marked at the front by a row of brown-leafed elms and behind by the dormant orchard.

Affection welled up in her at the sight of her home. It was a good place to come back to, in the dark, after tramping on the hills—or after sojourning in the high cold halls of Logres.

Over the thrumming wind, someone called her name.

Blanche wheeled. In the dim dusk, the grey-clad figure was hardly visible against the hillside. As he came closer, something about his loping stride warned her that he was not from her own time. But up here on the hill there was nowhere to run. Blanche stood her ground until he was close enough for her to see his face.

"You again!" she whispered, and put a hand to her heart, which began to hammer now that the threat was past.

Sir Perceval inclined his head. "The King sent me," he said.

"How you frightened me!" said Blanche. Then, as she remembered her manners with a rush: "I am so sorry. I mean, good evening. But why have you come?"

"The King sent me," repeated Perceval, raising an eyebrow.

"For what?" Blanche took a second look at him and felt a wild impulse to laugh. Mail and surcoat were laid aside, and he was now correctly garbed in coat, waistcoat, and trousers. But they fitted badly, and the fault was exaggerated by his brown face and rumpled hair, which the buttons and starch only made look wilder.

Perceval said, "The Lady of the Lake has taken Sir Ector and her damsel to speak to the King. I have come to guard you in their place. They have told your people that I am your cousin, which is partly true."

It took Blanche a moment to realise that by *her people* Perceval meant the servants. To her, they were only the help. Blanche said: "Do you believe there is danger, then? Here?"

"We hope not," he said with a smile.

"But Morgan le Fay knows where I live."

He nodded. "The Lady says her rift has been repaired. But we do not know her full power, and Sir Ector has been called away." He grinned. "Do not fear. I am here to serve you, as I promised."

Despite the fit of schoolgirl giggles that had seized her in Carbonek when he first proposed to be her knight, his assurance annoyed her now. "You inspire me with almost perfect confidence," she said, honey-sweet. "With a few more years and experience, you would make a capable guardian, I'm sure."

"And you an amiable ward," he said, bowing again.

He spoke so courteously that Blanche had walked on five steps before she realised that he had insulted her. "I'm sure you were the obvious choice," she said, gesturing to the house below as it sat snug in its garden glowing with light, "given the magnitude of the present danger."

"The present danger, which is that the Witch of Gore, as you say, knows where you live."

Blanche shuddered and thought it a rather brutal reminder. They went on in silence, but now the house below seemed less comforting and more ephemeral, and the cold wind blowing against them reminded her of the void between the worlds, into which, as the horrible premonition struck her, it was the doom of all such pleasant and homely places to fall forever.

Would Night swallow them all in the end?

"But you are willing to risk your life for me?" she said at last, more earnestly.

Perceval repeated the words he had spoken in the King's solar.

"If mortal strength can save you, I will."

They reached the gate to the orchard. Blanche watched Perceval open it, the hair on the back of her neck prickling to remind her what had happened last time she and Nerys had crossed that portal. When they had passed safely into the orchard, and the gate was closed, Blanche said, "Why?"

"Why…?"

"Why will you…" she grimaced at the theatrical words "…save me?"

"The King—"

"The King sent you. I know."

They walked on between the shadows of the apple-trees. Blanche tried again.

"Aren't you afraid of what is coming?"

He laughed. "Pshaw!"

"What, do you like the—the pain, and the idea of dying?"

Perceval said: "No. But it is better than the idea of a life without any kind of danger, without any kind of victory."

Blanche shuddered. "Everyone fears death. What makes you so eager to face it?"

"I had rather keep my word sworn to you in Carbonek, and obey my King, than prove myself faithless." He thought a moment. "So I find that I am afraid, but of something worse than death."

That made her laugh. "Worse than death! Thanks! You are very comforting!"

They came through the gate at this side of the orchard and into the garden. Perceval said, "Does it trouble you, having me here?"

"No," Blanche admitted. Then, after a moment, she said, "Shall I tell you what I think?"

He bent his head in assent.

"Each time I have gone to Logres, or needed help, you were there. It reminds me of what Vicar says, about Providence. I always thought it was a nice way of saying that everything is for the best. But after the last few months, how can I think that?"

"You know what destiny looks like," said Perceval at last.

"I do now."

"A mysterious plan, too strange to be happenstance. I too see it unfolding around us."

Blanche said: "But that is what frightens me. What seems best to Providence horrifies *me*. What if it takes me far away from home? What if it drives me into deeper danger? What if it…" she swallowed, "what if it wants to hurt me?"

They came out onto the lawn below the house, where light streamed out onto the grass, and Perceval looked at her. "Why, damsel," he said, with surprise and ineffable disappointment in his voice, "are you afraid?"

"Yes, terribly"—she bit back the words and glanced back the way they had come. The last light had faded out of the west and even the trees hardly seemed blacker than the sky. "I am sorry," she said at last. "The darkness made me afraid. In the light I will be brave enough."

Perceval looked out at the night and his answer, when it came, shook her. "I know what you mean by fearing the dark," he said. "The tales I heard of Logres spoke of it as a beacon of light. But I found it sieged by shadows." He glanced back at Blanche. "I, too, fear the future. I fear that Logres is doomed to flicker and die, leaving only the dark, and that nothing I can do will stop it."

Blanche stared at him. "Do you mean that Logres is in danger?"

"It has always been in danger," he replied, with a smile.

"From Morgan le Fay?"

Perceval shook his head. "She is only the foremost of our enemies. Britain is full of sorcerers, barbarians, brigands, raiders, and rebels. It is the work of the Round Table to resist and subdue them, to shield the little people against them. Had you not heard this?"

"I—" Blanche began, and then fell silent. She could not truthfully say she had been ignorant of it, and suddenly, sickeningly, she was ashamed of herself. "I had heard it," she said, in a voice she hardly recognised. She laid her hand on Perceval's arm. "But what are you going to do about it?"

He smiled encouragingly. "The task at hand. The King said that the fate of Logres rests on your safety."

"That's what the prophecy said. But how?"

"You are his heir," said Perceval. "The one who will inherit Logres when he is gone. The one who will fend off the night. But you knew this too."

"I did," she said in horror. "But I never thought of it this way before. I never knew what was at stake." For a moment, the evening dark pressed in like the enemies of Logres; ahead, the windows of her own house gave off a comforting glow.

Blanche looked Perceval in the eye. "I am mortified," she said. "Here I have been telling you my own selfish woes, while you are trying to save a civilisation."

Perceval opened his mouth to speak, but there was the sound of a gong from within the house.

"It is dinner," said Blanche with a shaky laugh. "Let us go in."

IN THE LIGHT, AS SHE HAD predicted, she felt stronger. It was good modern gaslight streaming from lamps mounted on the wall, and with the addition of a good solid butler like Keats to fill glasses and pass plates, Blanche felt even better. But the vision which had filled her imagination a moment ago on the lawn, of a kingdom besieged by primeval chaos, still weighed on her mind.

She fought it with forced mirth.

"So the railway has your box, Cousin Percy," she said in Welsh as Keats swam in with the soup. "You had better hope they disgorge it soon, or you will be wearing Sir Ector's clothes all the way back to Merthyr Tydfil. Our gentlemen's outfitter in the village is not the thing at all."

"No, not the thing," said Perceval, playing along valiantly, although he evidently did not understand one word in three.

"When we have a moment, you must tell me all the news. Thank you, Keats." Blanche took a feverish spoon of soup and was grateful that Perceval had apparently learned some table manners in the last few months.

Perceval spoke. "They say the new Bishop of Trinovant nearly burned down the cathedral by mistake during the winter."

"My goodness," said Blanche. "How extraordinary. Keats, will you close the curtains over there? I feel the dark coming in. The cold," she corrected herself, and afterwards fell silent.

After dinner, in the drawing room, Perceval wandered to the corner and inspected the bookshelves. Blanche sat down at the piano and tinkled a few bars of the *Well-Tempered Clavier*. Surprised, the knight whipped around to see what had caused the strange noise. Then he relaxed and came off guard like a dog coming off point, grinning as though he hadn't convinced her for a terrifying moment that some enemy had silently entered the room behind her.

Blanche banged the lid shut over the keys.

Perceval held up a book. "Tell me what this is."

"It's a book." She took it off him and flipped it open. "See inside? Writing."

He peered at it. "The little words. I never learned the trick of them."

"You never learned to *read?*"

He shook his head. "We had no books in the cave. And no parchments."

"The cave!" Blanche pressed her hand to her forehead.

He laughed and gestured to the piano. "It had no lamps or singing machines, but it was warm if you kept the fire going."

She had to let go of her dismay and laugh. "No, no, I'm sure it was lovely. Only I just remembered that the dinner party is tomorrow night. And you were brought up in a cave."

"Yes."

She said: "Well, at least Emmeline and I can speak Welsh. And at least the Welsh have a reputation for being half-savage, because I think we're going to need it."

BLANCHE SWISHED ACROSS THE HALLWAY AND tapped on the door of the room that had once been Sir Ector's. Silence. She tapped again. "It's me."

"I think," said Perceval from within, "you had better help me with this gorget."

She opened the door and found him struggling with his collar. "Do try to remember what I told you," she said, brushing away his hands and pinning the collar on. "Say how-do-you-do to the guests, watch which forks and spoons I use, and avoid all subjects of religion and politics. There's the bell. They're here."

Kitty Walker and Emmeline Felton were in the hall removing wraps and hats when Blanche and Perceval came downstairs to meet them.

"Blanche, you look *delicious*," said Kitty, kissing the air by Blanche's cheeks. She glanced at Perceval. "Why, you coy thing, you never told me you were expecting anyone *else!*"

"I wasn't," Blanche said repressively. "This is a cousin from Merthyr Tydfil, Perceval de Gales. He only speaks Welsh."

Kitty looked at Perceval and giggled and said, "*Noswaith dda.*"

"Good evening," said Perceval in the same language.

Blanche hissed in English, "I thought you didn't speak Welsh?"

"Welsh nanny," said Kitty. She switched back to Welsh, sidling up to Perceval. "I haven't spoken the language for years. Do tell me if I say anything very funny."

Blanche sighed. "Hello, Emmeline dear."

The Vicar's daughter squeezed her affectionately and said, "I am so sorry you are going away, Blanche. We'll miss you."

"Oh, Emmeline, and I never thought—I'll miss your wedding. If I'm still here when Mr Pevensie comes back from London next week, you must bring him to visit."

Keats ushered in Mr Corbin in immaculate evening dress. The sight of him threw Blanche into confusion. She had meant to ask his advice. Kitty had probably let him know that she urgently wanted to speak to him. But now that she stood face to face with him, she had another twinge of conscience. She'd already told him about Logres, about her parents, about everything. She did not have the time to reason it through; only sudden doubt hit her that it had been wise to reveal so much.

"Don't fib!" Kitty's delighted voice sliced through the hall, startled back into English. Blanche turned to see her dissolving in helpless laughter. "Blanche, darling, he says there are dragons in Wales."

Perceval laughed along with Kitty, as if enjoying her mirth. Blanche stood wordless.

"They *are* more difficult to find than they used to be," he said to Kitty in Welsh. "The giants, on the other hand, grow more numerous." She went off into fresh peals of laughter.

"Miss Pendragon, good evening," said Mr Corbin's soft amused voice at her side. "Where did you find such an original?"

She turned to him, forcing a smile. "M-my—" and then she caught herself. This man had nothing to do with Logres, and her guardian and Nerys had gone to great lengths to keep the servants and others in Gloucestershire from knowing where they had come from. Her conscience nudged again, and she heard herself continuing smoothly:

"A friend of my guardian's, come down to keep me company. Percy de Gales. Of the Merthyr Tydfil de Gales."

"Will you introduce us?" said Mr Corbin.

"Oh, I'd love to, although he doesn't speak English."

"That need not hinder us," said Mr Corbin in perfect Welsh.

Blanche stared. "I suppose you had a Welsh nanny too, then," she said feebly.

"No," he said, smiling. "My nanny was a woman from Carlisle. But I learned the language years ago conducting a study on conditions in a Welsh ordnance factory. And now I'd very much like to meet your friend."

There was nothing to do but lead him over and make the introduction. "Percy, this is Mr Simon Corbin. He—what *do* you call the profession, Mr Corbin?—he writes letters to *The Times* about education reform."

Blanche, watching the two of them exchange politenesses, wondered if it could be possible to find two more dissimilar men. Even the tentative air she detected in Perceval, as he tried to conceal his ignorance of Gloucestershire manners, could not veil his open face or chill his laughing eyes like the mocking and secretive melancholy of Mr Corbin.

Then Keats appeared to announce dinner, and Blanche asked Mr Corbin to escort Emmeline. Kitty took Perceval's arm. He solemnly offered the spare to Blanche, and she took it, the better to surpervise his conduct on the way into the dining-room.

Entrée and soup. Kitty, making desultory conversation with Perceval, wanted to know if he had been up to Llanstephan at all, and didn't he adore the little town? Perceval said No, but fame of its beauty had spread throughout Merthyr Tydfil and the countries around. Emmeline was talking to Mr Corbin about the war, in Welsh for courtesy's sake.

Main course, lamb cutlets. "I don't think it's right at all," Emmeline was saying. "Poisoning the wells, burning the houses, and shutting up the women and children in camps? This is not a just war."

Mr Corbin smiled. "How else do you propose we shall win, Miss Felton? We are fighting a mobile and well-supplied guerrilla force. The Boers buzz about our ears like gnats, and while the generals make futile attempts to swat them, hundreds of men are dying of typhoid."

Emmeline looked beseechingly at Blanche. But Mr Corbin went on: "You think me heartless, Miss Felton, but I assure you I am not. The families in the camps are being cared for; outside, they would only starve. Meanwhile, it behoves us to take every advantage in this struggle. Is it not better to win at once and end the suffering, than to continue locked in stalemate?"

Emmeline bowed her head, but said, "If the Boers thought so, they would already have surrendered."

"If the Boers thought so, there would not have been a war," said Mr Corbin with a laugh. "In a perfect world these sad decisions would be unnecessary."

Perceval had been following the conversation, and now he spoke. "Yet in fighting, as in anything else, Christian warriors must act in accordance with their prayers. *Adveniat regnum tuum sicut in caelo et in terra.*"

"Christians? Mr Corbin is a *nonbeliever*, Percy," said Kitty with a laugh.

Mr Corbin raised a conciliatory hand. "Yet I understand you, I think, sir. You mean that the citizens of heaven must act as though they were in heaven. But this is my point. God knows—if He exists—where heaven is, but it certainly is not on the earth."

"Augustine says—" Blanche began to object, but Mr Corbin had not finished.

"This is the real world, sir. Save your ideals for heaven."

"I say that a battle which cannot be won without treachery and dishonour is a battle not worth winning."

"It is a pretty idea, certainly," said Mr Corbin with a smile which even Blanche thought was rather provoking. "But *I* think that if you were a fighting man, de Gales, you would find the model difficult to put into practice."

"It can be done," said Perceval, sitting back in his chair with arrogant ease and folding his arms.

"Can it? Let us try it ourselves, now. Cast me as the villain in a melodrama, de Gales. Having crippled you with a cowardly blow, I turn to condemn one of these adorable ladies—" he turned with half a bow to Kitty, who giggled—"Miss Walker, for instance, to death, or a fate worse. I twirl my moustache. Miss Walker faints. And you, sir, recollect that you have a weapon concealed on your person."

Perceval shifted in his seat. Blanche read his face like a book. Oh dear. He *did* have a weapon concealed on his person.

"Do not deny, Mr de Gales, that to preserve her you would take your last chance. You would bury your knife in my back without a second thought, without a warning, no matter how unchivalrous that might be."

Perceval, less arrogant now, stared mutely at the table. At last he stirred and said, "It would depend—"

"Sophistry, sir!" Mr Corbin thundered. He went on: "Ah, but even now you fail to understand me. What if it were not the villain doing these dastardly deeds, but your colleague, or your commander?"

Perceval looked up with quick displeasure. "What do you mean?"

"I mean," he said, "that by your own showing, the greatest threat to heaven comes from within the ranks of the angels themselves. Before you can prove to me that heroes can defeat villains with nothing but the purest chivalric ideals, you must convince me that heroes do exist, and that villains are not a fanciful tale for children. You must tell me, sir, if you dare, that you are incorruptible, and that your colleagues and commanders are as pure as you. Your health."

And Mr Corbin took a sip of wine. Perceval, with a furious scowl, stared at his plate. Blanche herself was suddenly angry with the schoolmaster. It hadn't been a fair fight; Mr Corbin was so much older and so much more worldly than Perceval. But she could not take up the argument on his behalf. For one thing, she had been lax in her duties as a hostess in not diverting the conversation sooner. And for another, if she was honest, she was inclined to agree with Mr Corbin.

She searched in vain for some lighthearted joke to dispel the blunt force of his words. But nothing came, and she rather awkwardly said, "Tell us what you have planned for your birthday, Kitty."

LATER, IN THE DRAWING-ROOM, BLANCHE SAT alone with her cup of tea. Emmeline was at the piano, playing country airs, and Perceval stood with his head inside the instrument, asking questions and keeping Kitty in giggles. Under the music, the hum of voices, and the laughter, Mr Corbin came over to sit on the stool by Blanche's feet.

"Let me have your reproaches," he said to her in English. "You will not find me unrepentant."

Blanche tried to determine whether he was joking or not, but failed, as usual, to read his expression. "It was very wrong of you."

"Poor lad," he said, smiling. There was a moment's silence, and he went on, "He is not from the Wales we know, is he?"

Even if she had wanted to lie, Blanche's face would have given her away. "No."

"Perhaps I am jealous of them," said Mr Corbin, under the piano's melody, so low that she had to lean forward to hear. "Those half-savage warlords and unwashed illiterates who would take you away from us."

"I—" Blanche's protest died away.

"Your guardian told us you had gone on holiday," Mr Corbin probed. "I didn't believe it. You went *there*."

She gave him a look of mute appeal.

"Remember," he said, "they can't force you to live there. It's your choice."

He was going to try to prevent her going to Logres if he could. She supposed she should be grateful for his help. But a sudden unease gripped her, a feeling like a bad conscience.

"I used to dream," she said, and swallowed. "I dreamed I was there, in a meadow with the sun shining on banners and armour. And it wasn't like what you say. It was beautiful." She remembered the night in the slough in Gore, when in cutting wind she had determined to die uncomplaining, with her face to the free hills, and tried to put the splendour of that moment into words. "Now that I know such a place exists, I can't help wondering...*what if it is true?*"

"Blanche, no."

"What if they need me?"

"*Need* you? Blanche, who has been worrying you?"

"No-one," she said, bewildered.

"Don't make the best of a bad bargain, my dear."

He was still fighting for her. She felt a quick rush of gratitude, and dropped her voice. "I can't think of any way to avoid it. Besides—"

And she caught herself.

"Besides?"

"It's nothing."

"You said, 'What if they need me'. They can't need you to destroy yourself by flinging yourself into their brutal world."

"But what if they do?" He looked puzzled. She tried again. "If my sacrifice can preserve them—"

"Someone else will do it."

"They said—" This time, although she caught herself, she permitted herself to go on. She glanced at Perceval and dropped her voice a little lower. "They said they need me."

"Nonsense. They'll make do with someone else. Besides, to them, you're only a woman. How important can it be?"

"I'm to guard the Holy Grail."

Mr Corbin's lips pressed together and turned white. "So," he said at last, "not content with spiriting you away to primitivism, they're making you the high priestess of their bogus cult."

"I—"

"Blanche, look at me and tell me that if there was a way to stay, you wouldn't take it."

"I—"

"I can find a way. Tell me you aren't interested, and you need never see me again."

"It would depend on the way," she whispered at last.

"Then promise me you won't go before you've seen me again," he said.

It's I will keep me a maiden still,
Let the elfin knight do what he will.
Lady Isabel and the Elf-Knight

he days stretched out with no sign of Sir Ector and Nerys. Kitty was busy on her party business, and Mr Corbin did not call again. There was little to do that week except to amuse Perceval, but he took a great deal of amusing. Hitherto Blanche had been glad to muddle through life doing a little reading, a little handiwork, and a little visiting, but Perceval could not read, visit, or tat, and quickly grew restless without work to do. For most of the day he occupied himself working with the horses. Sir Ector had ridden Malaventure to Logres, but Perceval spent hours riding in circles on Rufus and Florence, training them to respond to the lightest pressure of rein or heel and gaining balance and rhythm for himself. Then he rigged up a makeshift quintain for ring jousting, and pounded white-painted wooden pegs into the ground which, approaching at a gallop, he aimed to spear and carry away.

In the evenings, Blanche found him a knife and knots of wood to whittle while she read aloud, mostly in Latin, and they had far-ranging conversations as knotted bowls or dragon-handled spoons took shape under Perceval's hands.

"How much longer do you think Sir Ector will be?" Blanche asked one evening in the drawing-room.

Perceval kept all his attention on the wood in his hands, a block of dark walnut. "Time flows differently here than in Logres. But I know it will take them a week of that time to travel from Nimue's gate to Camelot and return."

"So if time moves more slowly here, which it seemed to do while I was at Carbonek, we may look for them in a little under a week from now." Blanche stared into the fire and wondered if she would get the chance to speak to Mr Corbin again before she left.

She said, "Do you think Mr Corbin was right, about the necessities of war?"

"No," Perceval said, frowning at the walnut. His knife scraped against the wood three times before he asked it, the question she'd been hoping to avoid. "What did you talk to him about, the other night?"

"He doesn't want me to leave," she said at last.

"Why should he have a say in it?"

Blanche laughed. "You really don't like him, do you?" she baited.

Perceval didn't take the hook. "He bested me in argument," he admitted. "But he was wrong."

"He made me promise to see him again before I leave." Blanche was probing in earnest now, wondering what Perceval's reaction to this would be. But once more he spoke calmly:

"He will be at the damsel Kitty's dance three days from now, surely. There's no reason you should not speak to him then, if the Lady tarries."

Blanche wondered if Perceval really was not suspicious of Mr Corbin's intentions. But she let it lie, and because Kitty's party was to be a fancy-dress affair, she began mentally searching her wardrobe for a costume.

KITTY'S ROEDEAN FRIENDS CAME DOWN FROM London for the occasion, and Blanche, entering the ballroom on Perceval's arm, felt Kitty had done due honour to the splendour of the occasion. The place was blazing with light reflected from silverware and crystal, decorated with tinsel and silk roses.

"It's marvellous, isn't it?" Kitty asked. She was dressed as a fairy princess, with gossamer wings and a glittering crown. "Mamma let me do what I liked. We had Madame de Lorraine come down to decorate. Ooh, Percy, what a wonderful costume! Where did you get it?" she added in Welsh.

"My aunt Lynet made the surcoat," Perceval said, which was perfectly true. "Many Happy Returns."

"And who are you, Blanche?"

"Marie-Antoinette."

"Is that why there's an hourglass around your neck?" Kitty screamed. "Oh, how horrid! And you must be Sir Lancelot, Percy."

Perceval glanced down at his glittering mail and red-and-gold surcoat.

"Must I?"

Kitty clapped her hands. "Oh, excellent! 'Must I'! Did you hear, Simon?"

"Most amusing," said Mr Corbin, who had just come in, and showed his white teeth in tribute to the joke. He gave Kitty his best wishes, and then moved on to Blanche and bowed.

"Good evening," she said, giving him her hand. "And whom do you represent, Mr Corbin? The Duke of Wellington?"

"His nemesis, I'm afraid."

"Napoleon Bonaparte!" Blanche withdrew her hand with a laugh. "I don't know if I can shake hands with you, sir."

"Simon, ask her for that ghastly hourglass as a keepsake," Kitty, who had been welcoming other guests, interjected.

Mr Corbin looked at the pendant and smiled his secretive smile. "I shall ask her for a good deal more than that tonight."

Blanche glanced at Perceval, a little guiltily. But of course he had not heard: the thing was said in English.

"To begin with," Mr Corbin went on, "this waltz."

Blanche said, "Excuse me," to Perceval and allowed Mr Corbin to lead her onto the floor.

"I am not a good dancer," he said, a smile crossing his melancholy face—Blanche murmured a polite disagreement—"But I know that when one has an assignation at a ball, one puts pleasure before business."

They moved into the flow of couples. Mr Corbin had been quite correct. The pleasure would be all his: of the two of them, he had the better partner. Blanche relaxed and let him guide her where he wished. There would be more opportunities for dancing later.

"We make a pretty picture, I'm sure," she said. "The last of the *ancien regime* and the first of the new."

"Thesis and antithesis," Mr Corbin said. "What comes next is synthesis."

They threaded a narrow passage between two other couples and drifted on up the room. Blanche said: "I have heard of this before. The thesis is received doctrine. The antithesis is some new and revolutionary idea. And the synthesis—"

"Is what happens when thesis and antithesis marry."

"And I thought philosophy was unromantic," said Blanche, smiling.

The music ended. Mr Corbin snatched a pair of champagne *coupes* and offered his arm to Blanche. "Now for the business. Shall we step outside, onto the terrace?"

It was a clear, cold night, and Blanche, folding her arms, hoped the discussion would not take long. "How cold it is!" she said, glancing at the moon.

"Winter is trying her teeth," Mr Corbin said. "But tonight she is only a pup: when she is old, ware her bite."

Blanche turned to him with an inquiring shiver. "I promised not to go away without seeing you."

"And I promised to find you a way to stay in this world, if you chose to take it."

"Tell me."

He said with more than his usual solemnity, "I hope you do choose to take it, Blanche. I don't wish to lose you."

He should not have been using her Christian name, Blanche thought. But another shiver of excitement and cold danced down her spine, and she thought she knew what was coming.

"Blanche Pendragon, will you join me in my life's work? Will you forsake your guardians and homeland, and join your purpose with mine? In a word, will you marry me, and free yourself to claim a new heritage, a new world bright with the hope of reason and brotherhood?"

He spoke with gleaming eyes, and lips that curved in a smile as the words rolled from them. It was what Blanche had expected—but not quite what she had expected, and a faint cloud of disappointment fell over her. She had dreamed of being addressed in an enraptured whisper, not in measured apostrophes like the lines in a play.

Still, perhaps the tender passion struck some men differently.

"I hardly know what to say," she said. "Dare I?"

"As my wife, you would be answerable only to me—and that only if you wished," said Mr Corbin. "You would be protected not only from the will of your guardians but also from the diplomatic marriage they no doubt intend for you."

Blanche paled. "That hadn't occurred to me."

"Blanche," he was saying, "do you hear me? I am offering you a sure way to defy your fate. And my entire regard and affection into the bargain."

Blanche stood motionless, speechless, as though suddenly deprived of will. *Did* she want to marry Simon Corbin? Three months ago, she would have thought she did; she would not have cared that it would break Sir Ector's heart. *Did* she want to escape the burden of Logres? A week ago, she had—before Perceval had come, and unmasked her for a selfish coward.

The consent was trembling on her lips. But when she spoke, in a suddenly choked voice, she surprised herself as well as Mr Corbin.

"I can't."

"Can't what?" he cried. "Cannot defy the selfishly-imposed will of a family you've never seen? Cannot free yourself from the superstitions of barbarism?"

Blanche put her hands to her head. "I despise myself, but not for that. When I thought I had no choice, I bemoaned my lot with the satisfaction that I would be forced to do the right thing in the end. Now you present me with an alternative, and I say...I say that I thank you, Simon, and beg your forgiveness. I have trifled with you. I have allowed you to make this declaration, when I should have known that I could never accept it."

She fidgeted with the hourglass around her neck and looked at him timidly, sure that he would be hurt and offended. But his face had not changed. Only his voice became challenging. "Why not?"

She would have had to fight to abandon Logres. Now her indecision had guaranteed that she would have to fight to go there, and she knew she had only herself to thank. "I should have known that I could never grieve my guardian so," she said, lifting her chin. "Then...we are not suited to each other. Our difference of outlook would keep us from agreeing, and besides, there is the question of my duty to Logres."

"None of these things need bind you," he said. "If you will not marry me, let me spirit you away to some place where they will not find you."

"I don't expect you to understand," she said with a strained smile. "You have put a choice before me, my friend. And I am grateful. But I choose to be bound. I will go to Logres, and do what is asked of me."

"So be it," he said gloomily. "We shall lose you, and Blanche Pendragon will be known no more among her friends and cavaliers."

Blanche remembered the pendant around her neck. She tugged the ribbon loose and held it out to him.

"I think you had better take it back. Remember me by it, if you like."

Simon Corbin took the hourglass from her hand and held it up to the moonlight. A bitter smile curled his lips.

"It has run its course," he said, and dropped it underfoot and crushed it into the pavement.

Blanche drew a swift breath of shock at the sudden controlled violence of his movement. But she had no time to speak, for Kitty's voice frothed out of the ballroom followed in a moment by herself.

"Simon! Yoo-hoo, Simon!" When she saw Blanche standing there with Mr Corbin, Kitty put her hands to her mouth with a gasp. "Oh! I am so sorry! It's nothing, really."

Behind Kitty stood Perceval, a tall upright figure, mail-shirted, with his sword swinging from his hip. After the last five minutes, the sight of him was as welcome as reinforcements in the heat of battle, and her shoulders dropped in relief. She looked past Mr Corbin, past Kitty, and smiled at him.

"Don't wait for me, Mr Corbin," she said in Welsh.

He bowed to her and offered his arm to Kitty. They passed into the ballroom and Perceval came forward to lean against the baluster of the terrace beside her.

"I see you have spoken to him," he said.

"I have," she said. "I keep no secrets from you, my deputed guardian. Mr Corbin has made me a proposal of marriage, and I have refused him."

"This was his attempt to keep you here?"

She smiled sadly. "He said that if I married him, I would be able to defy Sir Ector. I said I chose not to do it. He was angry, I think."

Perceval laughed. "Let us not mind him."

His dismissive tone grated on Blanche. She had cherished Simon Corbin's good opinion. She had even, once or twice, dreamed of accepting him. Did Perceval think it was an easy thing to spurn such a man's protection? Did he think that the choice was so obvious, between the dangers and hardships of Logres, and the comfort and freedom of her home?

"I am sorry I had to do it," she said in a sharper voice. "If my fate were any different, I should be glad to have him."

Perceval looked incredulous. "Be glad your fate is wiser than you, then."

"Oh!" said Blanche, "just because you lost an argument to him, you must act as though no woman could like him."

"What?" Perceval yelped. "I deny it. Someone may someday love that dirgeful face, but never you."

Blanche could not think of a good retort, so she snapped open her fan and turned to re-enter the ballroom. But Perceval called her back, gently. "Lady. Stay a moment."

He rose from the terrace baluster, and took her hand. "I did not come to quarrel with you, Blanchefleur."

She did not trust herself to speak, and therefore only raised an eyebrow.

"Forget about Simon Corbin. Look elsewhere for one who would serve you and guard you."

"To you, of course." But his earnestness disarmed her, and the words came out with less hiss and spit than she wished.

"Yes, to me." His thumb traced over the back of her fingers and touched the red-gold ring of Ragnell. "I told you once that I saw a kind of destiny in our acquaintance."

"Please don't…"

"It was you and no-one else in the pavilion, in the courtyard, and at Carbonek," he said. "You are perilous and fair. Is it any wonder you should run in my mind?"

Blanche stared back at him for a long moment, her mind a whirl of conflicting thoughts. "Why, Perceval," she said at last with a shaky laugh, "are you jealous of him?"

The earnestness slipped away from him, and he laughed. "Jealousy implies doubt," he said with the boundless arrogance she detested. "I never doubted you for a moment."

Blanche flushed. "Doubt me? What right could you have had to doubt me? What am I? Your sweetheart?"

The instant the word was out of her mouth, Blanche could have bit her tongue off with mortification. Perceval looked down at her and slowly smiled, a dog's smile, all teeth.

"Are you?"

"Don't be odious. Of course not," she snapped, more vexed with herself than with Perceval. "It was a figure of speech. I mean," she went on, less angrily, "you and I would *never* suit. We do not share an intellectual level at *all*. And please don't bring up that scene in the pavilion again. I thought we decided to forget the whole business."

Perceval stuck his thumbs in his belt and whistled. "Oh, lady, be kind," he said, and grinned.

He opened the door for her to return to the ballroom, and she passed through with trailing robes of displeasure. But if he felt it, he gave no sign.

Therewith the Giant buckled him to fight,
Inflam'd with scornful wrath and high disdain,
And lifting up his dreadful club on hight,
All arm'd with ragged snubs and knotty grain,
Him thought at first encounter to have slain.

Spenser

Four more days passed, and Perceval spent less time with the horses and more time pacing around the house, watching the hills.

"Are they late, Perceval?" Blanchefleur asked him one morning as she saw him pass the library windows for the second time.

He opened the French doors and wandered in, frowning. "I cannot tell."

"I'm sure someone will come eventually," she said with resolute cheerfulness.

"Yes," he said, "the Lady—or the Lady's bane."

"What does that mean?"

"It means, the thing that killed her." And he prowled out by another door.

The following afternoon Emmeline and her young man visited. Blanche felt the cloud lift. They went with the sun, and so did the brief gaiety they had brought with them. That night was cold and clear, with stars glittering overhead. Dinner was hushed. Perceval ate sparingly, coiled like a spring, Blanche thought.

"If they do not come tomorrow," Perceval said, "we must forestall them and take a door to Logres."

"The wardrobe in the hall goes to Carbonek," said Blanche.

"Only with the right elf-key, I think. The damsel Nerys left it with me.

We'll take it tomorrow."

Blanche retired early, but found sleep beyond her. She turned up the lamp and settled in with Augustine. For hours there was no sound but the periodic chime of the downstairs clock, which struck nine o'clock, ten o'clock, and a quarter to twelve before she began to feel sleepy.

It was nearly midnight when Blanche heard the wind. It came screaming from the west like a bird of prey and gripped and shook the house. Blanche listened to it for a moment with puzzlement, then rolled over again and went back to reading. She had ceased to hear the storm when there was a tap and the door creaked open. It was Perceval, armed *cap-a-pie* with his sword drawn, moving more quietly in his steel harness that she would have thought possible.

"What's wrong?" Blanche gasped, rising and snatching the woollen cloak from Carbonek.

"Softly," he said; but he moved quickly and had pulled her halfway to the door before she could draw breath.

"Don't—give me a moment," Blanche whispered, struggling.

She went to turn back, but Perceval caught both her wrists and wrapped his arms around her. There was a noise like thunder and the outside wall of the bedroom exploded inward. Blanche screamed. Huge jagged shards of glass from the window sank into the wall around them. Through the gaping void, Blanche saw stars in the sky. Then the raging wind whipped her hair across her face and blinded her.

Perceval, whose armoured body had shielded her from the blast, was speaking in a murmur. "Listen," he said. "Get the servants out of the house—out the front. I'll deal with the giant."

There was another rending crash and the corner of the room, with some of the floor, crumbled agonisingly away.

"Giant?" Blanche whimpered.

Perceval pushed her out the door, out of the wrecked room. She paused staring as he stepped to her bedside, picked up the heavy lantern, and smashed it against one of the bedposts. Burning oil rained across the coverlet and melted into the carpet, caught and spread by the wind. He had no time to do more. A hand, horrifying merely for its hugeness, came out of the night, gripped the ragged broken wall, and strained. Then a massive figure, blacker than the sky itself, rose against the stars.

Perceval, lifting his shield, sank into a crouch.

Blanche fled. Downstairs, some of the servants had already shuffled into the hall, blinking and yawning. Keats was there with a candle, and

Lucy the housemaid, armed with a trembling poker. "Fire," Blanche gasped, before they could open their mouths. "Where's Cook? And John? And Daisy? We must all go at once."

She drove them before her out the front door into the storm.

THE GIANT CLAMBERED INTO BLANCHE'S ROOM, more than twice man-height, bent like an immense cloud to fit below the tall ceilings. A battle-axe like a short polearm, dagger-pointed at the end of the haft, dangled from one gnarled hand. Perceval, shifting from foot to foot, kept his eyes on it. The giant could not swing his weapon easily in the narrow confines of Blanche's room: when he saw the knight, he rammed the axe at him point-first.

Perceval slipped aside to avoid the dagger-point, stepped lightly onto the axe-blade as it whistled toward him, and launched himself forward. Behind, another wall splintered as the axe punched through. Perceval landed in a crouch under the giant's outstretched arm and swung back and lashed at the inside of the massive elbow. *Clank.* His blade, which should have bit deep and drunk, rebounded with a harsh whine; his arms jolted.

The creature was wearing armour.

The giant kicked. Perceval was already moving to the side, but it got him on the shield. The shock travelled up his arm, and Perceval thought he felt an old wound split open. He staggered back, falling to one knee. Then the giant wrenched his axe out of the wall: more plaster, dust, and splinters hummed through the frantic air. The flaming mass which had been Blanche's bed licked out a tongue of flame and ignited the dust. The whole room flashed with a puff of flame. Through it Perceval heard, rather than saw, the axe-blade come swinging toward him. He scrambled up and flung himself for a corner, the pain in his arm forgotten.

The axe bit into the wall next to him. Again, debris and flame filled the air, and the house groaned and trembled in the wind. Perceval knew he hadn't much time.

BLANCHE STOOD ON THE LAWN OUTSIDE the house, watching the glowing windows.

"Is everyone here?" she yelled over the wind, trembling violently, but whether from cold or from fear she could not tell.

"I think—" said the cook uncertainly, and began counting on her fingers.

"I think the gas pipes behind the house must have blown," Blanche heard herself say. It was true, too, with half of the back wall smashed in. "It's dangerous—we must keep clear of the house."

John, the coachman, unlike the others, was alert and unpanicked. "I'll ride and fetch the fire brigade, miss."

"I suppose you had better," said Blanche, for she could think of nothing else to say. But if the fire brigade came at once, would Perceval have time to deal with the giant? "Wait," she called after him. "The horses! They are still in the stables! If the fire spreads—"

John and Keats set off for the stables.

"Miss, miss," gasped the cook, fighting the shawl she'd snatched to wrap around her, "Mr Perceval—he's not here."

Blanche looked at her, trying to think of something to say.

"He must be still in the house," said Daisy.

"I'll fetch him," the cook volunteered.

"No! You mustn't!" Blanche put her hands to her head. She could not tell them to sit back and watch the house burn down with someone still inside. And she certainly could not send anyone in after him.

There was only one thing to do.

"I'll go in and find him."

"No, don't!" sobbed Daisy. "I'll run for Mr Keats."

"Don't move," said Blanche, and turned the full force of her look on the housemaid; to her surprise, Daisy shrank back, looking almost frightened. But they had to obey her now; it was desperately important, and she had nothing but her voice and her eyes. She stiffened from crown to heel and said: "Listen, all of you. *Stay here*. I will fetch my cousin."

"But—" the cook protested.

"You can't. Not with the smoke, and your bronchitis. *Quiet!* You will obey me."

She had never spoken like this before. They stared at her dazedly, but they neither moved nor objected. She fixed them with one last glare, then turned and ran through the gale to the house. Her thoughts thrummed to the time of her feet:

"I must make a plan. I must make a plan."

PERCEVAL GROANED AND COUGHED, FLUNG OFF the flaming waste which had followed him into the depths, and rose unsteadily to his feet. He looked around. The floor of Blanche's room, once it collapsed, had dropped them among fiery wreckage into the library, and the bookshelves had blossomed into flame.

He was in poor case. His armour still kept him whole, but his right hand was scorched and the smell of singed hair, as well as improved visibility, told that his helm was gone. There was blood and smoke stinging his eyes; he rubbed and blinked the tears away.

Over in the corner, the colossal enemy reared to his knees and glanced around. Perceval, still shaking, lifted his shield, but the giant ignored him, climbed to his feet, and swung his axe at the wall.

Blanchefleur was the true quarry, and if that wall gave way the giant would be out of the house, free to move, able to snatch her and crush her in a moment. Perceval howled and lunged. The giant waited for him to come in range, then swung an iron fist. Perceval ducked to the floor, came up and jumped. The giant's armour was crude mail; there would be a chink somewhere. He clung to the massive body for only half a second before being brushed off, but in that half-second he stabbed deep into the giant's armpit. There was a bellowing roar and a shake that sent him tumbling across the room. The giant lifted his axe again.

Perceval was up and out of the way in the nick of time. Again he dashed in close, within the giant's reach, and circled round, drawing his poniard in his left hand. The long, slender knife, he hoped, would do the trick; he waited for the giant to straighten a little to turn, and then he plunged the blade screeching between the chain links of the creature's mail, into the back of the knee.

The giant bellowed again and his leg snapped shut with a convulsive kick, trapping Perceval's left hand in the hinge of the knee. He felt the bones in his hand grinding together and then the knee opened. He left the poniard wedged into the giant's mail and slithered to the ground.

So the enemy was crippled now, but savagely angry. Perceval snatched up his sword from the floor and ran into the corridor.

INSIDE THE HOUSE BLANCHE HEARD WUTHERING wind, roaring fire and the commotion of battle mixed into a thunderous symphony. Heavy smoke and flakes of paper gusted on the air.

In the hall she put her hands to her head and tried to think. Perceval had smashed her lamp and set fire to her room, either to help him defeat the giant or to destroy all signs of the fight. Did he have a plan beyond survival? Blanche looked up at the wardrobe which led to Carbonek. On the other side of that door was safety and shelter and the Holy Grail. She dashed to it and pulled at the handle. Locked, and Perceval had the—elf-key, as he called it. Desperate, Blanche snatched up a letter-opener lying on the side-table by the front door. It only took her a moment to slide back the tongue of the lock and fling the door open.

Beyond hope she saw two narrow walls of rock running away into the darkness. There was a puff of cold, fresh air and the scent of earth. She could run away and be at Carbonek long before morning; it was only a short scramble down the rocks. Perceval would deal with the giant and, if he survived, be collected by Sir Ector and Nerys when they came.

She put a foot inside the wardrobe, onto the path. It flashed into her mind that Carbonek had a will of its own: it seemed not to need keys or even doors, it had yielded gracefully to a lock picked with a letter-opener—it wanted her, and its goodwill leapt toward her through the dark.

Yet still she hesitated. Then a flake of burning wallpaper drifted down from the upper landing, and the hall-carpet smouldered where it fell. Blanche peered up through the murk to see a flicker of red at the top of the stairs. Then there was another crash, and the house shook.

She found herself standing motionless, listening and waiting for the next sound. Was he still alive? There came a muffled bellow from the corridor that led down to the library. Yes. Blanche took one more long-ing look at the dark cleft inside the wardrobe and pushed the door to, propping it open with the paper-knife. Carbonek could wait for Perceval.

Blanche wrapped her cloak more closely around her, crossed the hall and stepped into the corridor, full of thick choking smoke with a dull yellow glow at the end. She felt the house trembling around her with a succession of thumps. Then out of the halo of smoke Perceval appeared, running toward her. He had lost his helm, his surcoat was scorched and tattered, and his face was covered in soot.

He skidded to a stop when he saw her and almost stumbled into her arms. At the same moment, the library exploded into the corridor with an ear-shattering crash and a tide of wind and fire, and Perceval, regaining his feet, shouted, "Get out!"

He turned to face the giant. The massive enemy crawled into the pas-sage, reaching out his hand, while the flaming walls groaned around his shoulders.

Perceval tightened his two-handed grip on his sword, hefted it to his shoulder, and ran. The outstretched hand snatched at him, but he swerved to one side and skidded under it on his knees. A look of foolish surprise crossed the giant's face as he realised that he had missed his tiny foe. Then Perceval plunged his blade into one stupefied eye.

All this had barely taken a few moments, and Blanche had not stirred. Thus she saw the death of the giant: a spurt of blood, the eyeball tumbling out, and the final, desperate struggle as it died.

Perceval wrenched his sword back and came reeling up the corridor to Blanche, scarcely evading the thrashing arm which tore through the walls and flung the fire further. Blanche stepped forward and caught him just as his knees buckled.

"Stand, sir," she commanded. "The house is falling. We must go."

They staggered out into the hall. There was fire here now, too, and Blanche, treading with thin slippers, sucked in her breath as something seared her foot. Perceval hardly seemed conscious and she had almost his full weight to bear. A short dash through the flames would take them to the wardrobe. Blanche hesitated, coughing, balancing on her unburned foot, trying to blink back the tears of pain. Then, just as she gathered herself to stagger forward, a sconce which hung from the high ceiling above fell crashing to the floor, followed within a heartbeat by the beam it hung from. The way was blocked.

Blanche cast one last despairing look at the wardrobe, barely visible through flame and smoke, then pulled Perceval's arm around her neck and half-dragged him a step or two to the back door. She fumbled with the latch. Then the door banged open, driven by the wind, and she staggered down the steps and into the garden.

In the biting gale, Perceval revived somewhat. "Further," he rasped. "Into the orchard."

They fell to the ground at last beneath a pear-tree, in grass wet with dew. Perceval groaned in pain as he relaxed. Blanche leaned back against the tree and gasped for breath. Here, at the foot of the rise behind the house, they were just high enough to see the whole place wrapped in flames, and the hills lit up with a lurid light.

"My home," she said. "And our door back to Logres!"

Perceval grunted in reply. Pain stabbed through Blanche's foot like a reminder and she turned to him in concern. "Are you badly hurt?"

He grinned. "I don't know."

Blanche clutched her hair. "Oh, what are we going to do? The wardrobe is gone and I can't *imagine* how I shall explain you to the servants."

"I still have the key," Perceval muttered. Then something caught his attention. He struggled to his elbow and said, "Hark!"

It was a low rumble, shivering up from the ground. Blanche froze. Then, with a rolling, thunderous crash, the house collapsed. Yellow and scarlet flames shot up into the sky, illuminating everything. A moment later, when the glare died down somewhat, Blanche could see the little huddle of servants on the front lawn. There were John and Keats, holding the horses; there was Cook, fallen to her knees with her handkerchief to her mouth, and Lucy and Daisy clinging to each other in terror.

"They think we are dead," said Perceval, and fell back with a sigh. Blanche went to rise, but he raised his hand. "No," he said. "More trouble may come. Wait."

He fumbled for his sword, trying to wipe the blood off onto the grass. Blanche, seeing how it hurt him to move, said, "Let me." She cleaned the long blade gingerly, then slid it back into the scabbard.

"Let me see your hands," she told him, and eased the gauntlets off. His left hand was bruised and swollen from being caught in the giant's knee, and his right hand was burned shiny red through the tattered glove. "Oh, dear."

"The rest of me isn't much better," he said cheerfully.

"I haven't even ointment to put on the burns," Blanche sighed. She took a handkerchief from her cloak's pocket and dabbed at a welt on the side of his head. "Oh—that's nasty."

"It hurts." He twisted his head and grinned up at her.

"Oh, you're enjoying this," she groaned, blushing.

He gestured to hands and head, looking innocent. "What, this?"

She laughed, but a moment later she bent and kissed his forehead. "Thank you. Again."

Perceval cocked his head to look up at her, but then, on the wind, they heard the beat of galloping hooves. Instantly he struggled to his feet, gripping his sword. "Someone's coming."

The hooves rushed closer, as if blown on the wind. Through the shadowy orchard the fire's red glare struck glittering off mail. Then they saw the rider more clearly—a knight, sitting an outstretched white horse easily with slackened reins, his flashing sword whistling in the wind. Perceval snatched his own blade out of the sheath, but the knight had already reined in, throwing his horse into a sliding stop and coming to a dead halt within inches of Perceval's trembling swordpoint.

Spatters of mud settled back into the grass. With a titanic surge the horse regained its feet. The knight snatched off his helm and Blanche said in a voice that was half a sob:

"Sir Ector!"

Her guardian wiped his bloody sword against the saddle-blanket and shot it back into the sheath. "Blanche, my dear. Thank God we are not too late."

For the first time, Blanche saw two women who followed the knight and checked their horses more slowly. Nerys was one of them. The other, she guessed, must be the famous Nimue.

This was the one who spoke. "What happened here, sir?" she said, addressing Perceval.

"The servants think we are dead," he said. With the coming of their friends all the tight-wound vigilance had gone out of him, and his words slurred and stumbled against each other in weariness. "It was a giant. I don't know who sent him. He sleeps yonder," and he pointed to the flaming wreck of the house.

Sir Ector slid off Malaventure and gathered Blanche into his arm. "Well done," he said.

Perceval bowed his head. "What now? The servants have our horses. And I think you too have been hard-pressed."

Nimue said: "We were followed from Camelot, God knows how, for only the Council knew our errand. We went out of our way to shake them off, but Morgan and her men surprised us when I had opened the gate."

"Was there a fight?"

"For a while," rumbled Sir Ector, and Blanche shuddered at the fearful light in his eyes. "But her giant passed us easily enough."

"We put the others to flight and hastened through. The door is still open for us to return. As for the horses—" and Nimue put her hands to her mouth and sent a whisper into the wind. There was an answering whinny from the front lawn, a rush of hooves, and helpless gesticulations from the coachman's little black figure. A moment later, Rufus and Florence stood panting before them.

"Let us go," said Nimue.

In the sudden silence that followed the Lady's words Blanche glanced up to see that all of them had, almost involuntarily, turned to look at her. It took a moment for her to remember that she had once insisted on staying. A wry smile cracked the hot tight skin of her face.

"Yes, let's go," Blanche said.

Part II

The · City · of · Light

Impious war in Heaven and battle proud,
With vain attempt.

Milton

In a rush of cold air Blanche saw huddled bodies on the ground, saw the glimmer of dawning light off broken spears and discarded shields, and felt Florence rise beneath her and fly smoothly over the heaped ruin of a dead horse. Before she could turn her head away, or close her eyes to block out that horrible sight, the forest swallowed them and flowed away to the south.

They were galloping much too fast for her comfort. Her burned foot throbbed in the stirrup. Blanche let the reins fall slack in her hands and curled white-knuckled fingers around her saddle-horn. Next to her, riding bareback with the wind in her hair, Nerys somehow sat straight and smiling. To her, this was a homecoming. To Blanche, it felt more like going into exile.

After half a mile Sir Ector, in the lead on the flying Malaventure, slackened the horses into a rolling canter which lasted until the sun rose above the treetops, flooding the forest with wintry light.

In a sheltered glade at the head of a valley where a little dark spring welled from the ground and rushed down the hill, Sir Ector pulled Malaventure to a standstill, craning in his saddle to look back the way they had come, lifting a hand for silence. They listened to the dawn.

No pursuit came to their ears.

Sir Ector nodded and dismounted. "We are safe here for a moment. Let us take counsel."

Blanche glanced around at her companions. Nimue urged forward to speak to Sir Ector. Nerys smiled at Blanche, as sunny as the morning itself, then winced as she slid to the ground. She had transferred her saddle to Florence for Blanche's use, and the long bareback canter had taken its toll. Perceval climbed stiffly off Rufus and fell to his knees by the water's edge, hesitating a moment before plunging his whole head into the icy stream.

Blanche slid her injured foot out of the stirrup and dismounted gingerly, trying not to put weight on the burn. She limped toward Nerys. "Where are we going?"

A rare delight flickered in the fay's eyes. "To Carbonek."

Blanche glanced at Sir Ector and Lady Nimue as they exchanged hurried words with frosty puffs of breath. Then Sir Ector called to the others:

"Here we part: the damsel Blanchefleur is called to Carbonek."

Perceval reared up, flinging drops of water from his head. "Carbonek! There is no place I had rather see."

"Nor I," said Sir Ector. "But only the damsel Blanchefleur is called there, and only the called will find it."

Perceval said, "She will need an escort. Protection."

"*Only* the called." A smile flickered in his eyes. "Were I the Knight of Wales, I would go in quest of a herbalist and a warm bed."

Perceval grimaced. The Lady of the Lake said: "Nerys will go with the Grail Maiden. We others have our own tasks to accomplish. The Queen of Gore's rift must be mended again. And one must take word to Camelot that the damsel Blanchefleur is in Logres."

"There is your work, if you will have it," said Sir Ector. "But first we will rest and eat." And he led Malaventure to the water.

The food was plain and tough—hard bannocks, a battered cheese, and strips of dried venison washed down with water. They ate without fire or warmth, sitting on the bare stones by the spring. Then, as Nerys filled the water-bottles and divided their remaining food between the two parties, Blanche moved over to Perceval.

"Well, I suppose this is goodbye," she said, making a shield of her light and careless voice. "Thanks again for everything, Percy."

He laughed and groaned. "Call me anything, but not that. …So I cannot follow you to Carbonek."

"Believe me, you're welcome to go in my stead."

"Oh, I would make but a poor Grail Maiden, damsel. Well, I will get myself to a sickbed, where if you come running to me for help I shall turn over and go back to sleep. So keep clear of trouble."

"I'll try." She wove her fingers together and wondered how she would survive in this place without him. "I don't *like* to get into trouble, you know. Or to be any inconvenience to anyone."

He laughed at her. "I tease! Lady, you carried yourself tonight like the true heir of Logres. Any king might be proud to call you his daughter. Any prince might be glad to win you for his wife. A plain knight may serve you for the moment, and consider himself raised by the honour."

She said, "Tonight? It was nothing. I could not have acted differently." She loosed her fingers and took a deep breath. "Perceval, you know I'm very grateful to you, but—that's all."

He grinned back, unabashed.

"True. I have no right to your undivided regard." The words sank into the dewy morning world before he added: "Yet."

Sir Ector moved to Blanche's side; she sagged a little with relief. Perceval glanced up at him and smiled, then turned again to Blanche.

"Godspeed, lady. We will meet in Carbonek, before the Grail."

"There is a monastery in the next valley," Sir Ector told him. "Go there and stay until your harms are healed, sir knight. Then there will be time to think of Carbonek and the Grail."

He drew Blanche away and smiled at her with mingled affection and sadness. "Ah, Blanche! When I see you again, you will be another man's daughter."

But whose? For the first time it struck Blanche how entirely her whole future hung on that question. How much more dangerous would Logres be if even the protection of the Pendragon's name was taken from her?

"You will always be my dear guardian," she said, trying to sound playful. "Even if the rest of the world disowned me." And she found herself looking at Perceval as he wrapped up his burned hand with some ointment from the saddlebags.

Sir Ector followed her look. "He works quickly, this young knight," he said thoughtfully.

"A little too quickly for me."

"Then say the word and I will see to it that he holds his tongue."

"No, no," said Blanche, horrified. "There's no hurry. He must find me in Carbonek before he can speak to me again. Maybe he will change his mind when he knows me better." When all of Logres knew the truth about her birth. "In the meantime, it pleases him to serve me. Please don't tell him to stop."

Sir Ector nodded, and she breathed a sigh of relief. "He will do great deeds for you, Blanche. Courtesy in accepting them is fitting."

Nerys came toward them, leading Florence and her own horse. "All is ready to leave when you will," she said to Blanche.

"Then lose no time. Go now," Sir Ector told them.

BLANCHE AND NERYS RODE ALMOST AT random, aiming more or less north-west into Wales but allowing valleys and hills to divert them. They met few others, friend or foe. That night they awoke in great fear to see a fire blazing on a nearby hill, with gigantic figures looming around it. The following day they met a knight-errant named Sir Lamorak, who shared his store of food with them, and bent his journey toward the monsters. Then there were the howls of wolves one evening, and that night they sheltered in a cave with a barricade of fire at the mouth, watching by turns.

To Blanche, it was a nightmare, and the thought of Carbonek at the end of the journey was hardly more comforting than the weary present. She remembered what Simon Corbin had said of Logres, how he had implored her not to waste herself on a barbaric land. At the time her head had been full of grand visions of duty and rigour, of an endless war between light and darkness, and it had been easy to brush off his concern. Now she envisioned a pointless death among wolves in the wilderness, or being carried off by some paltry ailment in Carbonek.

In a few days, the men and beasts faded away, and they rode through lifeless hills.

"Tell me about Camelot, Nerys," she said one morning, for it had begun to take form in her mind as a place of ease and warmth.

"I was only there for the council," Nerys said. "But it is a beautiful city, standing on a hill, full of trees and gardens."

"I should like to see it one day."

"By favour you will. After the Quest."

Blanche sighed. "I am willing to do what I must, Nerys. But Carbonek, how dreary!"

"The King thought it best," Nerys said. "Though he knows of the hardships. What better way for you to prove the prophecy as your birth-right, than by guarding the Grail?"

"Is this a test, then? For his peace of mind?"

Nerys shook her head. "Of course not. It is not to him that you must prove yourself. It is to Logres."

"To the old wives and tittle-tattles?"

Nerys said: "If only it were so easy. Logres doesn't only have enemies outside, Blanchefleur. There are also enemies within. Pride, ambition, and schism. Can you imagine what trouble there might be if not everyone received you as the true heir?"

Blanche had not thought of this, but all the history she had ever learned, from Jane Grey in the Tower to the revolutions of the last century, rose up to rebuke her for overlooking something so obvious. "Trouble! Do you mean war? In *Logres?*"

"Why not? Did you not know that the first dozen years of the reign of Arthur Pendragon were filled with ceaseless war? Not only with the barbarians. King Lot of Orkney was Arthur's own brother-in-law, but he died disputing Arthur's throne. Uriens, King of Gore, the husband of Morgan, was another."

"His own kin opposed him?"

"Yes. And then there were those who stood with him. Gawain the son of Lot. Ywain the son of Uriens."

Blanche frowned. "Perceval's father is named Sir Gawain."

"Yes. Gawain was Arthur's man, even then, when they were both boys. He fought for the King against his own father. His own father, Blanchefleur."

"And you think that it could happen again. With me."

"Of course." Silence fell before Nerys spoke again with aching regret in her voice. "There has even been war in Heaven, Blanchefleur."

That reminded her of something she had heard before, and despond gripped her. "The greatest threat to heaven comes from the angels themselves. Mr Corbin said that." She rubbed her aching forehead. "Oh, Nerys. Please."

The fay kneed her horse closer. "What is it?"

"If everything goes wrong… Nerys, I'm here to do what I can, I promise. But if everything were to go badly wrong, so badly that there was no more hope at all—would you send me home again?"

Nerys wrinkled her brow. "To Gloucestershire? Perhaps. If there was no hope at all." Then she reached out and touched Blanche's hand where it lay on her horse's withers, and the light in her eyes broke across her whole face. "But take courage! There is always hope for those who walk in darkness."

LATE THAT AFTERNOON, KNIFED BY THE cold wind, the two of them crested a snowy hill and stood looking down dull grey screes to the winter ocean.

"We must have missed it." Blanche sagged in the saddle.

"Wait." The fay put her hand up to her eyes and scanned the shore. "Look down there."

Blanche followed Nerys's pointing arm. Down on a rocky outcrop above the sea, hardly visible against the tumbled stones of the shore and the white-crest waves, a ramshackle castle stood. Blanche said:

"*Carbonek?* Here?"

"They call it the Wandering Castle," said Nerys with a laugh. "It is never to be found in the same place twice. Come!"

This time as they neared the castle, Blanche saw that the keep stood intact, the battlements were cleared of nests, and—strangest of all—tiny human figures went to and fro on the rocks outside, or sat with a fishing-line kicking their heels above the waves.

"There are people."

"There always were," Nerys reminded her. "Only, like the castle, they are not always found."

A thin wailing shout went up from a child as they approached, and then more folk came swarming out of the castle. All the way up the road to the gate, and through the shattered courtyard, Blanche stared into hopeful, hungry eyes. All the people of Carbonek were thin and threadbare, from the youngest children in garments so patched that they had almost lost their original shape and colour, to the hollow-cheeked knights whose battered chainmail hung off their wasted frames like the sloughed skin of bigger men.

Did Carbonek take its desolation wherever it went?

She dismounted in the courtyard, all of a sudden fiercely glad that over her sooty nightgown she was still wearing the embroidered wool cloak Naciens had given her on her last visit to this castle. It was the one thing she had saved from the fire. She had admired the garment, but its real value had not even crossed her mind.

Now it did.

These shivering and threadbare people had tended the sheep. Shorn the wool. Washed, carded, spun, dyed, woven, cut, sewn, and embroidered it, all by hand. And at the end of it all, they had given it to her, who had more than she could ever desire. How could she have faced them, knowing she had thoughtlessly lost their gift?

There was a hot smoulder in her stomach. Maybe it was shame. Maybe it was anger at her own conceit. Whatever it was, it stiffened her spine.

Someone came forward to take Florence's bridle. Nerys smiled at her and gestured for her to take the lead. Blanche took a deep breath and marched up the steps into the hall, followed and surrounded by a breathless crowd. Inside, she found the hall full of noise and light. A fire glowed in the big hearth and two squires were playing at the chessboard. Torches lit the tables, and servants hurried up from the kitchen bearing plates heaped with fish and bread.

A hound rose from where it lay under the high table and came toward them, tail wagging politely. Every bone stood out on its snake-like head, and the fur on its lean sides was dull. It wrapped its tongue around Blanche's chilly fingers.

How much she had missed before!

The table on the dais was already full of people. There was Naciens the Hermit, rising up from his seat. And there on a couch in the midst of the table lay an old, old king, propped up with pillows and looking frail enough to be slain with a feather.

Beside the ancient king, Naciens did not smile, but his eyes beamed welcome. Blanche went forward to meet him between two tables running the length of the hall. A hush fell over the company. One of the squires at the chessboard shouted "Checkmate!" before he realised that his voice had fallen upon silence. He turned scarlet and sank back to watch.

The voice of Naciens filled the whole silent hall. "Name your name, wanderer through the Waste."

In the hush, with every eye fixed upon her, she paused, keenly aware how unfit she was to take up the high duty being offered to her.

And yet it was being offered to her. And since nothing else would repay them for their gift, she would do them this service.

She squared her shoulders and said:

"Blanchefleur, of the realm of Logres."

15

And after many days she came
To that high mountain, where are built
The towers of Sarras, carved and gilt
And fashioned like thin spires of flame.

Gosse

he aged King stirred on his couch and spoke in a gentle, creaking voice like the closing of a badly oiled door.

"Be welcome to Carbonek, damsel," he said.

Naciens spoke again. "Name your errand, Blanchefleur of Logres."

Blanchefleur said, "I have been sent to guard the Holy Grail."

"And do you accept this task?"

"I do."

"Then you are twice welcome," the King said. "Naciens."

The hermit lifted his voice. "Nerys the Fay. Branwen, daughter of Culhwch."

Behind her, Blanchefleur heard rather than saw the quick gesture of surprise Nerys made before she stepped forward. With the second name there came a long silence. In the hush she clearly heard a breathless whisper— "*Me?* Oh!" and then a rush of footsteps as the owner of the whisper darted to her side—a girl perhaps a little younger than herself, all flaxen hair and nervous energy.

Naciens said: "The number of the Signs is three, and the number of the keepers is three. Do you, attendants of the Grail, bind yourselves to faith and obedience; to give eternal knowledge freely to any who seeks it, and to guard the Signs with your lives, as grace shall be given you?"

"We do," said Blanchefleur, and felt the voices of the others echoing in and around her own. Naciens lifted his hand and blessed them with a

124

smile, and then there was clapping and cheering from the castle folk, a sound like the fall of waters. Seats were found for them at the high table and someone passed them each a rusk of bread topped with stew. Then the talk rushed on around them.

Blanchefleur glanced to her right. There sat Nerys, eating but apparently not tasting the food, for she looked ahead into an unseen realm, silent and solemn. She turned to her left and saw the girl from Carbonek staring at her with excited awe.

"Welcome to Carbonek," said Branwen.

"Thanks."

"Dame Glynis said I might show you the castle."

"Dame Glynis?"

Branwen's hands fluttered. "She is the steward's wife, and oversees the women. She does like to run everything, for the King will never say her nay, and his daughter, the Lady Elaine, is too ill to bother with household things. But we all like her, even if she is a mother-goose."

Blanchefleur said, "The King has a daughter?"

"Yes, but she only came back to Carbonek a little while ago. We have not had a real Grail Maiden since she first went away."

"She was the Grail maiden? Why did she leave?"

Branwen shook her head. "No one ever speaks about it. I asked once but Mother said it was gossip."

"I didn't know you could leave Carbonek."

"Oh, yes, any time. Finding it is the hard part. Mother and I only stumbled upon it by mistake when we were lost, after the wild men burned our house down. It happened when Father went to visit the High King at Camelot, and we haven't seen him since. I do miss him. Have you met Heilyn?"

"Heilyn." Blanchefleur struggled to keep up with the girl's quicksilver chatter. "No."

"One of the squires here. One day, when the Grail Quest is achieved, he will go to Camelot and tell Father all about it, and Father will come and collect Mother and me. And I will see the flowers and fruit again on the apple-trees in the spring," she went on, in a dreamy sing-song, "as I remember doing when I was small. There are no flowers here in Carbonek."

"Never?"

"Never. But there are other things. There is the Grail, which is something, isn't it?"

"I—"

"And do you see that chess-board?"

Blanchefleur looked over to the fireplace. "I know it well. Perceval was about to destroy it when I came in."

Branwen giggled. "Well that you prevented him! For that is the chess-board of Gwenddolau son of Ceidio, and the pieces will play by themselves. It is one of the Thirteen Treasures of the Island of Britain."

"How does it work?"

"I cannot tell. A wise smith must have made it." Branwen shrugged. "I wanted Heilyn to take it apart to find out how, but King Pelles did not allow it."

Beyond Nerys, on Blanchefleur's right, stood the couch of the old King of Carbonek, who was speaking to Nerys in his weak, reedy voice. Blanchefleur turned to hear what she could of the old King's words, but she only caught a snatch of them: "—there is nothing any of us can do, you understand. When the Grail Knight comes— "

But the rest of his sentence was lost to her, for Naciens pushed back his chair and rose, beckoning to Blanchefleur, Nerys, and Branwen to follow him.

Naciens led them through the hall doors, down a passage, and up a long winding stair to a little low door at the top of a tower. Behind this door was a chapel jewel-coloured with stained-glass light. Tall slim windows walled the chapel on three sides. A low table stood near the eastern windows. Here rested the heavy wooden platter she had seen once before, now heaped with bread; above it on two hooks suspended from the ceiling hung the spear, dripping slow drops of blood which vanished before they reached the ground. Overhead, the roof soared high, seamed with narrow honey-coloured ribs, painted blue with gilt stars.

Not all the light in the room came through the windows. And indeed the tower was built more like a lantern than anything else, and the riotously coloured windows seemed meant less to let light in, than to pour light out. For beside the platter on the table stood the Grail itself, a heavy plain brass cup of unmistakeable age, covered in a scrap of white samite to temper and diffuse the blinding light within.

Blanchefleur hesitated, struck with abashment in the presence of so much light and beauty. But Naciens, moving to the table, called to them with a smile. "Come and eat."

"Eat?" Blanchefleur lifted a hand against the light. "Of *these*?"

"Even of these. *Potestis bibere calicem quem ego bibiturus sum?*" he quoted.

"It is not only your right, but your duty."

She looked doubtfully at Nerys, and saw the fay's hand gripping the lintel of the door with white finger-tips. She kept her eyes on Naciens, and made no sign to Blanchefleur, but there was longing in every line of her body.

Blanchefleur swallowed her awe and dropped her hand. The light struck her full in the eyes.

"Then we are able."

IN THE FOLLOWING DAYS BLANCHEFLEUR SETTLED into the rhythm of life at Carbonek, unsure what her work as the Grail Maiden might require beyond tending the chapel and holding herself ready for some future summons. Meanwhile she lodged in a tiny closet set into the wall of the Grail Chapel above the door, just big enough to house a mattress, a shelf, and a chest to hold her things, separated from the chapel itself by a heavy tapestry and a door. That tapestry, like everything else in the chapel, was wild with colour and images, depicting Christ sitting throned in heaven above the words *Data est mihi omnis potestas in caelo et in terra*.

She spent most of her time away from the Chapel, however, on a busy course of study—learning physics and surgery in the infirmary, where everyone was shocked to discover that she did not know how to set a bone; spinning and weaving in the solar, where her clumsiness with spindle or loom made watching her a favourite pastime; and reading chroniclers and philosophers with Naciens, in which alone she could show the beginnings of competence.

In Carbonek, for the first time in her life, Blanche Pendragon felt a dunce.

Caught in a constant stream of work, struggling to grasp a hundred new names and faces, with hardly a spare minute from morning till night, the past faded out of mind and Blanchefleur almost forgot everything that had gone before: the witch trying to kill her, the giant which had nearly succeeded, the question of her parentage and legacy, Perceval and the Quest...

Until one night not long before Christmas, when she awoke from troubled dreams to find herself standing in golden light on the peak of a mountain.

THE ROOM WAS BUILT OF STONE seamed with gold, pointed and spired in unimaginable complexity like a finger reaching up toward heaven. There were window-openings, without glass, opening onto the sky above, but this was like no sky which Blanchefleur had ever seen. It was dull flat gold like the sky in an illuminated manuscript.

The three Signs, as Naciens had called them, were there on the east wall, but here their numinous glory clung to the sky and the whole land, so that they themselves appeared unremarkable. The old spear had a rusty stain on the blade which might have been blood, and the Grail was uncovered, for here it did not give out light but received it.

The chapel's roof rested on window-outlining pillars which twined to-gether like trees above Blanchefleur's head. The floor, like that of Tintern Abbey in Monmouthshire, was covered in a thick living carpet of grass, and in the centre was an opening onto winding stairs. Blanchefleur went to one of the windows, and looked out, and caught her breath.

She stood in something like the steeple of a cathedral, looking down at a roofless church on the ground. This itself stood on the highest peak of a mountain covered with ancient buildings, so that the whole mass formed one labyrinthine city. Few of the houses and halls had roofs and from this vantage Blanchefleur saw that the same thickset velvet grass carpeted every floor. Instead of tapestries or stained-glass windows, instead of knotted carpets and curtains, the city was furnished with trees, vines, shrubs, flowers, fruits, and bulbs.

Down in the crossing of the cathedral a clear, bubbling spring welled from underground. It spilled from its basin and flowed through the open doors and across the terrace. It tumbled down the slope, joined by other springs. It threaded like silver ribbons through a thousand canals to water the whole city. Miles off, at the very foot of the mountain, it gathered itself together again into one splendid rush which split into four arms and flowed away through every kind of tree and flower, in each direction, until distance confounded the eye.

Blanchefleur stood wordlessly staring at the whole earth spread out at her feet. The majestic rivers, the riotous fecundity of the whole country-side, the mazelike intricacy of the city itself, full of arches, spires, court-yards, fountains, walls, windows, waterfalls, and buttresses, the dizzying height of mountain, cathedral, steeple, and spire, struck her immovable, speechless, and all but sightless.

She did not know whether she had been standing there five minutes or five days when at last she stirred her stiff body and went down the steeple stair. On the ground, wandering beneath the leaping arches of the great cathedral, it was the silence which struck her. The place was not ruined, but tended; roofs and windows had been left off, not because of decay or fire, but because in this country there would never be cold or storm.

Were there inhabitants? Blanchefleur remembered the silence of Carbonek when she first came there, and went on, out of the church and down the slope, into an endless maze of courtyards, halls, and gardens. All was hushed and still, but she had never seen such beauty either in building or gardening. Robed caryatides stood knee-deep in flowers, bent gravely beneath the weight of walls and balconies. Nothing here was dead or diseased; more than one hall she passed through mingled the grass with herbs that gave off a heady scent when trampled, and she saw pillars supporting twining tomatoes or grape-vines. Further on she wandered through an orchard rich with the scent of apricots, and then a courtyard with a deep pool surrounded by orange-trees and daffodils.

It seemed to be spring and autumn here all at once.

At last Blanchefleur came out into an open courtyard decked only with amber-red maples. She stopped and put a hand to her heart when she looked inside. There was a great red winged serpent—a dragon!—lying in loops and folds within the garden, and on the blood-slimed grass beside the dead monster's severed head a knight was resting. He had thrown his helm and bloody sword aside, as well as his shield the colour of silver, which bore a dragon even brighter red than the one on the lawn. The knight sat with his bearded chin in his hand, but when Blanchefleur paused under the arch leading into the courtyard, he lifted his head and saw her.

Blanchefleur went toward him, a little timorous, but not fearful. He smiled up at her and she felt faint surprise to see his brown hair and beard now plentifully streaked with grey. Time had beaten, but not bowed, that head.

Even so, she remembered him well. It was the King from her dream of the meadow. Tears filled her eyes. It was true, after all. It was true, and all good dreams had come true in this land.

He watched until she stopped in front of him, her head bent before all the might and glory of the name of Arthur. Then he said simply, "You look like your mother."

Guinevera, casta vera, she thought, and for once she dared to believe it, and lifted up her eyes. "I do?"

"Very like." He wiped his sword clean on the grass and rose, returning it to its sheath. "Well, my dear daughter, is it the Grail that brings you to Sarras?"

"Sarras?"

"It is one of the names of the City on the Hill. This City."

"Then I suppose it must be the Grail that brought me here," said Blanchefleur. "I thought I was asleep in my closet at Carbonek…"

"I know I am asleep in my chamber at Camelot," returned the King.

The silence spun out a while, companionably. Blanchefleur marvelled how familiar the King seemed to her in manner and tone of voice, as if she had never left him or forgotten him. She sought for something else to ask, but all words had drained from her. What *did* one say to the High King of Britain, the august lord of Logres, the rumours of whose glory had blown through the wind between the worlds and become woven into all histories, even the ones in which he had no true part?

"Tell me what it means, sire," she said at last. "This city."

"It is our compass-point," said the King. "Every polity is built on a pattern, Blanchefleur. And not just every polity, but every life, every family, the church in every village. Everything imitates something. The only question is, what will it imitate? Something eternal, or something earthly?"

Blanchefleur turned her face to the peak of the mountain, where far above them the roofless cathedral shot up to touch the heavens.

"Sarras," said the High King of Britain, "is the pattern for Logres. Some would say that Logres *is* Sarras, but that is an error. Sarras is more, immeasurably more than Logres; yet perhaps one day, Logres might hope to become a part, an outflung border, of Sarras."

"By imitating it, you mean?"

The King nodded. "Yes."

Blanchefleur tore her eyes from the dizzying peak above her and said: "But I have never seen anything like this in the waking world. How can we hope to achieve this?"

"Our hope is not in ourselves," said the King. "And yet we have more hope than we did at the beginning of our labours. Remember what Augustine said about the City."

"*Et de caelo quidem ab initio sui descendit.*"

"That was the passage I meant." He fitted his shield onto his arm, and took up his helm. Blanchefleur, watching him, felt desolate.

"Are you leaving?"

"Yes." He gestured to the headless dragon. "I have done what I came to do. But I have not been able to deal with every danger for you. Harden your resolve, dear heart."

He passed his free arm around her shoulders and drew her to him.

"When I see you again in Logres," she said, "will you remember this—Sarras?"

"Not when I am awake, dear heart." Blanchefleur felt his lips brush the top of her head, and his arm released her.

She blinked the tears from her eyes. Arthur of Britain had gone. But she was not alone.

Under the arch leading into the courtyard stood a tall slim black-haired woman, clad in red so sulky-dark it was almost black.

"Fair niece," she said, and smiled with all her teeth, "at last we meet in the flesh."

16

I saw pale kings and princes too,
Pale warriors, death-pale were they all;
They cried—"La Belle Dame sans Merci
Hath thee in thrall!"

Keats

For Blanchefleur, all coherent thought stopped. Still smiling, the Witch of Gore sauntered into the garden and paused to look at the headless dragon. "Well, well, well," she breathed.

With an effort Blanchefleur summoned her thoughts. She wasn't dead *yet*, and that was more than she had expected ten seconds ago.

Suddenly her surroundings jolted into clarity. The luminous dull-gold sky, the molten-red dragon, the violence of splashed blood and splashed maples against emerald-green mossy ground and wall, struck her with an almost tangible blow. She was *alive*, and life had a terrible splendour.

All this in the fraction of a second. Then Blanchefleur laughed, and said:

"Not what you expected? The dragon headless and the maiden entirely unsinged?"

Morgan lifted her head slowly, and her eyes held wariness. "Not quite," she said.

She paced on, roving restlessly as sea-water, to and fro, up and down, and Blanchefleur, without thinking, moved as well to keep distance between them.

"Tell me what happened here," said Morgan.

"I think you know."

Morgan shrugged and rolled her eyes. "As you like. *You* did not deal with it, at any rate. So much is clear. Who was it, your champion? The

132

Yap-Mouth of Wales?"

Blanchefleur realised that Morgan meant Perceval, and frowned. If Perceval did like to talk, at least he did what he boasted. "Maybe it was. Your dragon gave him no trouble, at any rate."

A smile. "Oh, do tell."

Her voice, smooth as samite, said nothing plainly but inferred anything at all. Blanche attempted hauteur. "I don't see why I should tell you a thing."

"Dear niece, even if I were interested in your little intrigues, I'm hardly likely to disapprove, eh?"

"Intrigues—what? What do you mean?"

Morgan arched a thin brow. "Oh, don't try to deny it. I saw you in his arms."

Blanchefleur flushed scarlet. "What? That was my *father*."

Morgan smiled. Blanchefleur realised she had been outwitted and lifted her chin a little, trying not to care.

"Ah, my dear. Still so much a child, to be matching wits with *me*. To be guarding the Holy Grail." The tip of her tongue flicked out to touch her lips. "So, my dear brother rode to your rescue, like the perfect gentle knight he is." Her tone had been offensive, but now her eyes narrowed, and her voice dripped malice: "Or did he? Did you *see* him kill it? Arthur Pendragon, who gathers better men to his banner to do the work he is incapable of himself. Lancelot. Gawain. Bors. There lie the real powers of Logres. And he boasts of it."

They stood facing each other, having worn one or two circles in the grass, and at this moment Blanchefleur was nearer to the door in the green garden wall. She had not taken her eyes from Morgan since the first moment she saw her, but now, without a word, she turned on her heel and went to the door.

It was a reckless thing to do, and her shoulders clenched tight in fear of a blow as she walked away, but it had suddenly occurred to her that she had no reason to stay and hear poisonous words.

Besides, short of stabbing her in the back, what could Morgan do? Run after her? Shout? But Morgan had far too much pride to run or shout, and had spent too much time talking to intend violence.

Beyond the mossy courtyard, Blanchefleur found a main road running up to the cathedral at the peak of the mountain. She forced herself not to look over her shoulder, but moved as soundlessly as she could, listening, listening. In the deep living silence of Sarras, only her own footsteps sounded against the street. Then, far away, there were other footsteps like the drip of rain, needling at the edges of her calm... Blanchefleur quickened her pace a little and fixed her eyes on the cathedral spire.

Where was she going? Was it foolish of her to lead Morgan to the Grail itself? Or could the spire be fortified somehow? She sorted through panic-tangled thoughts, forcing her breath into a slow rhythm. If Morgan killed her it would not take the witch long to find the Grail, in any case. And since there were two things to guard—the Grail, and her own life—it seemed reasonable, with no other plan, to put the two in the same place and stand or fall together.

Then, too, there was the irrational feeling that the Grail meant safety.

She looked back, once, when she reached the roofless cathedral. Morgan was not fifty paces away, and when she saw Blanchefleur turn back, she lifted a cheerful hand.

Once again, Blanchefleur wondered if she was forgetting something. If she was walking into a trap. But she set her jaw and went up the staircase to the Grail, breaking into a run as soon as the stair took her out of sight of the church door. Her feet seemed unharnessed from her heart; what should have stranded her halfway up the stair, doubled and gasping, beat serenely on while the steps flowed away beneath her feet. She mounted to the high chamber as if on wings, swift as thought, exultant.

Yet all this way she saw nothing that could be used for protection. Here in the spire there was the Spear, to be sure, but she knew the story now. It had been used once before, decades ago, by Sir Balyn. He had snatched the spear down and wounded King Pelles in the Grail Chapel itself, and with the stroke Carbonek had been laid waste and cut off from mortal lands. The same consideration prevented her snatching up the platter and bouncing it off Morgan's head as she rose through the stairway.

But the Signs lay on a massive wooden table, with skirt-boards reaching to the ground. Blanchefleur flung her arms around it and pulled, and to her great joy it came grating slowly across the floor. She shoved and strained at it and within a handful of breaths had it across the stair's opening, leaving only a space of a few inches at each side. Even as she eased the table into place, there was a rush of steps from below, and Blanchefleur, looking down into shadowed darkness, saw the gleam of Morgan's eyes.

And Morgan laughed, seating herself on the steps below. "Well," she said, "your methods are crude, no doubt, but effective."

Blanchefleur leaned on the table, just in case, and said, "I'm not moving. What are you waiting for? Are you trying to *bore* me to death, now your pet dragon is gone?"

"My dear, what makes you imagine that *I* had anything to do with the dragon?"

"But you—"

"Did I not inquire what happened? It was honest curiosity."

"But you sent the giant."

"Alas, yes." A sigh, soft as the wind on a midsummer's day. "I *said* it was a waste, but was I heard? No."

"A waste? What? What are you saying?"

"That killing you was never part of *my* plan. I swear I am the most ill-used woman in Christendom. To think that I taught the creature everything I know." Suddenly, there was a whip-crack of hatred in her words. "And now he turns my own power against me!"

Blanchefleur swallowed. Moistened dry lips. "He? Who's *he?*"

Silence fell upon the steeple. At last Morgan's voice slid out from beneath the table with the calm and sinuous grace of a serpent. "Oh, I *would* tell you. I am willing to tell you. I am waiting to tell you."

Instinctively, Blanchefleur recoiled. "Never mind," she said. "You would only lie to me, anyway."

"Would I? Think! I, the Witch-Queen of Gore! I, the Enemy of Logres! I, Morgan, the slave of my own—*creation*. Fetching and carrying! Morgan, send a giant to another time! Morgan, that paramour of yours is growing fat and lazy in Gore, send him to murder a woman! Bah! Even *I* would not stoop so low!"

Her voice rang with genuine injury. "And all of it bungled and botched beyond recall. Do you wonder how I hate him?"

Blanchefleur clutched the edge of the table. A chill crawled over her scalp. Morgan was speaking again:

"You, Blanchefleur. You will help me destroy him. You will set me free."

"Set you *free?* Never."

"Did you not hear me?" Morgan put her eyes up to the space between stone and wood, gripping the skirt of the wood. "Killing you was no plan of mine. You will die, or he will. That is the only choice you have."

The panicked tangle in her mind was getting bigger. Blanchefleur swallowed and whispered, "What are you doing here in Sarras? Another errand?"

"He sent me to fetch you. Dead or alive, he said. He didn't tell me about the dragon."

She picked up that thread and tried to follow it through the maze. "So you say. Why wouldn't he tell you?"

"Why would he? He has never admitted me to his counsels."

"Tell me his name."

Below, in the shadows, Morgan moved restlessly. "I hardly dare… Lilith!" she swore. "Why am I talking to you? Why do I not finish you now? You would never believe me—and when he learns that I am plotting against him, he will kill me."

Blanchefleur remembered to whom she was speaking, and came back on guard. "Let me know when you make up your mind," she said with a hard edge in her voice.

"A game," said Morgan.

"What?"

"A game of riddles. If you win, I will show you who my master is. If I win, you will agree to come with me—alive."

Blanchefleur said: "Nonsense! I'm not playing any such game."

"Then I'll kill you now."

Blanchefleur frowned, weighing the odds. There was the table to navigate, and she had assumed Morgan was unarmed. But then, she was a witch, and a powerful one.

Again, Blanchefleur wondered if she was being a fool, but there was no time to sort out all the possibilities. "All right. If you win, I'll go with you, but you must give your word to do everything to keep me alive. If I win, you tell me who your master is and then you go away and leave me in peace. Agreed?"

"Agreed." And Morgan gave the first riddle:

> *A father's child,*
> *A mother's child,*
> *But no man's son.*

Blanchefleur, braced with outstretched arms over the table, slackened with relief, for the answer seemed obvious. "A daughter," she returned. When Morgan did not reply, she gave one of her own:

> *In the garden was laden a beautiful maiden*
> *As ever was seen in the morn.*
> *She was made a wife the first day of her life,*
> *And she died before she was born.*

"Eve," Morgan said, after only a moment.

"Yes."

Morgan said:

> *I sought for it, 'twas easy its finding:*
> *The thing that God never found and never can find.*

Blanchefleur swallowed. "Repeat it?"

"You heard it once," Morgan said, and there was the gleam of eyes from below.

But then the answer came. "An equal!" Without stopping to hear whether her answer was correct, she rushed on, nervous now:

> *What has six legs, two heads, four ears, two hands,*
> *But walks on four feet?*

Again this hardly seemed difficult to Morgan. "A man riding a horse—a knight."

"Yes—right."

Morgan chanted:

> *What does man love more than life*
> *Fear more than death or mortal strife*
> *What the poor have, the rich require,*
> *and what contented men desire,*
> *What the miser spends and the spendthrift saves*
> *And all men carry to their graves?*

Blanchefleur bit her lip. A corner of her mind was screaming that if she could not answer, she was bound to shift the table aside and go down to Morgan, to be delivered to a far worse enemy if she was telling the truth, or to be killed out of hand if she had lied.

She clenched her teeth, slammed a door on the inner scream, remembered the last six words of the riddle, and gasped in another breath of freedom. "Nothing."

The silence stretched out, and Blanchefleur knew again that she had guessed correctly. And more calmly now she picked another riddle, dredged it up from the mists of lower memory with words still hanging in the golden air.

What is the best furniture for a man's house?

This time there was no answer. The long seconds passed, each in silence. Blanchefleur peered down past the table to see whether Morgan was still there.

"Well?"

"A moment."

More time passed. Blanchefleur felt her fingernails beginning to hurt and, looking at her hands, saw that she was gripping the edge of the table so hard that her knuckles showed white through her skin.

"I have it," said Morgan suddenly. "A hearth."

Blanchefleur closed her eyes. "Wrong," she returned. "The answer is a daughter. A daughter is the best furniture for a man's house. But you wouldn't know that." And she braced herself against the table, half-expecting Morgan to attack the barricade.

Instead, Morgan's voice came up like an audible shrug. "You win, then. Reach down and take my hand."

"You were going to tell me his name. Your master."

"I never said that. I said I would show you who he was. Take my hand."

Blanchefleur stood back from the table. It was happening, it was happening, the thing that she had forgotten or overlooked or failed to account for when she drove a bargain with a witch. It didn't matter that she had no idea what it was. All that mattered was the certainty gripping her by the throat, that in winning she had lost.

It was her own fault. At the time it had seemed the only thing to do, but she had agreed to the riddle game and must keep her word. She fell to her knees and reached through, into the dark, out of the light of Sarras. "Jesu, protect me—"

A FIRM HAND TOOK HERS. IN an instant the steeple was gone and Blanchefleur stood by Morgan in a cloistered walk on a starry summer's night in—*where* were they? Not Sarras, although the lofty foliage of elms and oaks was visible beneath the stars beyond the cloister. They stood on the high balcony of a mazelike castle with the wind sighing through branches and banners. Two figures came down the passage toward them, and as they approached, Blanchefleur glanced unbelievingly at Morgan.

The Witch of Gore looked back with a ghastly smile on her empty face. Blanchefleur turned and looked into the young eyes of the High King of Britain. Beside him, clinging to his arm, Morgan walked, scarcely more than a girl, as Arthur was scarcely more than a boy. She was speaking in tones too low to hear; their heads bent together, curiously trusting.

Blanchefleur turned away with a cry, and the scene dissolved to the tower in Sarras. "You're lying," Blanchefleur gasped, jerking away from the opening in the floor, but Morgan's hand yanked her back. Her voice was even.

"Keep still. There is more to see."

"No!" Blanchefleur strained away, but Sarras vanished and once again they stood outside at night. Now it was a drab early spring, all mud and stinking puddles in the fields outside a castle wall. A door in the wall opened, then slammed again. Morgan stood there alone, head drooping, carrying a little bundle in both arms: a baby. She looked up, and on her face was a bitter inscrutable smile.

Moving stiffly, Blanchefleur turned her head to look at the older Morgan standing beside her. She hated herself for even asking, but she had to hear it from Morgan's own lips. She had to know for sure what Morgan meant to tell her. "A child?" she mouthed.

The bitter smile touching Morgan's mouth hadn't changed in the intervening decades. She said: "If it comforts you, he didn't know we were brother and sister at the time."

There was a jingle of harness. The long-ago Morgan looked and saw a horse fastened to a ring on the wall. It was difficult for her to mount carrying the baby, but she managed it, and the plod of hooves carried her away.

Blanchefleur knelt on the stone in the tower at Sarras; it seemed her mouth and heart and every limb had turned to ash.

"I'll never believe you," she groaned.

Not until then did she feel her arm hanging limply down into the stairwell. Morgan had gone.

17

There the cavaliers of Britain roam,
Valiant in arms, with knights of other lands.
...
Valour is needed by all those who come,
For here a knight his death, not glory, stands
To find.

Ariosto

n the little monastery where Sir Ector and Nimue left him to recover, Sir Perceval ran a fever for two days and afterwards was as weak as a kitten for a sennight. Outside, the winter bit deep and snow fell on the hills, but the monastery lay snug in its valley, steam rising from low thatched roofs.

One late afternoon ten days before Christmas when Perceval began to feel more like himself, he was sitting on a rail in the stable feeding Rufus a handful of oats when from outside he heard a commotion. A moment later his uncle Sir Gareth came bounding in with his destrier and some of the brothers trailing behind.

"Well met, fair nephew!" he said. "I had been questing, and returned to Camelot, and lo, there was nobody to greet me but my own Lady Lynet, for everyone has gone on a very great hunting-trip after the White Stag, even the Queen. And my lady told me from Sir Ector that you lay here in a fever. I pressed on to see you."

"Then you might have spared yourself the trouble," Perceval laughed. "I am sound as a bell and just about to ride to Camelot myself."

Sir Gareth fiddled with the straps of his horse's bridle, giving the task only half his attention, and making a nuisance of himself with the quiet monks. "No need," he declared. "Camelot stands nigh-empty. Only Sir Mordred's squire arrived home yesterday to say that his master would be

140

back by the week's end, and rather than await his coming, I have decided to run an errand for Lynet. Will you ride with me?"

Perceval grinned. "I may be persuaded. What's the nature of this errand?"

Sir Gareth threw up his hands and collapsed onto a haybale. Behind him, the brothers breathed a sigh of relief and began untangling the harness. "Lynet is with child, and she *must* have dragon sausage," he said. "Welsh dragon sausage. Pork, beef, *Cornwall* dragon—not good enough. What do you say, nephew?"

Perceval put a hand to his head with a sudden memory. "I would come, but I have no helm. I lost it in the other world, and have nothing with which to buy another."

"Careless of you," Sir Gareth said. "Then ride with me to find a dragon. There will be enough gold in its hoard for a hundred helms."

The next morning, and with the monks' direction, they armed and set out riding north-east at an easy pace. It was on the second day, as they paced up the western bank of the Wye seeking a ford, that they saw two other knights riding south down the eastern bank.

Here the river was narrow, twice the distance of a stone's throw across. It was easy to see the markings on the shields of the two knights, and to his great surprise, Perceval recognised one of them. It was a sable shield, bearing a silver dragon. The second knight had the similar-hued bearings of argent, a bend sable.

Perceval acted without thinking, pulling Rufus into the lee of an oak, watching through the leaves. Sir Gareth joined him without a word or a sound. When, after a little time, the knights on the opposite bank of the river turned and made their way under the shadows of the trees, Perceval turned to Gareth and cried,

"He is still alive, then!"

"Yes, and on his way to Camelot for Christmas." Gareth laughed.

"You mean Sir Breunis?" Perceval asked, a little confused. "Is he now a member of the Table?"

"Sir Who? Oh, you mean the knight with the silver serpent? But I have never seen that device before. No, I meant the other one."

"Did you know him?"

"Mordred. Our cousin."

Gareth spurred his horse back to the path and lead the way up the river. "Tell me what you know about Sir Breunis," he said over his shoulder.

"He was a common wayside robber," Perceval said. "I passed my sword through him and the King gave him his life when he begged for it. He vowed to mend."

"It has happened before," Gareth told him. "There was Ironsides, the Red Knight, whom I fought on my first quest, and for many years now he has been a true knight of the Table. And your mother's brother, who served with us seven years after the Queen of Gore's enchantment was broken. Depend upon it, when we come to Camelot, we will find Sir Breunis's name on a siege as well."

Perceval glanced at Gareth, and saw a crease between his eyebrows giving the lie to his words. "Do you really think so?"

The crease deepened, and then smoothed away in a smile. "Let us hope!"

It was in a valley on the other side of the river that they found the little desolate village the monks had spoken of. Here they were pointed to a nearby well, where the trees and the ground were all blackened with fire and the gnawed bones and bootless weapons of unhappy villagers strewed the ground.

In the dim sunset Perceval looked the glade over and said, "Does your lady wife think so little of sending you out on deadly errands?"

Sir Gareth unstrapped the blanket from behind his saddle. "It's our fourth child. I've grown accustomed to it."

"Of course," Perceval said with a grin, "even dragonfire might burn less hot than my lady aunt's temper."

Sir Gareth cuffed Perceval across the ear. "For that piece of insolence, youngster, you take the first watch. And be glad you are so tender in years that I dare not risk my honour upon you in single combat to prove my Lynet as sweet-tempered as she should be."

"Tender in years? What, and my wounds not yet healed from a battle you would have trembled to see?"

"Dare not accuse me of cowardice, child."

"Dare not call me a liar, ancient kinsman."

"Enough!" With a snap, Sir Gareth shook out his blanket and sank down between the roots of an oak-tree. "A week after Christmas, then, in the meadow outside Camelot, we will joust. And God have mercy on your soul."

The moon rose high above the trees as Sir Perceval kept watch. Gareth snored under the shadowy oak. Apart from this, the only sound came from flittering bats and the snuffling of a passing badger. Perceval stared at the well in the moonlight, and was happy. Happy to be active again, happy to be back in the company of his brother-at-arms, happy to be home, with his sword on his hip and his shield on his arm, as they should be, instead of hidden away at the back of a wardrobe.

He stretched a little, and his mail made metallic whispers that echoed away in the night. But then they went on, even though now he was stock-still; and then came a little snort and a few more scuffling noises, and he knew that the dragon was coming.

He rose to his feet as quietly as possible, and drew his sword.

The dragon rippled out of the well in dark liquid folds, a stripe of moonlight running down its scales. Perceval bent at the knees, lifting his shield, raising his sword. A twinge plucked at his shield-arm and the certainty struck him that helmless and weakened as he was, he could not hope to face even this small dragon alone.

It lifted one of its two long snouts, sniffed the air, and saw him.

"*Gareth!*" Perceval bellowed, and then with a lash of the dragon's tail he went down. At once he was struggling up again—too slow, too slow—then a crushing weight landed on his chest and wrestled him back to the earth. Perceval felt a blast of heat in his face and looked into a pair of toothy maws, each with a red-hot glare rising in the throat.

But Sir Gareth, shieldless and unhelmed, was already on his feet, yelling "Orkney! Orkney! A rescue!" The beast merely lifted one head and roared fire. But Gareth was no newcomer to dragon-killing. He dove to one side, surged up unscathed, and struck off both the dragon's heads with one blow of such force that they went rolling across the glade and the blade scythed deep into the ground by Perceval's head.

Perceval grunted as the twitching bulk of dead dragon toppled onto him. Fumes choked him. In the sudden dark that followed the flaming blast, Gareth was laughing.

"What cheer, nephew?"

It was Christmas Eve when they returned to Camelot with the dragon, heads and all, to which cause the remaining villagers had gladly contributed a cart and driver. Fierce weather froze the road solid enough for easy passage.

They kept the cold at bay with talk and laughter. Gareth's tended to revolve around what he was going to do with the jingling bag in his pack, the gift the villagers had made him out of the little dragon-hoard.

But all talk of new arms and horses faded when at last they came out of the woods to the snowy meadow and saw Camelot rising on the hill above them, no less gracious and welcoming in the leafless nakedness of winter than in the green robes of summer.

There was the dragon to deliver first, which Sir Gareth, with a sudden impulse for theatre, did in the Great Hall itself, where, with an air of desperate candour that convulsed all watchers, he called forth Lynet and laid both the dragon's-heads at her feet. One of the ladies screamed at the grisly sight, and some looked queasy, but Lynet had the stomach of a man, and received the gift with a pretty speech followed by a clout on the head, which Gareth repaid with a kiss.

With the comedy finished, it was time for dinner. After, Perceval and some of the knights he knew dragged chairs to the fire to finish a conversation. Sir Gawain joined them, but when the other men one by one drifted off to see families or horses or armourers, he rose and beckoned to Perceval.

The King's solar was full of the scent of fir and spices. The Queen filled cups with mulled wine from a pot hanging over the fire, and the King sat by a chessboard, strumming his fingers on the arm of his chair as if working out a problem.

He looked up and smiled when he saw Perceval.

"So you are returned, Sir Perceval," said the King. "Sir Ector has already told me the manner of your leaving the house in Gloucester. I am greatly in your debt."

"Sire, I was glad to win this honour of serving you."

The Queen handed wine to the two newcomers. "Be seated," she told them, and sank into her own chair. Perceval obeyed with a sudden solemn premonition. This was not a council meeting, yet the air was oddly formal.

The King said: "What was your estimation of my daughter's nature, Sir Perceval?"

"We have lived so long without her," added the Queen, as if to soften the blunt force of the question. "Tell us all you can."

Perceval opened his mouth—and then, perhaps for the first time in his life, thought better of it, and closed it again. He stared at the tapestry on the wall for what seemed an age before, at last, he said: "At worst, thoughtless. Too wrapped up in herself, and a little disdainful of Logres, I think. She was loath to come here at first, Sir Ector said, and so I found her. But then her conscience began to reproach her, and she listened to it."

Perceval could not read the Queen's face, for she held her cup like a mask before her mouth. But he saw something a little like disappointment in the King, and rushed on, bubbling out some of the warmth he had bottled in a moment ago. "There was a man in that other place, who I think had made her half in love with him. He offered her his protection and hand, but she refused him. For Logres. When the house was burning around our ears, she would not save herself without me and if not for her, you would have seen the letters of gold fade from my seige at the Table. When she listens to her conscience, the Lady Blanchefleur is better than an army."

The King said, "I am glad to hear it." He paused. His next question, when it came, was even more daunting. "And what is her estimation of you?"

The Queen gave him no help this time. She placed her cup on the table and waited for his reply. Almost in a panic, Perceval glanced at his father. Sir Gawain looked back solemnly, and in a flash Perceval realised why he and his father were sitting here speaking to Blanchefleur's parents. He remembered the last time he had sat in this room, and the King asking Sir Gawain if Sir Gawain objected to his son's guarding the King's daughter—

Perceval almost laughed with relief, and said, "Sire, I will be plain with you, for I catch your meaning. It has now and again come into my mind to win the regard of the Lady Blanchefleur, although I would not do so while she was under my protection and before I had your consent to it. As to her opinion of me, she is not ill-disposed toward me, and if you will give leave, I hope someday both to gain and to deserve her favour."

A gleam of amusement shone in the King's eyes. "Then you have my leave to try, on one condition. The Lady Blanchefleur is in Carbonek, guarding the Holy Grail. When the time comes and the Grail Knight appears, go in quest of the Grail. Achieve that quest, and when you meet the Grail Maiden in Carbonek, you will be free to speak your mind. But fail in the Quest or turn back, and with your hope for the Grail, relinquish your hope for the lady."

Perceval nodded. Sir Gawain said, "This is a reasonable condition, if you ask me. The Quest will prove the true citizenry of Logres. And why should the Pendragon's heir have to do with anyone less?"

Perceval said under his breath, staring into the fire: "There will be the Grail Knight too."

"The Grail Knight?"

"Yes." None of the others were saying it, and if they were discussing

Blanchefleur's future, and what would be best for her, then it had to be said. "Sire, your words to me today have been kind. But one may come with a better claim than mine."

The King lifted an eyebrow. "The Grail Knight?" he said. "Of course he will be the best of us all. But would he come looking for a wife?"

Perceval said: "Forgive me the question. What *will* he come looking for?"

Sir Gawain said, "From the earliest time we have known about the Holy Grail, and the promise of the Grail Knight. Those who participate in the Grail participate in the will of God Himself. That is what the Grail Knight will do—he will lead us to the Holy Grail. It is his privilege to drink of that cup."

"I thought it was for all of us," Perceval said.

"In a secondary manner, yes. But we have other work. That is why we need the Knight. We do not expect him to be so worldly minded as to think of marriage."

Perceval felt none so sure. But the King said: "In any case, when the Quest is fulfilled, it will be clear to all of us what the Grail Knight has come to achieve."

LATER, IN THE RUDDY FIRELIGHT IN Gareth's rooms where a handful of the knights had gathered to talk, Perceval took a chair by his uncle.

"Have we news of Sir Breunis?"

Gareth ran a hand through his hair and sighed. "I asked Lynet. Mordred came back alone and the name of Breunis is missing from the Table."

Sir Gaheris, another of the Orkney brothers, leaned over. "Are you talking about Mordred?" he asked.

A slow silence fell on the room.

"What about Mordred?" asked Sir Lamorak from where he lay stretched out on the hearthrug.

Gareth said: "It's nothing."

The fourth and youngest Orkney brother, Agravain, spoke up from a corner. "You have never liked him, have you, Gareth?"

From the look on Gareth's face, Perceval guessed he had forgotten Agravain's presence.

"Agravain—"

"You know that no one has ever accused Mordred of illdoing."

"I do," Gareth said miserably. "But what *has* he done?"

"Nothing!" Agravain shot back. "Nothing at all!"

Gareth leapt to his feet. "You said it! *That* is what concerns me!" He stopped, stamping down the fire of his temper. "It concerns me about all of us, friends. When the Grail Knight comes, will we be ready for him? Or will he find us too busy doing nothing?"

Agravain said, "The Grail Knight? What? We are talking about Mordred."

Sir Lamorak said, "Doing nothing? What do you mean, Gareth? You just delivered a village from a dragon."

"I know, I know." Gareth waved an impatient hand. "But is there not a certain hope we have in the Grail Knight? *Adveniat regnum tuum sicut in caelo et in terra...* the transformation of Logres. It is good to deliver villages from dragons. But that will not be the Grail Knight's task. Sometimes I wonder..."

He laid his hand on Perceval's shoulder. "What if the Grail Knight had already come, but nobody knew him? What if one of us, here, now, in this room, is the Grail Knight? You, Perceval? You, Lamorak?"

Lamorak laughed heartily.

"I don't see what this has to do with Mordred," said Agravain. "Unless you are blaming him for not being the Grail Knight."

"The boy has a point," said Gaheris with a smile.

Gareth pursed his lips. The passion in his eyes went out and he sat down again.

Perceval bowed his head and said, "I am not the Grail Knight, Gareth."

"Perhaps not," he said with a smile. "But you *could* be. Mordred? No."

Some of the men laughed.

Perceval said: "Why are you so sure? Gareth, he must have done *something* to earn your distrust."

"Well, then," said Gareth, "my reasons are three. First, his parentage. Second, his face, which is as close and secret as a grave. And finally, eight days ago on the Wye River, I saw him riding south in the company of Sir Breunis, who you tell me was a villain and robber until you fought and all but killed him."

"The first two are not firm evidence, brother," said Sir Gaheris. "But to see him in the company of Sir Breunis? Perhaps an answer can be found therein."

"I am leaving Camelot in a week," Perceval said. "When the King gave Sir Breunis his life, it was on condition that he mend his ways. If he does not, I owe him death. Let me go to see whether he has kept his oath, and perhaps I will also discover what Mordred does in his long errantry."

"Good! A plan is better than talk," said Sir Lamorak.

"Bring me back word," said Gareth, "and if Mordred is cleared of fault in this, let me never speak another word against him."

Sir Caradoc had been listening to the conversation and now said: "I wonder you do not take it to the King."

"The King esteems Mordred," Gareth said. "And I am no backbiter, even if I distrust him. If we find any evil in my cousin, then we will go to the King, not before. Let us not add needlessly to his troubles."

Sir Lamorak sighed. "He is no longer young. I fear he grows weary under the weight of Logres."

Agravain said: "Does he? Sitting at feasts and tourneys while the rest of us spill our blood in the marches of Logres? Surely he could weary himself to better purpose."

Someone hissed in a breath and the whole room went suddenly very cold. The youngest son of Orkney seemed to shrink a little. At last Gaheris spoke: "Agravain! You know that is false. The King has never neglected the good of Logres—and he is never idle."

"It worries me," Agravain said sulkily. "What if there was another Saxon invasion? Would the King lead us to victory then, as he did when he was young? Or has he grown old and fond of comfort?"

"*O tu minimae fidei!*" said Sir Gawain, putting his head in at the door. "You speak as if he were half in his grave, Agravain, rather than occupied with other matters. I am going down to the chapel, Perceval. Come with me."

Perceval clapped Gareth on the shoulder, left pinched silence behind him, and followed his father down uneven tunnel-like corridors to the little chapel. Camelot castle was overbuilt and twisted, and hundreds of years had bowed it in on itself. But the chapel, to one side, stood straight and fair.

Its spear-pointed stained windows would come alive in the sun, but they loomed dead and dull in the clouded night. Only two candles gave light from the altar, flinging shadows overhead like tall watchers bending to stare at them.

Until now Perceval had stood in the chapel only in services among a throng of people. But here, in the lonely dead of night, he bent his head and saw that upon the stone by his foot was written a name.

King Pellinore said the stone, and then the other stones of the floor crowded upon his view, whispering. *Sir Cador. Sir Balan. Sir Galehault. Sir*

Hoel.

"Do you see the names?" Gawain asked, bringing light. "Look."

And he saw a name upon every stone in the floor, and more names on the stones in the wall.

"What do they mean?" Perceval breathed.

"These are the knights of our brotherhood who have gone from us," said Gawain. "For they shed their blood like water in defence of the defenceless."

"How many?"

"All, in the end." Gawain laid his hand on his son's shoulder. "Sir Perceval, when the priest reads the lesson, he says that he who would save his life must lose it. Good words for any man, for there are moments when cowardice will bring death more surely than boldness. But the ordinary man knows, when he goes out to meet the wolf in his road, that he may yet come home in peace. Not so the knights of the Round Table. We win through one deadly peril only to face another. If we banish one evil, we must go on to the next and after that, to the next—until death meets us in the path. We yield up our bodies every day, not for glory and fortune but so that those weaker than ourselves may live. Do you understand?"

"I do," said Sir Perceval. "And I say that there is no nobler calling. I am content." But then he thought of the Lady Blanchefleur kissing his brow on a night of fire and blood, and with a sudden ache of grief told himself that even a hundred years of peace would not be enough time to spend with her.

18

Sweet lord! how like a noble knight he talks!
Tennyson

even days later at dawn Perceval stood in the courtyard, huddled into his cloak but fiercely happy to be questing again. As much as he liked the warmth and ease of life at Camelot, it still took an effort for him to come off his guard there, to feel less hemmed in and surrounded. Now, despite a cold wind knifing through all the layers of wool, steel, and leather he wore, Perceval's spirits soared.

Dame Lynet handed him his shield. "Go with God's favour," she said. Perceval turned and grinned at her.

"May it also be with you. I'll be back at Pentecost to meet the young one. And take care of Gareth. I fear I have sent him to bed for a month."

Lynet wrinkled her nose. "Yea, you inflict the deadliest of bruises."

"Sir Gareth of the Black Eye. It sounds well. As I watched him tumble from his horse the third time—"

"Another word, fair nephew, and an aunt's revenge falls upon you," she warned.

Perceval swung to Rufus's back. "Then call the retreat!" he laughed, and setting spur to his horse, clattered out of the courtyard and down the hill.

His first aim was the little valley in the north where he had fought Sir Breunis. Here he came one icy January day under a colourless sky, and wondered at first if he had wandered into the wrong valley. Then he saw the raw stump where the oak-tree by the castle gate where Sir Breunis's shield once hung had been cut down and carted away. Perceval stared at it in surprise and urged his horse toward the castle. His first visit to the valley had shown an overgrown, ill-kept country, and Sir Breunis's men had slouched out of the castle and village in stained and slovenly clothes. Now everywhere he saw signs of industry and care. A little way up the hill, on the other side of the village, a mill was being built over the stream. Perceval spurred Rufus into a trot and went to examine it.

Sir Breunis's men worked about the gaunt and skeletal structure. Not a head rose at the traveller's approach. The overseer, a short, heavy-featured man of middle age, strode about in the cold to keep warm, shouting into the wind. When Perceval checked his horse and shouted "Ahoy!" the man finished a string of directions to his men and then stumped over to the knight and planted himself before Rufus, thumbs stuck into belt, face impassive.

Perceval undid his helm and leaned down. "Ho, there, fellow. Tell me about the work."

"Flour-mill," said the overseer, and his mouth clamped shut.

"This land does belong to Sir Breunis, doesn't it?"

A grunt of assent.

"Where is he? Might I speak with him?"

"He's not in the valley."

"Your magniloquent response fills me with mingled joy and disappointment, my good fellow," Perceval said, his temper wearing thin. The only reply this time was an uncomprehending stare. Perceval looked downhill to the little village and pointed at another new structure. "What have you built there?"

"Schoolhouse."

It was Perceval's turn to struggle over an unfamiliar word. "A what?"

"*Ludus.*"

"Really?" Perceval looked from one to another of the buildings. "Sir Breunis had you build these?"

"Yes." Was there a shade of hesitation in the answer? But then two men strained by beneath a great oaken beam, and the fellow wheeled away, shouting directions for them. Unwilling to disturb the labour, Perceval reined around and rode back down to the castle. Here the overseer's words were confirmed—Sir Breunis was away.

Perceval left the valley feeling stern with himself for the disappointment he felt. Part of him had looked forward to settling accounts with Sir Breunis today—just how much, surprised him. It was all to the good, he told himself, if the man had kept his word and begun to live honestly, making provision for his people.

And then there was the fighting he had done a few days ago, when he met Gareth in the meadow outside Camelot. Nor had it ended with Gareth: he had unhorsed five more knights before the bell went for Vespers, and on the way back up the hill to the castle he had overheard Sir Culhwch suggest matching him with Sir Lancelot. The most renowned knight of Logres was on some far-roaming errantry, or maybe Perceval would have had his chance then and there.

Breunis? He had no need to prove his valour on mean men.

North he rode, seeking out the loneliest places, and meeting soon enough with adventures. He rescued a countess transformed by an enchanter into a pig, struck the gong of Hafgan, slew two of the Three Brothers of Iscoed and crippled the third; and, meeting Sir Ywain in Gaerlleon, helped drive back a party of Pict raiders that had come down the coast to plunder the monastery at Wigan.

Here he rested a week, weathering out the last icy blasts of February. It was early in March, and beginning to smell like spring at last, when Perceval and Ywain set out together for Carlisle, the capital of Gore and the seat of King Uriens.

"Every two years my father holds a tournament," Sir Ywain explained. "Most of the Round Table will be there."

"And your mother?" Perceval asked.

Ywain shook his head. "Carlisle is the last place she would show herself. Many years ago I caught her about to kill my father as he slept. When I snatched the sword from her hand, she said it was not premeditated. Only a moment's passing impulse."

"And you believed her?"

Sir Ywain looked at him with shadowed eyes. "I did and do. She was never able to forgo a chance of mischief. But I was able to convince my father that he should keep beyond the reach of her whims for the future. She has her own place and her own servants to the south."

Carlisle itself was filled to bursting when they arrived, and had he not come in Ywain's company Perceval would hardly have found lodging. As it was, he was able to sleep in a corner of the great hall, and have Rufus fed and housed in the stables. Knights who had arrived earlier or with more attendants and money stayed in rich houses of the town or pitched pavilions outside the city walls. Nor were these the only visitors. The roofs of Carlisle sheltered men of every estate, from kings and lords to bondmen and beggars, from priests and farmers to smiths and shoemakers.

The tournament itself lasted three days, and Perceval's cool nerve and steady hand won him victory after victory. On the second day he had a moment of shock when, charging toward him through the melée, he saw a shield with a device that had never completely left his mind since the first moment he saw it. It seemed that he stood again in a courtyard, only half-armed and half-trained, facing Sir Odiar of Gore through sheeting rain. But there was no time for fear: the champion of Morgan was already upon him, all swinging mace and lashing hooves. Perceval admired that killing accord of heavy arm and deft horsemanship even as he wrenched Rufus aside and lashed, out and back, with his sword. Then the melée swept them apart, and there was no more chance to fight that day.

That evening Perceval had to take his bridle to a blacksmith to repair a buckle, and while he was waiting he went out into the street and strolled down toward the city gates, with half a mind to get out into the open and look at the Emperor's Wall that barred Carlisle from the north. The street was busy, full of mummers and minstrels, torches and braziers, and cries of "Hear" or "Buy". Anonymous in leather jerkin, without armour or identifying blazon, Perceval grinned to see four players re-enacting one of the day's high points: the Knight of Wales knocking Sir Persides, Sir Aglovale, and King Colgrevaunce off their horses without drawing rein. Perceval was, as usual, light of purse, but he spared a silver coin for the players.

It was just as he turned away from the circle of cheering watchers that Perceval looked up and saw a man retreating through the evening gloom. He thought he recognised the figure and gait well. It reminded him of some familiar form he had studied closely in the past, and wondering if there was another of his Camelot friends here, perhaps disguised, he called and ran after him.

Others drifted between them in the thickening night. Perceval lost sight of the man, and when he finally caught up with the one he thought he was following and shouted a cheery "Halloo!" the man turned upon him a face he felt sure was unfamiliar.

"Well, good evening," said the stranger in a stiff and surprised voice, and Perceval saw the pale bearded face of the knight pointed out to him at a distance in Camelot as Sir Mordred.

"I ask your pardon," Perceval said. "I thought I saw someone I knew."

"We are strangers, I believe," said Mordred. He checked in the midst of a motion to leave. "But I remember. You are the son of my good cousin Gawain, are you not?"

And despite the primness of his voice, there was a friendly flash of white teeth from within his black beard.

"Perceval of Wales. You must be Mordred," said Perceval, and held out his hand. Mordred bowed.

"Even so." He straightened from the bow and put out his hand to take Perceval's just as Perceval returned the bow.

"I am glad to meet you," Mordred said, glancing awkwardly at his hand. "Gawain often speaks of you, always with such pride." He dropped his hand to his side and looked up with a smile. "It is good to see. Gawain was so unhappy in his own father."

Perceval opened his mouth to ask about it, but Mordred raised a hand and forestalled him. "Forgive me for bringing up the old family history, cousin. Are you fighting tomorrow, as well?"

"Assuredly," Perceval said with a grin.

Mordred bowed again. "Then we shall not see each other. I am riding out on quest tomorrow evening, but I will be at Camelot for Pentecost. Farewell!" And he walked on and was lost in the crowd.

Perceval turned and went back to the smithy, thinking that Sir Mordred his cousin was hardly the sinister figure he imagined from Gareth's warnings. He was collecting his bridle when a boy ran in with the news. Sir Lancelot had arrived with Sir Gawain.

He lengthened his stride on the way back up the hill to the keep, and found his father in the great hall.

Gawain beat Perceval on the back. "They told me you were here! Northern air has done you good, I see. What have you been up to all these months? Hunting and haunting bowers, I'd wager." But there was a twinkle in his eye.

"Discovered! Alas," returned Perceval, straight-faced.

Gawain laughed. "And you slew the Brothers of Iscoed on a day that you had nothing better to do, or so I hear."

A grin stole over Perceval's face which he could not have reined in if he tried. "Just to keep in training."

Sir Lancelot strolled over from where he had stood speaking to Sir Ywain. "I hear fair things of you, son of Gawain. One day soon I shall have to break a spear with you."

Perceval tried not to betray the flush of delight that went through him at Lancelot's words. The Knight of the Lake never jousted with young or untried knights. Breaking a spear with Sir Lancelot meant a reputation as a seasoned warrior.

Beside him, Gawain, though one of the few knights of Logres capable of matching Lancelot, seemed no less keen. "Tomorrow?"

Lancelot turned to Perceval. "I am captaining the King of Northgales's side tomorrow, against King Carados and the Scots."

"Agravain and I have been fighting under the King of Northgales," Perceval said. "I had rather fight with my kin under you than against you for now, sir. If nothing else I may watch and learn."

For a moment Perceval wondered if Sir Lancelot was offended, he seemed so surprised. But then he bowed as if to a king. "Your son has bested me in courtesy, Gawain," he said. "If he is as skilled in arms, my star will set." He turned back to Perceval with a smile like sunshine. "And the King of Gore tells me you have shown yet unmatched skill these past two days."

"Well, *yet*," said Perceval. Then King Colgrevaunce came walking by and called Lancelot over to talk. Perceval turned to his father.

Gawain said: "You are a wiser man than I," and he did not smile, but the praise in his words was better than anything Lancelot had said. Perceval kicked the rushes underfoot and changed the subject.

"I wondered," he said—and it was true, in the last ten minutes he had been wondering—"why you never mention my grandfather much. What was he like?"

Gawain was taken aback. "Why do you ask?"

"I should dearly like to know something about him, sir."

His father looked, not at him, but through him. At length he stirred as if floating to the surface of memory and said, "It is a long story, and not one to be told in this company."

"You can tell me another time."

"Yes," said Gawain. But there was something secretive and shamefaced in his father's manner, something so ill-suited to his temperament and renown that Perceval found, for the first time in his life, a mystery he did not care to solve.

THE NEXT DAY, SEEING SIR LANCELOT and Sir Gawain cut through the press, Perceval felt with a bittersweet twinge that the decision not to fight Lancelot today had been the right one, not just for courtesy's sake but also for pride's. Then, when the day drew toward the afternoon Perceval saw the blue boar of Odiar again. This time the knight of Gore checked his pace, kicked his horse round, and laid his spear in rest.

Perceval fewtered his own spear, spurred Rufus into a gallop, and met his old enemy with a crash. There was a nauseating blow to his body, and

Perceval hit the ground. When he slid to a stop, gasping with pain, he went to push himself out of the mud and instead passed out.

HE SWAM TOWARD THE MURMUR OF voices. Light broke above him. Slowly, his father's worried face came into focus.

"What happened?" Perceval whispered.

"You've lost far too much blood," Gawain said. "But you'll mend. Odiar was lucky. He ran straight through the mail and grazed the tenth rib."

"Not lucky," Perceval gasped, although his head was swimming and he felt sick. "Stronger. Faster."

Gawain said: "Tell that to the judges." And he hefted a clattering purse.

Perceval had no strength to speak. He only opened his eyes a little wider.

"When the day was over, the prize was declared for Sir Lancelot. But he had gone, and could not be found. You were judged second-best."

"Pentecost," Perceval said. "Give it back. Not mine."

Gawain shook his head. "Calm yourself. He wouldn't take it. He conferred an honour upon you last night, but you refused it." He chuckled. "Old Lancelot had to have the last word."

There was someone else in the room, who now moved between Perceval and the candlelight. "Drink this," said the voice that was not Gawain's, and Perceval gulped down a warm, salty draught.

IT WAS APRIL BEFORE THE SURGEONS released him. Frantic to get out of doors and be part of the spring, Perceval scudded up and away, straight north, past the Emperor's Wall, into the wildest country he had yet seen. Here were adventures to be found in plenty, but he clung to the road north in the unexpressed hope of reaching Orkney, the islands of his fathers. Long before he reached the north seas, however, one evening high up in the hills, he went toward the light of a blazing fire and found there an ancient man with a donkey.

"May I share your fire tonight, good father?" Perceval asked him, sliding off his horse.

"You have far to travel, Sir Perceval of Wales," said the old man.

"But not tonight, I hope," he said with a grin, and went to tie Rufus to a tree. The man spoke again.

"Pentecost draws nearer," he said. "The Grail Knight is at hand. The Quest will begin. Ride back to Camelot."

Perceval turned back to the old man, the hair rising on the back of his neck. "Who are you to say so?"

"I am Naciens, the Hermit of Carbonek."

The Quest! Perceval sat by the fire that night, watching for dawn. The spring-fever that had driven him so far north seemed a small thing compared to what came upon him now at the thought of the Grail. It was time. At last, it was time.

He saddled Rufus again before the sun rose, but turned to ask one last question of the Hermit.

"Tell me, did she come to Carbonek safely, the heir of Logres?"

"Yes."

"I am glad to hear it," said Perceval, and rose back into the saddle. "Until we meet in Carbonek, fair sir."

But no smile relieved the harsh gravity of the hermit's face. "Beware," he said. "You think that you stand. Beware of falling."

"Sir, I will," said Perceval, much struck by the old man's earnestness.

He reached Camelot on the first day of summer, three days before Pentecost. Perceval found the royal city full and overflowing, much as Carlisle had been, but for a different reason. From all corners of Britain the Knights of the Table were returning to their citadel for the feast, but a steady stream of men of all estates followed them. For rumour had been busy, and it was afoot that the Holy Grail drew close to Logres. Pavilions burst into silken bloom up and down the riverside meadow outside the gates. At every meal Camelot's great hall was packed with guests, and Perceval and the other knights were kept busy hunting boar, venison, and fowl to feed them.

In the greenwood by day, riding down the black boar with his brother-knights, lightly clad in leather and linen, throwing the slender darts he had not forgotten to make, now and again hearkening as in the distance a sweeter horn blew and other hooves with dim crying of hounds came and rushed away just beyond eyesight, or finding a merry troupe of maidens with hawked wrists to accompany; in the high hall at night, scented with spring flowers and hung with blazing banners, as more people than he had ever seen before in one place supped and laughed and listened to the songs of minstrels—in those brief days, Sir Perceval moved in a hushed awe, and wished that it would never end, that no matter what happened hereafter, in some quiet corner of Britain King Arthur would still hold his court at Camelot, and Logres would reign bright and ageless in strength and beauty.

On the evening of his arrival Perceval went looking for the King, and heard from a page that he was in the garden.

The castle garden occupied the eastern slope of the Camelot-hill. It was not a big one, but its designer had made the most of the space, filling it with trees, hedges, and riotous spring flowers. In the mazelike middle of the garden a fountain gushed water which streamed away to join the river girding the castle. Here, amid the scent of daffodils, under trees hung with tiny lanterns, the King paced with a hound at his heels, speaking to Sir Bedivere.

Sir Perceval paused at a distance until the King looked up and called him. At the summons he started forward and bowed and gave his news. "Naciens the Hermit of Carbonek spoke to me in the Scots' land. And I heard that the Grail Knight will be here at Pentecost."

Before the King could reply, another step fell on the path, and the three looked up to see bars of argent. It was Sir Bors, a cousin of Lancelot's.

"Sire," he said, with the breath of a man who has been hurrying, "I saw Naciens the Hermit in Lyonesse, and he told me that the Grail Knight would come at Pentecost."

"I can well believe it," said the King with a smile.

"I rode five days without drawing rein to tell you," said Bors.

Silence fell. The only sound was the soft splashing fountain. Above, moon and stars. Around, perfume. Beyond, the wild faint thread of a nightingale's song.

"Earth is weighed down with Heaven tonight," said Perceval, almost in a whisper.

The King stirred. "The noontide of Logres," he murmured.

"Not so, by my faith," said Bors, "but the dawn."

"Good Bors, the son of succor!" said the King. "But I stand here in fear and trembling for a thing I cannot fathom. Who can say if the works of our hands will endure before the glory that is coming?"

On his way back to the castle, Perceval saw a figure moving through moonlight and shade, and recognised it as Sir Lancelot. With a murmur of apology he left Sir Bors and followed the Knight of the Lake's shadowy form into the labyrinthine garden.

The sense of awe was still upon him, and he walked softly, almost breathlessly, lest by some loud noise or sudden movement he should break the spell of that graceful garden. Too softly: before he had gone more than ten paces from the path, on the shadowed border of a moonlit clearing he paused with a sudden sense of mistake. There was a ghostly apple-tree, covered in white blossom. Below it walked like a silent vision three others, rippling in and out of moonlight and shadow. At the approach of Sir Lancelot, one of them came forward. In the full moonlight, her hair and skin and samite gown shone like silver. Only her eyes were invisible, thrown into shadow, black pools of distance.

The Queen.

Perceval stood immobile. What had he stumbled upon? Unbidden, the words of the Lady Nimue came into his mind. *She would be burned.* Before they had flashed through his memory he wheeled around to hurry back the way he had come. He took only two steps into the bushes and came face to face with his father's youngest brother, Sir Agravain.

Perceval stared at his uncle, his stomach churning, feeling like a sneak and a spy. But even in the grip of that dreadful moment he recognised the same look in Agravain's twisted features.

Only for a moment. But as they both mastered themselves, it came burning hot into Perceval's mind that Agravain must have been following Lancelot on purpose and not, like himself, by accident.

A rush of anger sluiced through him like floodwater. Afterwards, Perceval could not determine whether what he did next was right or wrong. "Agravain," he cried out, in a voice that tried to be jovial, but choked on the horror of the moment. "Have you come to speak to Lancelot too? I saw him walk this way."

Agravain, who had opened his mouth to speak, almost flinched as Perceval's voice split the night air. "I—" he faltered.

"What a surprise," said Perceval, still at the top of his voice and grinning madly, "to find you here. Shall we go on together?"

"I was just going back to the castle," Agravain muttered.

"The evening is yet fair," said Perceval. But as he sang out the words, footsteps approached, and the Knight of the Lake stood by them, straddling the path with his hands on his hips.

"I hear my name called," he said with a gleam of laughter. Agravain conquered himself with an heroic effort and spoke a greeting. Then, so soundlessly that Perceval thought he was dreaming, under the dappled moonlight behind Lancelot the Queen appeared like a white shadow.

"Well," she said, and her voice, like herself, was cool and silver. "I did not look to see such a gathering when I craved a moment of time from the Knight of the Lake."

At the sound of the Queen's voice Lancelot stepped aside with the measured grace that marked all his movements, but Perceval knew from the way he had stood blocking the path from them that he must not have expected her coming. And yet, such was his perfect self-command that not an eyebrow flickered when she spoke.

The Queen came forward flanked by the two other damsels Perceval had noted earlier. Lancelot, if outwardly composed, nevertheless stood speechless; Agravain's eyes narrowed; Perceval, watching them all, felt like one waking from the dead. For had the Queen's tryst with Lancelot been guilty or secret, she would not now stand before them, uttering a gracious word to each.

He realised that she was speaking to him.

"And I am glad to see you, Sir Perceval, still upon your feet," she said. "For it was told to me that you took a wound at Carlisle."

"Madam," he said, sagging with relief, "and I also am right glad to see you here." Whether she caught the double meaning or not was not apparent. She dropped her lashes, smiled, and moved on.

19

O servant of the high God, Galahad!
Rise and be arm'd: the Sangreal is gone forth
Through the great forest.

Morris

n the day of Pentecost the High King of Britain held festival at Camelot.

Even that morning, latecomers still straggled in to the bursting castle. Sir Gareth and Sir Gaheris arrived before breakfast, having ridden south a few days on a quick patrol. While they still stood stretching their legs in the courtyard, Sir Kay returned from Trinovant with Sir Ector and the Bishop of Ergyng. Then at mid-morning, just after church, two kinsmen of Sir Lancelot came riding in on horses stumbling with exhaustion: Sir Hector de Maris and Sir Lionel. Through gulps of water, they told the others that they had ridden night and day since escaping from the dungeons of the Castle Nigramous. Finally, a short space before midday, with the feast about to begin, Perceval rode through the keep gate and saw Gawain on the ramparts above, staring up the river with shaded eyes.

"Is all well?" Perceval called, reining in his horse and speaking through a thicket of white blossoms. Nine of the Queen's maidens had carried him on a last-minute maying, and his arms were full of the thorned flowers.

"Sir Lancelot went away with a damsel after sunset last night," Sir Gawain told him, "and he is still gone."

"Did he not say when he'd return?"

"Not a word."

"I am mounted and ready. Shall I ride after him?"

"No," Gawain said with a laugh. "I've seen Pentecost feasts before. If he does not come, let me ride out. Though it will be a pity, for his is the only siege empty, saving the Siege Perilous." He turned and scanned the landscape again. "Wait!"

A single knight came trotting out of the forest, bearing the familiar argent and gules. When Gawain stuck two fingers in his mouth and whistled, he waved his lance in the air and spurred his horse to a canter.

"He is in a good mood," Gawain said, leaving the ramparts to join Perceval in the gate. On reaching the keep, Lancelot reined in beside them and pulled off his helm, revealing a flushed and grinning face.

"Perceval was worried about you," Gawain told him very seriously. "Where have you been?"

"I knighted a boy," Lancelot said through the grin, and trotted on, up the hill, to the stables.

"So ho, a boy." Gawain cocked an eyebrow. "I wonder if that has anything to do with the old story... Give me your horse, Perceval. I can put him away while you take those flowers inside."

Sun flooded the great hall of Camelot with midday light, striking sparks from hurrying women in finery and serving-men in refurbished livery. Perceval dumped his mayflower on the Table and jumped aside to avoid a page spreading fresh rushes on the hall's floor. Fetching up against his own siege, he folded himself into the seat so as to be out of the way as he watched Lynet and her sister hanging the new Pendragon banner on the wall behind Arthur's chair. Then someone came up with fresh tablecloths, and Perceval vaulted across the Table to avoid her. He landed gently on the rushes inside the Table, opposite his own seat and the Siege Perilous, and turned laughing...

Perceval stopped laughing. The Siege Perilous had been as blank as a practice shield ever since he had first come to Camelot. There were fiery marks on it now, words of gold.

"Lynet," Perceval called. "You can read."

She came over and stared at the siege. As the others in the hall crowded around them, Lynet read:

"On the day of Pentecost this seat shall find its master."

"Call the King," someone said.

When Arthur came, he stared at the words for a while, and then sent for a cloth of samite. "So the Siege Perilous will be filled at last," he said. "Let it be veiled until it is claimed."

When the hall was finished, the doors opened. In came the ninety-nine knights of the Round Table and sat in their ninety-nine seats, each with a name written on it in words of gold, from the King at the head of the Table facing the hall doors, to Sir Bors and Sir Perceval facing him on each side of the shrouded Siege Perilous. In jostled the visitors, the servants, and the people of the town to sit at the four long tables on each side of the hall. Above, the galleries flooded with silk and the laughter of ladies. Perceval looked up and searched for those he knew—his aunt Lynet, Lyones wife of Sir Gaheris, Guimier wife of Sir Caradoc, and the Queen of Logres. A twinge of sorrow struck him for apparently no reason, and it took him a moment to realise that he hoped and half-expected to see his mother there. It was not her face that broke upon him through the rippling colour of the gallery, however; it was Nimue's, as subtle and secretive as ever, that looked down on him, and bowed in greeting, before turning away again.

Even the Elves had heard of the Grail. Even the Elves had come to see.

Then the food came in, and Perceval gulped as he inhaled the fragrance of boar, beef, venison, pheasant, and game of all kinds cooked in stews, in pies, or roasted. Someone passed him a flagon of wine, and he splashed out a cupful; since the first time he had tasted it, in the pavilion more than a year ago, he had gained the stomach for it. Bread came around next, soft fluffy brown rounds still warm from the oven to serve as plates and soak up gravy. There were apples and carrots, parsnips and onions, whole roasted mushrooms and long strips of crisp smoked bacon, nuts and barley, all mixed together beneath a huge boar stuffed and roasted and propped up on a platter. There was a pie full of mutton, sweetened with plums, nuts, and apples. There were ten enormous wheels of cheese, blue-mottled inside, whose smell failed to fight off the knights gathered to do them injury.

Perceval had no idea how he would even begin to taste everything. But his dilemma was put off. Just as the Bishop rose to say grace, a page ran into the hall waving his cap. "Sire! Sire!" he cried. "Here's a great marvel!"

After the discovery of the words on the Siege Perilous, Camelot was athirst for any news. A breathless silence fell on the hall. The page skidded to a stop, turning red.

"Will you not come out and see it?"

Then everyone moved, jumping up with a rattle of chairs and following the page outside, down the hill, to the river running around the foot of Camelot-town. In the water below the bridge floated a not-quite-square stone, like the keystone of an arch. A sword had been thrust point-first into the rock. Here it had floated, and here it waited as if to be drawn, bobbing on the current.

Perceval saw the King's hand go hesitantly to his own sword, Excalibur, then fall back again as Arthur remembered that the sword in the stone which had made him King so many years ago was long broken, and the one he wore now was the gift of the Lake.

The King leaned out over the parapet and read the second prophetic message of the day, chiselled into the stone.

"Never shall I be drawn, but by the best knight of the world."

By Perceval's side, Sir Caradoc murmured "What, bar none?"

The King looked up with a smile. "Well, Sir Lancelot. As it appears, someone has sent you another sword."

Lancelot shook his head. "It was not meant for me, sire." The King waited for more explanation, but Lancelot bowed his head and stood back.

"Sir Gawain?"

"I fear that only the right owner of this sword will lay hands upon it and escape harm," said Gawain. "Nevertheless, I will try." He stepped onto the bridge, leaned over, and knotted his hand around the hilt. Grunting, he drew it up an inch or two—but the stone clung to the blade. Gawain let go and the sword slid, bobbing, back into the water.

The King turned and surveyed the crowd. "Will you try, Sir Perceval?"

"I am sure that this sword was meant for the Grail Knight," Perceval said. "But I will try if you wish."

He stepped up beside his father and closed his hand around the hilt. In that moment he wondered, with a sudden thrill, if the sword would move in his hand. But the stone stuck with the sword, and although he put forth all his strength, the further he drew it up the heavier it became, until the pommel slipped through his fingers and the stone splashed back into the river.

"It will not come," he said, gasping air.

"Then let us wait for the coming of the Grail Knight," said the King, and they all went back to the feast.

Perceval was settling back into his seat, and the Bishop was just drawing breath, when there was a sound like trumpets, and the doors of the hall slammed open. Some of the knights started to their feet, hands going to swords and daggers. But Perceval grunted in surprise, and glanced up at Bors on the other side of the Siege Perilous. It was the old man they had both seen questing in the night: Naciens, the hermit of Carbonek. He came over the threshold, under the leaping arch of the tall door, leading by the hand a young man of Perceval's age all clad in red armour, but with an empty scabbard and no shield. In perfect silence the hermit led the young man to the seat by Perceval's, and drew off the white cloth. And now on the Siege Perilous appeared the words:

"This is the seat of Galahad the High Prince."

The young knight unclasped the white cloak from his shoulders and laid it over the back of the Siege Perilous as calmly as if it had been any ordinary chair. Then he sat down in it.

Not a breath stirred the silence. A knight of Gaul had sat in that chair once, and been consumed in flames. But nothing happened to the new knight, except that he glanced at Sir Perceval and gave a tight-lipped smile.

Perceval remembered how he had felt when first taking his own seat at the Table of Camelot and thought incredulously: He is shy of us all. He, the best knight of the world.

Then, in the hush, the Bishop of Ergyng saw his chance and took it. "*OREMUS! Benedic Domine nos, et haec tua dona, quae de tua largitate sumus sumpturi; per Christum Dominum nostrum, Amen.*"

That was the signal to begin eating, and the people of Camelot busied themselves with food. Perceval lunged for a pie as it went past and ladled some of it onto his trencher, thinking to give the Grail Knight a few more moments' grace before the attention of Camelot fixed on him again. He was surprised, then, when the boy said very quietly under the clatter:

"I am Galahad. Have you been a knight of the Table long?"

"A year, more or less," said Perceval, handing him the pie. Sir Galahad took it from him with pale scholar's hands, but Perceval saw dauntless goodwill behind the shyness in the young man's eyes and felt that here was a courage deeper than lay in his own power. "You are really the Grail Knight? Have you seen *it?* Is it near?"

Galahad shook his dark head. "No. I have come in quest of it, just like everyone else."

His smile, something in the set of the teeth and the cock of the head, reminded Perceval of someone he knew. "Were you the boy Sir Lancelot knighted this morning?"

The smile fled. Galahad looked down at his trencher. "Yes, that was I."

Perceval cried, "He's your father, surely?"

"Is it so easy to see?"

"Huzzah! I am Perceval, the son of Gawain who is more than a brother to Lancelot. And now let no one marvel at your being the Grail Knight. The best knight of the world could only come from one father."

At that Galahad looked so uncomfortable that Perceval tried to think of something else to say. "I never knew Sir Lancelot had a wife."

"He has none," said Galahad. "I am a bastard."

He said the word softly, but when he raised his eyes to Perceval they were level, candid, neither bitter nor defensive. Perceval said: "Oh." After that he could think of nothing to say at all. Only the food no longer smelled as good.

Sir Bors, on the other side of Galahad, claimed the young knight's attention. Perceval looked around the Table. Sir Gawain was neither talking nor eating; he only sat still with his arms folded, a look of deep joy in his face. The King opposite also seemed to be feasting his soul, not on the food but on a sight never before seen under the high windows of Camelot: one hundred knights, none greater in the world. Was he glad, as Gawain was glad? As Perceval watched, Arthur lifted a hand and passed it across his eyes.

Sir Lancelot, for once, both spoke and laughed as though it was the proudest day of his life. He boasted of his son and Gawain's, and said that today the keeping of Logres passed into hands mightier than his own. And cleaner, too, Perceval thought with a rush of something that was almost anger.

The Queen had come down from the gallery to speak to those eating at the long tables on each side of the Round Table, and stood with bowed head speaking to the young Bishop of Ergyng. Sir Ector, at the head of one of those tables, sat with chin sunk deeply in hand. Above, in the gallery, the Lady of the Lake had come forward and leaned upon the baluster. Her gaze burned into Galahad's shoulders next to him, not his own, but Perceval almost flinched back from that white-hot pressure.

When Nimue saw his motion she drew back, veiling her eyes, and turned back into the crowd. But her pale fingers had left dents in the oak baluster.

At last the whole company rose and went down to the water again. There stood Naciens on the bridge with bent head, looking at the marvellous sword. The crowd reached him but did not overwhelm him, standing back as if some instinct warned it of the ancient hermit's high authority.

Naciens looked up, up the hill. The crowd parted and waited. At last, walking slowly, Galahad came down from the castle between the King and Sir Lancelot. The Grail Knight reached out his hand and took hold of the sword-hilts. Immediately the stone sunk into the water, and Galahad lifted up his sword.

Naciens lifted his hand and said, "This is the sword of Sir Balyn, who struck the Dolorous Stroke. Now it is yours, Sir Galahad. Bear it to good fortune and God's glory."

Galahad went down on his knees, and Naciens blessed him. Then the little, bent old man untied his mule from the castle gate and went away. Perceval watched his brown and battered form shamble into the woods, resisting the urge to run after him and offer his protection. Naciens, of all men, did not need it.

Galahad rose to his feet and brushed futilely at the mud on his knees, only succeeding in working it further into the mail he wore. When he looked up, he met Perceval's eyes and laughed.

Perceval wondered: Where did one learn such humility, not even to resent such wrongs as Galahad had been born to?

The company went back up to the castle. Sir Lancelot called, "A joust!" and others took up the cry—"A joust! Put the new knight to the test!" Perceval lengthened his stride and reached the keep ahead of the main body of the crowd in time to find a pageboy to saddle his horse. Then he dashed up to his room, wrestled into his leather and mail, and came running out again, buckling his sword on over his surcoat as he went.

Most of the knights had gone to arm themselves as well. Only Galahad, who was already armed, stood in the empty Great Hall speaking to the King. Perceval went over to them and the King smiled at him, reached out, and gripped his shoulder.

Perceval said to the Grail Knight: "Will you break a spear with me this day?"

He did not expect Galahad to look down on him from Lancelot's immense height and say, gently, as if he knew it must disappoint, "Sir, I cannot."

"No? Well, there are others to fight," said Perceval, trying not to show how vexed he felt to be denied the honour.

"Not for any lack of love," Galahad added. "But for the regard in which I hold you, Perceval of Wales."

Courtesy, Perceval thought, almost in a panic. It would be easier to break a spear. He said, trying to mean it: "Your kindness is better than any fame." And then, with a rush of more sincere feeling, he added, "I ask your pardon for falling so silent at the Table today when you told me of your birth. It meant no disdain. I can imagine no harder thing befalling a man, than to be cast off by his father."

"I knew you thought no ill of me," said Galahad. "And of your kindness, think not much ill of him either. So far as the matter lies between him and me, we have killed and buried it."

And again, although he searched for it, Perceval saw no trace of bitterness in Galahad's eyes.

So when Perceval sat by the side of the meadow with the others whom the Grail Knight had refused to joust, Lancelot and Bors, he did so with no shadow of resentment for Galahad's sake. There was good sport, for Sir Galahad knocked Sir Lamorak, Sir Gareth, and Sir Tristan off their horses in quick succession. Perceval whistled as Gaheris went down like a ninepin, and glanced sidelong at Sir Bors. "He strikes like a thunderbolt. And I thought him scholarly!"

The older knight smiled. "I am no longer sorry to be passed over," he said.

Perceval laughed and remembered the tourney at Carlisle.

After Galahad unhorsed everyone he would agree to fight, however, it was Perceval's turn to take the field. After a year as a knight, his skill had grown to match the wit, strength, and audacity that had assisted him from the beginning. He went through Sir Tristan, Sir Lionel, Sir Lamorak, and Sir Aglovale almost as easily as Sir Galahad had; only Sir Tristan came close to unhorsing him. He was just leaning down from Rufus to help Gaheris off the ground and shake his hand when the people lining the town walls and the grassy bank above the lists began shouting and cheering in good earnest, and Perceval turned to see Sir Lancelot trotting up.

"May I beg a breaking of lances?" asked the king's champion.

Perceval agreed and drew back, his stomach suddenly full of Marchflies. As he laid his spear in rest, the sickening jolt of his fall at Carlisle came back to his mind. Perceval fought down the nausea and dug resolute spurs into Rufus. If he kept thinking of that, he would have to hang up his shield and take to farming, for his spear would never keep him again… Ahead, Lancelot thundered down on him, and then there was the familiar double shock, and with some resignation he went rolling through the green grass of summer.

Perceval staggered to his feet, vaguely aware of the crowd's yelling, and looked around for the victor. But Lancelot was not far away. He, his helm, and his saddle diversely littered the ground. His horse wandered, confused and shocked, on the other side of the lists. Perceval tore off his own helm and went to shake hands.

"Well struck. No, not again: another such fall might cripple me," Sir Lancelot gasped, and struck Perceval between the shoulder-blades with painful goodwill.

THAT EVENING THE HUNDRED KNIGHTS OF the Round Table gathered in the Great Hall with their guests, and with the last light of the day came the Grail. Late in the afternoon it had begun to rain, and the clouds gathered thick and angry over Camelot, but the wind changed at sunset. There was a great cracking and pealing of thunder, as though Camelot itself was broken and thrown down; then, through the western windows of the hall the sun flickered and gained strength and struck the floor in the midst of the Table's ring. And there floating in the sunlight was a vision of the Holy Grail, all covered over but burning with unbearable light.

In that marvellous light the knights stirred like sleepers waking. Perceval saw faces turned to him which seemed fairer than mortal flesh, as if remade in some new mould.

A subtle, mazing scent stole through the air, as if all the spices in the world were there. Suddenly—impossible to see how—the table was full of food and drink. And then the wind blew the clouds together, the sun sank, and the vision was gone as quickly and heartbreakingly as it had come.

In the sudden dark, the King drew long breath. "Now," he said shakily, "let our Lord Jesu be thanked for what we have seen this day!"

The meal was almost done when Sir Gawain rose from his seat.

"Brothers," he said, "we have eaten of the Grail's bounty, but it was veiled from us, and not explained. Wherefore I vow that I shall labour in quest of the Holy Grail for a year and a day, or more if necessary, and never shall I drink in any other name than in the Name of that cup until I have seen it more openly. And if I may not prosper, then I will return as one that may not set himself against the will of our Lord Jesu Christ."

Perceval stood. "And I make the same vow."

He was followed by a great number of the knights of the Table. But the King buried his face in his hands.

"Alas!" he said. "For all the years we have longed for this day, my heart misgives me at last. Fair nephew, you have well-nigh slain me with this oath. For you have dispersed the fairest fellowship in the world, and where might I find others to take your place?"

PERCEVAL SET OFF THE NEXT MORNING after matins, taking only Rufus, his arms, a bottle of water and a packet of hardtack, and a blanket rolled up behind his saddle. He rode as far as the bridge with Sir Gawain, Sir Lancelot, and Sir Galahad, and halted with them by a meadow still pockmarked with the hoof-prints of the day before. It was a grey, drizzling morning and few of the people had ventured out of doors to wave them goodbye.

"Well," said Perceval.

"I am going north," said Sir Galahad. The early morning light on his pale face suggested that he had not slept, but a mood of piercing keenness burned in him.

"I will go straight into Wales," said Perceval. "That is where I found Carbonek in the autumn."

"I mean to wander as the wind blows," said Sir Lancelot with a smile, and held up a finger to test the air.

But Sir Gawain put up his hand to shade his eyes and squinted. "Is that Sir Mordred, going west?"

"Is he going after the Grail?" Perceval asked, with a friendly impulse.

"Most are," said Gawain.

Galahad shook hands with Perceval. "Farewell, fair brother. We will meet again. Goodbye, Sir Gawain. Goodbye, Father."

He turned his horse and went trotting up the river. As the road bent, he turned and waved before he went on. And so went the Grail Knight from Camelot.

Lancelot grinned after him, slapped Gawain on the back, and with a shout sent his horse plunging towards the forest.

Sir Gawain rubbed his shoulder. "He'll be my death someday. I expect you to avenge me, when it happens, Perceval."

Perceval laughed. "I shall slay him in kind, with thumps on the back." He paused. "You knew, didn't you? That Lancelot had a son?"

"It was no secret. We had forgotten it, out of courtesy."

"But I thought there was a penalty for adultery. Burning."

"The penalty is only so harsh in the case of certain high ladies, as we read in the laws of the ancient commonwealth. In any case, it is within the King's discretion to show mercy. Lancelot was judged penitent."

"And so it was forgotten." Perceval frowned. "So easily."

"He has lived a blameless life since."

Perceval remembered what he had seen in the moonlit garden. "And if I knew that he had not? If I knew that he—or anyone—was to blame for something *now*? Should that be forgotten, too?"

Gawain glanced at him. "What! Do you mean that you know any ill of Lancelot?"

"No. No, sir."

"If you think ill of any man, keep your tongue in your head. If you know ill of any man, speak boldly. Pursue the enemies of Logres, wherever you find them, and leave good men in peace. This is no more than you have always done."

"That's true. Well, farewell, Father."

Gawain looked at him under grave and shaggy eyebrows. "Come back safely. Find the Grail and your lady, or not, but come back."

"And you, fair father."

He turned, as Galahad had done, when he stood on the threshold of the forest. But Gawain was already out of sight. Perceval turned back to the road and ambled on, Rufus's feet squelching on the soft wet road, the chill breeze blowing against his right cheek. He wondered how long it would take to find Carbonek.

20

Who will help me? who will love me?
Heaven sets forth no light above me:
Ancient memories reprove me,
Long-forgotten feelings move me,
I am full of heaviness.

Rossetti

No summer warmth found Carbonek. That spring some of the weeds clinging to the rocky soil of the Waste put out stunted flowers, but although the bitter teeth of winter lost their edge, the year passed without sunshine or birdsong into a foggy, watery summer. And Blanchefleur, shivering in her closet one midsummer night, thought that the weather reflected her mood.

She was glad of all the work that fell on her shoulders in Carbonek. Gone were the days of leisure and tatting. When Naciens was not out on one or another of his errands, she read with him in languages, philosophy and the sciences. But it was her apprenticeship to Dame Glynis, the castle's housekeeper, that drained every dreg of her strength. After a long day shadowing the old lady from laundry to infirmary, fumbling with distaff and spindle in the solar, candle-making in the kitchen or poultice-brewing in the infirmary, she should have been glad each evening to take the long trudging journey up to her closet in the Grail Chapel.

But instead, when she had pulled the covers up to her nose and tucked her feet into the hem of her smock, there was all night to think and worry. Months of work and study had already passed since her meeting with Morgan in Sarras. But after dark, all this faded away, and the past crowded closer than the present.

Once again she closed her eyes and relived those hectic moments inside Morgan's memory, the sudden, queasy shock almost like fainting that took her from waking in Sarras to waking in Carbonek with a stomach clenched in horror.

She had thought Logres a dreamworld. She had been wrong. For the first time in her life she was really awake. No longer were all her senses drowned in sleep. Now delight spun like a dance, worry gripped like a fist, fear cut like a knife. Could she stand and not fall on this trembling earth? Could she drink this wine and not stagger?

And Arthur the King, as lightning, fell from heaven... "It is a lie," she whispered to the empty dark of her closet, just as she had that first night. But the aching cold knotted tighter and heavier in her gut. What if Arthur—that giant looming behind all the history and legend of Britain— what if he really was, as Morgan claimed, guilty of such gruesome things?

"It is impossible," she said aloud, remembering the gracious lord she had met in Sarras. Then a voice in her ear murmured, "But such a man would know how to dissemble." Implacably, her doubt built a gallows on which to hang him: Perhaps she was not really his daughter. Did the King of Logres think not? Had he sent Morgan to kill her, to dispose of an imposter without sparking war? Was he capable of calling her "dear-heart" while measuring the time till his assassin arrived?

She rolled from one aching side to the other, trying to smooth out the knot between her shoulder-blades. She was awake and the wind between the worlds had carried her, like *Comus*'s Lady, into the blind mazes of a tangled wood. And yet she had known. She had *known* that Providence was a lion in ambush.

Only she had never imagined a thing like this.

It was, oddly enough, the memory of Perceval that shook the suspicions out of her. No one in his right mind would send Perceval, however young and unproved, to guard anyone intended to die. And she laughed at the thought.

"It is a lie," she said to herself, each night alone with the glimmer of starlight and Grail-light shining like Hope through her closet window. But that did not keep what she had seen from gnawing on her mind. There must be a grain of truth at the bottom of this bitter cup. What was it, the one truth on which Morgan had built her lie?

Tonight she rubbed her goosefleshed arms and considered telling Nerys what had happened in Sarras. But these days Nerys was seen only in passing; some business of her own kept her from both the quiet industry of the solar and the chatter and bustle of the Great Hall at meal-times.

And if she found her? If she asked a moment of Nerys's time, and found a corner in which to breathe new life into Morgan's lies, or dare to name such crimes as murder, incest, goetia?

She shuddered again. Ah, they were lies, and not to be dignified with credence.

Inside, Blanchefleur relived the past in Sarras. Outside, seasons wheeled away and the landscape changed as the castle faded from one place to another.

Wherever it went Carbonek took desolation with it, from gorsy moor to silent fen, from splintered pine-forest to blackened and blasted garden. And yet despite the drear surroundings and the endless shortage of food and fuel, the castle-dwellers themselves yielded to no melancholy. It was difficult to pine away in the company of Dame Glynis or Branwen.

One midsummer evening, gathered with some others around the chess-board in the hall, Blanchefleur was listening to the squire Heilyn debate a theory of polity with one of the younger knights when Nerys came and laid a hand on her arm and said, "Come with me."

Blanchefleur followed reluctantly. "What's the matter, Nerys?" she asked when they had left the others out of earshot.

Nerys turned to her. In the months since they had come to Carbonek, the fay's agelessness had grown more evident, as if the veil that shroud-ed her was burning away under some influence stronger than herself. Blanchefleur shied away from looking into her eyes, which had become windows into vast cosmic spaces, never as unearthly as now. Her words were fewer these days but heavier, and today they fell like crushing weights from an immense height:

"There is a lady dying who wishes to see you."

Blanchefleur tried to think who Nerys could mean. In Carbonek, no one ever seemed to fall ill.

"Her name is Elaine," Nerys added. And Blanchefleur remembered King Pelles's daughter, who had been the Grail Maiden before herself, whom she had never seen.

"Oh," she said softly. "Of course I'll come."

Nerys led up the stair toward the big, warm rooms on the south side of the castle. "I have attended her often in her illness," she said, and Blanchefleur wondered if that explained the fay's intensified *other*ness. "She is no longer herself, and her humour is bitter. But she wishes for you."

Nerys paused outside the door of a room not far down the corridor from the solar. Her tone was oddly pleading. "Be kind to her, Blanche."

"Of course."

Elaine of Carbonek's chamber was as shabbily furnished as any other room in Carbonek, but clearly every available comfort had been provided. There was a fire in the hearth burning to fend off the cold even now in midsummer. Dim tapestries lined the walls, and somewhere, rugs had been found to cover the floor. Chests marched against the wall, a heavy curtain shrouded the window, and the canopied bed was covered with a new blanket.

One of the other women of the castle, the wife of one of the knights, rose from the bedside with a murmured word, bent gracefully, like a streamer in the wind, and left them. Nerys beckoned Blanchefleur to the bed.

Elaine of Carbonek was forty, maybe, with a sharp pale face nearly as white as her pillow. Against that deathly pallor, the shadows of her purple-rimmed eyes and her grey-streaked dark hair sprang into violent contrast. Blanchefleur, seeing how desperately ill the woman was, did not see the dislike in her eyes until Elaine said, in a soft husky voice like an accusation:

"You are Guinevere's daughter. You have her face."

"Yes," Blanchefleur said. "Did you know her?"

"No." Something too hard and sharp to be a smile crossed her lips. "But I know her face. Come closer and let me see you."

With an inarticulate fear Blanchefleur looked at Nerys standing like a tombstone by the end of the bed. Nerys lowered her head. Blanchefleur moved closer to Elaine, leaning forward a little, and forced herself to look into those frankly, coldly searching eyes.

"I cannot tell," Elaine said at last, with a frown. "Perhaps there is a little of him in the jaw."

Blanchefleur shot another helpless glance at Nerys and said, "A little of whom?"

Nerys opened her mouth to say something, but Elaine saw it and forestalled her: "The Knight of the Lake. They say he's your sire."

The tone, and the look that crossed her face—a curious mixture of gloating and despair—stung Blanchefleur into familiar words: "It's a lie!"

Elaine smiled. "Is it? Lancelot betrayed the King of Carbonek. Why should he hesitate to betray the King of Logres?"

Blanchefleur's first impulse, as in Sarras, was to turn on her heel and leave, but then she remembered that Nerys had asked her to be kind. Also Elaine was not Morgan; she had been the Grail Maiden, too, once.

So she swallowed the jagged lump of anger in her throat and said: "Pardon my hasty words. Please, I have no wish to rake the past."

Elaine frowned. "And yet you are all too ready to speak in ignorance."

"I beg your pardon."

"Then listen to me." Elaine went to struggle to her elbow, but sank back gasping. Nerys moved forward to prop the dying woman up a little higher. Elaine looked at Nerys as the fay lifted her in strong arms and laid her back on the pillows; the hostility faded out of her eyes. "Nerys," she murmured. "You will outlive us both. What do you want with years? If I could only take some of yours!"

"If I could only give them," Nerys said.

She retreated to her former station and Elaine, turning her head, looked at Blanchefleur. She lifted a finger to point. "I bore the Grail Knight to Sir Lancelot. And I did it wearing *that* face."

Blanchefleur recoiled. "How?" she asked, before she could stop herself or think better of it. But Elaine had already gone on, as if she had not even heard the question.

"I was happy until he came, wandering through the Waste to Carbonek," she said. "Once I saw him, my peace of mind was gone. But he, poor fool, he loved the Queen of Logres. It was wrong of him, and he knew it. Then it was said that from us would come the Grail Knight, the deliverer we had all so long awaited. He was rightfully mine: mine, not hers…

"I knew he meant to leave us, and my heart was already breaking. So I went to the Castle of Case, and the witch of Case gave me aid…I said I knew your face, maiden. I saw it in the mirrors of Case, when Brisen had clothed me in the form of Guinevere. How I hated that ashen hair and those pale-blue eyes! I could cheerfully have taken my nails to them. But I knew my revenge would be far more subtle a thing."

Blanchefleur turned away. "I have heard enough," she said. But Elaine's voice murmured on.

"Did she hear of it, far off in Camelot? Did she hear how it dawned upon him what he had done—when everything was over, and he saw my true face? Or how the realisation drove him mad, and he fled under the knowledge of the manifold betrayal of every trust he had borne? Faithless to God, to King, to lady, to host, to me! And I was glad, because he would not love me.

"I could never find my own way back to Carbonek. But how else would the Grail Knight have come into the world? My son was born, and grew stout and strong, like his father, who found his mad way back to us in Case. We drew him back to health, but he could never stomach the sight of me. He went away as soon as he could sit a horse. When my son was a little older I gave him to a monastery for his raising, and Naciens brought me here."

"You were penitent, then," Blanchefleur said, struggling not to show her loathing. But Elaine's mouth tightened with resentment: in the flickering candlelight, Blanchefleur saw for the first time that there were deep stubborn lines scored from nose to mouth.

"Never! I was like the Lady Eve, cast out of my home for a sin Fate demanded of me."

Blanchefleur rose to her feet. "How can you say such a thing?" she said, fighting to keep her voice down. "There would have been another way. There is always another way." She remembered something Perceval had said once, a long time ago. "A thing that cannot be done without dishonour is not worth doing. If we are citizens of Heaven—"

She started as Nerys's warning hand fell on her shoulder. In the tight-stretched silence Elaine smiled bitterly.

"You are a proper Grail Maiden, damsel. I hope you may never see the underside of life, for it may strip you of your comforts. At least I have seen the daughter of Lancelot before I died. Take her away, Nerys; she tires me."

They left, Blanchefleur choking back her rage with clenched teeth, Nerys apparently without expression or emotion. The fay closed the door after them and stood in the shadowed passage for a moment with her head bent. At last, when no sound came from the room they had left, she lifted her head and murmured: "Alas! I may never die, but I am better prepared for it than she. Oh, if I *could* take her place…"

All the indignation went out of Blanchefleur in a rush. "Oh, Nerys! You are so good, and I am so…very…angry."

Nerys sighed. A breath of cold air drifted down the passage and she lifted her hand to guard the candle she carried. "If I had known what she meant to say, I would have spared you."

"But it's true, what she told me. About the Grail Knight."

"Yes."

"Could she be right then?" Blanchefleur grasped Nerys by the elbows, relieved to speak freely on this, at least. "About Lancelot? If a false Guinevere—then why not the true Guinevere?"

"I—"

"You think so too!" choked Blanchefleur, and remembered her worst nightmares about Arthur.

Nerys spoke coolly. "Look at me." Her ageless eyes, like abyssal depths, dizzied Blanchefleur. "I think, if it came to that, it would depend upon the true Guinevere." She smiled. "Take the candle. I must go back to Elaine."

Blanchefleur began climbing to the Grail Chapel, but halfway up the stair the heart went out of her, and she sank down onto the steps. Perceval had once called her the true heir of Logres. What if she wasn't? Until now, despite all the doubts that weighed her down, she had been able to brush the thought away like a nightmare upon waking. Now she wondered. What would the King do if he knew? What would Perceval do? Would they feel deceived?

A tear slid down her cheek, and then another. She was crying. She was crying for Logres, because she wanted to belong here and she was afraid she did not.

She felt a numb wonder. When had this happened? When had *Logres* become her home?

And why, in the midst of all its intrigue and scandal, did she look to Logres for all her hopes and desires?

She was still sitting on the stair when she heard steps coming up from below, light tripping feet that suggested Branwen. As they came nearer, Blanchefleur rose silently to her feet and continued to climb.

"Oh! Blanchefleur! There you are!" Branwen's breathless voice broke upon her. "Where have you been? King Pelles is asking for you."

Blanchefleur adjusted her face and turned around. "Really? I was just going to my closet."

"I think he only wants to speak to you quickly."

"Of course. I'll come."

When Branwen led Blanchefleur into the crippled King's chamber, they found him lying on his couch by the fire whittling a juniper fish-hook. Some of his knights were sitting nearby, and the hum of conversation fled at their entrance. Apparently undaunted by their attention, Branwen called, "Here she is, sire."

King Pelles blinked up at her. "Ah, damsel. They tell me that you have spoken to the lady Elaine."

Blanchefleur twisted her fingers together behind her back and wondered if she was in trouble. "Sire, yes, I have."

"She was ever a headstrong girl," he said apologetically. "I pray you will not allow any of her wild words to disturb you."

"No, sire," said Blanchefleur, in surprise. "She is very ill." The moment she said the words, she realised that they might be taken in two ways. She rushed on: "If anything, sire, I fear I was the one to give offence."

"I am sure you cannot have done anything of the kind. She always was most…er, ha." His reedy voice wandered into silence and he changed the subject. "Have you every comfort you desire, Lady Blanchefleur?"

Gaslight. Hot water. *Tea.* Blanchefleur said: "Everything I need, thank you, sire."

"We look forward to a better time," said the King. "The Grail, after all, should never have been ours alone. Nor even Logres's alone. With the Grail Knight will come new hope for all of us."

Blanchefleur remembered the odd circumstances of the Grail Knight's birth, and said, "What if the Quest fails?"

He blinked at her. "What?"

She flung out a despairing hand. "What if none of the knights find Carbonek?" Another possibility struck her. "Or what if something happens to the Grail?"

King Pelles's jaw sagged. "I have perfect faith in your capacity," he said at last, somewhat uncertainly. "As I have in the Grail Knight."

"I'm sure we'll both do our best," said Blanchefleur, and the endless winter grey seemed to sink into her bones.

It was three weeks later that Nerys told her Elaine of Carbonek was dead.

21

We have seen the City of Mansoul, even as it rocked, relieved.
Chesterton

Autumn came to Carbonek with the gracious rigor of a monastic rule, alternating stern, still, frosty nights with the benison of balmy days. Glimpses of the sun, rare throughout summer, now melted away some of the castle's ingrained chill. On one of those lucid days a foraging-party returned with sacks of apples and pears gleaned from a deserted orchard behind a ruined farmhouse, and Naciens, in addition to the usual bag of conies, brought a parcel of nuts slung over his mule when he reappeared from his latest wandering. These additions to the castle's stunted fare seemed delicacies even to Blanchefleur's fastidious taste, and lent festivity to every meal.

On a sunny afternoon in the solar, Blanchefleur sat by the window spinning. Her fingers were more deft now than they had been when she first came to Carbonek, and although she fumbled with the spindle now and again, it was no longer a living thing struggling to get away but a tool with a rhythm that could be mastered. Blanchefleur plucked a little more wool from the distaff and marvelled at the difference that a short year had made in her.

"Do you ever think of going back to Gloucestershire?" she asked Nerys, who was sewing on the other side of the room, the only other soul sharing the warm quiet.

Nerys shook her head. "I sometimes think of going back to the Isle of Apples, Nimue's country."

"Your home?" She had never thought of Nerys having her own country to return to.

The fay's pale fingers stilled with an exhalation of breath. She sat quiescent and statue-like for a deathly moment, then breathed in again, and the needle went dipping back toward the cloth.

"Home is a place I may never see. But in Avalon, for a little while, one might forget, and in a night's slumber wear out an age of the world."

"How is it found? Is it far?"

"Further than the land's end; nearer than Hy-Brasil."

Blanchefleur paused to wind thread onto the spindle, and her mind returned to Gloucestershire. "I sometimes think of going back, just for the fun of it," she said. "To see what they would all say if they could see me now—Kitty, and Emmeline, and the rest." She did not have the courage to mention Mr Corbin, although he was perhaps foremost in her mind. No doubt he would be sickened by her acceptance of Logres ways and Logres fashions. But then, it had been months now since Mr Corbin's opinions had mattered. And she loved the Logres fashions. She shifted her shoulders, delighting in the free slide of her skin against loose linen and wool.

"Do you miss them?" Nerys asked gently, keeping her eyes on her work, not pressing for any answer.

Blanchefleur wrinkled her brows together. "I miss Perceval," she said at last, surprising herself. "We had such good talks. The others…none of them would understand about Logres. Except Emmeline, maybe."

Nerys had no chance to reply, for the door opened very slowly and Branwen came in, brows puckered, juggling three apples. "Look!" she squeaked, and then one fell to the floor with a thud and rolled into a corner.

"I'll have that one," she offered, diving after it, and brushing the dust off against a cat that lay snoozing on a chest near the window. The animal gave Branwen a scowl and began to wash itself. Branwen handed Nerys and Blanche an apple each and bit into her own with a *scrunch* of relish.

"Thanks," Blanchefleur said, laying down her distaff, and—as one of them did every so often—went to the window to peer out. The solar overlooked the castle gate and whatever landscape a visitor would ride across to reach it. Today it showed low hills covered in scrubby gorse and heather. Not a sign of movement betrayed life, and Blanchefleur turned back to the solar with a sigh.

Branwen did not need to ask what she was looking for, or whether she had seen it. Instead she gave a bright smile and said, "After so long, it almost frightens me to think that the Grail Knight will come soon. Even King Pelles can hardly remember what Carbonek was like, all those years ago, before Sir Balyn and the Dolorous Stroke."

She hauled the cat into her lap and plopped down cross-legged on one of the chests. Blanchefleur started across the room to her, swinging her arms, for spinning tired them without frequent rests. But she never made it to Branwen. A sudden dark mist arose before her eyes and she sat down with a bump on the bare stone floor, gasping air. From a long way away, Nerys said, "Blanchefleur? Are you ill?"

She tried to answer, but her tongue would not fit around the words. Darkness blotted away every sense.

The world would never be warm again, or glad. Someone was crying little stifled sobs a long way away, and had been doing it since the beginning—a grief as old as the world, that not even the passing of yet unfathomable aeons could wipe away.

The dawn was still young, and dark human shapes loomed up like ancient ruins in the morning mist. All of them moved together, ranks of men each one in his mail with his sword by his side. Beyond them Blanchefleur sensed a great press of people, on whom silence hung like an interdict. The only sound that bled through the slow tread of many feet was the weeping that would never end.

She was covered with nothing more than a white smock. She shivered. Two tall shapes, neither of them armed, marched at each elbow, and one of them swung the cloak from his back and settled it around her shoulders. She looked up into a narrow kind face etched with heartbreaking pity.

She spoke, seemingly without effort of will, and in a voice that was strange to her own ears: "Sir, Christ bless you for standing a friend to me today."

He pressed his lips together as if too stricken to speak, turned his head away, and paced on by her side. Blanchefleur wondered if this was a funeral procession, and who was being mourned. Her feet, numb with cold, dragged a little. Only the jolt of pain as she stubbed her toe through thin shoes proved there was life in them.

They turned off the hard road, now, and went through the wet cold grass of a meadow. Ahead, three torches spat pale yellow flame into the morning air. Only then did Blanchefleur see it: the stake, piled around with wood.

The armed escort divided and stood to each side, becoming granite statues but for the white puff of breath from helm and visor. But she and her two guides walked on, and with a slow cold creep of horror Blanchefleur understood what was happening. And still her feet did not falter, and her mouth would not open to cry out, until they stood at the very foot of the stake, and the man at her side lifted the cloak from her shoulders.

The horsemen hit them like a hurricane. They swept up from behind on steeds with muffled hooves and were among the escort with swinging swords almost before they had been seen. The man with the cloak went still as ice when he heard the commotion; he looked up and stared at the newcomers with a bittersweet welcome in his eyes. Then, like an iron-shod wind, a horseman rushed down on them. There was a flash of steel, and her friend crumpled beneath it.

Suddenly she was able to scream, staggering back, lifting hands to mouth. The horseman wheeled his steed. Its flailing hooves hung in the air over her head for a breathless moment and then the rider leaned down from the saddle. His steel arm went around her waist, flinging her to the saddlebow. The great sword scattered red as it swung again. Gasping and retching, she looked down and saw only blood on the ground. Then all sound faded away and for the second time, black veils muffled her sight.

PAIN AND DARK DISSOLVED. THE COLD that had clung to Blanchefleur's bones for months melted into warmth. She opened her eyes on the dull-gold sky of Sarras and rolled dizzily to her elbow, half-expecting to see signs of the battle she had just left. But there was no fog here in Sarras, no dawn gloom, no blood—only the soaring cathedral walls, and the grassy floor, sweet and pure.

She fell back to the ground, pressing a hand to her heart, and muttered, "What *was* it?"

The living silence of Sarras did not reply. Blanchefleur closed her eyes on the bright glory around her, but behind her eyelids an image of blood and ruin lingered. She shuddered and opened them again. Was the night-mare something of Morgan's making? But no: Morgan was not yet here and the vision had come between Carbonek and Sarras. What had brought her to Sarras so swiftly and silently last December had chosen this time to drop her, for a moment's detour, into some other time and place. But for what purpose? Was it a warning of some kind?

She thought of the fire, of the blood, of the awful screams of pain and anger that she had heard, and shuddered again. Was it a warning? Would she one day live what she had just dreamed?

She would wait and remember. In the meantime Sarras claimed her attention, and if she had guessed rightly, there would be work to do.

She rose to her feet and went to the cathedral doorway. Once again the sight of Sarras struck her with staggering sweetness. The dizzying mountain, seamed with silver where the river twined through its streets and gardens, rushed into the sky like a fountain of stone, flinging out tree and flower and flying buttress like flecks of spray. Despite the silence, the ancientry, and the sheer indelible weight of her stone, Sarras seemed a living thing, not merely vigorous but impetuous.

She turned reluctantly and re-entered the church. Up in the steeple, the three Signs had neither been disturbed nor tended. She blew some dust off the platter, and looked at the bloodstained bowl of the Grail with pursed lips, wondering if it should be covered. But no such cover had been provided.

One thing *had* been provided. A trap-door had been fitted to the stairway opening, a gate of wrought iron so wisely crafted in the shape of lilies and leafy vines that she could imagine it to have grown from the earth. A lock and a key lay beside it on the grassy ground. Blanchefleur took them up for a closer look. Both were made of a metal that looked like silver but was both paler and heavier, etched with lilies to match the gate.

It was as she lifted them from the floor, however, that a puzzling thing caught her attention. In the diffuse golden light of Sarras, both the lock and the key cast a faint shadow on the floor. But her own hand did not. Nor did her hair, gown, pouch, or anything else that had come with her from Carbonek.

"Curious," Blanchefleur thought, and the thing slipped from her mind. She went a few steps down the stair, closed and locked the gate, and after a moment's thought slid her hand between the bars to lay the key on the floor above, where it could be reached but not seen. Then she went down the stair to the terrace before the cathedral.

Here, murmuring across the grass, flowed the stream which watered the whole country. Blanchefleur bent down to drink from it. The taste was fresh, of course, but that seemed a bare and niggardly word: this was a freshness beside which all the water of the world forever after would taste stale and salt. At the first drop on her tongue she knew she would never drink again without remembering and grieving for Sarras, and so the sharp joy of that wonderful water came twinned from the first with sorrow.

When she straightened with dripping mouth, she saw Morgan on the other side of the stream on the edge of the terrace, outlined against the sky and distant countryside, which for a moment gave her the appearance of a giantess. At the sight of her aunt's smile—thin and red, like blood running down the groove in a sword—hair prickled on the back of Blanchefleur's neck.

Morgan said: "Well! I am here." She folded her hands into her wide sleeves. "My master was displeased when I returned without your blood."

Blanchefleur recoiled a step. "What did you tell him?"

"The truth."

"What?"

"That I had driven a bargain with you, and lost."

"And?"

"As I said. He was displeased." Morgan's eyes narrowed. "I begin to think I must cease to protect you from him."

"No!" Blanchefleur blurted the word out with something like panic. Morgan burst into laughter.

"Oh, your face! Exquisite! Never fear, you may yet live to see his fall. But what have you done about him?"

"Done about him!" Blanchefleur gestured despairingly. "What *could* I do? Even if I had the courage, I would never know where to begin."

There were orange-trees on the terrace, heavy with fruit. Morgan strolled to one of them, picked an orange, and dug her thumbnail into the flesh. "What is there to perplex you?" she asked. "Two words whispered in the right ears, and you should only have to sit back and watch the poi— watch the physic work. No one need ever know you had a hand in it."

"If it's so easy, why could you not do it?"

Morgan shook her head. "He would know at once whom to suspect. Besides, I have tried it once or twice already. No one believes *me*. Now, if the Grail Maiden said it—!"

"But I am so frightened of him, and I am trapped in Carbonek," Blanchefleur said, tears starting to her eyes. "What could I say to harm him there? Would God I were as safe from him!"

Morgan looked at her incredulously. "You are too frightened to do this simple thing?"

"You are, too! What chance do I have? I am only a simple girl, and I have no skill in deception."

Morgan spat an orange pip onto the grass and said, "If you can be so little use to me, I might as well kill you now." And she drew a long, glittering knife like a stiletto from the jewelled sheath hanging at her belt.

Blanchefleur felt she had forgotten how to breathe. "Good aunt," she whispered at last in a choking voice.

Morgan laughed. "Where is your Welsh pig-boy now?" She darted forward and caught Blanchefleur by the neck of her gown, lifting the knife to strike. Blanchefleur's knees gave way; she sank to the ground and cried, "Aunt, please—"

"You refused to help me."

"I'll do whatever you ask!"

"I cannot use a chicken-heart like you."

"Anything!"

The word broke painfully, violently out of her throat and hung on the air, echoing from the cathedral walls. Morgan checked, and a glint of craftiness struck from the depths of her eyes.

"Anything?"

Blanchefleur gritted her teeth shut and nodded.

With swift decision, Morgan dropped into a crouch by her side. "Then listen," she hissed. "We may not have much time. There is a way for me to destroy this master whom I hate, who sent me to kill you. His downfall is assured, his death is certain. You need do nothing, only give me what I need to accomplish it."

Blanchefleur looked at her in fascination. She felt horribly aware of that gleaming knife, so motionless when it had threatened her life, but now forgotten, clutched in a white-nerved hand that shook like a leaf.

"Yes," she breathed. "Anything."

"You want him gone as much as I do."

"As God is my witness—"

Morgan clapped a hand over Blanchefleur's mouth. "*Lilith!* Will you utter that name *here? Now?*"

They crouched in silence under the golden sky. Morgan shook even harder, staring up, waiting. Not a breath moved in the air. At last she relaxed her strained vigilance and went on. "All will be well, once I have it. You may change your mind, if you like, and try to fight me. No one will say you did less than your duty. And remember that you are afraid of me," she added, laying the knife's blade against Blanchefleur's cheek.

Blanchefleur felt the steel trembling and breathed: "Yes."

Morgan's voice dropped to the thread of a whisper. "You know the Thing I mean."

"Yes." Blanchefleur shuddered in her own time, a counterpoint against Morgan.

"Then come."

They rose and went into the cathedral. Morgan gripped Blanchefleur by the arm, with the knife dangling from her other hand, but it seemed to Blanchefleur that she clung close more out of fear than an intention to do her injury. They reached the stair to the steeple in safety. Here, Morgan seemed to regain some of her nerve, and they went up the stair almost at a run.

They stopped at the trap-door. Morgan yanked at the lock and said, "The key! Quickly, now!"

"I have it," said Blanchefleur, and her hand went to the little pouch that hung from her belt. Then she stopped.

"Oh, Morgan, and I am its keeper!"

"Yes, but hurry!"

"Tell me what you mean to do with it."

"Not now!" Morgan's whisper was almost a scream.

"Only tell me, and you shall have it!"

Morgan lifted her hands to her head in despair. "Listen, then! It is possible, with the right learning, to use the hair, or bone, or blood of a man to make another man—a, a *simulacrum*, a double."

"Blood." Blanchefleur felt her stomach turn over. "The blood in the Grail? *That* blood? A double?"

"Yes!" Morgan returned, and the smile that passed across her face struck ice into Blanchefleur's veins. "But—*not heavenly*. Something so powerful that even my master could not resist it. And now I have the art of bringing a child to manhood within days. I cannot fail in this."

Morgan's words faded into the dusk of the stairwell. "The key," she said, remembering.

Blanchefleur, who had been stooping close to Morgan, flung herself to her full height and laughed. The sound rolled up and down the tower and rang, to her tight-wound nerves, like thunder. But like thunder, it cleared the air.

Morgan remembered her knife, and lofted it. "Hush, hush," she cried, but some premonition of defeat clouded her eyes.

Blanchefleur did not flinch. "Why, I don't believe you have a master at all."

"Give me the key!"

"Search me if you like. You won't find it," Blanchefleur said, holding out her hands with a smile. "Dear aunt, I have tricked you abominably, I fear."

In the dim air of the steeple, amid a black halo of rioting hair, the whites of Morgan's eyes shone ghastly-pale.

"It was foolish of me not to guess the truth at once," Blanchefleur went on. "I only come to Sarras when I am brought, and I am only brought when the Grail is in danger. You never intended to kill me; you must have wanted the Grail. Had you come here for some other reason, you could have strolled through these garden-palaces until Doomsday without laying eye upon the Grail Maiden. No! In the end I saw it all. I only wanted to know *why* you needed the Grail."

"Give me the key," Morgan said again, but her voice was scratched and chipped like an ancient blade.

"Now that I know your plans?" she cried. "Dear aunt, be reasonable. You profess to have a master you hate already—yet you mean to create some sort of infernal prince, ten times worse?"

"I am desperate," said Morgan, and she had gone beyond rage into calm.

"You are a liar," said Blanchefleur contemptuously.

Morgan did not speak. Only, with viperish speed, she lifted her knife and drove it into Blanchefleur's heart.

O they rade on, and farther on,
The steed gaed swifter than the wind;
Until they reach'd a desert wide,
And living land was left behind.
Thomas the Rhymer

Sir Perceval hunched down under his spaulders and stared into the desolate valley through a drifting mist of rain. Summer and autumn had passed. Winter, although sometimes he had almost despaired of it, now seemed about to do the same. And in those months he had travelled up Wales and down again, and having crossed the Severn Sea near Caerleon now passed through Dumnonia in a mood of despondent stubbornness. At first, all those months ago, that wet summer morning when he had left Camelot, he had felt sure of finding the Grail within a month or two. Now Carbonek seemed so far away that he had ceased to be able to imagine arriving there at all. And yet time slipped by, and soon the year and a day set for the Quest would be over.

Perceval suppressed the quiver of urgency that crept into his mind at this, and thought: All the better. With fewer than four months left, if he was to find Carbonek at all, it must be soon.

Rufus, head down, plodded down the slope into the shrouded valley. Perceval shifted back in the saddle, shook water out of his right gauntlet, and hunched again into thought. It was more than a year since he had last seen the Heir of Logres. More than a year since his promise in Carbonek before the Grail's coming, to serve her a year and a day—

How stupid his behaviour had been on that night of miracles! To turn his back on the Grail and run! Could that foolishness have anything to do with his difficulty in finding Carbonek now? God knew he had repented

189

of it often enough.

—There was no way of knowing, and Perceval turned his thoughts back to Blanchefleur. The term of service had expired in the autumn, and when he next saw her he would return her silver moonstone ring, which even now he wore on a thin leather thong around his neck. But no matter, he would continue to serve her as long as he had it. And he could not help grinning as he remembered all the ruffians and brigands whom he had vanquished and, by way of penalty, sent to kiss the hands of the lady Blanchefleur and undergo the reparation she commanded of them. That was common enough; there was always a steady stream of knights coming to Camelot to kneel before one lady or another and declare that her champion had sent him to greet and wait on her. But the men he fought would not find Blanchefleur at Camelot. They must go on quest, in search of the Grail, and the benefit to their souls and to the peace of Logres, Perceval thought, must be tremendous.

He came back to the present to sniff the air. Some faint stench rose out of the valley to greet him. Perceval loosened his sword in the scabbard, gripped his lance, and went on more watchfully. Then he began to see them: bones, stripped bare and gnawed by gigantic teeth. Down here the fog lay thicker, threaded through the rocks and concentrated above the scummed stream at the valley's nadir.

Perceval drew his sword. The stink grew: sulphur and rotting flesh and putrid eggs. Then there was a grey glint of scales through the mist, and Perceval came to a bend in the valley and saw the dragon. The massive coils of its body filled the gorge; its wings rose beyond sight into the sky, like iron towers.

Its fire was dead. The ravens were already at work on its eyes and tongue. They also clustered on the body of the knight that lay by its gaping maw, but their beaks rapped against mail and plate in vain.

Perceval shot his sword back into the scabbard and dismounted. From the festering smell, the knight must have been dead for weeks. Surcoat and plume had been scorched away; only the steel harness was left. His shield was split and blackened, but Perceval could trace the outline of the passant lion and crosslets of a man he knew.

"Sir Lamorak."

The words hung heavily, like the foetid fog, on the air. Perceval went to the dragon and found Sir Lamorak's sword thrust through the roof of the monster's mouth, into its brain.

He dared not stay long in the valley, but lifting up the body bore it to higher ground and found a place to raise a cairn. When the stone mound was tall enough, he planted the knight's sword at the top and hung the shield on its hilts. He paused and prayed awhile and then, throat dry and head aching, rode on looking for a place to rest.

Sir Lamorak at least would never find the Grail, he thought. Had he failed the Quest? Or had he found a better reward?

The rain drifted to a stop and the last light of day shone out beneath the clouds. Perceval rode down into the next valley, a place of gentle grassy slopes, budding apple-trees, and ruined stonework glimpsed through the undergrowth. He wondered who had lived there, before the dragon came.

Then he heard the clink of harness ahead, and looked up to see a horse and rider coming down the green path to meet him. The knight, too far away in the gloom to be seen clearly, reined in and settled his helm on his head. Perceval closed his hand on his lance, and for a moment the two knights sat facing each other.

"Will you joust?" asked the knight. Perceval did not recognise his shield: snowy argent, bearing a cross in blood-red gules.

"Gladly," Perceval said, and they backed their horses and laid their spears in rest.

It never occurred to him that he might lose. A year ago he had matched Sir Lancelot, and now in the full tide of his strength, he thought he could stand against any knight of the world. As he laid his lance in rest and spurred Rufus into a gallop—the war-horse, weary with constant travel, nevertheless scented battle and charged eagerly—Perceval moved with practised precision, with the accustomed confidence of a strong arm and a true point.

Yet the buffet he received plucked him from the saddle and flung him to the ground with a wrenching force he had not thought possible. He lay stunned and sick, with hot blood running from his nose, while the stranger's hoofbeats dwindled into distance.

Perceval clawed himself off the ground, surprised to discover that he was still whole. He staggered to his feet and called Rufus. Night was upon them now, and there was no chance of following the stranger knight to demand another match. So Perceval limped to the ruined manor, drank from its well and found a sheltered corner in which to spend the night.

The morning dawned bright and balmy, fresh with the scent of coming spring. Perceval woke, breathed it in, and felt suddenly young again, as young as he had felt two years ago when he left his mother's house. He rolled to his knees, throwing off the cloak he used as a blanket, caught his breath and laughed a little at the bruises that ached when he moved, and found a strip of dried meat in his saddlebag to chew on.

Where had the stranger knight gone? Perceval buckled saddle, bridle, and bags onto Rufus and went back to the path. The knight's hoofprints were clearly visible here, and he followed the trail all day, finally losing it in the tumbled stones by a river. That was a disappointment; but he thought the last of the trail pointed upstream, and he went up the riverside looking for a place to cross.

That night he came to a little cave in the side of the river-valley, where a spark of light suggested some inhabitant. He found there an anchoress who offered him a meal and a place to rest for the night. The food was better than anything he had eaten for days and the old lady was good company. At length he told her everything that had happened on the Quest, how long he had wandered without finding anything, and how he had finished by being unhorsed by a stranger. Then he saw that she was laughing, and his tale died away.

"Oh, my poor boy," she said, "that was Sir Galahad. Did he have no shield of his own at the Feast of Pentecost? Yet now he rides with the shield of Joseph of Arimathea. He crossed the river at noon."

"Oh," said Perceval.

"Do not seek your chance to even the score," said the old lady. "It was your injured pride that sent you after him to me. But your Quest is not to seek your own glory."

"Then I will follow him still," said Perceval, feeling himself flush red, "and ask for his fellowship upon this Quest."

The anchoress said: "Follow as you will, for we must all follow some-one. But take care, for temptations and evil enchantments await you, Sir Perceval. Only be humble, and pure of heart, and who shall say? You may yet come to the Grail Castle and find your heart's desire."

Perceval sighed and nodded, and choked his impatience down again. But in the early foggy morning as he departed, he felt the first glimmer-ings of a hope that had been missing the other day as he sweated above the dragon's valley building a cairn for Sir Lamorak. It had maddened him to miss not only the Grail, but also the dragon. Yet he did not really wish to lie in Sir Lamorak's place beneath the stone cairn, and the knowledge that there was a man in the world who could best him was oddly cheering. There was a just order of things into which he could fit; there were men above him, and men below. He was not alone, and if he was not the first to find the Grail, then perhaps by almighty grace he would be fifth, or tenth, or last—and it did not matter which.

So cheered and uplifted, Perceval rode on in a haze of contemplation through which ran like a scarlet thread the hope of his lady and the Grail. But then he rounded a bend in the road and almost walked his horse into the midst of a troupe of footmen who had formed a solid barrier across the road, and sat eating and drinking there as if they owned it.

"Oi! Sir knight!" shouted one. "What's your name and errand?"

Perceval, in his surprise, did not answer. The man wore a sign he recognised, the badge of the argent dragon. But how could these be Sir Breunis's men?

The mass of men before him moved like restless sea-water, hands clenched on bills and bows, bowls set aside, chinking spoils dropped back into bags and pouches. Perceval, suddenly alive to his danger, reined Rufus back a pace or two.

"Whom do you serve?" he challenged them.

"Saunce-Pité!" yelled one man. But their captain raised his hand.

"We ask the questions here," he said. "What's your name and errand?"

Perceval stripped sword from sheath. "If you do not know my bearings," he told them, "then all you need know of me and my errand is that I serve the High King Arthur, and where I find his enemies unlawfully in his land, there do I slay them."

He was answered with a shout and an onrush, and spurred Rufus upon them, striking left and right, each stroke biting home and biting deep. They pressed close against him, but fell like mown grass beneath his scything blade—and despite the bloody swath he carved, he fought smiling. There were little farms and villages that would dream on, undisturbed, beneath the winter moon because he struck true today. Thinking this, he had laid six men in the dust already when they slew his horse beneath him.

He felt Rufus shudder as the cold steel went in. The noble beast, his since the quest of the Queen's cup, went down with a scream. But the churl who had stabbed him fell also, head split by lashing hooves.

Perceval flung himself away from the wreck—fell, saw the rabble come running, and surged to his feet, gripping his sword. He had no time to lament the horse. In a moment he was surrounded, with nothing but his armour to protect his back, and he knew it was like to go hard with him now that he had lost his mount. But the son of Gawain was young, and strong, with the blood of mighty Orkney in his veins, tempered by the subtle and strange blood of Avalon. Taller than his father's brothers, more terrible in battle was he, and though now a score of men came against him and pressed him on every side, still he fought, until the blood ran down his sword and splashed his arm to the elbow.

For all that, he was wounded and flagging when help came like iron-hooved thunder. A knight, all in white and red, sliced through the mob, scattering them right and left; then cut back again, his sword hissing in the teeth of the wind, until those he left alive broke and ran for the trees. Perceval saw his rescuer's shield as the knight checked and turned and wheeled back to chase the survivors, and he knew it was Sir Galahad. Perceval followed at a stumbling run, calling Galahad's name, but the Knight of the Red Cross vanished into the forest driving the rabble before him, and Perceval felt the ground heave and buck beneath him. He fell dizzily to his knees.

For a few minutes he rested there, gasping through clouds of pain, until his head cleared a little and he could climb back to his feet and cast up accounts. The sums came out discouragingly. He had his life, but little more.

He salvaged food and water from Rufus's saddlebags, rested a while, bound up his wounds, and then walked away. Later, there would be wild beasts, wolves or lions, among the dead, and in the aftermath of battle, he was too feeble to fend them off.

At first, Perceval hoped to find a castle where he could beg a night's lodging for charity's sake, and perhaps bargain for a horse. But this was a deserted place, and the path soon gave out among stones and scrub. Night came dark and cloudy, howling with wind. Perceval wrapped himself in his cloak, wedged himself into the roots of a great oak, and swallowed cold food and water.

He intended to watch. The pain of his wounds, the cold and the rain, and the fear of wild things, whether beasts or men, should have kept him waking.

But suddenly, a crack of thunder made him start, and he opened his eyes on blackest night. A moment later there was a flash of lightning and he saw quite close to him a lady of towering height, muffled in dark robes, with eyes that glinted in the fitful moonlight. She led a black horse, richly furnished. The blaze of lightning stamped its image across his mind. Sir Perceval had seen horses worth a king's ransom, great war-horses of the dying Roman breed, eager for battle, swifter than wind. But he knew that he had never seen one to match this horse.

"Sir Perceval," the lady said to him, her voice lashing through the storm, "why do you lie here?"

He rose stiffly to his feet, trembling with cold as the wind caught him. "Be well, damsel. If I am in your way, I am sorry, but my horse is dead and I cannot travel fast."

"You are wounded," she said.

He lifted a palm in a gesture of resignation. "That also."

"Then I take pity on you," said the lady. "Only promise to do what I shall ask of you, and I will give you this horse. He will carry you to the ends of the earth."

"Damsel, if it is a thing I may do with honour, you have only to ask and it is yours."

Her voice in the darkness was oddly mocking. "Only care for him, and return him to me in my home."

He would have given far more for the chance to sit such a beast, if only for an hour. "Gladly. Where is that?"

"He knows," she said, rubbing the proud black arch of the neck. "He will bring you to me. There! He is yours."

"My thanks," Perceval said, and took the reins from her. She remained with a hand on its nose as he mounted with difficulty—it was a tall beast, and his wounds caught him as he moved. The horse stood still as graven stone until the lady took her hand from its head, and Perceval touched his spurs lightly to its sides. With a deafening scream, it reared into the air, so that Perceval loosed his feet in the stirrups to jump. But it came back to the earth safely, shied at a shadow, neighed again, and leaped forward.

Perceval had never thought such speed possible. He crouched low on the horse's back to avoid being swept off, moulding his hands to its withers and rising in the stirrups a little to disconnect from its rippling back. The countryside blurred away.

Perceval remembered the reins and pulled them, gently at first, to slow or turn aside. But the horse fought his hand with an iron mouth, neighed and gathered speed—how was it possible?—running smooth and straight as an arrow. Then suddenly they left the trees behind and flew across a stony waste, yet faster and faster; the wind plastered Peceval's hair to his skull and shrieked in his ears, and he had to turn his head to open his eyes; and then he saw all things fall away behind him, and only the moon above kept pace.

The minutes went by as they rushed on, and became hours, and Perceval, exulting at first in that marvellous, sure-footed speed, perceived that the horse would never tire but went on unceasingly; it was certain this was not a horse of flesh and blood. And now he had travelled further in a handful of hours than in all the last week.

And Perceval began to fear, for if the beast would not tire, and if he could neither check it nor turn it aside, then beast or fiend he was at its mercy. So he put up his hand to shelter his eyes from the blast, and looked ahead. There was a river before them, deep and dark, running with a mighty current that churned and spun. The horse never paused or slowed, but gathered itself to leap into the torrent. Perceval yelled, kicked his feet out of the stirrups, and made the sign of the cross. With a horrible scream the horse checked and reared and Perceval had a heart's beat of safety. He took it, flinging himself from the saddle and crashing down among the stones at the water's edge. Then the horse plunged on, and Perceval lifted up his dazed head to see it borne away by the current; and was it only a trick of his bleared eyes, or did the water burn behind as it went?

"Surely the horse and the lady were both fiends, and would have carried me to Hell," Perceval said to the cold night air, and trembled to think how close he had come to death. The rest of the night he spent wakeful by the water's edge, sometimes praying, sometimes fixing his eyes on the imperceptibly lightening East. Yet in the aftermath of terror he felt more encouraged than ever. Surely, to be attacked in such a manner proved that he must be coming closer to the object of his Quest.

Morning came at last, and just as the sun's rim touched and gilded the barren horizon, Perceval saw the lion.

Its hide was dusky in the half-light as it came prowling down to the water's edge to drink. Perceval held his breath, watching its measured movements and the ripple of the cold dawn wind in its mane. Only when the lion suddenly raised its dripping muzzle did he see the intruder. It was a snake, coming down from the rocks, a gigantic beast; he doubted he could fit both arms around it. Despite its size, it moved soundlessly but for the rasp of its skin over the ground, and its beady eyes fixed on the lion.

The lion saw it, moved in and crouched down, growling in its throat and lashing its tail. The snake in answer reared up a diamond-shaped head, swaying warily from side to side. Then the lion sprang, all yawning red mouth and reaching claws. But quick as thinking, the snake threw a coil of its body around the lion, and they rolled together among the stones. The lion snarled and clawed, trying to get its teeth in its enemy's neck; the snake moved easily, throwing another coil around the tawny body. Paws bound, the lion followed the serpent's swaying head, snapping uselessly and growling with pain and anger. Perceval knew it would die quickly without help.

His whole body protested as he scrambled stiffly to his feet and made a fumbled cut at the snake's tail. That got its attention. It flicked around to face him, hissing and spitting venom that smoked on his shield. All Perceval's weariness fell from him, and he rushed forward with a good will. One furious blow, and the serpent fell to the ground lashing wildly, half beheaded; another, and the head left the body altogether.

The fire of battle left Perceval bent and exhausted, with pain sluicing through his body. He collapsed onto a nearby stone. The lion clawed its way out of the writhing coils and came to Perceval to rub against his hand, breathing out a deep and bone-shaking rumble that he thought might be a purr. Perceval slid off his gauntlet and buried his hand in its mane.

"We are the same, you and I," he told it. "For by the grace of God we are both saved from the serpent's belly."

The lion rumbled a little more and then bounded away on heavy paws. It returned in another moment with a stone-grey rabbit dangling from its mouth, laid the animal at Perceval's feet and a few minutes later, brought another. Perceval built a fire, cleaned the rabbits, and within an hour was eating the best meal of his life. The creatures were thin and wiry, but Perceval could not imagine anything tasting better. He gulped down the hot meat, licked his fingers, and left the fire to burn out among the stones. Then, slowly, with the lion following at his heels, he set off downstream. He had no idea where he was or how far he had come, but that, too, was a hopeful sign. Perhaps, here in the waste, at the end of all his means, he would find the Grail Castle.

She show'd me a cup o' the good red gowd,
Well set wi' jewels sae fair to see;
Says, "Gin ye will be my lemman sae true,
This gudely gift I will you gie."

Alison Gross

ir Perceval trudged through utterly deserted lands filled with the silence of stone and gorse. He turned his face to the sun and spoke to the lion to keep his thoughts off the pain of his wounds, which were not serious but galled him as he walked.

Its ear twitched companionably as he told it of the Grail, which he sought, of Sir Galahad and his father and the rest of the Table, all out looking for it, and of how soon he hoped the Quest would be achieved. Of Blanchefleur, whom he hoped to meet at Carbonek carrying the Grail. And of all the things he hoped might come from that meeting.

There were dreams. One night, he thought he stood on the cold riverside where he had killed the great serpent, but the creature was alive now, and an old woman, dressed with great splendour in scarlet, sat upon it. The lion was there too, and with her hand buried in its mane stood a young damsel, who came to him and said, "Sir Perceval, my lord greets you. And my lord sends word that you make yourself ready, for you shall fight the strongest champion of the world. And if you are conquered, you shall come to no harm, but be shamed for ever until the world's end."

"Damsel, who is your lord?"

"The greatest lord of all the world," the damsel said, and left him suddenly.

Now the lady that rode on the snake spoke: "Sir Perceval, you have done great wrong to an unoffending lady."

"Madam," he said, "surely not."

"Surely you have," she returned. "I had in this place for a long time a serpent which served me, and you have slain him. The lion was not yours to defend; tell me why you slew my servant?"

"Only that I thought this lion the gentler beast," said Perceval. "But how shall I make amends?"

"There is a way," the old woman said. "I have lost one servant. Now you will be my man."

"I may not grant it," Perceval said.

"No, truly!" said the old lady. "For you cannot, since you serve the Lord, Jesu Christ. Be sure that in whatever place I find you off your guard, sir, I shall take you, for you were once my man."

Perceval woke that morning with an eager sense of impending threat. But the day passed uneventfully, as did the day after. Days became weeks. Spring grew stronger, warmer, and his wounds mended. And yet the land changed, the desolation grew less, and there was still no sign of Carbonek.

One day the lion brought him one last meal, rubbed against his hand, then turned and went back the long way they had come. Perceval sat down on a stone to skin the rabbit it had brought him, and watched it go. Suddenly, he could almost taste the loneliness. Even animals were better company than the trees. After his last hot meal, he climbed to his feet and went on.

He wandered in a wood now, full of spring green and flowers. After a few days the countryside became more hilly, and when he climbed the tallest peak he saw a great expanse of blue sea not far away to the West. But he journeyed mostly in the valleys, feet pounding a dull rhythm. He thought of Sir Galahad, galloping around on a good horse knocking people off right and left. Had the Grail Knight already achieved the Quest months ago, and gone home with Sir Gawain and Sir Lancelot and the rest of them, while he, Perceval, wandered on blindly in forsaken hills?

Perceval stopped and sat down. His stomach growled. There was one last rubbery piece of hardtack left, but he felt as if a single bite would choke him. Well, and was he not good enough? Had he not toiled and travailed like the rest of them for the last ten months, and on foot? Was it all some maddening joke? Sir Perceval of Wales, lost in the wild and wandering in circles while the Sir Borses and even the Sir Kays of the world tore past in glad hordes crying, "I have seen the Grail!"

The mood no sooner came creeping in than he pushed it back, and just to prove his resolve, crammed down some of the remaining hardtack and went on. He would find Carbonek, however late, regardless of the distance. But despond came in like the tide, and the weariness of holding back those waves ground him down at last. After two days fasting on water and a few of the edible herbs he found by the way, he reached the sea and sat on the sand watching the waves breaking endlessly on the shore, and the water stretching out to the hazy horizon. And nothing to see but trees, and water, and shore between them as far as the eye could reach. No Carbonek. No food, no shelter, no company. He must climb back to the top of the low sandy bluffs he had slithered down, and he must do it soon, for the water was creeping in and there was nothing for him on the shore.

He toiled back to higher land, hampered by his armour and sweating under the bright morning sun. At the top he straightened wearily, tried to brush off some of the sand, and went north along the cliffs.

He did not look at the sea again. The delight that had once struck him at every glimpse of that limitless silver road had vanished, and the water seemed almost to mock him. He shifted the empty saddlebag and water bottle he wore on his back, keeping his eyes on the hills. Here in the forest, if he found an ash-tree and sat down with his knife, he could make darts and hunt food as he had in the years before he left his mother's home. But some impulse drove him on, hoping against hope to find some dwellings, some company, something kinder than unseasoned meat and the naked sky.

When he heard it, he knew what it was that he had craved all these lonely weeks. A human voice.

He turned and looked and saw a damsel coming through the trees toward him, all in black with a white veil that blew sideways in the wind and showed a face of perfect beauty beneath hair as yellow as butter. "Sir knight," she said again, as she came nearer, "be you that Sir Perceval who rides in quest of the Holy Grail?"

Of all the things Perceval had hoped or expected to see in this place, such a lady was the last. He became aware that he stood gaping like a fool, and bowed. "I am, damsel."

"Then," she said eagerly, "know that I am a poor disinherited lady wandering alone, cast out by my enemies. And of your quest I know little, save that Sir Galahad passed this way only yesterday, and asked me if I had seen Sir Perceval, greatest of the knights of God. He is resting at a hermitage not far from here, and tomorrow I will take you to him. But come now and rest; you have travelled far with little comfort."

She spoke quickly, almost breathlessly, and now paused, holding out her hand with a welcoming smile. Almost in a daze, Perceval took her hand and allowed her to lead him through the trees to where, in a green glade by the clifftop that looked out onto the sea, a pavilion had been pitched and richly furnished. A little table with a chair stood in the sun outside. Here she seated him and brought food: fine white bread, fowl, wine, and plums.

"Eat only a little," she told him, "for you have fasted long." The food, sweeter than any he had eaten for weeks, woke his great hunger and he ate it all. Meanwhile the lady sat down to embroider at a frame and chat, pleasantly, of small things. Perceval felt that he had slipped into an altogether fantastic world, sitting as he did surrounded by gentle midday sun, the lady's murmured conversation, and the domestic chatter of birds. Where there had been desolation and emptiness a bare moment ago was nothing now but comfort and ease.

Hunger had kept his eyes open the night before. Now, with his appetite blunted and the warm sun pouring upon him, he yawned.

At this the Disinherited Damsel started up and insisted that he rest. She took him into the pavilion and fussed over him like a dove, worrying that the little couch might be too hard or too small for his lanky frame. Perceval, drowsy and contented, submitted quietly to her ministrations. The pavilion was even warmer within than the sunny glade, and the light, filtered through red and yellow silk, made the place glow like the inside of a jewel. He tried to remember what it put him in mind of, but the lady talked on, saying that she would help him disarm, and that if there was anything, anything she could do for him, he had only to ask "—for," she said, helping him draw off his mail shirt, "I know that you have helped many poor unfortunate ladies like myself, and if I can show my thanks in any way, I must."

"Thank you," Perceval said, for he was a mannerly man.

She dug into a chest and drew out a furred, embroidered robe to wrap him in. She gathered up his armour and weapons into her arms, and told him she would clean them while he slept. Perceval lifted a hand to object as the pavilion's silken door whispered shut behind her, but then he dropped it and laughed a little. Danger was banished to the hard hills, and in this exquisite light and warmth was no lurking terror.

Perceval sank onto the couch. How long had it been since his body tasted such comfort? For months, every night, he had slept on the cold ground in his mail. Now, lapped in samite and furs, he could almost believe himself far away, in Camelot…It was hours before he woke.

He started up, not recalling his surroundings, all his senses jangling. The heat was oppressive, the red walls felt suffocating, and he leaped to his feet and tore the robe from his body before he remembered the damsel, and the fear bled out of him. He sank to the couch again and sat bathed in rosy light, savouring the rest that still clung to his aching bones.

He pulled on his shirt and leather jerkin, and went outside. The first thing he saw was a table of food the Disinherited Lady had prepared. The second thing was the sun, low down in the West near the world's rim. It shone gloriously, red and gold; the pavilion's shadow ran black against the yellow-lit grass and splashed up against the forest's edge. By the table, the Damsel said, "I have cleaned your armour of mud and rust; it lies over there," and she pointed to where his arms were heaped by a tree. "Now come and eat."

"Lady," Perceval said, "it is not for you to serve me thus."

"Ah," she said, throwing up her hands, "I am nameless and landless here; who shall say what is for me anymore? But you have travelled and travailed, and in any place you would make a name for yourself as honourable as the name you have in Logres. It is a small thing I ask, to render you some of the service you have rendered to others."

"Then if it pleases you, I yield," said Perceval, and went to sit at the table with her. There was wine, meat, bread, and fruit of all kinds, and the lady to sit by him and talk. She drew his story from him—the tale of hardship in the wilds, the villainy of Saunce-Pité, the black horse that would have borne him to perdition, and the thing he sought, which remained so far beyond his reach. Pity swam in her eyes.

"I have spoken enough," Perceval said at last. "Tell me your own tale."

"Let us sit in the pavilion," she said, and beckoned him to follow her. She seated him cross-legged on cushions inside the door, with the curtains looped back so that they could see out—could see the sunset and the blazing sea, and hear the waves murmuring against the cliff below. The damsel poured out heady muscat wine for both of them and sank onto the rug beside him.

"There is so little to tell," she said with a bittersweet smile. "I was the richest lady in the world; I wore fine scarlet, not sombre black; in the East was my city and all the kings of the earth brought me their trade and begged for my love."

Perceval leaned closer. It was hard to hear her and her head was cast down. "What happened?"

"One lord I refused," she whispered. The scent of her hair was making him dizzy. "So he took his revenge on my lands and my wealth, but I escaped. He could not take his revenge upon *me*."

"Tell me his name," Perceval said. "He will be a mighty man indeed to overcome—"

With a quick soft intake of breath, she laid a finger against his lips. "Have a care, Perceval, and speak honestly, or not at all. I have wandered long, but now at last I come to Logres. Perhaps, among the brethren of the Table, I might indeed find a knight to win back my kingdom."

He caught her hand and pulled it down gently from his lips, although after a moment he could not remember why. Her fingers laced into his, and she lifted drowning eyes to him.

His voice rasped across the silence. "You will surely find one to help you."

She raised her other hand to his cheek and then gently, hesitantly, she kissed him. Only the lightest touch. Sir Perceval went still as stone; his head was heavy and drowsy and now his heart seemed to have stopped. She kissed him again, more deeply, and his blood began beating again. Her hair tangled between his fingers.

"Lady," he whispered, "you are passing fair."

"Sir Perceval…There is no other knight in the world I would rather have to serve me."

"I…"

"Say you will," she murmured in his ear. "I know you can help me, Perceval. And if you do, if you'll swear to serve me, I and mine will be yours forever, as long as the world lasts."

There was nothing in the world left but her hair twisted into his hand and the red lips that pleaded for his help. "I will," he said in a dry mouth. She lifted the cup in her hand, with the wild sweet muscat inside. "Drink in my name," she whispered.

Perceval said, "I pledge—" and then the words faded on his lips.

For through the pavilion door the last rays of the sun as it sank shone upon his armour, lying beneath the tree, and upon his sword, leaning against the trunk. And it caught the sun's light and reflected it like a blazing cross, lancing his eyes with pain. Then in an instant Sir Perceval remembered the Holy Grail, and the Lady Blanchefleur, and the Lord he served, and was stuck with a thousand different thoughts at once. For how could he drink of any other cup, in any other name, when he had vowed he would not, but seek the Grail? And how could he love any other lady than the one to whom he had sworn service, Blanchefleur? The damsel beside him turned and flung her arms around his neck as he shrank away from her, but then with a keening wail a cold wind rose out of the sea and blasted the last cobwebs from his mind. He wrenched away from the damsel and stumbled outside, onto his knees, and crossed himself. The lady screamed. Suddenly, Perceval was cold and sweating.

"Fair sweet father Jesu, let me not be ashamed!"

The Disinherited Damsel screamed again, her face twisting into a mask of hate. "Traitor!" she howled, and came at him with clawed hands. But the winds veered and clashed overhead. The trees threw up their hands and bent their heads; and then the wind turned and blew the pavilion, the damsel, and all out over the sea, the lady screaming and cursing him and the pavilion twisting like a wreath of smoke. And the water of the sea burned after her.

At that moment the sun sank below the world's rim and suddenly the evening was grey and cold. Perceval lifted his hands to his head. What had he done? What had he done? What had he been *about* to do?

All those days he had toiled in the wilderness, prayed, hoped, swallowed every bitter twinge of impatience and disappointment, fought himself into trusting patience. And now he had thrown it all away. What could cleanse his guilt? He thought of his horror when he had thought evil of Sir Lancelot and the Queen, and his stomach turned in self-disgust. "I am not fit for my calling," he thought, and ran to his swordbelt, and drew his poniard with some wild idea of paying in blood.

But the gleam of its point sobered him. It was another's wounds that must clean him. And he was not his own, but was bought by another. Even now, was it his treachery to lady and Lord that he deplored, or the injury to his own honour? He slammed the blade back into its sheath while shame, like a serpent, twisted in his gut.

Where would he go now? What would he do? "Oh, *miserere*," he breathed, and lost all other words.

Night fell and dragged, and Perceval sat slumped on the grass, staring at the sea. At last, when he thought the sun had perished, a gleam of light shot into the air. Perceval armed himself with stiff fingers and stood on the cliff, watching colour steal into the grey sea. Then the sun rushed up, rose and gold, and in that clear light he saw the white sail of a ship in the south. It skimmed over the waves on a breath of warm wind that smelled of spring flowers. Perceval watched it dully, then stiffened as the sail furled and the ship came to rest, like a white bird, on the water below him. He spied a man moving on the boards of the ship. There was an arm lifted in greeting, and a shout from below, and with numb and at first uncomprehending surprise, Perceval recognised the shield of Sir Bors.

"BORS!" PERCEVAL WINDMILLED, FELL, SLID, AND staggered up again at the foot of the cliff while stones rained around him. "Bors! *Bors!*" Sand sucked at his feet, and then he was in the water. A wave slapped his chest, forcing grit into his eyes, but through tears and seawater he saw the white planks of the ship and Sir Bors leaning over the rail, reaching out a hand. He thrashed through the waves, caught his brother-knight's hand at last, and rose over the side, dripping and weeping, to land on the deck.

Bors seized him in a bear-hug, slapping his back and shouting. When he let go, Perceval collapsed to his knees. Worry checked Bors's welcome. "Perceval! What is it? What's amiss?"

"Nothing!" He hoped the water running off his head would disguise how recklessly he was weeping and laughing. "Not a thing! Oh, God, fair Father! Nothing's amiss!"

Then wind whipped into his face and Perceval, dragging the back of his hand across his eyes, saw for the first time that the ship's sails and anchor had run up while he greeted Bors, and now the rudder moved without human hands, steering them out to sea.

"The ship," he said, and let the words hang while he gulped down his tears. It was a morning of marvels. There was no need to ask questions. Nor to rise from his knees. They wanted to be on the deck right now; there they were happily humbled.

Sir Bors's teeth flashed in his brown beard with a deep and contagious joy. "Sir, I perceive this ship is as great a mystery to you as it is to me. But when I first came on board, I found the hermit Naciens here. And by his counsel, we await but one other."

Perceval dragged in one cautious breath, and then another, before venturing to ask. "The Grail Knight?"

"The Grail Knight."

But yet, I say,
If imputation and strong circumstances,
Which lead directly to the door of truth,
Will give you satisfaction, you may have't.
Shakespeare

Blanchefleur feared the nights. Sometimes she fended off drowsiness and knelt, hour by slow hour, in the chapel. But even here in Carbonek her body had not gone beyond the need of sleep. It came sooner or later, and she wandered through the land of dreams besieged by the spectres of her own imagination.

Morgan plunging a knife into her breast. The searing pain, the sudden hot gush and shudder of a heart losing pressure. Dizziness as life drained away. Jangling nerves telling her to panic, to fight or run even as her knees folded beneath her. That day she had wakened gasping in the infirmary, her physical body uninjured by Morgan's shadowy steel but with a heart that still believed it was dying. Dame Glynis was there, and forced bitter potions between her teeth to slow the staggering heart. But in the dreams there were no potions, blood sobbed from the gash in her chest, and terror woke her to a cold sweat.

Yet the worst dreams came when Morgan did not stab her. Instead, by one stratagem or another, she broke into the tower of the Grail and snatched that wonderful cup, and Logres became a desert of corpses.

Sometimes she dreamed of Perceval, and sometimes these dreams were like the memory of fire in wintertime. They were children running through a summer countryside, climbing trees and eating apples. Sometimes, though, fear threaded through these dreams as well. She was back in that cold vision of the stake, and looked up from the saddlebow to see her rescuer's face: it was Perceval's, grey in the dawn and freckled with blood. Or she saw him as he wandered endlessly in a naked land, stalked by lions and serpents. He was buried under a cairn above a valley of bones by a dragon's lair, his homeless spirit wandering among the stones. Or he found a new love, a lady willing to return his ardour: in a jewel-coloured pavilion by the sea he sank into her embraces, and forgot Logres, the Grail, Blanchefleur.

She woke after this last dream and gave a groan of disgust. Here was the Grail, in danger from a cunning and deadly foe from whom she had escaped only by heavenly grace and the quick wisdom of Dame Glynis—nor had the danger passed; it was six months now since the last attack, with the muted spring struggling to bloom in the Waste, but she knew in her bones that Morgan would try again, and soon, before the Quest was achieved—and yet, as if all this was not enough, her thoughts must go wandering after Perceval.

Perceval, whom she had treated, she realised, with barely-disguised scorn. In the cold and the dark she was suddenly hot all over, remembering the words she had used more than a year ago on the terrace outside a lighted ballroom, when he had teased that she was his sweetheart:

"We are not on an intellectual level *at all*."

She pressed her hands to her blazing cheeks, seeing it all unfold before her—the ignorance she had discovered in herself every day of her life in Carbonek, unfolding in kitchen-garden, infirmary, solar, even in Naciens' study. Then she remembered the evenings she had spent with Perceval in Gloucestershire, companionable hours of reading aloud while he whittled knotwork and interrupted with questions and observations. She remembered his quick understanding, his heedful memory, and how often he had had to pause and explain his comments in simpler words when her mean store of Welsh or Latin left her struggling to grasp his meaning. Another wordless frustration seethed from her throat. "Not on the same level!" she muttered to the darkness. "Indeed!"

Careless jibes she had made at his expense and at the expense of Logres came back to haunt her now. They had felt like teasing fun at the time, but after more than a year in his world, they echoed ignorant and condescending in her memory. And yet he had met each one of her barbs with courtesy.

She could not blame him, she thought, if he found a lady to value him more highly. Even if he had as good as promised that he would earn and claim her regard. She closed her eyes, she saw him kissing that yellow-haired woman, and she realised what it was that had stamped that image as it were on the inside of her eyelids.

Jealousy.

She hissed air like a sluice of cold water through her teeth. How was it possible? That after all this time, he should still haunt her dreams? That within the space of the same breath, she should drown in such despairing self-contempt and then in such furious anger?

She was not good enough to stitch his surcoat or sand his mail. Inconstant wretch that he was.

And Lancelot. And Arthur. Was there no honest man in the world? Was every house founded on sand?

"I shall go mad in here," she said, and dragged her cloak around her shoulders and went out, into the Grail-light.

Day came dark and cold, and that afternoon, as soon as she could flee solar and infirmary, Blanchefleur took the key Naciens had given her and went up to the hermit's tower-study. Book-lined, crowded with all the paraphernalia of arithmetic, geometry, astronomy, and music, this was the lair she longed for today. She half-expected to see Naciens there, but the room was empty. Blanchefleur reached for the *Republic*, the book she was meant to be studying. But even Plato could not dull her worry for long.

Socrates said:

"To the rulers of the state, then, if to any, it belongs of right to use falsehood, to deceive either enemies or their own citizens, for the good of the state."

Blanchefleur thought of the High King. Did he hide the truth for the good of Logres? Had he lied to her, that day in the gardens of Sarras, exercising some divine prerogative? She slammed the book down. Perhaps, if she herself was not caught in such a tissue of lies, truths, and half-truths, she would be friendlier to the philosopher's words. As it was—she reached blindly for words to embody her thoughts, and said, "*Veritas liberabit vos...*"

Hurrying footsteps from below broke into her train of thought. She went to the door and opened it as Heilyn, panting, reached the top of the stair. Something had stamped elation into every line of the squire's face, but for once he had no breath to speak. He gasped at her a moment, then bent double and wheezed.

"Heilyn! What's happened?"

"It's—," he gasped, and then went back to huffing.

"The Grail Knight," she cried.

"No—"

Blanchefleur threw up irritable hands. "You asked Branwen, and she said yes."

"*What?*" He gulped another breath and straightened, shocked back into his usual gravity. "No, no, not that. We have guests. Knights."

"Their devices! A pentacle, gold on gules?"

Heilyn wrinkled a brow. "I believe I saw such a device, yes."

"Perceval." Blanchefleur forgot everything else and bolted for the stair.

Heilyn called, "Lady," before she was two steps down. Blanchefleur wheeled. "The books," he said apologetically. "You know he likes us to leave the study as we find it."

"Oh, please, won't you do it? This once?"

"I don't know where—"

"I'll show you." Blanchefleur dashed back up the steps and into the little tower room, thrust the *Republic* into his hands, cried "There!" pointing to the correct shelf, and rushed back to the landing. "And snuff the candles for me!" A twinge of conscience trailed her dizzy flight down the stair. Heilyn *never* left the astrolabe or the compasses or anything else he used the fraction of an inch out of place.

Evening dusk hid under the rafters of Carbonek's Great Hall, but the torches had been lit and supper was coming in on platters. Most of the castle folk were assembled, ready for the meal. Branwen caught at Blanchefleur's arm as she came through the door and said, "Blanchefleur! Did you hear? I sent Heilyn for you!"

"I know, I heard!" she cried, and half-dragged Branwen toward the great press of people at the big doors. There was a glint of gold and gules, but when the crowd shifted Blanchefleur stopped in her tracks. The face she saw was narrow and battered, with deep-etched wrinkles and fair hair streaked with grey. Half a century of war and struggle had passed over that head, so that he was old before his time: the fire in him had consumed his weary flesh. Then she saw his shield, and recalled that Perceval's had borne a three-pointed label above the pentacle. She was looking at Sir Gawain, who came walking into the hall of Carbonek beside another man whom she did not know, bearing a device of red and white stripes.

Disappointed, Blanchefleur turned and slipped through a side-door. Branwen caught her.

"Where are you going? Supper is ready."

"I won't eat. I am going to the Chapel to get ready. You had best come. Where is Nerys?"

"In the kitchens, I think. And I am *famished*." Branwen threw her a despairing glance.

"Oh, well, eat something, and bring Nerys up."

Blanchefleur went upstairs and shook out the white samite tunic of her office. She pulled it on over her dress and knelt, but there was a great burden of weariness on her shoulders. She forced herself to pray anyway. Half an hour later, heralded by galloping steps on the stair, the other two arrived. The door opened and Blanchefleur gaped at the sight of Nerys standing there with flushed cheeks, laughing back over her shoulder down the stair.

"You win!" Branwen's giggles echoed from below. "It's not *fair!*"

Wordlessly, Blanchefleur stared at Nerys. They were *racing?* The fay pretended not to see her astounded look, but a small and catlike smile tugged her lips as she shrugged into her own tunic. Then Branwen came trudging up the steps, smoothing back limp strands of hair from her face.

She said, "Oh, Blanchefleur, you should have been there. A fig for Sir Lancelot! Sir Gawain is the most perfect knight in the world."

Nerys pretended to look solemn and quelling, but her voice shimmered into laughter. "And more than twice your age, withal."

"Oh, pfft! *You* know I didn't mean it that way."

"Sir Lancelot?" Blanchefleur asked Nerys. Somehow, without meaning it, her voice fell like a little cold brass snuffer on the hilarity of the room.

Nerys said, "Did you not recognise him?"

"I saw Sir Gawain," Blanchefleur said. "The other was Sir Lancelot?" A little flame of warmth sprang into her. "But this means the Grail Knight is yet to come." And Perceval had not yet failed the Quest for lack of time.

Branwen emerged tousled from her own white tunic and said: "We offered both of them food, and Sir Lancelot ate, but Sir Gawain did not!"

"Even though you all teased him," said Nerys.

"Oh! He was discourteous, and refused our hospitality, and declared himself our enemy, or so we all said." Branwen giggled again. "And, Blanchefleur, he bore it all in the most knightly manner imaginable!"

"But why should he not eat?" Blanchefleur asked.

Nerys said hesitantly: "There is another supper for him to partake of. And these knights have sworn to refuse any other communion, with any other King, until they have found it."

"It is a test!" said Branwen. "And Sir Gawain has passed it!"

Blanchefleur lifted the Grail from its table and paused. "But Sir Lancelot. Has he failed?"

"Let us see," said Nerys, and took up the Spear.

When the three of them, walking in almost-tangible light, entered the great hall of Carbonek, Blanchefleur at once saw the stranger knights sitting at table. One was asleep, his shaggy dark head turned away from the Grail, burrowed into his arms. The other rose to his feet as she entered the room. It was Sir Gawain, and the way he stood with his chin upflung and his shoulders set square reminded her of Perceval. But in the Grail-light she saw with preternatural clarity a difference. This man was stubborn, unsubtle, bellicose. A good man to have at one's side, if he could be kept there.

She went down the hall toward him. Sir Gawain stepped away from his chair and called in a voice with all the ringing gold of a trumpet, "Maiden of the Grail, in God's name show me what these things mean!"

A sigh rippled across the hall like a harpstring that has been plucked and released. "Follow, and learn," Blanchefleur told him. He left the table and paced after them, Naciens rising from his own place to bring up the rear. But when they had circled the hall, and just as the doors opened for their exit, Sir Lancelot stirred and lurched to his feet and followed with sightless, sleepwalking eyes. All the way up the stair to the chapel, his shuffling feet sounded on the steps behind them.

In the Grail Chapel they laid the Signs on the altar and Gawain went to his knees in prayer. Naciens closed the door after them, and Blanchefleur drew breath five times before she heard the soft groping of the sleep-walker in the dark, at the door. She touched Naciens's arm and whispered, "Shall he fail the Quest utterly?"

Naciens saw the pity in her eyes. "Do as you will."

Blanchefleur went and opened the door. Lancelot knelt there on the threshold. Was he awake, now, or still asleep? Certainly he never saw her, but stared past her to the Grail. She looked down at him, with his sharp-drawn face and the eyes that seemed a little too weary even for sleep to cure. She had been ready to resent this man, she realised, for the question-mark on her lineage. But now all she thought of was the piteous story of Elaine.

He shouldered suddenly up and forward, his eyes fixed on the Grail, as if to enter. Without thinking she darted out a hand to grip his arm. "No! Remain where you are, Sir Lancelot, for it was not given to you to enter here."

He sank back to his knees, looking up, seeing her for the first time. Like Gawain, he was battered more with war than age, and though he must have been handsome once his face was now marred by weather and scars. They looked at each other, and something in Lancelot's eyes recoiled, wounded; his lips framed one word: "Guinevere?"

She pressed her lips together. "No," she said, and turned her back on him, leaving the door open for him to see. Further in, under the wash of Grail-light, the fire in him burning yet more brightly, Gawain was kneeling. While the Knight of the Lake saw only the Queen of Logres, what did Gawain see, beyond human sight and knowledge?

She remembered the question asked in the great hall, and said: "Sir, this is the blood of Christ, and the grace of God, given for you. Ask, and you shall receive."

Gawain stirred and stood like a sleepwalker himself, reaching out a trembling hand to the Cup. Some of the light passed from his face. Then, as if afraid, he drew back and went again to his knees.

"Let one who is worthy drink. The Grail Knight cannot be far."

Was it motion that caught her attention, or only the wing-beat of a bitter mood? Blanchefleur glanced at Nerys and saw that she had bowed her head; disappointment lay in the bend of her neck. Naciens sighed and said: "Because you have asked to know what these things mean, the waste lands shall be healed of their blight. Long have we waited for this deliverance."

"It is well. When I am dead, let that be the deed for which I am known." Gawain rose to his feet, and stood a moment longer before the Grail. A look of longing passed across his face; then he turned resolutely away, and went out of the chapel. Outside the door Sir Lancelot had sunk down on the steps in a deathly faint. Without a word Sir Gawain bent, lifted him, and carried him down the stair.

For twenty-seven days Sir Lancelot lay in a stupor and could not be roused. Meanwhile, Sir Gawain stayed at Carbonek, and meanwhile, for the first time in Blanchefleur's experience of the place, summer descended with blue skies, flowers, and warmth. The castle's kitchen garden erupted into plenty. And one day a herd of wild sheep with overgrown coats wandered into the valley where Carbonek for the present stood. In a hum of activity they were shorn, butchered, and smoked, while the women busied themselves with the fleeces, washing, carding, spinning, and weaving. The curse had lifted at last.

One soft and golden afternoon a week after the knights had come,

Blanchefleur took her distaff and went to relieve the damsel who was watching Sir Lancelot. With all of Carbonek quickening into renewed life, Blanchefleur felt an odd kinship with the ill knight. Of all the castle-dwellers, they two alone faced an uncertain future.

She wedged herself into one of the chamber's windows, sun and breeze at her back, tucked her distaff under her left elbow, and began to spin. The motion quickened her dull mood and with a quiver of anticipation she wondered what would come next, whether it would be Morgan or the Grail Knight, and whether she would see Perceval again.

The door opened and she slid down from the window as Sir Gawain entered. Although Blanchefleur had seen him in passing at mealtimes and in passageways, she had not spoken above five words to him since the Grail Chapel. Out of the light, did he recognise the Grail's keeper?

He bowed to her now and went over to where his friend lay on the bed. "No change?" he asked.

"None, sir."

He turned away with a sigh and stood looking at Blanchefleur. A smile softened his harsh features. "So you are Arthur's daughter."

"I believe so," Blanchefleur said, but her eyes went involuntarily to the man on the bed.

If Gawain saw her confusion, he made no sign. Instead, he took her hand and touched the gem she wore. "Well, well. The old ring."

Blanchefleur looked at the red stone on her finger and said, "That was Perceval. He gave it to me."

"As I gave it to his mother," said Gawain.

"He told me the story," Blanchefleur said. Sir Gawain beamed at her paternally for a space. She blushed. It was not as though Perceval was actually paying court to her, she thought. And would Sir Gawain think so kindly of her if he knew how she had treated his only son?

She smiled awkwardly and said, "I thought I would come and watch Sir Lancelot for a while. One hears so much about him."

Gawain laughed and glanced at the bed. "If he could hear you, he would crave your pardon for lying like a felled log in the presence of such a lady." He turned to Blanchefleur again more seriously. "You do not know him, lady, the best man in Logres, saving only our lord King. Have you seen him in tourney? I, I press on wherever battle is thickest, but he will stay back, if there is a young or untried knight, and let him triumph. And so he gains the more glory by his courtesy than I do by my arm."

"A woman might love him for that," she said, greatly daring.

"Many have."

"I spoke to Elaine of Carbonek before she died. She told me the story, some of it."

When Gawain spoke again, his voice growled in his chest. "Elaine of Carbonek! Did she tell you that she bewitched him? Did she tell you that she almost destroyed him? Only by a miracle did he regain his wits."

"She said something like that," said Blanchefleur, a little wary of his passion.

"I know Lancelot. He could not have been in his right mind. He is incapable of dishonour."

"I—I beg your pardon, but I wish I could be as sure as you are." She looked at him pleadingly. "But I've heard it said that perhaps I am not Arthur's daughter."

"Who says so?"

The answer came back sharp and stinging, like a whip. Merciful heaven, there was a quick rage and an awful strength kept in hand there. She picked her words carefully. "People who hope it is false. Nerys, and the Lady Nimue, and others. They say Sir Lancelot loves the—my mother."

"That would be high treason." A dark flush spread across his face. "The Lady Nimue should know better than to spread such slanders, and if she were a man I would defend my Queen's spotless honour against her without fear."

She could not help smiling at that. Gawain softened and laughed with her, and the quick rage was only a memory that left the air cleaner and fresher for its passing. He said, "I know Lancelot better than to think him capable of such a thing. His love for the lady Queen lends him strength and spurs him on to the great deeds he does for the good of Logres, but he knows his place. I love him like a brother, but I would kill him without hesitation if I thought that he had touched her."

He turned to the bed and stretched out his hand above the sleeper. "Even now, where he lies! Not just for the sin. Do you not see what is at stake here, O maiden of the Grail? Lancelot's treason would utterly destroy us. Logres would rip in half between her king and her champion. And all the works of our hands would perish."

He turned back to her with the fire in his eyes gone, leaving them bleak and grey. Blanchefleur said, "Sir, you fill me with dread."

Gawain shook his head. "It is only a nightmare. This is the waking day."

"God grant you are right. But I cannot tell for sure, and I am afraid." Much as she feared his anger, much as she sensed the deep differences that lay like a gulf between them, Blanchefleur looked into his eyes and knew that he of all people would understand her doubts. She said: "I have learned to love Logres, or what I have seen of it here in Carbonek. And I have seen the holy city. I have shed my blood on its stones defending the Grail. I will go back there, and I will face the enemy of Logres, and I will die if I must to save her. It is unbearable to think that after this, by proving myself false-born, I might cause the downfall of Logres and all our hopes."

She took a deep and uncertain breath.

"But even if it does destroy us, shouldn't I know the truth?"

He looked down at her for a long moment. "Yes," he said at last.

"I dread passing myself off as something I'm not," she said with a faltering smile. "Nerys says I worry too much, but how in good conscience can I take such an exalted position without being sure?"

"You cannot." Sir Gawain frowned, but then his brows smoothed into a smile. "I say, seek the truth, lady. But I agree with the damsel: you worry overmuch. The truth is that you are true-born. That truth cannot hurt us."

25

Sunder me from my soul, that I may see
The sins like streaming wounds, the life's brave beat
Till I shall save myself as I would save
A stranger in the street.

Chesterton

Sir Lancelot woke from his stupor on a sunny morning in late spring, and the day after, he and Sir Gawain left Carbonek. Before they went, Lancelot asked to see Blanchefleur. She went down to him in the courtyard where Gawain was buckling straps and making stentorian farewells, and led him into the kitchen garden, where they walked between rows of cabbages like big blooming roses that reminded Blanchefleur of Sarras.

Lancelot walked with bent head and downcast eyes, hands clasped behind his back. "You are very like her," he said at last. "I would have mistaken you for her, if not for your colouring."

"Yes," Blanchefleur said. "Elaine—" and she caught herself.

There was a moment's silence before Lancelot spoke in a voice that seemed to come from very far away. "You saw her before she died?"

Blanchefleur looked at the cabbages, unable to subject him to her direct gaze. It was a strange world, she thought. Not only was this the most well-loved man in Logres, but he could have been—he could still be—her father. And yet he stood in the sun between cabbages and turnips, his eyes fastened upon the ground, looking like a whipped dog.

"Yes," she said. Then: "She told me the story. I know it wasn't your fault."

He looked up and said with desperate finality, "Yes, it was."

His flat voice warned her not to dig deeper, even if she had wanted to. Blanchefleur said:

"Take heart, sir. You came so very close to achieving the Quest."

But that was a double-edged comfort. When his eyes dropped back to the ground she wondered if it had cut too deep, and hurried on. "I can't imagine what it must have been like to be shut out at the end of it all. But you were there. You *saw* it. That is more than has been granted to any other man save Sir Gawain. And time is growing short. In a few weeks the Quest will be over."

"Yet I could have achieved it indeed," Lancelot said, "and mine is the greatest punishment that a man might suffer. I have followed too much the devices and desires of my own heart. And I shut myself out by my fault, by my own grievous fault."

Blanchefleur sighed, and scratched for words. "Have you no part at all in heavenly mercies?"

The silence stretched out. "I may hope," said Lancelot. But there was nothing hopeful in his voice.

After that, there was no more to say. They went back to the courtyard, where Gawain took his leave of her with the familiar fatherly gleam, while Lancelot bowed to her with the faultless courtesy that marked his every action. With her alone he seemed stiff and uneasy.

The knights dwindled to a tiny fleck on the road. Blanchefleur went back into the hall. With Gawain gone, the whole place seemed a little bigger, a little shabbier, a little emptier. She turned and went up the stair to the Grail Chapel, remembering some small tasks, some dusting and tidying, that had fallen due. But when she went into the blazing light of the lantern tower of Carbonek, she sat awhile on the floor, soaking up the light and the silence.

For the first time, she looked beyond the Grail Quest. Would the High King send for her? She thought again of her conversation with Gawain. At least he had believed her the true heir of Logres, she thought with a rush of gratitude, remembering the venom of Elaine. But if the opposite was proven? Would she meet with the same affection then?

What would it take to unleash the anger of Gawain?

Blanchefleur remembered the words she had said to Lancelot not half an hour ago—"Have you no part in heavenly mercies?"—and bit her lip and rose from the floor. There was work to do, she thought.

Dizziness hit her.

Now that it had come, she was surprised how little fear she felt. She clung to Carbonek just long enough to go to her knees. It was a bright, bright day; outside the chapel's stained-glass windows, sunlight reached in to mingle with Grail-light. If she failed this time, the dark would come; perhaps this was her last chance to see the light. She looked on the Cup for three heartbeats, just to fix it in her mind, and then she let go and slipped away.

BLANCHEFLEUR OPENED HER EYES ON GREEN beech-leaves and piecemeal glimpses of the golden sky of Sarras. She picked herself up out of the grass and brushed off her dress, searching through the leaves for a landmark she recognised. Then high above and far off, through weaving branches, she saw the cathedral and its spire. It would be a long walk up the mountain.

Meanwhile, she stood beneath a beech tree in a sloping corner of Sarras. A stream full of bright watercress chattered through deep banks to her left. Gigantic trees surrounded her, their bark flecked with tiny shelf-fungi, and uphill a short way she glimpsed a moss-covered wall. She swished through white and green snowflake-flowers and followed the wall to an arched gate of wrought-iron. Laying her hand on the latch, she glanced back into the shadowed loveliness of the beech forest and saw a gleam of white.

After the first jolt of shock, she dropped her hand from the latch and waited calmly for the stranger to move a little closer through the trees, revealing a breadth and height distinctively masculine. Not Morgan, then. She took a breath and unclenched her jaw. Then he stood before her, and Blanchefleur looked up into the boyish young face of a knight, black-haired, earnest-eyed, bearing upon his white surcoat the device of a red cross.

She had never seen him before in her life, but she knew at once, not only that he was no threat to her, but also that in the long-ago spark of goodwill which had first imaged their lives, they had been friends as strong as brother and sister. It was fitting, now, to slip into that predestined love. She put out her hand with a smile and said, "Good morning."

"*Is* it morning?" he asked, and took her hand and kissed it with an unselfconscious grace that reminded her of Lancelot.

"Doesn't it smell like it?" She lifted the latch and they went through the gate into the garden beyond. "I'm Blanchefleur," she prompted. "The Grail Maiden of Carbonek."

Here there were no trees to block the view. Sarras rose terraced and riotous above them, more sublime in glory than even she could remember. At last the knight tore his slackjawed gaze away from the cathedral at the mountain's dizzying peak and said to Blanchefleur: "I am Galahad, the Knight of the Grail."

"I *knew* it!"

He laughed. "Tell me the meaning of this place."

She remembered the words of the High King. "This is Sarras. The city on the hill. The pattern for Logres."

Delight shone from his face. "The City! Oh, to leave Logres and walk these streets forever!"

"But Logres needs Sarras too. Doesn't she?"

"Yes," and Galahad gave a laughing sigh. "Time enough to quit the mortal life when I am called. But however many years lie before me, I will remember this," and he turned his face again to the heights.

Blanchefleur felt a sudden flash of hope, "Why are you here in Sarras now? Have you come to help me?"

The way he wheeled toward her again, as if scenting danger, reminded her of Perceval. "Help you? Damsel, are you in danger?"

"Danger." She bit a lip. "She almost killed me, in the autumn, and yet *danger* seems somehow the wrong word to use of anything in Sarras."

"I understand," Galahad said gravely. "Nothing happens here that is not meant."

"And if she had killed me?"

"Then it would have been meant. But it was not."

"And therefore no danger." Blanchefleur tried for a moment to fit her mind around this, but there were corners and loose ends trailing out, and she had not the time to make them fit.

Galahad said, "This *she?*"

She gestured helplessly. "A witch. Trying to steal the Grail, and do—oh, horrible things! And I must prevent it…"

"Then this is for you," Galahad said, and drew a knife from the pouch at his belt. It was an odd little thing, T-hilted and small enough to fit into a woman's hand. Its translucent blade, only an inch and a half long, was bound with scrolling bronze wire to the bone hilt. "Have a care. Obsidian is sharper than anything else in the world, sharp enough to make sunlight bleed."

Blanchefleur weighed the shadowy blade in a doubtful palm. "What's it for? Not killing her, surely? I'd rather have your sword, if it came to that."

Galahad laughed and linked his fingers protectively over his hilt. "The knife was given to me by an anchoress dwelling by a river in Dumnonia.

219

She said nothing of killing."

She wrinkled her brow at the knife. "Well, I'm glad of that. After last time, I have no wish to come within striking distance of that woman. I'm sure Morgan le Fay finds it much easier than I do to stab people."

She sheathed the knife, tucked it into her pouch, and led the way through the garden into the streets. Questions itched on her tongue.

"Where are you, in the waking world? Are you far from Carbonek? Will you be much longer?"

But the Knight of the Grail shook his head. "I cannot tell."

Her questions were all futile, of course. "I'm sorry, of course you can't."

"But I think it will be soon." Eagerness snapped in his eyes. Before she could dredge up courage to ask the next question, he went on. "And yet I could wish it to be years in the future. So much of my life has been aimed toward this day. What shall I do when it is past?"

Blanchefleur looked at him with surprise. "Surely you came to do more than achieve the Grail."

"Oh, surely," he returned quickly. "That was never my whole purpose in the Quest."

She puzzled over that for a moment as they went up the hill. Blanchefleur, looking at the pavement beneath their feet, once again noticed the absence of any shadow. Neither she nor Galahad, it seemed, could disrupt the serene light of Sarras.

Sir Galahad did not look at his feet. He walked with his head lifted up, enthralled by all the beauty that surrounded them. Blanchefleur opened her mouth to ask for news of Perceval and then hesitated. Surely it was unlikely that their paths would have crossed?

Galahad spoke while she was still wavering in her mind. "My mother— is she well?"

"Oh," Blanchefleur said, halting. Galahad bent to look into her face. "Dead."

"Yes."

He stood statue-still for a moment, looking at something on the road. Then he lifted his head and went on up the hill, walking more slowly. "Naciens told me she was ill. I had hoped to arrive in time."

"I'm sorry." Blanchefleur tried to remember what she knew of those last days. "Nerys took care of her, toward the end."

With eyes narrowed against the light of Sarras, Galahad almost seemed to be searching the streets for something. He said, "I fear I do not know the lady."

"No one could have cared for her more tenderly."

They mounted higher in silence. Blanchefleur closed her eyes and saw once more the pallid face of the mother of Galahad, with the bitter lines scored into her face. At last the question almost burst out of her:

"Tell me what it means, Galahad—your birth."

There was a question in his glance.

"Did it have to happen the way it did? How can you know you won't be shut out of the Grail Chapel, like Sir Lancelot?" She swallowed, trying to dig deeper into the thing that troubled her. "How will such sinful people as your father, and my father, build *this?*" And she threw out her arms to encompass Sarras.

Galahad lifted his face to the cathedral. "We cannot."

Tears prickled her eyes. "Then why were we put on the earth?"

"To build Sarras." He smiled when he saw her blank perplexity. "It is no contradiction. Our inability does not excuse us. But hammer and nails need not be perfect, if they are wielded by a perfect workman."

"I don't know," she said. "Can any workman use such crooked, broken things?" But her words fell unheeded in the warm air. The street was empty. The Grail Knight had gone.

Her first reflex was another jolt of panic. She remembered too well that Morgan's first appearance had come immediately after the High King's sudden departure. She dug into her pouch and folded her fingers around the crosspiece of the obsidian knife. The shadowy blade did nothing to comfort her. She was not trained to use this or any weapon, nor could she bring herself to imagine using it.

A little thread of frustration curled through her thoughts. Once, she had turned up her nose at Christine de Pisan's recommendation that a lady ought to know the use of weapons. Now she stood in danger of her life, and by her ignorance was more likely to injure herself than her enemy.

The cathedral still loomed far above her on the mountaintop. Was Morgan already there, in the steeple? Blanchefleur broke into a run. Wing-footed, tireless speed greeted her efforts, but she mounted the hill and flung herself up the stair to the close-cropped green lawn of the cathedral with a breathlessness that came from fear.

She slid to a stop beneath the great doorway arch. No Morgan. She turned and scanned the terrace again with sudden doubt. Morgan *wasn't* here? Had she come to Sarras only to meet Galahad, then?

Unless Morgan was already ahead of her, in the steeple.

She started across the lawn to the stair. She had covered only half the ground when the steeple erupted. There was a flash of flame, a belch of smoke, a blast that knocked her down on her face. The whole cathedral hummed like a bell that has been struck. One of the stone saints on the steeple's spire toppled, tumbled head over foot for an agonising length of time, and then hit the ground with a dull *thump* that cracked off its serene and smiling head.

Blanchefleur choked, "Merciful heaven!" and staggered to her feet. Inside, the stair reeked of smoke and fumes and the smell of fireworks. But how did Morgan have *gunpowder?* She clutched the obsidian knife a little harder and pelted up the stair, coughing in the smoke. She lost count of the steps. Then the gate across the entrance to the place of the Grail suddenly loomed over her, and she fought herself to a stop just too late to avoid knocking her head against the iron.

She gripped the bars and shook them. Locked. Above, the wind had already blown much of the smoke away, but from the cramped steps below the trap she could not see the Grail. Only the great wooden table, blasted and blackened and swept clear, it seemed, of both Cup and Platter…

Blanchefleur reached up and groped at the ledge above the gate. The key was there where she'd left it last time, nestled into warm crackling ash that had once been grass. She snatched it and paused.

No flutter of clothing betrayed a presence above. No pursuing footstep echoed below. A whisper of sound dragged at her hearing, but then it came again and was only the wind. Blanchefleur waited no longer. She unlocked the gate, flung it back, and sprang into the chapel.

The place was scorched. The grass of the floor had turned to powder, where tiny fragments of bomb-casing still smoked and crunched underfoot. Blanchefleur barely heeded them. The Spear hung on its hooks, the length of its haft now charred and blackened. But the wooden table was empty.

She flung herself at it with a gasp like a sob, then scrabbled on the floor. Here was the platter, upside-down. The Grail had rolled beneath the table. Neither was even slightly harmed.

Blanchefleur collapsed to the floor, hugging the Signs, almost faint with relief.

Then a shadow spilled across the scorched grass, onto her lap. Blanchefleur jerked back with a cry as if she had been burned. Morgan stood not three paces away with her eyes fixed upon the Cup. Her feet were bare. And she had called that whispering motion the wind!

Blanchefleur put the platter down and rose up, clenching the Grail in her left hand and the sharp-enough-to-bleed-sunlight knife in her right. Morgan was breathing fast, her eyes bright with triumph, teeth showing. But she did not move.

"Give me the Grail."

Blanchefleur lifted her knife. Morgan's eyes slipped to that tiny blade and something damped the triumph in her eyes. Blanchefleur saw the infinitesimal quiver of the witch's jaw, and tightened her resolve.

"You know little of me if you expect me to do that," she whispered.

Morgan stood with her eyes fixed unblinkingly on the stone knife. Blanchefleur cleared her throat, backed a step, and said, "I am curious. What happened when you stabbed me in the autumn? You never touched the Grail, or we would know of it at Carbonek."

Morgan stirred, and her glare was knife-edged. "Sarras spat me out. I woke."

"Ah," said Blanchefleur. "I am brought to Sarras only when there is an attempt on the Grail. And if you kill me in Sarras, you put the Cup beyond your own reach."

Morgan tilted her chin, and her hand drifted to the knife at her own belt. "Tell me of yourself. Are you dead now, or living?"

"Do the dead guard the Signs of Carbonek?"

"Shall I pass my blade through you and see?"

Blanchefleur remembered that her mortal body lay in the Grail Chapel at Carbonek, far from the infirmary. Another wound like the last and she could die there, helpless.

Was death really too high a price to pay for the protection of the Grail?

She forced a smile. "Please, do that, if there is no easier way to rid Sarras of you."

Slowly, Morgan's hand fell from the knife-hilt.

Blanchefleur backed another step, away from the Table, toward one of the arrow-shaped openings that looked out on the mountain city of Sarras. The fall to the cathedral floor was far enough to kill her. She could go over clutching the Grail. Perhaps, by heavenly grace, she would not also die in Carbonek.

But it was a desperate gamble.

"Stop!" Morgan seemed to guess what was passing through her mind. "Why? Why die for it? It is only a cup."

Blanchefleur backed another step. "It is our only hope for Logres," she said, and remembered what Nerys had said so long ago. "And more than

Logres. The kingdom that shall never be destroyed."

Morgan bowed her head. The gesture hid the warning spark in her eyes. Then she sprang.

Blanchefleur reacted faster than she could have imagined possible, dodging to one side. Only let Morgan's impetus carry her to the window, and a single shove would suffice to kill Morgan and leave Blanchefleur in possession of the Grail. Her heart stood still as Morgan went past. Then the witch flung out a hand and clenched Blanchefleur's right arm. They staggered another step, to the window's edge, before steadying on the very brink. Blanchefleur yanked away, back into the room. But Morgan held her grip with fingers that bored into Blanchefleur's arm and reached for the Grail. Her left hand found the Cup and closed. They strained for a moment, then Morgan twisted the Grail and with it Blanchefleur's arm. She fell to her knees, whimpering in pain, and then lost her grip with one last jerk that tore the Grail free. It hit the ground too far away for her to reach. Morgan was on it at once.

Her shadow pooled beneath her as she knelt to retrieve the Cup. Blanchefleur saw it, and within the same heartbeat she saw the purpose of the knife that could cut sunlight.

Morgan rose to her feet, holding the Grail. Her shadow flowed across the ground. Blanchefleur hurled herself forward and sliced through the air at Morgan's heels. As the blade skimmed the floor, tiny ashen curls of grass parted and floated into the air, shredding into smoke. Through light and shade the knife flashed, and parted Morgan from her shadow.

Morgan whipped around, her face suddenly pale as paper. With a puff of wind, the shadow twisted like smoke and drifted away. Her hands, white to the knuckle, clenched on the Grail and trembled.

"No!" she whispered.

The Grail fell through her fingers into Blanchefleur's hands. Another puff of wind caught Morgan as it had her shadow; she floated a few steps, regained her footing, mouthed "No!" again, and was gone on the sweet warm breath of Sarras.

Blanchefleur rose to watch the wind carry her away. Then, moving very slowly, she set the Grail on the table, straightened the spear, replaced the platter, slid the stone knife into her pouch, and closed and locked the trapdoor.

The steeple still smelled of smoke, and the black grass was prickly and sooty, but Blanchefleur was too tired to care. She stretched herself out full length and for the first time in months, drifted into dreamless sleep.

26

Far in the Town of Sarras,
Red-rose the gloamings fall,
For in her heart of wonder
Flames the Sangreal.
…
But where the Grail-Knight entered,
Ah! me! I enter not.

Taylor

n a warm evening that smelled of summer, while the sun hovered low in a purple evening sky and the whirr of crickets underlined every other sound, the Grail Knight came to Carbonek. Blanchefleur heard the cry as she carried bread into the hall. The children were the first to race for the door with shouts of excitement; then the squires, with longer legs, outstripped them. One of them paused to hand Branwen a dish of mutton before dashing away. She squeaked in outrage, flung the gigantic platter onto the nearest table, and ran after. As a hush dropped over the emptying hall, Blanchefleur found Nerys standing like a statue with her arms wrapped round a stoup of wine.

"Nerys," she said. "What if it's him? At last?"

Sight slid back to the fay's fathomless eyes. She shook her head wordlessly and put the wine on the table.

Branwen swooped back into the hall in a storm of excitement. "Blanchefleur! Your knight is here!"

Relief bloomed in her tight chest. "Are you sure?"

"Oh, yes! Well, it would hardly be Sir Gawain again, would it? And anyway the device is labelled."

"And no one else?"

"Two others—"

"Is there the device of the red cross?"

"Argent and gules? Yes."

Blanchefleur took another deep breath. "The Grail Knight."

Branwen's eyes widened. Blanchefleur added, "I saw him in Sarras."

Nerys stirred. Her wonderment blazed like the light in a long-dead lantern. "You saw him in the City?"

Blanchefleur nodded.

"And never told me?"

"They're coming!" one of the pages yelped from the doorway.

Blanchefleur was struck with shyness. If she was going to see Perceval again, after all this time, she wanted at least the bulwark of Grail-light to strengthen her. "Let's go." She dumped the bread onto the table. "Stay if you wish, Branwen."

Branwen clamped her hands over her stomach. "I have no appetite."

Nerys and Blanchefleur looked at her in double concern. Branwen smiled weakly. "Let us see the end of the Quest first, and eat after."

"There's the Branwen we know," said Blanchefleur with a laugh. But then came the sound of many footsteps from the door, and she ducked into one of the side passages, trailed by the others.

With every step of the way up the winding stair to the Grail Chapel, the shining purport of what was about to happen weighed more heavily on Blanchefleur's shoulders like a robe of office. From Branwen's lip-bitten smile, and from the impression she had, every time she looked at Nerys, of deliriously triumphant music playing just beyond the borders of hearing, she knew that the others felt it too. In the chapel, bathed in light, they drew on their tunics and waited in a silence too glad to break.

At last Branwen said, "Can you believe it is happening at last?"

"Anything might happen if you wait for it long enough," said Nerys, with a smile.

"Not all of us can wait a thousand years," Branwen reminded her, "and then see our desires with our own eyes."

Nerys said: "The dwellers in the City, on the hill of hallowing, see their desires with their own eyes. And in their presence, all the selfsame threads they have spun in the web of their lives are drawn on, through men and deeds yet unborn and unthought-of, to the service of more mighty ends than even the dreams of the City could prepare them to imagine. It is the second of all joys."

Her voice faded to a whisper as she added half to herself: "We fays do not speak of the first; the memory is too grievous."

Silence unspooled. Blanchefleur gripped her hands together, thinking of the first time she and Nerys had talked about the Grail. "*Fiat voluntas tua,*" she said at last. "What threads will run from this day, Nerys? What will happen in Logres because of the Grail Knight?"

The fay lifted her palms upward. "Have I the eyes of Sarras? Like you, I can only wait and hope."

Blanchefleur thought of Elaine on her deathbed, Lancelot in the kitchen garden, Arthur and Morgan in the cloistered walk. That. That, she hoped, was what the Grail Knight would somehow purge away, although she could not think how.

"We must have stayed long enough," Branwen said.

"Then forward, in God's name." Blanchefleur stood and picked up the Grail for the last time. She rubbed its ancient ridged surface with her thumb, suddenly flooded with gratitude for its safety. After all her worry, after all the dreadful adventures of Sarras, here it stood at last, inviolate at the achievement of the Quest. Cradling the Cup in both hands, she turned and started down the stair.

In the hall at table, three knights sat silent and unmoving before untouched food. One of them was strange to her, a bulky man with calm level eyes and a red-barred device that marked him kin to Sir Lancelot. The next she knew: Sir Galahad, full of glad awe, leapt up like a tongue of fire. Beside him, more slowly, Perceval rose to his feet. He had grown broader since she saw him last, and beneath, in the piercing and perceptive light of the Grail, she sensed all Gawain's passion, but held in tighter check. And what had become of the easy bravado she remembered so well? He stared at her and at the Cup with almost grim reverence, and the whole eighteen months that lay between them and their last meeting seemed to rise up and cast its shadow on his face.

Then she recalled the burden she bore, and went on into the hall, walking in a light that no shadow would ever dim.

As they drew close to the three knights, Sir Galahad lifted up the hilts of his sword like a cross and called "In the name of Our Lord, stay a moment." Blanchefleur halted, and the Grail Knight came forward and bowed and kissed her cheek. For the fraction of a moment she gave him the wordless greeting of her eyes; then Galahad turned and took his place at the head of the procession. From the king's high dais, Naciens rose and said, "Now shall all true knights be fed. Take up the Maimed King."

Bors and Perceval went to the dais and lifted the couch of King Pelles.

An extra hand was needed to steady the head, and Naciens called the squire Heilyn. Then Sir Galahad led them all through the hall and up the long stair to the Grail Chapel itself, unhesitant, as if led by long-ago memory or a messenger none of the others could see.

From below, in the great hall, not a whisper of sound stirred the air. Carbonek, man and beast, sat breathless in expectation.

The chapel filled with people. Blanchefleur set the Grail on the table and stood aside, near Naciens. Branwen followed with the platter and then tucked herself out of the way by the door. Perceval, Bors, and Heilyn eased the King's couch through the narrow chapel door, laid it down in the middle of the room, and straightened. Sir Galahad rebuckled his sword and turned to Nerys.

"Damsel, if I may."

She put the Spear into his hands. He went to his knees by King Pelles. Blanchefleur did not hear their low words, but she saw tears spring up in the eyes of the grandfather of Galahad. Then the Grail Knight eased back the King's robe and unbound the wound he had suffered so long ago by the hand of Sir Balyn in this very place. It was partly healed, but festered below the surface. When Galahad poised the Spear above the wound, Blanchefleur quickly transferred her gaze to the window. Only King Pelles's groaning breath was audible as the Grail Knight sliced through the oozing flesh. Then the breath slowed and the smell receded. There was a soft murmur of surprise from Branwen, and Blanchefleur turned to see the King of Carbonek, tears streaking his face, rise to his feet supported by Galahad at one elbow and Heilyn at the other.

King Pelles put them aside, took the remaining three steps to the table alone, and knelt. The company in that little room was still watching him in silent wonder when Naciens reached out and lifted the samite cover from the Holy Grail.

A burst of light blinded all of them. Blanchefleur flinched and flung up a hand to cover her eyes, but before she had lifted it as far as her mouth her eyes hardened to the blaze and she stood poised in sudden joy. They were standing in the spire of Sarras with the whole world unfolded around them.

Perceval said, "*Mirabilis!*" Nerys lifted both her hands to her mouth; all the colour drained from her cheeks. Branwen, with wide unblinking eyes, moved over to Heilyn and slipped her hand into his. But Naciens said to Galahad: "Holy knight of God, take this long burden from my keeping, and release me from the vow I made to Joseph of Arimathea at the uttermost dawn of my life."

Galahad took the Cup from the hermit's hands, carefully, for it was brimming full of wine. He turned to the company. "Now the Quest of the Grail is achieved," he declared.

And he said: "Knights, and servants, and true children, you have come out of deadly life into spiritual life. I give you no new teaching. Only an old one, lest it be forgotten: *adnuntite mortem Domini donec veniat*, for this is the only true foundation of the City. Now take and receive the high meat which you have so much desired, for this night the Grail shall depart from the realm of Logres."

All of them received the Eucharist there at his hands.

When this was done, Galahad said: "Come down with me into the City."

"Gladly," said Perceval, and the nine of them followed the Grail Knight in silence down the stair to the grassy cathedral floor.

Blanchefleur stopped under the steeple and knelt to feel the ground for a tell-tale hollow. There it was, but the broken saint had been repaired, and stood again upon the spire of the cathedral.

The sound of feet and awed whispers moved away. Near her there was only silence until a voice spoke.

"What are you looking for?" Perceval asked.

She let the joy flood her face and ebb a little before she rose and turned around. "Proof I was not dreaming, when I was here last. ...It is good to see you again."

There was a little wry twist in his smile. "As I promised. Little knowing by what inexplicable favour I should be permitted to come at all."

His shamefast words struck her with mute surprise. He had indeed changed, and much for the better. She should keep silent, she thought. Or he might discover how far beneath him she truly was.

He held out his hand to lead her to the terrace and she took it with a wistful smile.

By now, surely, she should be accustomed to the grandeur of Sarras, but once again the view snatched her out of herself, so that she seemed unbodied and all but unpersoned before the sheer living presence of the City. And yet now new marvels appeared. Now, throughout the streets and halls, throughout the gardens and orchards, glimpsed through stone lattices or clustered by the riverside, walked and wrought a great company of people, like the stars of heaven for number.

When Blanchefleur became once again aware of nearby things, she saw Galahad at the foot of the steps leading from the terrace to the street beneath them. He was speaking with a man that loomed head and shoulders over him like a giant cast in brass.

"What is happening?" Blanchefleur whispered to Perceval with a sudden premonition.

The Grail Knight fell back a step. He and the man of brass bowed to one another with courtly grace. Then Galahad returned to where they all stood on the terrace. His look was solemn, but Blanchefleur sensed a wild gladness struggling beneath.

"Fair friends," he said, holding out his hands to them. As he stopped and fumbled for words, Blanchefleur understood, and it was like swallowing a lump of stone.

"You aren't leaving us?"

He looked back to her with all the earnest warmth that had lain between them since the beginning of the world. "I am given my wish."

In the silence that followed, only the hermit, Bors, and Perceval stood unconfounded. Among the others a blank distress hung in the air, until Blanchefleur spoke again with tears in her eyes. "Why? What about Logres? What about the rest of the Table? We were waiting for you to change everything."

Perceval, beside her, said: "We were wrong, Blanchefleur."

"I have done everything I came to do," said Galahad gently. "My work is over. Yours is beginning."

"Ours? Are *we* going to restore Logres?"

Galahad's silence flung the question back to her.

"Well, of course we are supposed to, but I thought you were going to help us."

"I have helped you," said Galahad. "Bors and Perceval remain."

Perceval said, "I know what troubles you. We all of us expected the Grail Knight to come and restore Logres. We waited too long. We believed that he would do our work for us. And when he did come to remind us of what we had forgotten, that the work is every man's, none of us were ready for him. None of us were ready for the Quest." Memory clouded his eyes. "Gareth was the only one of us who suspected…"

"The truth is, all of you are called," said Galahad. "All of you must drink of the same Cup."

"But it is leaving us," said Heilyn, speaking for the first time, and turning red when he had spoken.

Galahad smiled at him. "Fair friends, it was given to all of you. Continue to eat, continue to drink, continue to build on that foundation."

He moved restlessly and cast a glance behind to the one who waited like a statue below. Nerys, who had stood among them all this while without speaking, looked to the man of brass as well. There was a white-lipped desperation in her voice. "May I—may not anyone else go with you?"

The Grail Knight looked at her with pity. "Damsel, but one other. Naciens."

The hermit glanced up as if doubting whether to believe his ears. But Galahad beckoned to him, and he moved forward almost timidly. "Five hundred years I watched and kept the Grail. I rejoice that my task is done. Yet, damsel, I will watch a little longer, here on these steps, until your coming."

But Nerys kept her eyes fixed on the man of brass, and pleaded as if to him. "Sir, I remember well the day I first opened my eyes on the young cosmos. I am old now, older even than the Hermit of Carbonek. And I have not forgotten. For centuries beyond count I have waited in silence to know if, beyond this world, there is hope for me. At least show some sign that I may hope."

Not a muscle moved in that strange and splendid face. Then the head sank by an inch, as if to give acknowledgement or assent, but no word or look came to give comfort. Nerys let out the ghost of a sigh and turned away as if unable to bear his gaze.

Naciens came and gripped Blanchefleur's shoulder with one hand and Heilyn's shoulder with the other. "Fair children," he began, rasping, and then cleared his throat and spoke more briskly. "When you finish with Ptolemy, Heilyn, I meant to have you read Isidore of Malitus. And, Blanchefleur, read as you like, only never forget to snuff the candles. Christ keep you both."

Galahad embraced Bors and Perceval. To Bors, passing the sword of Balyn into his kinsman's hands, he said: "Fair lord, remember me to my father, Sir Lancelot, and bid him beware the inconstant world. I have nothing to give him, except this."

To Blanchefleur he said, "Sweet sister, as your labour is longer than mine, so your honour is the greater."

She flung her arms around him. "Not so," she said, her breath catching on a sob, "but as your honour is greater than mine, so your labour is the shorter."

"Let time prove that, Lady of Logres," he said, and then, gently loosing her arms, "The Messenger is waiting."

He and Naciens went down the steps into the City. Then, lightly and smoothly, those who were left stirred and breathed and looked at each other in the Grail Chapel of Carbonek, in the last grey light of day.

No one spoke in the fading memory of Sarras. With a pang Blanchefleur wondered whether she might ever see it again, or whether this day's golden memory must last her until the end—and she snatched hastily at glittering sands of remembrance… But they ran through her fingers even as she scooped them up, and already the seconds, like advancing waves, were washing them away.

At last King Pelles cleared his throat and said in a stronger voice than she had yet heard him use: "One more thing remains to be done."

He unbuckled the sword-belt at his waist and handed it, scabbard and all, to Perceval. "The last of the curse," he explained. "Heal the sword, and the wandering castle will be fixed again in her own valley."

Perceval let the sword slip out of its scabbard onto the empty table where the Signs had once lain. The blade was broken in two pieces. When he had prayed a while, he joined them together, and they gripped each other and became whole. Only the blade was marred by a scar where the two halves joined together.

"Ah," said the King. "You might have asked the question and healed the sword the first time you came to Carbonek, and the Quest would have been the easier. You did not, and therefore there is a mark. But keep the sword. I have no heir, and I am too old to fight; I leave it to you." He turned to Heilyn and Branwen. "Children, I am healed, but I think I will need your help down the stair."

"Wait," said Perceval. He unslung his own sword, and held it out to Heilyn. "Will you be my man, squire of Carbonek?"

Heilyn looked at the knight in awe. "Aye, sir. If my father favours it, sir."

"Speak to him," said Perceval with a smile that broke upon his solemn face like sun after rain. He turned to Blanchefleur. "It is cold and dark here, lady. Let us go."

Blanchefleur glanced at Nerys. The fay had not spoken since her outburst in Sarras and now she stood silhouetted against one of the windows, her face in darkness. Blanchefleur wished she could do or say something to comfort her. But could any mortal understanding comprehend the sorrow of aeons?

"Will you come down?" she whispered.

"In a while."

Blanchefleur touched her hand gently, and went to Perceval at the door.

He offered his arm and turned to go.

"Coming, Bors?"

"Coming."

The door to the lifeless chapel closed behind them. The Quest was done.

27

Lean on me, come away,
I will guide and steady:
Come, for I will not stay:
Come, for house and bed are ready.
Rossetti

Blanchefleur woke to bouncing.

"Look outside! Look at the sun! Look at the *trees!* There are apples! And *mountains!*"

"Branwen," she groaned, slitting one eye open to squint at her bedfellow, "*must* you?"

Branwen, haloed in yellow hair that tickled Blanchefleur's face, went on bouncing. "Your knight returned the castle to its true *locus!* I couldn't wait for the sun to come up and show us what it's like! Come and see!"

Further sleep was clearly impossible. Blanchefleur allowed herself to be dragged out of bed and herded to the narrow window. Here, in the first golden flood of morning light, she looked east down a long and winding valley clustered over with hundreds of apple-trees. Pools of molten fire betrayed the presence of water. Low, mossy ruins could be glimpsed among the orchards—foundations of destroyed houses, skeletons of sheep-pens, all blurred and softened by tiny flowering creepers.

"Isn't it lovely?"

Blanchefleur had almost decided to be cross. But the gorgeous land-scape and the mild summer air urged her against it. "Yes. It's beautiful."

"I know what we should do," Branwen said.

"Have breakfast."

"Oh, yes, but then we should all go out and *explore*. We can take food, and not come back until dark."

"Is that quite safe? Who knows what might be here after all these years?"

"Oh, bah! Nobody does villainy on a day like this. Race you downstairs."

"No. I want to go up to the chapel, first."

She ascended the winding stair, sunk in thought. Galahad gone. The work only beginning. What did it all mean? She thought of continuing for the rest of her life in a blind and desperate struggle like the one she had just endured with the Witch of Gore, and a tide of weariness swept over her.

She tapped on the door and went into the chapel. Nerys had not come down last night, even late, after Perceval had finished telling them his story, or even later, when Blanchefleur had lain awake waiting for her soft footstep and the unhurried swish of her skirts as she let herself into the room the fay shared with Branwen.

This morning, the Grail Chapel seemed less forlorn. Yellow morning light on thousand-hued windows painted the tiny room with colour. The King's couch was still there, although it had been pushed back against a wall with the rug folded tidily at its foot. Although the fay was nowhere to be seen, that rug bore mute and comforting witness to her hand.

"Nerys?" Blanchefleur called softly, then repeated herself, louder. No sound or motion answered from behind the hangings that masked her old sleeping-chamber. She pulled the tapestry back and peered inside. This, too, was empty, but the bed was neatly made—a thing for which Blanchefleur rarely, if ever, found the time—and the faint pleasant scent of Nerys hung in the air.

She climbed into the little closet, pulled on fresh clothing, wadded her old dress into a bundle and went back downstairs to the laundry. She found Nerys next door in the kitchen, grinding salt in the big mortar while Branwen ran back and forth between the hall and Dame Glynis with names and numbers for the exploration company.

Dame Glynis gave Blanchefleur three errands to do and then said, as an afterthought: "I shall have your things brought down from the Chapel. The Lady Elaine's room can be yours."

"Oh," said Blanchefleur, surprised. It was one of the best chambers in the castle, the kind reserved for persons of high honour. Like the Heir of Logres.

"My thanks," she said. "But I think I would rather sleep with Branwen and Nerys."

Dame Glynis did not understand. "There are couches for attendants in the room. I'll have them made up."

She left for the infirmary with a bundle of dried herbs under one arm, and Blanchefleur sighed. If only she could postpone being treated like royalty until she was sure of herself, she thought, fetching bread and meat from the pantry for lunch.

After breakfast the party of explorers set out. Sir Bors, Sir Perceval, and a handful of other knights from Carbonek had already scouted the countryside for danger. Closer to the castle, those who before the Dolorous Stroke had been farmers had been out since sunrise inspecting the ruins of their old homes, and now clustered by this or that pile of stones and timbers, gesturing or pacing out new foundations. Many of the men were too old now to hammer stone and fell timber, but their tall sons, grown in exile, multiplied their former strength. The village would rise soon.

Mounted on ponies or rambling on foot, the adventurers followed the stream down the valley beneath summer leaves.

Blanchefleur rode for the first mile or two. Ahead she glimpsed Perceval, armed for safety's sake and newly mounted on one of three horses provided, as he had explained last night, when he, Galahad, and Bors had left the white ship. Branwen, also pony-mounted, bumped along beside him chattering like a magpie. He laughed and talked and never looked back, or reined in, to speak to Blanchefleur. She tried not to care.

Instead, at the first opportunity she left the pony to a walker with tiring feet, and dropped to the back to speak to Nerys.

"Isn't it lovely down here?"

"Yes," Nerys said.

"The fruit-trees!"

"Yes."

"The wild roses!"

"Yes."

Blanchefleur tried to think of something else to say. Instinct had always warned her not to tread too close to a subject of grief. Only a very close friend could presume to share one's woes. But who was Nerys's friend, if not herself?

So she murmured, "Are you going to be all right?"

Nerys smiled very sheepishly. "Yes."

Heartened, Blanchefleur slipped her arm through her old companion's, and they walked on in amicable silence for a little way.

"I thought about it," Nerys said. "And then I was very ashamed of myself, because I stood there in Sarras, and asked for a sign. How many of the living have seen that City? To have stood in those streets is itself a sign."

Blanchefleur smiled. But after a moment she said, "I wish I found the events of yesterday as easy to understand as you do. The Grail Knight is dead. All our hopes. And only us left."

Nerys looked at her. Was there a glint of laughter at the back of those grey eyes? But of course, Nerys had seen uncertain victories before. And she had seen the hope that followed far more tragic defeat.

Blanchefleur blushed a little and said, "You're right."

Nerys smiled.

A little past midday they stopped to eat in a sunny meadow on the hillside. Blanchefleur distributed the food, and as they received, the others dispersed across the clearing in scattered, chattering groups until at last she and Perceval sat *tête-à-tête* over the empty baskets.

Blanchefleur ate in what she thought was silent awkwardness, but Perceval seemed not to know the meaning of the word. "What is this marvellous contrivance?" he asked, looking at his food.

"It's a sandwich. Didn't you have any in Gloucestershire?"

"I believe not." He took another bite and chewed slowly, eyes narrowed toward the hills. "Remarkable. Like a trencher, but with two trenchers. Do you know, these could be useful for quests."

"That's what we used them for," said Blanchefleur. "Well, not that we ever went on *quests*."

They sat for a while in silence, and then, between his first sandwich and his second, Perceval said, "You heard my adventures last night. Tell me yours. How have you fared in Carbonek?"

She thought back over the last eighteen months and shook her head. "It was not half so interesting as your story. Except for Morgan."

"Morgan? You had trouble with Morgan le Fay?"

"In Sarras."

She told him everything except Morgan's memories, and the things they signified—that Arthur was the father of Morgan's child; that he had manipulated his deadliest enemy against his own kingdom. It never occurred to her to voice them. Until they were backed with better currency than the word of Morgan of Gore, let them lie silent, gnawing on the edges of her mind.

None of the other explorers seemed in any hurry to move on from the drowsy meadow. Blanchefleur took her time over the tale, and Perceval—lying back with eyes shut against the sun's glare—at length stirred and said: "This interests me, Morgan's story about a master. You disbelieved her?"

"I did, when I found out she wanted the Grail. After she stabbed me, I was not so sure. She did seem desperate."

"I can go to Gore and ask questions, maybe." Perceval lay still a moment longer, brushed away a fly, and said: "Did she chance to mention the name *Mordred?*"

"Never. Who is that?"

Perceval drew breath to answer, but at that instant Heilyn came and said, "Will we go further down the river, before the sun sinks?"

"By all means," said Perceval. Heilyn went to collect the others. Blanchefleur stretched and then began gathering up baskets and discarded cloaks. Perceval went to help her.

She asked, "How long will you stay here, at Carbonek?"

He grinned. "As long as you want me to. Command me!"

There was the old Perceval, the one she knew so well. So he had not forgotten her after all. She laughed and teased: "But I thought you had errantry and questing to do. Do not stay another moment on my account."

He laughed and stood and offered her his free hand to help her rise. "Oh, lady, be kind."

They were the same words he had used so long ago on the terrace at Kitty's party, and Blanchefleur caught her breath. Kind! That was exactly what she had not been. For one companionable hour she had forgotten the bitter penitence of her sleepless nights. It all rushed back to her now and she looked up at him with all her regret in her eyes.

"I'll try," she whispered, in such a meek voice that she expected him to laugh at her. But instead, he replied in a voice just as soft.

"I am glad, for I have need of your kindness. There is something I must tell you."

She dropped her head and put her hand in his. They went together to where the horses stood, and he buckled the baskets on in silence and took the cloaks from her and tossed them over a pony's saddlebow. Then he took her arm and pulled her deeper into the trees, away from her chattering friends, where his own grey horse stood tethered to a chestnut tree. He reached across, past Blanchefleur, and knotted his fingers into the mane.

She willed her dry mouth to work. "What did you name him?"

"Glaucus."

"Well chosen," she said, and lifted her hand to rub the horse's neck.

The others were mounting up. Some of the ponies had already turned to plod back down the path to the river. Perceval cast them a glance and turned back to Blanchefleur, his hand tightening in the mane. He said, "I told you something, last night, about the Disinherited Damsel."

She traced her fingers through the dusty grey coat under her hand. "You did."

"You didn't hear everything."

In another moment he would confess, and she didn't want to hear him tell it. "You kissed her. Didn't you?"

"How—"

"I saw it one night when I was dreaming."

Branwen's voice came drifting through the leaves. "Blanchefleur!"

"We're coming," she called back. She looked Perceval in the eyes for the first time since he had offered his hand and saw that he had blushed red to the roots of his hair.

But he didn't move, and the determination in him never flickered. "Another moment and the Quest would have been lost. And Hell would indeed have taken its tithe of me."

Glaucus shifted away from them. Perceval's gaze broke at last; he seemed to realise for the first time how he was looming over her. He straightened and stared at his fingers, smoothing out the horse's mane.

"Damsel, now you know how to think of me."

She had to say the right thing, or anything could happen. One unguarded look, and this had come. Now what? If she forgave him, what would he say then?

She wasn't ready.

"Damsel?"

She looked up and laughed and turned up a palm. "It was a fiend. It might have happened to anyone."

He shook his head. "To Galahad?"

She kept her voice light. "You're sorry for it now. Don't do it again."

"By heavenly grace, I will not." For a moment he looked his gratitude. Then, to her relief, he lit up with mischief. "So you *do* mind." He swung into the saddle and held out his hand to her.

"I don't have to mind to tell you not to do it again." She stepped up and landed behind him.

"Oh, do you not? Shall I *make* you mind?"

"Why, you couldn't *possibly!* You're not heartless enough."

He threw his head back and laughed. "How right you are. Do you know, I might be insulted, but I have just achieved the Grail Quest. Would you love me if I was wicked?"

"Not a bit."

"Just as I feared."

SIR PERCEVAL AND SIR BORS LEFT Carbonek two days later.

The day after the ramble in the valley, Perceval asked to see Blanche-fleur, and she led him from the solar to her chamber, the one that had once been Elaine's, to speak alone. Blanchefleur saw Branwen's smile as they went, and groaned inwardly. Ready or not, it was too late to stave off the inevitable. And while part of her was laughing and singing because this moment had come, everything most cautious and most foresighted in her had dug in terrified feet and refused to move. Now, as she settled into her chair by the empty fireplace, holding distaff and spindle like a shield before her, she wondered which of them would win the tug-of-war that was her will.

Perceval lounged against her window, thumbs stuck into his belt, easy and indolent in the warm morning. Looking at him, it was hard to believe that he had faced a giant in the burning wreck of her home, or spent so long wandering in the most perilous parts of Britain, or made a name for himself even among the heroes of the Table.

But his voice was businesslike as he said, "Bors and I will ride back to Camelot soon with Heilyn. If you mean to come, best come now, with three of us to guard you."

"I hardly know," she said. "I think I had rather wait for the King to send for me."

"How so?"

Blanchefleur, spinning, picked her words slowly. "He may wish to pre-pare for my coming. Nerys said he hoped that guarding the Grail would be a way for me to prove my right to Logres, in case anyone disputed it. Well, I have guarded the Grail. Tell him about it, and let him send for me when he is ready." She smiled at him. "Besides, I don't know if Heilyn told you, but on the strength of becoming your squire, he asked Branwen to marry him."

"Oh, he mentioned it," said Perceval, grinning.

"She and her mother will travel to Camelot together by winter at the latest. I can ride with them."

"Still. I hardly like leaving you here, so far away, in such an uncertain world."

But just when she expected him to press the matter further, he changed the topic: "Do you remember when we met in the Great Hall below for the first time?"

Her hands fell idle. "I remember it."

"I said I would serve you a year and a day. Lady, it has been longer than that, and I have not always served you as faithfully as I should, but there is no lady in the world I would rather serve. Will you allow me to go on as I have?"

She suddenly feared that was all he wanted, and a stab of mingled disappointment and relief went through her. "Yes. Yes, of course."

She began to spin in a final sort of way, but Perceval did not take the hint. He walked over and, gently but firmly, took the spindle and distaff away. "Blanchefleur," he said, and his voice was so serious that she knew it was coming.

She stared at the floor by his feet. "What is it?"

"I have leave to ask you to marry me."

She did not look up or speak, and he dropped to a crouch so that she was forced to look at him.

"When King Pelles dies, if I live so long, Carbonek will be mine. I am no longer landless. And I love you best of all ladies in the world. I do not deny that at first mine was a boy's fancy. But I know both you and myself better than I did before, and I have all a man's devotion to offer you."

Blanchefleur did not speak. Only the tension in her shoulders snapped tight. But there was more at stake here than her own happiness, and she clung to silence like a lifeline. If he guessed what she felt, would he hear what she had to say?

He was still looking into her face, and a quick play of hope and fear passed through his eyes.

"Will you not give me an answer?"

"I cannot," she said at last.

"Why not?"

"Please," she said, rising from her chair and walking to the window, where she gulped a long slow breath to calm herself, "will you allow me a little more time to decide?"

"*Time?*"

"You—" She fought down the eager half of her and tried again, more stiffly. "You will admit that your fancy, as you call it, began long before I was inclined to welcome it."

He was silent for a moment. "You mean you do not love me yet?"

She could not bring herself to a lie of that magnitude. "Oh, no, no, it's…"

He moved toward her, and his purposeful step spurred her into speech.

"It's my birth," she said, turning back to him. "I cannot agree to marry you if I do not know who I am."

Perceval almost looked offended. "That! It cannot matter to me. It's you I love, not your pedigree. And here in Carbonek, I can offer you a home and comfort even if Logres should not want you."

He never looked more like his father than now, she thought. Sir Gawain, whose titanic temper stirred so easily even against friends and allies. How angry would he be if Perceval's wife, the purported Heir of Logres, whom he loved for his King's sake, should turn out to be a pretender?

"Perceval," she pleaded, "I only ask for time. I am not saying no. Let me find out for sure who I am, and then ask me again and see what I say."

He frowned. "Why should it make any difference? It cannot to me."

"I'm afraid…"

She could not finish the sentence. Not to the son of Sir Gawain. "Oh, Perceval, we are both young. What difference does a year or two make?"

"It makes a great deal of difference to me," he said. "I may not be alive in a year or two to ask you again."

Blanchefleur's stomach turned over. "Why, are you ill?"

"Ill? No." He looked at her in bafflement. "But you know how I live my life. By the sword and the lance. Sooner or later, I make no doubt, I will die by the sword, or by the lance. You ask for more time," he went on, softening, "and God knows that if I knew I had it, I would give it. But we may have so little time left."

A slow cold shiver ran down her neck. To her, Perceval, who faced death so readily with steel and laughter, had never seemed entirely mortal. "That did not occur to me," she managed to say at last. "But even so, I had rather lose you in waiting than act in foolish haste and regret it, perhaps for many years."

"I see neither foolishness nor haste in this," said Perceval, "and little reason to suppose you anything but what you are."

"But after what Elaine told me, before she died, I am no longer sure of myself. Maybe not now, but once, perhaps, Lancelot and my mother…"

Perceval shook his head. "I grant that. But I still say that I will have you, no matter whose daughter you are."

"It might not matter to you," she said, "but it might matter to others."

She might have told him who then, if he had not flushed dark and cried, "Others? What others? Who would dare—let any man raise his voice against my wife, and I will ram—"

"Don't say it," she cried in distress.

Perceval sighed, unclenched his fists, and turned away, running his hands through his hair. When he looked back, his voice was gentle.

"I must arrive at an understanding with you. For the last time, will you marry me? Say yes if you wish. Say no if you wish. But do not ask me to wait."

Blanchefleur felt inexpressibly weary. So this was the meeting in Carbonek after the glorious achievement of the Grail for which she had waited so long.

"Please don't…"

"I am asking you. Now. And I think you want to say yes."

She was wretchedly aware that she must have made some terrible mistake. But she could not put her finger either on what it was, or on how it could be repaired. So she said the only thing she could think of.

"No. My answer is no."

Part III

The · Shadow - blade

28

Now the day comes near and near
I feel its hot breath, and see it clear,
How strange it is and full of fear;
And I grow old waiting here,
Grow sick with pain of Guenevere,
My wife, that loves not me.
Swinburne

In the cold pre-dawn Blanchefleur tucked knees beneath chin and watched Nerys fold her blankets for the last time.

"Will you be safe travelling alone?" Blanchefleur spoke in a whisper, for on another couch in a corner of the room Branwen sprawled beneath a pile of bedclothes, dead to the world, and in these last minutes Blanchefleur longed to have her oldest friend to herself.

Nerys came over to sit on Blanchefleur's bed while she combed her long black hair. "I think so."

"I don't like it," Blanchefleur said. "No news from Camelot, and all those stories of disappearing travellers."

"I am riding west, not south," Nerys said, her pale fingers coming and going like moongleams in the dark cloud of her hair. "The road to the Apple Isle is long and chancy, but it will not take me near the Silver Dragon."

"They call him Saunce-Pité. He is only one man. Why doesn't the Table do anything about him?"

Nerys teased apart a knot, too busy to bother answering what they both knew—that neither of them could tell what the Table might be doing. Blanchefleur pulled the covers closer around her shoulders and said:

"I wish you were not going to Avalon."

Nerys said, "The rest of my people must know what I saw in Sarras. Now that the Quest is done, it is only a matter of time before the King sends for you. You no longer need my protection, or my counsel."

"Oh, Nerys," Blanchefleur said gratefully. "But can't I persuade you to stay? I will never have as much experience and wisdom as you. And I'm not safely home yet. Perceval went away at the beginning of summer, and we are still waiting to hear from the King."

Nerys reappeared from behind the sable curtain of her hair. "Some business must be keeping them. Unless the King's messengers have fallen afoul of Saunce-Pité."

"Your people can open doorways in space and time. Can't you get me to Camelot, Nerys?"

Nerys shook her head. "The elf-keys open doors between worlds. I can only take you out of Britain altogether."

She raked her hair to the back of her head and fixed it with a long silver pin. "Well! I am ready, and there goes Dame Glynis down the passage."

But Nerys lingered, clouding the air with thought. Blanchefleur waited. She knew that look, and braced herself.

Nerys said: "Blanchefleur, may I give you advice before I go?"

"Of course."

"If you see Sir Perceval again, treat him more kindly."

Blanchefleur felt her face grow hot. It was the first time the subject had arisen between them since she first told Nerys why Perceval and Bors had left the castle so soon, six months before.

"Oh, Nerys. I *had* to tell him no."

"No man can be toyed with in that fashion. Appeal to him, give your reasons, but either let him decide for both of you, or go your own way and let him go his."

"I thought it for the best."

Nerys saw the look on her face and said:

"I have pondered whether to say this. But I know you refused him against every inclination, and that you have been silent and melancholy since, and that despite the answer you gave him you still count the days until you see him again. You told him you would not wed him: Be not surprised if he takes you at your word."

Blanchefleur stared at her knees, drawn up under her chin. She supposed Perceval might eventually seek another lady. But what most worried her these days were his words at their last meeting in this very room—"Sooner or later, I make no doubt, I will die by the sword, or by the lance…"

She threaded her fingers together and said in a small voice, "I asked him to wait until I was ready. If he could only be patient!"

"I know, Blanche." She felt the wing-beat of the fay's sympathy in the air. "But he offered you an impatient man. If you wanted him, you should have said yes. If you do not want him, you must cease this pining."

Over against the far wall, Branwen shifted and sighed and sat up, pushing hair out of her face. Nerys stood, fastening her cloak at her shoulder.

"Consider this my last counsel to you, and think on it when I am gone."

Blanchefleur looked up, glad to put the conversation behind them. "You'll come back one day and see us?"

Nerys hesitated, but then a smile shone across her face. "Yes. I promise it. Look out your window on a morning in spring, ten or twenty years hence, and perhaps you'll see me coming."

"Twenty years! So long?" Blanchefleur sighed, and reached for a warm tunic to pull over her smock. "Oh, Nerys, I grudge every day of it."

The three of them went downstairs to say their final farewells in the Carbonek courtyard. And then there was nothing to do but stand in the gate and watch as the fay's dark figure dwindled on the road up the valley.

At last Nerys went over the crest of a slope in the road and was gone. Branwen stirred and said, "There are only the two of us now."

The words might have been wistful if not for her cheery voice. Blanchefleur felt a quick rush of affection for her. When the world frowned, Branwen went on smiling. There was a heart of steel under all that froth and bubble.

"You must be missing Heilyn," she said with a twinge of sympathy.

Branwen sighed. "Oh, Blanchefleur, you cannot guess how much."

Blanchefleur thought of Perceval and said to herself: Maybe I can. Aloud she said, "Never fear, he will come back for you one day soon."

"I hope so," said Branwen. "But he has chosen a dangerous life. I would have it no other way, but I fear for him."

Blanchefleur thought of Perceval again.

She sat in the solar spinning, and the thread humming between her fingers was fine and even, good enough to be dyed berry red or peacock blue and woven into woollen broadcloth for cloaks or tunics. It was the first really cold day of winter, a week or so after Nerys's departure, and on the hearth a fire was lit. As usual, Blanchefleur's attention wandered from the thread she spun to the window that looked out on the long pale road. She drifted from chair to window once or twice. The third time, there were two riders.

"Someone is coming," she called breathlessly. "He and his man both wear red, bright as blood."

"A knight, then," Branwen said.

Blanchefleur watched them come closer. She knew the same thought was humming in both their minds, but she said: "If he's a traveller he won't come here. He probably stayed the night at Case and had an early start. He'll keep going, maybe up to the Scots' land."

"Maybe as far as Orkney!" Branwen spoke lightly, but her words brushed close enough to their hopes to silence both of them.

"He's coming in the gate," Blanchefleur cried at last.

"Do you see his shield?"

Gold and gules. "It's Sir Perceval." Blanchefleur was surprised how normal her voice sounded.

Branwen flew to the window. Blanchefleur returned to her seat and went on spinning. The thread ran smooth between her fingers for a long time before the door opened behind her. Then the spindle leapt from her fingers and fell with a soft thump into the reeds on the floor. She reached to pick it up, but then thought better of it and rose to her feet and turned, looking at Perceval.

He had all his lean brown limbs and both his brown eyes. Something that had been pulled tight with worry in the back of her mind slackened in relief. But he was coiled tense himself, and spoke without greeting or preamble: "Lady Blanchefleur, we must leave at once. How soon can you be ready?"

Blanchefleur gripped the back of her chair. "What's wrong?"

He looked around at the others in the solar who sat motionless, staring. Then he bowed his head and said, "The Queen stands trial for her life."

For a moment Blanchefleur felt as though the floor had opened up beneath her. In the midst of this she heard her voice saying, "Within the hour, or sooner. Branwen, have Dame Glynis put up food and send to the stable for our horses."

"Don't leave without me," Branwen was already on her feet and moving to the door.

"Not if you are ready." Blanchefleur turned back to Perceval, almost pleadingly, conscious of the pain she had caused him last time they met. "I won't be long."

In her own room, she bundled a change of clothes, her comb, and some other necessities into a saddlebag while Branwen fluttered in and out with questions and suddenly-remembered last-minute tasks. At the last moment, only because it was the strangest and finest thing she owned, Blanchefleur dug into a chest and took out the obsidian knife, and tucked it into the saddlebag. Then she went downstairs.

In the courtyard they were saddling Florence, and a pony for Branwen. King Pelles was there to bid them farewell, and the rest of the Carbonek folk clustered around them: Branwen's mother, Heilyn's parents, Dame Glynis, and others whom she had come to know and love, and must now leave behind for another new life.

King Pelles said, "Lady of the Grail, in a happy hour you came to shelter under my roof. Go from it with God's favour."

She curtseyed to him and took her leave of the others. Perceval was waiting for her when she turned, and took her saddlebag without speaking, and helped her to mount. Then the four of them turned and went down the valley.

Blanchefleur turned once to see the tower of Carbonek which she had first seen shining with Grail-light in a desolate valley on a night of fear. Today it stood bare and homely in the winter sun, and the light of Sarras no longer shone in its windows. But it heartened her like a sight of the field of an old victory.

She urged Florence, sleepy and slow after two idle years, into a trot and drew level with Perceval. "Please. Will you tell me what has happened?"

He kept his eyes narrowed on the road ahead. "Surely. But let it not delay us. We have little enough time, and the wild is full of dangers. If you can bear it, we must ride through the night."

"I'll bear it."

"Good." His forehead crinkled in thought. "So, the Queen was found with Sir Lancelot in her chamber."

Something had plucked her heart out of her chest. "What?"

"Well, this is the way of it. There was a poisoning. Camelot," he added, "is not what it was. So many of us never returned from the Grail Quest, and the new generation knows not its father."

"A poisoning, go on."

"One of the pages tried to poison my father," he said with a sigh. "God knows why. Some imagined slight. But the dose went astray, and slew a knight of Gaul. This was at a banquet given in his honour by the Queen, and the Gauls blamed her. In the trial by combat, Sir Lancelot fought for her, and won. Only then did the page confess.

"That was when Sir Lancelot returned to Camelot. After the Grail Quest, he kept clear of us for months. Perhaps it was the shame of not achieving the Quest. Or perhaps he wished to kill his love for the Queen before he saw her again. Nevertheless, when the need arose, my cousin Mordred sent him word of the Queen's plight, and he returned in the nick of time."

"Then she has had one narrow escape already."

Perceval nodded. "It was a knightly and courteous deed of Mordred's to send for Lancelot. During the Quest, they say, Mordred was better than a right hand to the King's council. Then the King made him a member in the autumn, but the Queen threw all her influence against him. Of course, he may have aided her from policy, not love. But Lancelot defended the Queen, and the truth came out in the end, and all was well.

"Until, a week ago, my father's youngest brother Agravain claimed he had heard the Queen and Sir Lancelot in the garden, making an assignation."

"And? Was he telling the truth?"

"We have only his word; the Queen denies it. When Agravain went to the King with the news, privately, the King laughed and told Agravain to take Lancelot in the Queen's room at the appointed time—if Lancelot was there to take."

"Oh," said Blanchefleur, perceiving the rest of the story in a single flash.

"Yes. Agravain surrounded himself with a band of knights—for the most part young men, who have joined since the Quest." Perceval shook his head. "They seem like raw boys to me. Poor lads! Sir Lancelot was there, of course. But even in peace-garb, unarmed, he was more than a match for them. He got a sword and cut his way through them, galloped to his castle of Joyeuse Gard, and left Camelot full of blood and uproar."

"And you? Were you there?"

"I had ridden with the King to Caerleon-on-Usk." Perceval shook his head. "Agravain could not have chosen a worse moment, or a more lunatic manner. Had he gone alone and unarmed, Sir Lancelot would have treated him courteously. But met with naked blades and armed men? It was folly! And blood was spilled in the city itself." Perceval glanced at Blanchefleur, grim foresight in his eyes. "It was new blood he shed. But I fear a rift has opened within the Table, one it will be difficult to heal."

Blanchefleur shifted in the saddle. The day's end—whenever it came—

would leave her whole body aching. And there were long days of travel yet to come.

Not that it mattered. Not that anything else in the world mattered except that Logres was trembling and the pale and smiling queen of her earliest memory was in peril of her life. "You say that Agravain claims he heard the Queen and Sir Lancelot speaking in the garden."

"Yes."

"And the Queen denies it, but he *did* find Lancelot there with her."

"She says he came, but she never sent for him."

"Then there are only two possibilities," Blanchefleur said. Her breath hung on the cold winter air like smoke, and she shivered. "One, Agravain is telling the truth, and the Queen is guilty. Two, he is lying."

"Yes."

"If he is lying," Blanchefleur said, "then his behaviour was not lunatic. It was subtle—horribly subtle."

"And we are dealing with a cunning and dangerous enemy."

They rode on a few paces in silence before Perceval frowned and said, "At least, that is what I would say, if this was not *Agravain*. But I would not have imagined him capable of making and executing such a plot."

"You mean, being your father's brother?"

"I mean his character." Perceval flung up a hand. "He is not subtle. Bursting in upon Lancelot with an army is very much his way, as is being surprised and offended when the operation fails to run smoothly."

"I see." But it was an unconvincing excuse to her ears.

"I know what you are thinking," Perceval said. "To tell the truth, I could think so too. But with the blood of the Table soaking the city of the Table, the words of accusation against my own kin go sour in my mouth. Well, and so the Queen stands trial for adultery and, if she is found guilty, will go to the fire."

Another dull pang struck her. "And the King allows it?"

"He must do justice, even on his own wife, Blanchefleur. That is why Sir Lancelot and not he has always been her champion. A judge cannot argue a prisoner's case before himself."

"But Sir Lancelot did the killing. Why do they not deal with that?"

"They will. In time." Perceval fell silent. "But this matter has grieved the King beyond measure. I never thought I would see him despair."

Tears sprang to her eyes. "He can't find her guilty."

Perceval said: "If she is, he will."

Blanchefleur had not even allowed herself to consider this possibility.

She did now. "He will be forced to condemn his own wife to death. Sir Lancelot will never return to the Table. The prophecy of Merlin at my birth will fail. Logres will fall, and no one will be left to mourn her. And he despairs...Oh, Perceval...he believes it. He believes Agravain."

Perceval compressed his lips. When he spoke, it was almost in a whisper. "Yes."

So this was what she returned to Camelot to find: despair and disinheritance. The thought struck another cold shaft through her. "Perceval! Why are you taking me to Camelot? Why now?"

Perceval said: "I am not. Unless the Queen is already acquitted when we come there, I am taking you further, to Joyeuse Gard."

"To Lancelot! Why?" Because she was his daughter? "—*Why?*"

"I came to Carbonek without the King's knowledge," he told her. "My father said: The Heir of Logres, she should be here. But not at court, not until her position is assured. The Queen will scarcely be condemned, but if she is she will not go to the fire. Lancelot will bear her to La Joyeuse Gard. Take the Heir of Logres there."

Blanchefleur reined Florence to a stop. "But—to *Joyeuse Gard?*"

They were out of sight of Carbonek now, a little further down the valley where the road turned south, lifting into the hills. Above, a hawk screamed in the sky.

Perceval circled back to her. "Only if the Queen is condemned. Come, it's a long road to Eboracum."

Branwen's chatter and the murmuring counterpoint of Heilyn's answers came closer; the two of them passed, single file, and went on up the road.

She let Florence follow them, but she said to Perceval as they moved on, "Do you not see? If I go to Lancelot, everyone will think him my father."

Perceval laughed and shook his head. "Be at ease! The Queen will be acquitted. Or so my father thinks."

"God grant it." Blanchefleur shivered in the wind. "But if the Queen is condemned—"

"If she is condemned, my father said, then until the King can be brought to pardon her she will need all the comfort we can give."

"He said that?" Her voice warmed despite her misgivings.

Perceval grinned at her. "He is a good and kind man, Blanchefleur."

"Kinder than I thought." Kinder than herself. In her concern for the King it had not even occurred to her to think of the Queen's—of her *mother's*—feelings. Even now, she could not stir in herself more than a faint shadow of the pity she felt for the King... He was in so much despair at this betrayal. Could she add another blow to this one? Could she run in need to his rival?

Perceval said, "In this woe every road is equally dark. But I am content to do my father's will."

"What about *my* father?" Blanchefleur struggled to keep her voice calm. "What is *his* will? Surely he would have me with him. In Camelot." So that he could—

—Kill her? As he intended to do to her mother? She clenched the reins, blindsided by the thought. If Elaine had guessed rightly, if Morgan's word could be trusted, if she was ill-born and the King was the enemy, then he would condemn the Queen to death and she, who could not be proven one thing or another, might be murdered to clear the way for a new heir.

Because there was another heir, wasn't there? The baby in Morgan's memory.

"Blanchefleur? What's amiss?"

Perceval's voice broke into her thoughts. She glanced across at him and saw the big capable hands, one riding the hilt at his left hip and the other loosely clasped on his reins. Saw the bulk of shoulder and depth of chest that had come to him in the years since he first as a boy stood as the only wall between her and danger. And saw streaming like a banner above him the love of the man who had first sent him to protect her.

Arthur the King.

"Nothing's amiss," she said, and laughed at her fears.

"I said," he went on, "that my father thinks the King would liefer have you with the Queen."

She bit her lip consideringly and was astonished to find that she agreed. "I suppose he might. But what do *you* think?"

"I trust my father's judgement."

"But you think it's risky. Don't you?"

"Because of what people will think?"

"Yes."

Perceval fell silent. "You stand or fall by your mother," he said at last. "If she is acquitted, you will go to Camelot in all honour. If she is condemned, then there is no worse moment to bring you to court. Far better join your mother in Joyeuse Gard and wait for her restoration."

Just ahead of them, Heilyn shifted in the saddle and turned.

"Why go to either place? Why not take the lady to a nunnery?"

Perceval wrinkled his brow. "Is there one nearer than Almesbury?"

Heilyn shook his head. "You know the land better than I. Or find a monastery, one that will take women."

"It might do," said Perceval. Blanchefleur's heart sank to hear the hesitance in his voice.

"Please. Of course I don't want to abandon my mother. But surely it would stir up trouble to go to Joyeuse Gard?"

Perceval smiled at her. "We must ride to Astolat first. My father will send a man to bring word how the verdict falls. By God's mercy, we shall have no need of Lancelot."

And in herself she moaned "Too late, too late!"
Till in the cold wind that foreruns the morn,
A blot in heaven, the Raven, flying high,
Croaked, and she thought, "He spies a field of death."
Tennyson

Perceval led them south throughout the day and long into the night. At last they saw a wall rising out of the starlight above them and tumbled from their mounts to sleep a few hours rolled in blankets within the gate of Eboracum. When dawn came, despite King Aglovale's offers of rich fare and lodging, they mounted fresh horses and took the road.

"Was he going to send for me, the King?" Blanchefleur asked Perceval when they stopped to divide some waybread. "Before any of this happened?"

"Yes, when the land was quieter," Perceval said. "But there was so much trouble with the wild men, and with the men of the Silver Dragon. He meant to march north to sweep them out of the land."

"In a body? Could not a single knight of the Table deal with them? When we first heard of Saunce-Pité, three months ago, men spoke of a petty brigand."

Perceval nodded. "That he was, two or three years ago, when I fought him. The King gave him mercy, believing him capable of repentance."

She thought: Why could he not show the same mercy to his own wife? But the Queen was only accused, not yet condemned, and she would have the chance to face her accusers in the open court, and defend her innocence against the world.

Perceval went on speaking of Saunce-Pité. "Not until the Quest did I discover his reborn villainy, but I could do nothing against his men.

Whence these new tactics? To gather and train a body of footmen to fight as one, under a unified command, is a thing we have not seen since the old wars against Rome or the rebel kings. Sir Breunis has forsaken the rules of battle: he sends ants against lions, but in overwhelming strength."

"He is a real danger, then?" Blanchefleur asked.

Perceval shook his head. "Not an insuperable one. Fighting together, it was easy to win the war with Rome. Breunis can pick off lonely knights, but he will never stand against the full strength of the Table." He sighed. "If the Table were ever again able to ride north."

Day followed day and only the land changed around them. Blanchefleur fretted at their slow pace, but Perceval pushed on steadily and patiently, for he knew exactly how fast their horses could travel and live. Blanchefleur did not complain aloud, but as the miles rolled away behind them and the sun wheeled overhead, her stomach clenched harder and harder, so that with each day it was a little more difficult to choke down her food.

One morning she awoke and found that Branwen, who usually slept curled into her side, was gone. She, Heilyn, and Perceval stood overlooking the valley below. Hushed snatches of their voices blew back to her on the wind.

Blanchefleur went to stand beside them. Above, in the colourless sky of a winter dawn, black birds drifted on the chilling wind.

"If I had a bow—" Heilyn said.

"There are too many of them," said Perceval.

Blanchefleur rubbed sleep from her eyes. "What's wrong?"

"The ravens have been following us since Carbonek," Heilyn explained. "But this morning there are dozens of them."

Perceval pointed. "Look."

One of the ravens broke away from the circling mass and flew south down the valley. Blanchefleur remembered a night in Gore in the rain and felt a shiver crawl up her spine. "Morgan."

"Maybe," Perceval said. "And God grant it be none worse. Let us go on and take the adventure that comes."

Their path would have lain south, down the valley at their feet. Instead Perceval took them immediately west, across the hills. The raven army did not follow them, but from then on Blanchefleur was always aware of at least one black bird fluttering through the trees behind them.

It was on the last dingy, foggy day of the journey that they met the two knights. They had stopped in a glade, by a spring that had been walled around with stone, to refill water bottles and eat a scanty meal. None of them spoke until Perceval stretched and said:

"The Queen's trial began yesterday, if I count the days right."

Blanchefleur leaned over the stone parapet and stared at her reflection in the still pool. She was as pale and thin-worn as the others, she thought. The journey had not been an easy one for any of them: saddle-galled to the limits of their endurance, lashed by sleet in the hills, driven on relentlessly by anxiety for what might be waiting ahead or following behind.

And Guinevere, the Queen of Logres, stood trial for her life. She stared into her grey, watery reflection and tried to imagine what humiliation might taste like to the cool and proud temper she had felt in her dreams... Far better to sit here, stiff and aching in the cold wild, than wear the name of Guinevere. She stirred and said, "Have we far to travel?"

"No. Astolat lies a few leagues further, in the next valley. Camelot, four or five beyond." Perceval swallowed a last mouthful of waybread and rose to his feet, brushing crumbs from his hands. But then through the misting rain came a jingle of harness and plod of hooves. For a moment there was no other sound in the glade but the chirp of sparrows fighting over crumbs in the grass. Then two knights loomed out of the fog, the foremost carrying a blank shield, and Perceval's hand drifted to the hilt of his sword.

"Get the horses," he said to Heilyn without turning his head.

His tone struck fear into all of them. Heilyn moved at once, scrabbling for trailing reins. The taller knight pushed ahead of his companion and the sight of his device—a blue boar on a field of white—carried Blanchefleur back at once two years to a sunset in Gloucestershire, and the agony of terror she had suffered with each savage blow against the splintering door of the old house. It was Sir Odiar of Gore, Morgan le Fay's champion, who had tried to kill her.

Branwen could have no such memory, but Perceval's voice was portent enough, and perhaps she knew what the blue boar signified. She glanced at Blanchefleur in something approaching panic, and seized her by the elbow. Blanchefleur could not have told why that touch put such heart into her, unless it was the need to show courage enough for two. She hardened her face and rose to her feet, pulling Branwen after.

Sir Odiar was speaking to Perceval. "Sir knight, will you joust?"

"That I will, and gladly." Perceval drew on his gauntlets. Blanchefleur went forward in silence to lace on his helm.

She finished and stepped back. She could not see Perceval's face, but when he thanked her there was something abrupt and almost shy in his voice. She stared at the featureless iron and felt more keenly than ever the distance between them. Now. Now was the time to say what might be the last words he would ever hear from her.

"Fight," she said at last. "Win."

The words came out harsh with fear. Perceval swung away from her and said to Heilyn, "If I fall, you are the protector of these ladies, just as I am."

The squire nodded and, wasting no time on words, held out Perceval's stirrup. Blanchefleur looked from one to the other, worry itching in her throat. They were both so young, so very young. In the kindly world of her upbringing, Heilyn would be a schoolboy, and Perceval at Oxford dreaming up undergraduate rags. Today in Logres, both of them faced wounds and death in earnest.

If only there was a way to repay their sacrifice.

Perceval said: "Mount and be ready to flee if the battle turns against me. And mark well Odiar's companion, that silent knight with the blank shield. I think it will be good, if we meet him under some fairer guise, to know him again."

He swung into the saddle and gripped his spear with a shout. "Ho! I know you, Knight of Gore! What of the Witch of Gore, your mistress? Does she still send you to do her cutthroat work, as she did on a day I recall, in the castle of Gornemant?"

"And I know you, Welsh swineherd, well enough to weary of your babble. I have a debt to repay. Come, let me teach you how men speak, with steel, not mockeries."

"It is a tongue I love!" Perceval said, laughing and laying spear in fewter, and striking spurs into his horse.

The knight of Gore reacted swiftly; his horse gathered into a thunderbolt. Blanchefleur felt her fingernails bite into her palms, and waited with wincing-closed eyes for the crash of meeting. But the thunderstrike shocked them open again: fire flooded her veins and she hissed in one exultant breath.

Perceval's horse was flung back on its haunches by the shock of meeting: its head and shoulders strained up through air thick with shards of spear. Odiar's horse staggered back, almost stumbling to the ground, but the knight wrestled it to its feet, casting aside the splintered truncheon of his lance, fumbling for a new weapon. Perceval flashed out his sword, but Odiar caught up the mace at his saddle-bow and spurred his horse forward.

Morgan's man dealt the first blow, which Perceval fended with his shield and followed with a shrewd thrust. But Sir Odiar evaded the point with a twitch of hand and heel which sent his horse, exquisitely trained, dancing away.

"Lady, lady." Heilyn tugged at Blanchefleur's elbow. He had her horse's reins, and Blanchefleur, tearing her gaze from the combat, saw Branwen already mounted. She climbed to the saddle and turned back to watch the deadly two-rider dance.

Little as she knew of the arts of war, she saw Perceval reel under the hammer-blow of Odiar's mace when he could not turn his horse aside in time, and knew with a twist of her stomach that he was outmatched. Glaucus, his own horse, was still ahead of them at Astolat, where he had left it in return for a fresh mount on the outward journey. She knew what it looked like when man and horse moved together as one with the lightest shift of balance and weight. She saw Odiar doing it now, while Perceval maneuvered clumsily atop a jaded animal that did not know its master.

"Oh, kill his horse!" she groaned.

"That would be ungenerous." Heilyn sounded shocked.

"Ungenerous to whom? He's trying to kill us!"

She never knew if Perceval heard her words or not. But with his next blow a shard of steel from Odiar's armour spun through the air and chopped into the ground. Blood glistened on his blade. As Sir Odiar flinched back, Perceval dealt another stroke, lightning-fast, with such a minute backswing that only its effect betrayed what immense power went into it. The blade did no harm to Odiar, but split his shield in two and bit deep into the horse's neck.

"Well hit," gasped Heilyn, and fell silent.

Perceval backed, his breath loud in the sudden quiet. Sir Odiar raked his horse with the spurs, but the animal fell to its knees with a rush of blood and a crooked, broken neck. Odiar stepped to the ground, hefted his mace, and stalked forward without a backward glance at the thrashing horse.

"Cowardly struck," he spat.

"Empty words, coming from a murderer of women," Perceval said with a breathless laugh. And despite the blood trickling down his shield arm, he dismounted with a buoyant step, full of grace.

At last the sun had burned through the morning fog, and the whole forest glittered with water and light. Blanchefleur glanced at Branwen and Heilyn. Branwen had her face hidden, and trembled at every blow. Under level brows, Heilyn's eyes flicked back and forth between the knight of Gore and his companion, the knight with the blank shield who on the other side of the glade paced his dun horse to and fro like a caged lion.

Odiar was upon Perceval at once and they trod to and fro upon the grass—a step forward, a step back, a circle; again they moved like dancers, but Perceval was dodging the great mace now, sure and nimble on his feet. His sword flickered and bit like a fly, better at a longer range, and Sir Odiar soon bled from a half-dozen wounds. But then Perceval ventured in too close, and the mace crashed home, catching him in the hip. Perceval tumbled across the grass. With the same smooth movement he came back up to his feet, but with a dragging left leg. Then the mace fell again, and his shield shivered to pieces. Blanchefleur drew a breath like a sob.

Before she could blink, it was over. Sir Odiar, bleeding and flagging, recovered his blow more slowly and Perceval gathered his strength and was on him at once. His edged weapon, less potent than the mace against plate and mail, found a chink at the knee and slid in. The leg buckled.

Snatching out his poniard, Sir Perceval strode forward and stamped Odiar to the ground with a foot to his chest. With a flash of the knife he freed the man's helm and sent it spinning away. In one last titanic effort the Knight of Gore shouldered up, grabbing for the knife, taking an elbow to the face and then crumpling beneath Perceval's full weight.

Perceval put the poniard to Odiar's throat.

"Yield and cry mercy, sir, and your life is yours until you come before the King's seat for justice."

"I beg you," the knight of Gore ground out between clenched teeth, "not to mock me."

"No mockery, but Christian charity," said Sir Perceval. "Which, as you neither comprehend nor desire—" and skilfully he cut his enemy's throat.

He had not yet straightened when a rush of hooves brought the Silent Knight and a swinging sword upon him. Perceval, taken by surprise and unguarded on the ground, dove aside to save himself. With a shout Heilyn wrestled his horse in front of the ladies and fumbled for his sword. As his hand scrabbled for the hilt, Blanchefleur dug her heels into her mount and danced aside, baiting the attacker away from the unarmed squire, quickening to a canter. The Silent Knight turned his horse as if on a sestertius, and dashed to cut her off. But his path took him past Perceval again, and this time the Knight of Wales was ready. The great blade swung once more, but Perceval ducked to avoid it, reaching up almost at the same moment; hooked fingers around the knight's belt, and plucked him from saddle to ground. At the effort, rings strained and snapped on the mail hauberk across his back.

Blanchefleur, looking back, saw it happen and pulled her horse into a circling trot. She reined in, fell rather than stepped down from the saddle, and ran to Perceval as the stranger rose to his feet at swordpoint, though the blade trembled for sheer weariness.

"What is your name, and whom do you serve?" Perceval grated in a voice Blanchefleur barely recognised.

Heilyn slid down from his horse and came running, sword out, to face the stranger at Perceval's side. The knight went still, as if gathering himself for action. Heilyn tensed. Then the Silent Knight turned and fled, whistling to his horse. At a run, he caught the animal's neck and vaulted to its back. Heilyn shouted and ran, but the knight vanished from the glade and they heard his horse's hooves crashing through the undergrowth to the south.

In the sudden stillness Perceval groaned and fell to his knees.

It took another hour to wash, salve, and bind up all his wounds, though Blanchefleur and Branwen worked with hands made skilful by long hours in the Carbonek infirmary. His shield arm had burst open again along the old line, and was horribly bruised with mail links driven through the leather into the flesh. There was a great bruise on his thigh, too, just inches below the hip.

Perceval looked at it and whistled. "Now God be thanked. He was aiming to crush the hip and sever the artery, but glanced off the thigh. Wort and comfrey will mend this."

Blanchefleur felt sick as she realised how close she had come to losing him. It must have showed on her face, for with an effort at levity he said, " 'Tis nothing; you should have seen the wound I took in my side two years ago at Carlisle."

She cleared her throat. "I'm content looking at this one." She ducked her head and looked for salve in his saddle-bags. Perceval said:

"Heilyn, take Odiar's arms. As soon as I'm bound up, we will ride."

"Already?" Blanchefleur protested. "But look at you!"

"I'll travel easiest while my wounds are green."

She ducked her head again and went back to looking for the salve, but her sight had blurred over. She realised that she was crying even as the first hot tear splashed onto her arm.

Perceval said: "Come now! The last maiden I defended did not weep about it."

Blanchefleur froze. "What?"

"No, she combed her hair and then told me her father was very rich, and she hinted at a comfortable life as his son-at-law."

He laughed, but Blanchefleur's stomach turned over. "What did you say?"

"I told her I would seriously consider it."

"Did you?"

"Yes, I told her that. Then I gave her into Sir Kay's keeping and I rode for my life."

He laughed again and Blanchefleur was relieved enough to laugh with him. But when she found the salve, she handed it to Branwen and went away to pack the saddlebags, scrubbing at the tears in her eyes.

THEY SAW NO MORE RAVENS. BEFORE nightfall they reached Astolat, and were met in the courtyard by a young knight with a bow in his hand and a horn at his hip.

"Sir Perceval." He caught the knight's bridle. "Grace of heaven, man, who did you offend?"

"The Blue Boar." Perceval kicked his right leg over the horse's withers and winced to the ground. He glanced up and down the young knight and said in a voice that raised the hairs on the back of Blanchefleur's neck, "Were you out riding, Sir Bernard?"

The knight bowed his dark head. "I went hunting to the south."

"I recall seeing a fine rouncey in your stables. A dun. A good horse to hunt with, I thought."

Sir Bernard shook his head and reached out to rap on the stable door with his bow. "No. I took your Glaucus, thinking he needed the use." When the door opened, he said, "Bring out the horse, there," and immediately the grey charger, a little foamed with sweat, was led out ready-saddled. When he saw Perceval, the great horse dropped its head and butted against him with a nicker of greeting.

Perceval staggered back a few steps, laughing through a gasp of pain. When he spoke again to Bernard, his voice rang warm as ever. "And my father's messenger?"

Bernard shook his head. "Not yet."

Perceval glanced up at the westering sun, and then turned to Blanchefleur. "If we press on, we may meet the rider on the road."

"Press on?" Bernard glanced from Blanchefleur to Perceval. "You can hardly stand."

Blanchefleur questioned the Knight of Wales with a raised eyebrow.

Perceval set his jaw. "I can sit a horse."

"It's grown late," she offered, trying to conceal the blind fretful haste driving all her thoughts on, down the road, to Camelot.

"Yes. And my father's man should have come by now."

She gave a tight nod and shifted her aching bones in the saddle. "I have to know."

Bernard of Astolat looked up at her. Sudden recognition dawned across his face and he snatched off his cap and bowed like a lance coming to rest. "Lady of the Grail. Astolat is yours to command."

"Sir, my thanks. We will ride on this night."

Perceval was already unbuckling the saddle-bags from his borrowed horse. "Will you have my squire's horse saddled? We ride in haste."

THE SUN WAS STILL BURNING LOW in the West and they were scarcely a league from Astolat when Perceval, who had been riding in apparent weariness with his head sunk low, suddenly pulled Glaucus into a circle and then halted athwart the road, looking into the forest.

"What is it?" Blanchefleur asked him.

"The road is telling me a tale." At her look of concern a smile cracked his face. "I saw the scuff of horse-hooves on the road. Someone was riding to Astolat when he turned and galloped back the way he had come. Now he has turned aside into the wood. And a horseman rides after him."

Blanchefleur could only blink wearily. "Perceval, please. It's already so late."

But he spurred into the branches before she had finished speaking. Blanchefleur cast a despairing look at Heilyn and Branwen and plunged after him. "What if we miss the messenger?" she called.

Perceval was nowhere to be seen. Blanchefleur reined in, suddenly disoriented. Then she heard his voice.

"Too late."

She rounded the bole of a tree and looked down into a little hollow by a stream where Perceval sat with his shoulders slumped and his head bowed over the crumpled body of a man in the livery of gules and gold. And fixed in his neck, a gay-fletched arrow like the plume of a cap.

265

Blanchefleur's muscles creaked with pain as she slid off her horse and tottered down the slope to Perceval's side. He'd told Sir Bernard he could sit a horse, but at the moment that seemed to take all his strength; his eyes stared sightlessly into the distance. She gritted her teeth and knelt by the body. There was no pouch and no belt on the dead man's trunk, only a little straight slit in his tunic where someone had knifed the leather away.

Perceval said in a very tired and gentle voice, "Not *Bernard*."

Blanchefleur straightened and brushed her hands on her skirt. "You— you think *he*—"

"How should I know?"

"How long has he been with the Table?"

"A year." Perceval sighed. "He has Lamorak's old siege."

The footfall of horses stirred them into action. Perceval kneed his horse around and whipped out his sword. Above, Branwen's voice came drifting through the bare winter branches.

"There they are!"

"Sir?" called Heilyn. "Night is falling."

Perceval sheathed his blade and pulled Blanchefleur up behind him for the ride to the top of the slope where her own horse stood. "Then on."

As NIGHT FELL, FROST DESCENDED FROM a clear sky. Blanchefleur shivered in the chill, feeling that she had gone beyond weariness into extreme old age. She turned her head slowly—was there any part of her body that didn't ache?—and looked at the others. Branwen, huddled wrenlike into her cloak at the rear, met her eyes and managed a wistful smile. Between them, Perceval slumped in the saddle with his eyes closed and his hands slack on the reins. Ahead, Heilyn had taken the lead, his back straight and alert in front of her.

It was a little while before midnight when the road opened out upon wide rolling hills. A river looped through farmland and moated one low hill where a castle stood heaped up over a little town sleeping by its foot. The dim light of a gibbous moon reflected from ice on the castle roofs and struck silver sparks from the grass at their feet.

Heilyn halted them here, beneath the eves of the forest. Perceval jolted upright and whispered, "Let us avoid being seen, if we can."

Blanchefleur trembled in the cold wind. "Then this is—"

"Camelot."

She had dreamed of coming here. Dreamed of coming sulkily, determined to despise what she found. Dreamed of coming with curiosity to discover the beauty that wooed her even in her oldest memories. Dreamed of coming triumphantly, both servant and mistress, to the garden-city that was Sarras-in-the-flesh.

She had not dreamed of stealing past in the dead of night. She had not dreamed of shivering cold, numb feet, grey sky, and a tall stark finger pointed heavenwards from the meadow outside the city wall. She touched Perceval's shoulder and pointed at it wordlessly.

The stake…

No need, then, to ask which way the verdict had fallen.

Its inky shadow stretched across the white grass, fathomless, like the rift that had opened within Logres itself. Had she come so far only to witness the death of what was so strong and fair?

Perceval stirred and said, "Joyeuse Gard." He slung a sidelong glance at the rest of them. "There are no monasteries nearby. And I trust no one else."

Cold and age. Blanchefleur breathed on her fingers and said, "Well, then."

He led them south along the riverside. They forded out of sight of Camelot and reached La Joyeuse Gard a few hours later in the dead of night. Here, as not there, torches blazed and the courtyard swarmed with men preparing arms and horses.

As they dismounted at the door, Perceval offered Blanchefleur his hand. She took it but put no weight on him; he looked as if a breath would blow him away. But he would not go in until he had called the captain of the guard and given their exhausted horses into his care. Then only did he lead them through the door and up the length of the hall to where, in the glow of a lonely lamp, Sir Lancelot motioned his knights back and rose to greet them.

"Welcome, Sir Perceval," said Lancelot. He came around the table and took Blanchefleur's hand. "And the Grail Maiden. Since the return of the Grail Knights there is no lady in Logres held in higher honour."

She glanced sidelong at Perceval. Was that his doing? Apparently so; the corners of his mouth twitched up and she almost heard his silent laughter. Then he turned to Lancelot and the merriment was only a memory. "We saw the stake set up on the meadow at Camelot."

Lancelot nodded. "Gawain sent word it will happen at sunrise. We ride in an hour."

"Let me ride with you."

Sir Lancelot's eyes flickered in surprise, and he looked at Blanchefleur. She lifted her chin and made no sign. Perceval was as battered and weary as he looked, but he knew his limits better than she did.

"Your horse will be saddled," said Lancelot. "But you have travelled and fought hard already. Will you not stay behind and rest?"

"Where is my father?"

"With the King."

"And my uncles?"

"Also with the King."

"Then I will ride with you. My father would wish it. Let it not be said that no son of Orkney rode to his Queen's aid when she was falsely accused. Wake me, of your courtesy, before you ride." And bowing to Blanchefleur, he limped to one of the benches by the wall, stretched himself upon it, and was instantly asleep.

Blanchefleur went to cover him with her cloak. When she returned to the light, she saw Sir Lancelot looking at her.

He did not speak easily; the words seemed dragged from the innermost depths of him. "The lady is true. On my sword, which has never been dishonoured, I swear it."

"Thank you," she said, but when she looked at the young knights behind him and saw that one had turned away and was half laughing, half whispering into the ear of another, the words turned sour in her mouth.

"Either I will bring your mother to you alive," Lancelot swore to her, "or both of us will lie dead before Camelot."

She inclined her head. "I know it."

Maidens had come, ready to lead them away, to sleep. But Sir Lancelot did not break his gaze. "The lady is true," he repeated

"I hear," she said lifelessly, and allowed herself to be taken to a room glowing with fire, where the damsels gave her and Branwen clean smocks and put them to bed.

Toward morning she heard a voice crying *Gareth! Gaheris! Gareth!*

She woke and found that it was dawn and the fire had died; not even a coal was left. For a moment all she could do was lie still, listening to Branwen's even breath beside her. Then she remembered what she had forgotten.

The stake. The cold. The murmuring people. The dawn attack. Blood on the ground. The stake!

She was on her feet, reaching for a cloak, running to the window. But she already knew it was too late. Already the light was stronger than it had been in the vision of Sarras. She had misunderstood, she had missed the warning, and now whatever she had dreamed in Sarras had happened on the meadow outside Camelot, not to herself but to her mother, the Queen of Logres.

Too late.

Blanchefleur sank to her knees. In the cold, she began to shiver.

O madly right and madly left
Sir Launcelot blindly strake,
And helms and heads in sunder cleft,
To reach that deadly stake.

Buchanan

I t was a cold, dim morning. Outside, the frost had gone from the grass and last night's clear sky was veiled by thick cloud that drifted along the watery ground. Blanchefleur turned from the window and went to the foot of her bed to pick up her cloak. It was gone and she frowned for a moment before she recalled that she had left it with Perceval.

Branwen still lay abed; even in sleep there was a happy tilt to the side of her mouth. Blanchefleur dressed quietly, went to the hearth, and kindled a fire, not for the cold but for something to do. It would be hours before Lancelot and his horsemen returned with her mother. She laid the fire clumsily on purpose and kept getting up to coax it as it hovered on the verge of death.

All the same, she was glad when Branwen stirred, groaned, sat up to squint at her, and said:

"Good morning. Have you ever in your life been so saddle-sore? I feel as though horses have been riding all over me, instead of the other way around. Why, what is the matter? Is something wrong?"

Her face must have given her away. Blanchefleur gained time by digging through her bag for her comb. "I do not think any good can have come from last night's riding-out."

Branwen pushed hair out of her eyes and looked at her more closely. "What makes you think so?"

Blanchefleur frowned down at the comb, puzzling how to reply. Branwen rolled out of bed and said, "Speak to me, Blanchefleur, you frighten me. Tell me what has happened."

She replied reluctantly, loath as ever to air her worries. "One day in Sarras, I dreamed of fighting and death around a stake in a meadow. I thought it was something given to me for my own warning, but now I think it was meant for Lancelot. I do not know what is happening at Camelot, but I fear it is something dreadful."

Branwen crooked an eyebrow. "What manner of warning is that? Surely Sir Lancelot knew there would be fighting, or he would have gone alone and unarmed."

Blanchefleur shrugged hopelessly. "I don't know. How long till Terce, Branwen? They can't be back before then."

"An hour, perhaps. Let me fetch breakfast."

THEY WERE WALKING IN THE GREY and dripping castle garden when a trumpet blew and over the grinding of the portcullis they heard a clamour of horse-hooves. The two of them ran inside to the hall, and stood in the shadow of the door watching Sir Lancelot's fifty knights dismounting and unhelming in the courtyard. Blanchefleur looked for Lancelot or Perceval and saw the Knight of the Lake first, and in his strained mouth and hurried step she read confirmation of all her shadowy fears. He came leading a woman by the hand across the threshold of the Great Hall. Blanchefleur saw a rusty black cloak streaked by long gold-and-silver hair, and eyes like lunar seas, dark sleepless stains in a pale face.

Neither of them saw Blanchefleur.

She stared after them until Branwen laid a hand on her arm and gestured toward the courtyard. When she saw Sir Perceval, she thought he had been wounded again, and badly, for his face was gaunt with pain. With limping steps he made his way up to the door where she stood. The eyes he turned upon her were filled with horror.

"Perceval!" she choked, and reached out, but he did not see her hand.

"They are dead," he told her. "Gareth and Gaheris, my kin. And who knows who else."

Blanchefleur groped for words. "How?"

"Unarmed. They were killed in the rush...It was Lancelot."

Blanchefleur tried to speak, but words seemed useless, and before she could think of anything he had gone reeling up the hall to where Sir Lancelot stood.

"They were unarmed!" he shouted into Lancelot's face. "To slay unarmed men—oh, a deed worthy of the flower of knighthood!"

Lancelot's brows knitted, but there was grief in his voice too: "They already had the torches lit, Sir Perceval. I saw nothing else—"

Perceval seized his surcoat in both hands, shoving the Knight of the Lake back, rage-red. "Saw nothing? Saw *nothing*? *You should have!* Do you wield a sword or a broomstick?"

For a moment all the strength went out of him and he was shaking and slackened. Lancelot never broke his calm, and his hands closed like a vise over Perceval's wrists and plucked them from his surcoat. "You know me, Perceval. I should have lost my right hand rather than see it slay one of your kindred—and Gareth, Gareth whom I knighted. Whom I loved."

But Perceval lunged forward again. "I'll have it. I'll have both your hands and your coward head—"

Sir Lancelot stepped back a pace or two and bowed. "When you are stronger, I am at your service," he said, and reached out his hand to the silent Queen, who had stood without moving since Sir Perceval's intrusion. Mechanically, she took his hand and the two of them turned to go.

Blanchefleur hesitated to follow them, looking back to Perceval, who stood with his head flung back but his hands hanging uselessly at his sides and the hot anger on his face dimmed to a pale foreboding.

"I spoke rashly," he grated. "I see the good knights of Logres slaying each other wherever I look. I will not add needlessly to this strife. Until justice is done, let your own dishonoured name reproach you."

Lancelot did not answer, but his back became for a moment very still and quiet. Then he continued toward the stair, and the Queen followed. Perceval looked at Blanchefleur.

"Go to your mother," he told her.

Sir Lancelot led them to the best room in the castle, a snug chamber hung with thick new tapestries and heated by a fire of scented wood. Maidens within busied themselves in pouring a hot bath and setting a light breakfast over the flame of a lamp to warm. When Lancelot and the Queen entered, a stillness fell upon them and they sank to the floor.

"Joyeuse Gard is your realm now," Sir Lancelot said to the Queen, "and here is your chamber. The servants of your servant serve you. Have them bring whatever you wish."

For the first time Guinevere spoke.

"They may go," she said, and dropped his hand and moved further into the room. In a silken single file the maidens obeyed.

Only Sir Lancelot and Blanchefleur, with Branwen in the hallway behind, remained in the doorway. The Queen stood with her back to them, motionless. After a moment, she turned her head only and said in the same firm tone:

"Blanchefleur? Is that you?"

Blanchefleur looked up at Lancelot and he understood, stepping back and closing the door. When she saw his face it struck her that the Queen had not thanked him, but then the latch fell between them and he was gone.

"I'm here, Mother," she said, coming a few steps further into the room.

Still Queen Guinevere did not turn to look at her. Instead, with a graceful gesture, she shook the sleeve back from her wrist and took up one corner of her rusty-black cloak to dab at her face. Only then did she turn and look at Blanchefleur. If she had been weeping, every trace of tears was gone, and she was all coolness and distance and lofty carriage.

She reached out and one pale fingertip lifted Blanchefleur's chin. "How you've grown. I hear brave things of you, my daughter."

Not for the Queen of Logres a fond meeting. Blanchefleur swallowed a hard lump of disappointment and steeled herself to this woman's steely gaze. "From Perceval?"

"Yes." A tight-drawn smile fleeted across her mouth and the fingertip tapped the side of her jaw and fell away. "A man's loyalty is the sharpest of all weapons, Blanchefleur, and the hardest to find. Let me not hear that you have dulled it."

Blanchefleur blinked. "Did he tell you I refused him?"

"Yes." The Queen turned away from her and went to the window, where she stood with her fingers drumming on the sill. "Bear it in mind," she said in a voice that seemed to come from far away, "that a woman's shoulders are weak to bear the weight of a kingdom alone."

Blanchefleur folded lips and hands and did not reply. The Queen turned from the window and said, "That was why we sent you away, you know. For safety."

She lifted her chin and said what she would never have dared say to the King: "I wish you had kept me. In all the danger. I wish I had been there to share it with you."

"We could never have risked it. When she heard of the prophecy, Morgan le Fay tried to kill you."

Guinevere turned again and her fingers went on tapping the window-sill. Blanchefleur glanced from her stony profile to the nervous motion and back again, and for a moment she glimpsed under the stiff mask which the Queen of Logres wore clamped over her grief, and began to understand.

"I know," she said, taking a step forward and holding out her hands. "I know it was done from love for me. I'm only sorry I had to wait so long, so long, to meet you."

The tattoo on the window-sill hushed. Blanchefleur stood holding out her hands, willing the Queen to soften, to bend. No answering feeling stirred in that smooth pale face, but at last she came forward, put two cool hands in Blanchefleur's, and kissed her cheek. Then she drew quickly back and turned aside and went to the steaming bath, shrugging out of the black cloak.

Underneath, she wore a white shift smudged with soot.

The Queen looked at the cloak a moment, then folded it with careful deliberation and gave it to Blanchefleur. "This should go to Sir Gawain," she said, and though there was no discernible emotion in her voice, Blanchefleur felt a dull ache. "He would desire it."

Blanchefleur felt the texture of wool, smelled lanolin, rubbed oil against her fingers. All of it familiar. "This is Sir Gareth's cloak. The one he gave you, because you were cold…"

"That was the way of it. O Gareth! Ever the truest friend, laughing and loyal and incapable of a lie." Her voice ebbed and flowed with a rhythm that was all the expression she would allow of her grief. "And Gaheris. For whom shall I mourn first? The nine orphaned babes? The cold Queen of Orkney in her childless age? Gawain, titanic in love as in war?" She took a breath. "Or reeling Logres and her stricken King?"

Arthur. Blanchefleur's fingers tightened on the cloak. "How is he?"

The Queen's voice turned from elegy to flat distaste. "Barely the man I knew. You would think Mordred King now."

Blanchefleur remembered what Perceval had said of the Queen and Mordred. "He's one of the King's counsellors?"

"Worse," said the Queen, "one of his relations. Agravain is another. God knows what put it into that young man's head to accuse me. He had not the wit to do it maliciously, I think. But who egged him to it?"

"Could he have been truly mistaken?"

The Queen shook her head. "I never sent Sir Lancelot that ring, but a page brought it to him and he came at once. The page is a boy ten years old. Ten! All he could tell us was that a veiled lady gave him the ring. It was certainly mine. The boy cannot have been dishonest, and I, I never sent the ring. Another must have stolen it and given it to him. A woman certainly took part."

"Morgan?"

"I can think of no other." Arms folded, she was drumming again against her arm. "But the Queen of Gore has kept silence for months, and the new men of the Table have never had to do with her malice or her cunning. She is already half a story to them. My guilt was more credible."

She seemed to become aware of her jumping fingers, and dropped her arms to her sides, and spoke almost to herself. "What now? I should have died this morning, and with my death, as it was meant, the Table might have healed. But so long as I am alive, men will fight for me. Sir Lancelot makes pretty speeches, but he would never allow me to return to the King."

"Surely he has good reason," said Blanchefleur. "You don't really wish to be burned, do you?"

Guinevere glanced up at her sharply. "Yes."

Blanchefleur blinked.

The Queen moved with all the unhurried grace that marked her lightest motion: untying the cord at her shift's neck, stripping it from her body, stepping into the water. Her words were equally slow, equally clear.

"The Table is broken. The Table was broken the moment Lancelot blooded his sword in my chamber. And with the Table is broken the heart of the most glorious king of the earth. O Arthur! Better to die than to see such a lord destroyed on my account."

BLANCHEFLEUR WENT OUT BEARING HER MOTHER'S grimed shift and the cloak of Sir Gareth. As she paused in the great hall, looking for a servant to show her to the laundry, Sir Lancelot intercepted her.

"What of the Queen?"

"She is resting."

"I am glad to hear it."

Blanchefleur said: "What now? The King is not going to let you make off with her like that, is he?"

There was a wry twist in the corner of his mouth. "I have defied the King with force of arms. There can only be one response. By nightfall I will know when I may expect to receive him before my gates."

"The Queen spoke of going back to him—"

"Not to be thought of."

"No. Certainly not if she is innocent. But that must be proved, and there must be a reconciliation. If that is what we want, is it wise for the two of us to remain here?"

Sir Lancelot shook his head. "I fear if she is found elsewhere, she will be taken and burned."

"It wouldn't soften him?"

"It might have, once."

Blanchefleur looked up at him in mute distress.

"A man changes when he loses all the things that define him."

She pressed her lips together. "Even the King?"

Sir Lancelot looked down on her from his great height and said, "Even the King."

Tears itched in her throat. So many had lost so many things today. She stepped back and said, "How can I find Sir Perceval?"

"He is resting in one of the chambers. My steward will tell you which."

She curtseyed, trying to move with her mother's slow grace, and went to find the laundry. Perceval probably wished to be alone, she thought, to spend the worst of his sorrow in secret and present a stout face to the world. But it was hard to know he was so close, in so much pain. It was hard to have no right to go to him.

Branwen found her by the doorway into the laundry, staring into unbidden memories. She stood in her dream again and saw the fire, the fog, the gentle face of the man she now knew as Gareth. Then the memory was gone, and she was standing in the doorway in La Joyeuse Gard, and the shaft of thin morning sun coming in the window was barely four hours older than the light in her dream.

Branwen said, "You must still be tired. Go and rest."

Blanchefleur shook her head. "I will not sleep. Let us find work to do."

JOYEUSE GARD FILLED WITH PEOPLE ALL that day. Ox-carts trundled over the drawbridge with women and children huddled on top of their possessions and men trudging behind. Animals flowed bleating or lowing into the courtyard pens. In the smithy three men worked through the day making last-minute repairs to arms and weapons.

When Blanchefleur went into the hall for supper she found the room humming with new arrivals. More trestles had been put up and benches found to seat all the people.

She hesitated in the doorway and looked in vain for the Queen, or for any man she might recognise apart from Sir Lancelot, who sat in a cluster of strange knights at the high table.

She turned to Branwen, about to suggest that they eat with the Queen, when a dragging step sounded in the passage and she saw Perceval leaning on Heilyn. He had bathed and changed to a soft clean leather jerkin and linen breeches. Against the left side of his head the hair stuck up in unruly tufts as though he had fallen asleep while it dried plastered between head and pillow.

He said no word, but letting go of Heilyn bowed and offered his hand and led her up to the dais, limping heavily on his bruised leg. Before she sat, Blanchefleur caught his eye and smiled at him, trying to show some of the sympathy she felt. Perceval returned the smile, but tightly and distantly, as though he had no intention of letting her be concerned with his grief.

When she took her seat, silence fell on the table, and Sir Lancelot stood and lifted his cup. "Heir of Logres," he said in a voice loud enough for all his men to hear, "be welcomed. You are among true and loyal men."

She bowed from her seat and said, "Sir, I know it."

She was a little surprised when the knights around Lancelot drifted over and knotted around her. Perceval presented them to her: Sir Lionel, Sir Hector, Sir Alisander le Orphelin, Sir Pertisant. With the older knights, Lionel and Hector, Lancelot's kin, she could speak easily and graciously, but she had seen the younger ones smiling and whispering the night before. Tonight they were full of charm and laughter. She kept her guard up.

Elsewhere at the high table it was a quiet and sombre meal, full of talk of the war. She heard Sir Lionel say, "Of course Sir Gawain will be commanding the Table"—and she looked at Perceval, and wondered if he felt the same pang of foreboding. What hope had they, fighting against lords, fathers, and brothers? Victory or defeat would bear the same grief.

A stir at the doorway. A mailed step on the pavement. Sir Perceval rose from his feet and Blanchefleur looked up to see a man she recognised: Sir Bors, with grimy foam on his boots.

"Bors!" Perceval called, and the air was thick with cries of welcome. But before he would touch his food he told his news.

"The King called his council—all five that were left. Alas, cousin, that you slew the brothers of Orkney! Sir Gawain is furious beyond measure. We heard he went for horse and armour after you left, meaning to ride after and challenge you to combat. Sir Ironsides managed to get to him in time. They say that at the council even Sir Mordred could not slide a word in edgewise. No one else tried."

"And the King?" Sir Lancelot asked.

"Seemed to revive when he knew the Queen was safely away. But I cannot tell if he is angry or pleased. It is agreed with Gawain that he must besiege La Joyeuse Gard—so Mordred told me, and sent me to bring word that the King will come soon. Not so soon as Gawain would like, but before Sunday."

Slowly, Lancelot nodded. Blanchefleur stared at her trencher. She had hoped, against all hope, that the King would take some other course of action. The news seemed to drag them all one step closer to some terrible doom.

"You may defeat him," Sir Bors said. "There are yet more of the Table to declare for you and come to Joyeuse Gard."

Lancelot spoke sharply. "Declare for me? This is a private quarrel. I do not challenge the High King for his throne."

"You challenged his justice, which is the same thing."

"It was no justice at all, and that shall I prove upon the body of any who denies it. The King should know I had no choice. I had been a false knight had I done elsewise."

"Many may see it otherwise, even here, fair coz," said Sir Lionel. "If you wish to know how many, ask your friends here who *they* will have for king."

Sir Bors lifted his hands and said: "I am for Arthur. I am only here to defend true justice and to fight for whoever will champion it. But even if the Queen is proven innocent, cousin, your high-handedness has carried you into enmity with the King. What of Sir Clarrus, whom you slew on the threshold of the Queen's chamber? What of Gareth and Gaheris, who died this morning? None of them cold murder, I grant you, but Sir Gawain may certainly claim the right of a kinsman to see that blood avenged."

Sir Lancelot shook his head. "We will treat. There will be no fighting, so long as the King's grace is pleased to acknowledge his Queen."

After the meal Blanchefleur tugged on Perceval's sleeve.

"Come away," she whispered. "I want to speak with you."

She took him to her chamber, where she had sent Branwen to kindle a fire and mull wine. While the damsel whispered with Heilyn in the doorway, Blanchefleur turned to Perceval pleadingly.

"You should leave. Go back to your father at Camelot now, before it is too late. Bury your kin. Do not join Lancelot in his quarrel."

"It is already too late," he said. "I have lifted my hand against my King and must wait, with the rest, for his judgement."

"Surely your father will intercede for you."

"It is possible that he will."

She stared at him in amazement. "Is it possible that he will not?"

Perceval looked at his cup, brows crammed down hard over his eyes. "You heard Sir Bors say he would have ridden after Lancelot to fight him. Lancelot, his dearest friend in the world."

"All the more reason to leave this place! You mustn't be here when he comes."

"I cannot leave," he said after a long pause.

"Why? Why not?"

"I have a trust here which I cannot abandon," Perceval said, and bowed his head toward her.

She snatched off the ring on her hand and held it out to him. "I release you from your service to me. Take the ring and go."

He kept his head bent. "You may release me. Your father did not."

"My father?" She rushed on: "Then I'll go. We'll both go. It was a mistake to come here."

Perceval spoke slowly, as if battling to think clearly. "My father said you were best here…And after yesterday, with Sir Odiar, with the murder outside Astolat, I know he was right."

The words slurred and jostled one another with weariness. Silently, Blanchefleur reproached herself. Aloud she said, "Oh, Perceval, it isn't fair of me to push you on this today. But please think about it."

He nodded as if only half hearing her words, and set his cup down untasted on a table. "I will. Good night."

He limped to the door. Blanchefleur said, "Perceval."

"Yes?"

"I am so sorry about your kinsmen. I cannot imagine—oh, Perceval."

She had never known Gaheris or Gareth, so it was foolish to stand there with the tears rolling down her cheeks when Perceval, who had both known and loved them, stood looking at her with dry and stoical eyes. Yet behind them she could see that he was in pain, half-dazed with grief and in despair for the shattered heart of Logres. Worst of all was the certain knowledge that she could have spared him.

"It's my fault. I knew something terrible was about to happen. I could have prevented it."

He stared at her blankly and at last said: "Perhaps, and perhaps not. Do not spend tears on it. Good night."

He went out and Blanchefleur listened wretchedly to his limping steps fade away down the passage.

31

And terms of ransom they have laughed,
And truce to haughty scorn;
For dead to do Sir Launcelot
The fierce Gawayne hath sworn.

Buchanan

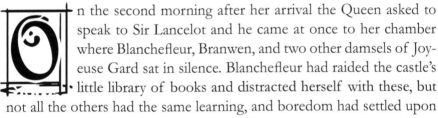

n the second morning after her arrival the Queen asked to speak to Sir Lancelot and he came at once to her chamber where Blanchefleur, Branwen, and two other damsels of Joyeuse Gard sat in silence. Blanchefleur had raided the castle's little library of books and distracted herself with these, but not all the others had the same learning, and boredom had settled upon them like a cloud as they watched the Queen sleep or sit for brief intervals staring out her window with her prayer-book drooping from her hand. Yet she never dismissed them, she never spent a moment alone, and Blanchefleur guessed why. They were her guard: witnesses for later inquiry, to speak to her conduct.

The Queen did not rise from her chair by the window when Sir Lancelot came, and she began without formality. "Sir knight, you have once again earned my most hearty thanks, and saved me from a shameful death."

From his place a step or two inside the open door, Lancelot bowed.

"Yet in preserving my life you have done deeds of violence against Logres. Now on my account a rift has opened within the Table, and while I live I fear it cannot be healed."

A sinew flexed stubbornly at the corner of Lancelot's jaw. "As long as you live, there is hope that your name may be restored with honour."

The Queen shook her head. "Do you think this is a matter of grace given on the field of battle? I was found guilty by the Table, not vanquished in combat. To redeem my name I must be acquitted as I was condemned, by the Table—and in snatching me from the flames, I fear you have but sealed their verdict."

"There is another way, if the King can be persuaded to take it," said Lancelot. "The Table found you guilty, but the sentence was passed by the King. He has the right to overlook your punishment. Let him cool from his first despair and his wrath against you. When he remembers the old days, he will take you back."

"He?" A faint red stain burned on her pale cheekbones. "Shall the High King of Logres stand before the world, cowed by an erring wife he has not the will to punish? No! If I cannot have my name cleared in the eyes of the world, let me submit myself to his justice." Each word whispered like a knife. "He would have repented of it soon enough. I would have been a martyr, instead of—what I am."

How like her, thought Blanchefleur with an itch of resentment, to think first and always of appearances.

"I will see you quitted," said Lancelot, passing a weary hand across his eyes. "Until then, I beg you, wait patiently. All that I have is yours."

"Let it outweigh the treasures of Ind; I would not take it. Not all the wealth in the world could console me for what I have lost."

It was Lancelot's turn to go red. "Despise me if you wish," he said. "Perhaps I deserve it. But had I not ridden to your aid, some other gentleman would have. And you would be in his castle, if not mine. And he would be preparing to lay down life, spurs, and honour in your defence, if not I. Be kind to me for his sake."

The Queen ducked her head, staring at her hands. At last, more gently, she said, "I do you wrong, my friend. But now that I am stronger, and have my wits about me, I do not wish to remain here. Let me go away to some nunnery, and send word to the King. He will do as he will. I do not think he will kill me."

Lancelot's mouth was a thin straight line. "No one will leave the castle," he said, and pointed to the window. "Look down the road to Camelot."

"What is it?" breathed the Queen, turning to see. But even Blanchefleur knew what the answer would be.

"The King is coming," said Lancelot.

THE ARMY FROM CAMELOT HAD GATHERED quickly and travelled in haste. It was small, just over half the knights of the Table and their followers, everyone who was not out questing or behind the walls of Joyeuse Gard.

But these were the best knights of the world, and Blanchefleur knew that not a man within the walls of Joyeuse Gard looked on them without disquiet as they pitched camp before the castle walls. Sir Lancelot, she knew, hoped to avoid a battle, and she added her prayers to his hopes.

Early that afternoon there came the note of a trumpet from below, and the other damsels in the Queen's chamber flocked to the window. Almost at once, Branwen wheeled to Blanchefleur. "Come and see."

The others fell back at her approach, and through the window she saw a small body of knights riding out from the camp of the army of Britain. Above them floated a banner she knew, the red dragon banner of Arthur of which she had dreamed as a child. Below, clearly to be seen, shone the gules and gold she knew so well, so that for a moment she thought it was Perceval himself.

Her throat went dry at the bravery of their show. "Are they attacking?" she asked.

"No, they are coming to treat," said Branwen. "See? They are bearing green branches."

Blanchefleur felt those clustered behind her stir and draw away, and turned to see her mother.

"Madam," said one of the damsels, "there is a balcony with a better view."

"This window is enough," said the Queen. "I will not appear to array myself against the King."

So the two of them watched from the window, where Sir Gawain's words reached them almost as clearly as they reached Sir Lancelot and his men over the gatehouse:

"Come forth, Sir Lancelot, dishonoured knight! Deliver yourself up to justice! For you have slain good knights of the Table Round, noble men and kinsmen, the like of whom shall never come again, and you have taken the Queen by force. Come forth, traitor!"

His voice was wild and cracked, and Blanchefleur felt the hair prickle on her scalp.

Sir Lancelot, near as he stood, spoke more softly, so that they strained to hear him: "My lords, you will not take this castle. And I have good knights with me, and if I choose to leave this castle you shall win me and the Queen harder than you well can bear."

A knight that rode with Sir Gawain took off his helm. From all that distance away, Blanchefleur could barely see his face. But from the Queen's indrawn breath, she knew it could only be one man.

"If you dare to come forth," said the High King, "you will meet me in the midst of the field."

She had thought Guinevere cold. But suddenly there was heat, high and fierce, pouring out of her.

Sir Lancelot bowed. "God defend! One of us might kill the other."

Gawain bellowed, "*Coward!*"

But Sir Lancelot went on, addressing the King directly. "Will you not hear me? I have slain your knights in the rescuing of the lady, Queen Guinevere, in fair fight and self-defence. As touching the lady, your Queen, I have only this to say: that I will prove it upon the body of any man breathing, save yourself and Sir Gawain, that the Queen is a true lady to her lord as any alive. And, my good lord, it seems to me that I should have lost all worship in knighthood had I suffered the lady, your Queen to be burnt for my sake. Have I not done battle for your Queen in other quarrels, and have I not the right to do battle for her in a just cause even against yourself? And therefore, my gracious lord, take your Queen unto your good grace: she is fair, and true, and good."

At that distance it was impossible to see how the King looked at this. Nor did he speak: Sir Gawain was beforehand. "False recreant knight! Know that my Lord King Arthur shall have his Queen and you, and slay you both if it pleases him."

"Is that my lord's answer?" Sir Lancelot asked.

Sir Gawain had only paused for breath. "As for my lady, the Queen, I will never say that she is justly shamed, and let it never be said that I quarrel with her, or gainsay what you say of her. But you, Sir Lancelot—what cause had you to slay my good brother Sir Gareth, that loved you more than all his kin? Alas! You knighted him with your own hands! Why did you slay him that loved you so well, while he was naked and undefended?"

"For that I make no excuse," Lancelot said. "But Jesu bear me witness, and by my faith to the high order of knighthood, I would as cheerfully have slain my kinsman Bors. Alas! I neither saw Sir Gareth nor Sir Gaheris in the rush."

"Liar! Do you indeed pretend that this is not of your engineering, that you unpeople the Table, that you make war against Logres, that you drag the very name of knighthood in the dust? Flower of knighthood, they say! Traitor and miscreant, rather! I will make war to you while I live!"

"I hear you," said Lancelot. "But what does my lord King say?"

The King appeared to stir himself. "This: That your crimes remain.

Open your gates and lay down your arms."

"Sire, I will do so, and submit myself to your justice, when I have your assurance touching the lady, your Queen, that you hold her guiltless and true."

Gawain cried: "Shall we allow this oathbreaker to dictate terms? Does he think to hide behind the lady Queen, and so escape my hand?"

Another voice, fainter, came from the knot of men clustered with the King. "Moreover, there can be no question of our lord holding the Queen guiltless, when that question is settled by others and not by him."

In the window, Guinevere was thrumming against the sill. "The true son of his mother."

Sir Lancelot said, "Those are my terms. My lord, I beg you—"

Gawain cried: "Have you not heard the words of Mordred? The lord King cannot accept your terms, even if he wished to. Coward, slayer of unarmed men! We will bring you to battle, will you, nill you!"

Silence hung over Joyeuse Gard while the King sat wordless. At last, Lancelot bowed his head. "Then we will receive you," he said, and left the gatehouse.

Blanchefleur turned to the Queen in distress. "What has happened to Sir Gawain?"

Her mother looked out the window with eyes the colour of iron and spoke under her breath. "What has happened to my lord?

"It seems to me," said Branwen, "that Sir Gawain is looking for an excuse to fight, and cares not what that might be."

The Queen murmured again. "He takes it so hard, so hard."

Blanchefleur swallowed. "I wondered if Gawain had something of the sort in him."

Guinevere turned from the window. By her side, one hand clenched; the knuckles went white, as if she forced all the pain out of her face and voice and into her fingers. "I speak of my lord. It is not like him to stand by while others speak for him."

Blanchefleur heard the dull crash of a mailed foot in the corridor. "Someone is coming."

In one fluid motion the Queen reached out a hand, took up Branwen's needlework, sat, and began to embroider. Branwen made a startled proprietary snatch, then subsided into decorum as the door opened and Sir Lancelot entered.

He stood inside the door. The Queen did not look up; she held the hooped linen like a shield.

"Alas!" he said. "I must fight."

"Let me go back to him," said the Queen, head bent over the linen. "He will not have me burned."

"Your life is no longer the only thing at stake, O Queen. The siege will continue even if you do return to him."

"If it makes no difference, I will go."

"It makes a great deal of difference. I have said I will not return you without an undertaking to treat you in all honour, as guiltless. Or I should be required to rescue you again."

"I give you your service back," said the Queen. "I forbid you ever to rescue me again."

Sir Lancelot said: "I am your true servant, lady, but if I must disobey you, I will."

For the first time, the Queen lifted her head and looked directly at him. "Must I find another protector to rid me of you?"

"Do so! If there is some gentleman rash enough to take up all your quarrels, then I shall hand you to him. Or if I may find some way to give up my care of you honourably, without delivering you into danger, you may be assured I will take it. Until then, you are under my care, and will accept it."

Guinevere seemed to grow taller in her seat, and her lips thinned and her eyes narrowed, but Lancelot gave her stare for stare. She said, "Well? Am I to consider myself your prisoner?"

She flung the word at him like a dart. A flicker of triumph came into Lancelot's eyes and was as quickly gone again. "It might be best if you did," he said smoothly, and bowed, and left.

When the door closed behind him the Queen threw the embroidery aside and bolted to her feet. In the silence she drew a long sharp breath of surprise. For all the world, Blanchefleur thought, as if a favourite dog had turned and bitten her. She was still thinking so when Guinevere flung a look out of the corner of her eye to her, so cold and shuttered that Blanchefleur nearly flinched back, wondering for a moment if the Queen had heard her thought.

Guinevere said no more. For the rest of that afternoon she sat by the window with her back turned on the rest of them in a complete and forbidding stillness.

Blanchefleur was lying awake at dawn the next morning when the first assault came. She heard a confused clamour, distant trumpets, and then a pounding like thunder, with shudders that ran up from the foundations of the castle and thrummed in her bones.

At first she could not guess what the noise might be. Only when she slipped from the couch where Branwen was sleepily stirring and ran to the window did she see the ram, like a gigantic caterpillar, swung by two lines of men against the gates of Joyeuse Gard.

Branwen woke with a start and nearly fell off the couch. "It's begun!" She spoke in a whisper, for the Queen still lay motionless in the big canopied bed in the room's centre.

Blanchefleur was scrambling into her clothes. "I didn't see Perceval last night. He was captaining the watch on the south wall. Where will he be now, Branwen?"

"God knows, and he'll be busy."

"I have to find him."

She thrust her feet into shoes, yanked a hasty knot in the laces, and rushed downstairs. There was little coherent thought in her mind, only a certainty that she needed to see Perceval, because since everything had gone wrong he had needed her. She should have gone to him yesterday. It might already be too late.

In the great hall, and outside in the courtyard, Joyeuse Gard swarmed like an ant-hill. Lancelot's men crowded the gatehouse. Two of them, staggering on each side of a cauldron of boiling water, went past as Blanchefleur craned her neck for Perceval. The courtyard seethed with men and horses; knights waited by their steeds testing buckles and straps while squires ran with a shield or vambrace from the armoury.

The gates groaned as the battering-ram shook them again.

Someone stepped into her path, a man-at-arms holding up his hand. "Back into the hall, lady."

She gave him her mother's stony glare. "Do you know who I am?"

He didn't move. "Yes, lady."

"Then you should know better than to stand in my way."

She went down the steps as if to walk through him, and he stood aside saying, "Lady, be not overlong. If harm comes to you—"

His voice faded into the bustle and shout of coming war. Blanchefleur knew she had won only a brief space of time. She began to work her way around the courtyard, keeping to the walls where in the dawn twilight she might go unnoticed. Then suddenly, her heart jumped. There he was, slumped on a haycart in a quiet spot near the pig-pens, eating an apple and staring at Glaucus.

"Perceval?"

He slid down to the ground and limped toward her, swallowing a bite of the apple. "Blanchefleur! You ought not to be here. There's about to be a charge."

"They're riding out, then? It's a sortie?"

"As soon as the gates fall."

"And you? You're going with them?"

He stiffened into expressionlessness and spoke as if repeating a lesson. "Yes. The Queen needs defending. Lancelot's manslaying can be dealt with after."

"She doesn't want to be defended. She says that if she had died, the Table would still be whole."

He slid her a dead stare. "With innocent blood raining down like fire on our heads?"

She knew him well enough by now to be distressed by that wooden look. Perceval never bothered to hide vigour and high spirits; what deep hurt lay behind this stoic front? She gazed at him wordlessly.

Perceval took a last aimless bite of apple and tossed the core to the pigs. They grunted and squabbled for it. In her thoughts, Blanchefleur said, "Must you fight? Come back, come into Joyeuse Gard, and wait for it to end."

She could not say it. By now she knew him well enough to understand the insult it would be to him. So she said: "Please, Perceval, please. Come back safely."

"If I can."

Could he not hear the pleading in her voice? She said: "Don't do anything rash. Don't lose everything the Grail Quest achieved. Logres needs you."

He laughed, a mirthless sound as grey as the air. "This is a battle. Who can tell what may happen?"

"There are greater things than the Queen's honour to give your life for."

"Lady, if you are troubled, pray for my soul."

"I will not! I will pray for your safety…" She swallowed a little more of her pride and reached pleadingly through the cold dawn murk. "You worry me, Perceval. You're so quiet these days. I know how you feel! I know that you have friends on both sides. And loyalties on both sides too—and that people are going to die. Perceval, don't you dare die, no matter what happens today."

He looked at her from behind the wooden mask and said, "I will try.

Farewell."

"Farewell, and God go with you," she said, and knew that none of her words had lifted him out of his apathy.

He turned, gathered up his reins, and reached for his stirrup. The horse blew a white cloud of warm breath and shifted restlessly at the sound of coming battle. Blanchefleur stood shivering in the frosty air, knowing that in another moment Perceval would be gone, perhaps forever—almost certainly forever, unless she could give him a reason to live.

She said: "I love you."

The words unloosed blinding pent-up tears. Then Perceval was there in front of her again, and his hand lifted her chin.

Words gushed out as fast as the tears. "Please forgive me. I should never have sent you away. I don't want to lose you. And I don't mean to play with you, like the Queen does with Lancelot, only I was afraid…"

He cleared his throat and said raggedly: "Silly maid! I *knew* it," and she knew that the mask was down.

He waited for her to wipe her eyes and then said, "You are going to marry me."

"If you live."

He snorted. "No more excuses."

"No, Perceval."

"We are getting married."

"Yes, Perceval."

"Tomorrow, if possible."

"If you think it best."

The sound of a trumpet jarred them back to the courtyard of Joyeuse Gard. Lancelot was calling his men to horse and Sir Bors, striding past from the stables, looked at them incredulously, abrupt with haste. "What is she doing here? Get her inside and mount up."

Perceval threw back his head, snuffed the air like a war-horse, and laughed. Then he whirled Blanchefleur into his arms, carried her to the door of the great hall and swung her down again at the top of the steps.

"Everyone is watching," she gasped, face red, finding her feet again.

"Good," said Perceval. "Witnesses. Wait for me after the fighting is done."

Sudden seriousness fell on him when he mentioned the battle. Blanchefleur said, "Do you still mean to fight?"

He hesitated. "Yes."

"Then come back to me safely."

"If I may, I will."

He laid his hand against her cheek and brushed the corner of her mouth with his thumb. The world seemed to hush; Blanchefleur saw his eyes move to her lips. Then his hand dropped again.

"Kiss in haste, repent at leisure," he said with a laugh. "I can wait. God be with you, dear love."

"And with you."

For a moment, the limp was gone. He ran down the steps, vaulted to his horse's back, and spurred forward to join the other knights drawn up before the straining gates. From the top of the stair Blanchefleur kept her eyes fixed on his gules and gold.

Crash. The castle shuddered again; the gates cracked; Blanchefleur thought of the night in Gloucestershire when the door of their house was battered open by the champion of Morgan. That knight now lay mouldering in a clearing to the north. At what great cost would Perceval, still bearing the marks of that combat, win through to her at the end of this day?

Crash. Was this the same battering-ram that shook her awake this morning? Were the gates still standing? She was someone else altogether now—five minutes in the open air and her life had changed. Perceval vanished within the ranks of his fellows. She turned and went up to her mother's chamber, feeling herself poised uncertainly on the brink of an abyss of joy and terror.

"The sun is risen," said Guinevere.

She sat half in light, half in shadow, wearing black like night against which her hair shone pale and tangled. There was a silver mirror in her left hand and a white bone comb in her right, but these lay listless and unmoving in her lap.

"Will you watch from the window, madam?" Blanchefleur asked.

Voice, like hands, was listless. "No."

Blanchefleur bent and took the comb from her fingers. "Then let me comb your hair."

They did not speak again. The Queen closed her eyes as Blanchefleur teased the knots apart with skilled fingers. Now and then her lips moved. Blanchefleur found her own thoughts turning to the men on the field below. There had been a splintering crash when the gates fell, and then the shouting had started. Crashing steel she could hear, the high whinny of horses, the screams of the dying.

Was it true that she had once thought the fierce cry of swords the bravest sound on the earth? She blinked back more tears and saw her hands again. Soft and graceful, adorned with the great golden ring of Orkney, one twined into her mother's hair and the other clasping the carven comb. And outside, men were dying.

DOWN BELOW, SIR PERCEVAL HAD MOVED in a trance that was half daydream, half nightmare until the gates burst. Then everything became sharp and clear again. Lancelot's men were drawn up in the courtyard, ready to charge, and when the gate fell they spurred recklessly forward, cutting through the men outside like a scythe through grass. Then they reached the field, with iron-bladed destruction reigning on every side. Yet, to his horror, Perceval found it like any other battle he had ever fought. There was sweat trickling down his face and down the furrow of his spine between his aching shoulders, there was a roar like falling water in his ears, and his own throat was inexplicably parched and ravaged, although he could not remember having joined in any battle-cry. And the blood ran through him like molten iron with the mad and merciless lust of battle, while men who had been his brothers crumpled beneath his blade. For a while, he gave himself over to the single desperate purpose of death.

But then came a lull in the tempest. He found himself the only living man in that part of the field. As he glanced around, feeling cold and tired in the sudden quiet, he saw for the first time the shields and livery of men that he had known well—some that he had loved. Some that he must have killed, with as great a joy as he had once killed thieves and murderers...

Their shields reproached him. There was Sir Persides. There was the young son of Aglovale. There was Bernard of Astolat, who for a short while had been a friend, who now would never have the chance either to prove his innocence or suffer for his guilt in the matter of Gawain's messenger.

He looked at the stark forest, naked branches like grey smoke against the bleak blue sky. It flashed into his mind that he could set his spurs to his horse and vanish into their shadow. Instead he reined Glaucus away, back toward the battle. If he fled, it would unmake him; do that, and he might as well die a coward's death on his own sword.

There was nothing to do but follow the path he had decided with such painful debate to follow. Gareth and Gaheris, he reminded himself. He knew—had known as soon as he saw them lying there in the trampled mud—that they were only the beginning.

He was sucked back into the melée, and it was then that the worst came. Suddenly he saw before him the shield he had been dreading, the gules and gold that he mirrored. There was nowhere else to go, nothing else to do. He lifted his shield and dropped his sword-arm.

It seemed like an age that he stared at the cold and terrible front of his father's helm. But an eddy in the fight bore them past each other, and he thought that Sir Gawain had hesitated too, sword hanging slack in his hand.

Perhaps, then, his father knew why he had to be here, fighting for the Queen's name.

Perceval spurred forward, willing away the ache in his bones and the pain that still throbbed in his shield-arm and his hip where Sir Odiar had struck him. The battle-fire had left him now, and he fought with his mouth pressed into a thin line, more for survival now than for bloodshed.

In front of him, two knights crashed together. Sir Bors, helm missing, the battle-fire gleaming in his eyes, dismounted and staggered to the knight he had just unhorsed.

"Lancelot! Lancelot!" he cried hoarsely, drawing his poniard. "They have killed Lionel and Blamor, our kin! Lancelot!"

Perceval saw the fallen knight's device. The Pendragon.

The Knight of the Lake rode out of the melée, blood dripping from the mace in his hand. "I hear you, Bors."

Bors had his elbow hooked around the King's neck, struggling to keep him on his knees. The pale sun gleamed on his blade.

"Tell me, cousin. Shall I end this war forev—"

"God forbid!" Lancelot was crying like thunder.

The dog reached Bors before Lancelot or Perceval could: a grey wolf-hound, armoured, blood-streaked. Bors went down under its snapping teeth and the King sprang back to his feet, drawing his sword.

Lancelot was on the ground facing him; as the King rose, he flung his sword to the ground and went to his knees, throwing up empty hands. "Sire and dear lord, I pray you, cease this destruction! Your Queen is innocent!"

The King stood motionless and faceless among the bloody ruins of the chivalry of Logres. At last he said, "Will that restore to me my dead knights?" He took a step forward, grip strengthening on the hilt of his sword. "Will that heal the Table and undestroy my kingdom?"

"Let me be punished. Death. Exile. I'll take it gladly. Only say you will spare the Queen's grace. You are the King: you can pardon."

"And you say she is innocent."

"I call Heaven to witness she is. But sire, you cannot continue this slaughter, even if she is not."

The King was silent for a moment, and then lifted his helm. Beneath the iron his face was pale, with deep pouches below the eyes. Perceval, looking at him, then understood some of the despair he must have felt.

"No," he admitted. "I cannot."

"Then I throw me on your mercy, sire," said Lancelot, and lifted his sword, and offered the hilts to the King.

Arthur stretched out his hand and touched it. As he did so, his shoulders straightened, and a little of the strain left his eyes and did not return.

"I receive your sword, and ask you to keep it for me a while longer. Bedivere, Bleoberis, sound the retreat."

This is Modred, the man that I most trusted.
Morte Arthure

They went out to the King that afternoon with fifty knights. Sir Lancelot, riding with the Queen at the head of the column, had shed his armour for sombrely magnificent peace-clothes of fine broadcloth and velvet; the other knights followed his example—even Sir Bors, whose face was torn and bleeding from the war dog of Arthur. Only Sir Perceval, who had spent the past two hours on the battlefield directing the work of burial, remained armed. The Queen herself did not change her black robes, but Blanchefleur and the three other damsels with her were given bright silken tunics for the occasion.

The four damsels each rode pillion behind a knight. Blanchefleur was perfectly satisfied, for she had Perceval. Despite all that had happened that morning, they did not speak on the short ride to the King's camp: everything they had to say to each other was so important that it could not be wasted on this brief, crowded ride. But from Perceval's weary smile when he pulled her onto his horse Blanchefleur knew that, terrible as the battle must have been, he had come to some kind of peace with it.

And so she sat behind him in silence with one hand on his shoulder so that he could look out the corner of his eye and see her there.

They crossed the battlefield and Blanchefleur made herself look. The ground was ploughed by hooves, stained by blood, heaped with carrion. Women moved among the dead; carts were brought out to collect bodies; squires sat or stood, heads bowed, by fallen lords. Over all, the watery sun shone through leaden clouds.

A funereal silence hung over the royal camp. All those left alive were out on the battlefield, carrying on the work, and apart from the sentry who admitted them to the camp there were few souls to be seen peering out of tents or hurrying by on business. But then the party from Joyeuse Gard came in sight of the King's pavilion, hung in silver and scarlet, to find a gathering of men-at-arms assembled.

Sir Lancelot's company dismounted and stood holding their horses, facing the King's men. Blanchefleur felt the silence stretch tight between the two companies; it was as though all the blood spilled on the field between camp and castle lay between them. Lancelot, Perceval, and Bors conducted the Queen and her damsels through this gauntlet of dagger-pointed stares, down the aisle between the two companies to the King's pavilion.

Inside, Blanchefleur glanced across the men assembled there, seeking the young king of her earliest memory, or the knightly father she had seen in Sarras. The man who sat by the folding camp-table in a furred robe with his sheathed sword resting across his knees looked old and worn by comparison, with silvered hair and a weariness in the eyes that reminded her of Perceval as he had been this morning in the dawn. The great grey dog that lay under his chair heaved to its feet when they came in, and bared its teeth and growled.

"Down, Cavall!" The King spoke softly, but the dog heard, and crawled back under the chair to lick the blood-streaks in its fur.

Behind the King many knights had crowded into the pavilion to witness the peace, but two took precedence. On the King's left stood a slim pale young man with a silky black beard and a gloomy complexion, and Blanchefleur dimly wondered if this was the Sir Mordred of whom she had heard. On the King's right stood Sir Gawain, and the change in him was more painful to witness than that in the King, for he stared at Lancelot with hot and ugly bloodshot eyes. He was far more obviously in the last stages of exhaustion, burning with anger, battered and bloodied. There seemed little remaining of the kindliness and humour with which he had glowed in Carbonek, gladdening the Waste Land.

All this she observed in the few short breaths that passed as the party from Joyeuse Gard halted within the pavilion and took silent stock of their reception.

Then before anything else could be said Sir Lancelot took the Queen by the hand and knelt before the King. "My lord king, I bring you your Queen, and beg you to receive her. For she is true, and that I will prove on the body of any knight that denies it."

The King rose and lifted the Queen to her feet. "I take it as proven. Lady Guinevere, I thank the King of Heaven and these good knights for delivering you from the fire. If I have done you wrong, I beg your pardon."

"With all my heart I give it to you," the Queen said. With that the King drew her into his arm and kissed her in the presence of all. But Blanchefleur noted the King's words carefully, and that *if* troubled her. Was he receiving her back, with so fair a show, in continued suspicion of her faith?

But then her own cue was given, for Guinevere turned from him and held out her hand to Blanchefleur. "Your daughter, my lord."

Blanchefleur took a breath to calm her suddenly quaking heart. As she went to move forward, Perceval took her hand and she had the same feeling she had had once or twice before, of reinforcements in the thick of battle. She lifted her chin and said, "Here, sire."

Perceval said, "Right joyful am I to deliver her up to you after all this time of waiting."

The King smiled at her, and it was as though the sun came out.

"Lady Blanchefleur, I am sorry to have passed all these years without your company."

All the foreboding she had felt crossing the battlefield seemed to roll back like storm clouds. This was the father she remembered from their meeting in Sarras—and now, as then, he accepted her. Forgetting that he had no memory of the City, she went on an impulse and hugged him. Surprise crossed his face when he realised her intention, but then his arms went around her shoulders and pulled her closer.

She broke away and looked to her mother. Guinevere took her by the shoulders and kissed her cheek. Then the Queen went to Perceval, smiling, and gave him her hand with such a show of friendliness that Blanchefleur almost envied him.

"Sir Perceval. You have served us well."

Perceval bowed over the Queen's hand. "That shall be seen, madam." And he went down on his knees before the King.

"My dear lord," he said, "I have taken up arms against you, and will abide your just wrath."

"I do not pardon you," said the King.

Blanchefleur turned to him with a sharp breath of protest. But he went on:

"Rather let me seek pardon. You believed yourself fighting in the cause of true law and justice. The same cause which, in prolonging the strife of this war, I fear I have injured. Let me always have such men about me."

Gawain spoke, hoarsely, for the first time. "Heaven forfend. Unnatural whelp! What of your kin?" He transferred his attention to the Knight of the Lake. "Truce or no, I counsel you to make your peace with Heaven, Lancelot."

Perceval looked at his father with mute reproach. But Lancelot replied before he could gather words: "Fair brother, for such you have been to me, you slew my cousin Sir Lionel today. There is your revenge, if you will take it."

But Gawain's voice rasped with contempt. "What is Lionel to me?" He turned back to Perceval. "And you! Did you strike a blow in defence of your kin, yon morning before the gates of Camelot? Were you not a son of mine, the word for such an act would be treachery."

Perceval stood blankly staring under Gawain's lashing words. Blanche-fleur knew he was distressed, but Sir Gawain misread the look as insolence. "You rode in that charge," he said. "Did you watch them die? Did you approve the thing?"

"God knows I did not."

"You did by your deeds today!"

"Then should I have stood there like they did, to bring an innocent lady to death?"

Gawain flushed red. "How *dare* you?"

But Perceval had sparked, and his words poured out. "Of course I brought the Heir of Logres to Joyeuse Gard. In obedience to you. Of course I rode to deliver the Queen from death. You wished it. Since the day I left my mother's cot to seek you, in everything I have done I have only sought by pleasing you to prove myself a worthy son to you."

"So prove it. Will you avenge your kinsmen's blood?"

"No!" Perceval shot back. "I will see that the justice of Heaven is served, but not an inch further will I go. From now on I follow my own conscience, and I tell you—"

"I have heard enough." The thunder of Gawain's voice rose above Perceval's. "From this day you are no son of mine."

"Enough," said the King. Softly, but there was a note of authority in his voice that instantly quenched both father and son. "This is a woeful day, but wrongs have been righted and it is no time to quarrel. Sir Gawain, you sought this day's battle as revenge for your wrongs. For this I will not punish you, for I too was at fault. But you will accept the death of

Sir Lionel—once your friend, alas—as settlement of Sir Lancelot's guilt."

Gawain opened his mouth as if to protest, but the King went on. "There will be no more talk of revenge. Or of casting off sons. Remember, Gawain, why your mother and not yourself rules in Orkney today."

Gawain pressed his lips together until they turned white. "I do remember it," he said, and looked at Perceval with bitter tears. "O, I am well punished for the sins of my youth."

Perceval flinched at that. "Punished? What can you mean?"

Gawain said: "In the days before my father Lot of Orkney yielded his claim on the throne of Uther Pendragon, I fought under the banner of Arthur. My father died refusing to see or speak with me."

There was deadly silence for a moment, until Perceval spoke. "Why did you never tell me?"

"The regrets of youth pass. I looked to the future. To *you*."

"And left me to repeat your mistakes? How was I to learn, unless you taught me?"

Gawain looked at his son incredulously. "Do you dare to blame me for your own insolence?"

"Sir, you did say you were punished in this, though it was none of my own doing."

The air was full and heavy—layers of grief, suspicion, and now anger. Blanchefleur felt it pressing on her chest, too heavy to breathe. She had always sensed Gawain's temper, she had always feared it turned against the man she loved. But Perceval was his father's son, inheriting more sins than even he was aware, she thought. In a way it was worse that he could hold his own so well.

Before she could think of any way to smooth over the quarrel, the young man in black behind the King's chair stirred and gave a faint cough, a tiny sound that recalled both the combatants to their surroundings.

Gawain glanced around. Sir Lancelot stood by in silence and the sight of the man who had been his friend seemed to remind Gawain where his real quarrel lay. He swung back to Perceval and said with harsh briskness, "Then do something now. I am going to Camelot to bury my kin and swear an oath on their graves. Choose! Follow, or stay! And if you stay, do not presume to call them kin again."

Perceval looked at the King. "I know the oath you mean, and I think you were just forbidden to make such an oath, sir."

But Arthur, looking at them both under level brows, showed no sign of speaking. Gawain looked at him, gave a hard bright laugh, and turned back to Perceval. He pointed at the golden pentacle on Perceval's surcoat. "Find a new badge to wear, boy."

He left defiantly, head thrown back, shoulders straight. Inside the pavilion, Perceval sagged, pale under his tan, more defeated than Blanchefleur had seen him since the night Mr Corbin bested him in debate. The tent was full of men, but in the wake of that quarrel none spoke.

"Sire," Perceval said at last, appealingly.

"He heard what I said about revenge," said the King. "But I say nothing to your quarrel."

Perceval bowed and stood back. In the quiet, Sir Bors stepped forward and threw himself upon his knees before the King. "Gracious lord, I have raised my hand against you. Here are my spurs. Here is my belt and sword. What is your will?"

His words reminded them all why they had come, and the last five minutes' storm faded away leaving only a scent of relief. Under the King's chair Cavall the hound growled again at the sight of the man whose face he had marred in battle. But the King smiled at Bors.

"My will is to clemency today. I know you, my trusty Bors, loyal to your kin before your lord, and that is right. And in battle wise men may speak foolishness and blasphemy, let alone treason. There is a man of God on the island of Iona. Take your belt and spurs to him and pay their weight in gold as a ransom. Then, if you desire to serve me, come back to Camelot, for if I see rightly we will need you again."

"My true and gracious lord," said Sir Bors; then his voice failed. He rose and bowed and left. Iona was far away.

The King stirred and looked at his rival.

"Sir Lancelot."

"My lord."

"You have land in the north of Wales, I think," said the King. "For the manslaying of Sir Gareth and Sir Gaheris, which was done in confusion and darkness, not lying in wait, you shall go there and stay within your borders until a new Bishop is appointed in Trinovant."

"I will obey," said Sir Lancelot. Blanchefleur thought she felt an ache in his voice. The present bishop was only a young man, likely to live longer than the Knight of the Lake.

Sir Lancelot went on: "But, sire, a boon. One last matter of counsel, if you will hear me."

"Speak."

"You did not hear me speak at the trial of the lady Queen," Lancelot said. "Then I do not think I would have been believed—"

"Now is not the time to bring evidence."

"Sire, I grant it. Yet allow me to speak before I go. You know that I have been the champion and servant of the lady Queen for many years."

The King bowed his head. "I know it."

"During that time I have done errantry and questing on her behalf."

"I know it."

"In the winter of last year the lady Queen wished to learn more of a certain knight of the Table of whom she suspected—nothing, at that point. Only a thing she had from Sir Gareth made her curious to know his loyalties better. She asked me to follow him to the tournament at Carlisle, and to mark all his actions going and returning. This man left the tournament after two days, and travelled south into the waste. I was forced to vanish likewise."

Blanchefleur saw Perceval, who had been standing apart with drooping head, stiffen and lift his eyes to Lancelot.

"I hunted my quarry to the citadel of the man known today as Breunis Saunce-Pité, where I saw him received with all show of friendly courtesy. In the following days, the two of them viewed new-built houses and mills in the valley, and had a foundation laid out for another. Such seemed to me at the time a good argument of their well meaning. And so when I returned to Camelot I reported to the Queen what I had found, on an evening in the garden that Sir Perceval and Sir Agravain may, I think, remember."

Perceval said: "I remember it, sir. The lady Queen was there, with attendants, and I might give you their names."

"Then the reputation of Saunce-Pité grew," said Lancelot. "And we now hear that he is the same Sir Breunis. This puts a different complexion upon his fellowship with a knight of the Table."

"It was," the Queen added, "the reason I warned you against receiving this knight into your councils, my lord."

The King looked at her in sharp surprise. "What, are you speaking of Sir Mordred?"

She returned his look steadily. Sir Lancelot said: "Yes. And I believe that he has stirred up this strife and war to remove your Queen, a threat to his rising power."

The King turned to the pale young man at his side. "What do you say, Sir Mordred, to these things?"

"They are a convenient excuse, surely."

Perceval said: "It is true! He knows Breunis Saunce-Pité. Gareth and I saw them travelling together last winter."

"I grant it," Mordred said. "I knew Sir Breunis, and sought to dissuade him from his evil ways, until his obdurance made it wiser for me to avoid his company. But tell me, I pray, how the fact of my acquaintance with Saunce-Pité makes me a conspirator against the Queen's grace?"

"It gives you reason to so conspire," Sir Lancelot insisted. "You knew the Queen distrusted you. You knew she threw her opinion always against yours with the King."

"It is the prerogative of ladies," said Mordred with a smile, "to take dislikes to those who would rather be their friends than their enemies."

A new voice called from a young man bearing the double-headed eagle of Orkney. "Why not ask her what grudge it is that she carries against my cousin?"

"Good cousin Agravain, I think not—"

But Agravain, with a hot rush that reminded Blanchefleur of his brother, spoke on: "Ask her! For years the whisperers have hinted that you are the King's son, Mordred, and she believes them and is full of malice toward you."

In the silence that followed this, Blanchefleur reached out and grasped Perceval's arm. "Who is Mordred's mother?" she asked in the ghost of a whisper, so that she thought he might not hear her. But he turned and mouthed the very name she had been dreading.

"Morgan."

Her fingers closed a little harder on Perceval's arms and she stared at the King with dismay.

But others in the pavilion seemed less aghast. One knight said, in a rather bored voice, "For shame, Agravain! Not here."

The King frowned. "Your rash suspicions have already flung this realm into war, nephew. Learn to bridle your tongue and not repeat idle tales."

Agravain twisted his mouth sulkily and retreated. Mordred said to the King, "My lord, let not such things turn your favour from true and loyal men."

"Rest assured they shall not," said the King, but he looked thoughtfully from nephew to Queen. Then his eyes fell on Blanchefleur and he said, "Step forward, daughter. Mordred, salute the Lady of the Grail, the Heir and coming queen of Logres. Will you serve her, honour her, and uphold her as you have her father?"

"Lady, I swear that I will."

Under the King's gaze Mordred bent over her hand to kiss it. Blanche-fleur, still shaken by Agravain's blurted words, could not restrain a shudder as his lips brushed her hand. At that he glanced up; she looked into piercing grey eyes and knew him.

She could not have said what it was that triggered her memory. Whether by a trick of stagecraft, or by some art of his mother's, he was different. Bearded, mail-shirted, grey-cloaked, carrying himself upright and honestly as he had throughout the whole meeting, she could have been in his company for months without guessing his secret. Perceval, after all, had known him and not recognised him. How had he given himself away? Was it that moment of calculation when he felt her tremble and looked up to assess her mood? Or was it something else, the unnatural perception which had been hers since Carbonek, the ability to see and sum up a man's character with the blink of an eye?

Be that as it may, there was now no doubt of the thing.

Her voice, when she spoke, was strained and faint.

"Simon Corbin?"

The doubts that were so plain to chase, so dreadful to withstand—
Oh, who shall understand but you; yea, who shall understand?
Chesterton

he look that flashed into Simon Corbin's eyes when she said his name frightened her, for it was the sudden desperate fighting instinct of a cornered animal. His grip on her hand hardened just as Blanchefleur, seeing that ugly impulse, jerked away from him so that his white-knuckle fist grasped air. She spoke almost without thought, so that only once the words hung in the air did she perceive their full meaning: "You're Morgan's secret master! *You* ordered her to kill me."

Already he had the upper hand of himself, and faced her with smooth puzzlement. "Lady, surely you are mistaken."

But now she had seen him with his mask down. Perceval stood by her side, and with a glance at his face she knew he too had recognised the man Corbin.

"Impossible. Do you expect me to forget the face of the man who was for six months my friend and for one evening my suitor?" One realisation collided with another. "Merciful heaven! Everything you said was meant to keep me away from Logres!"

Perceval sounded almost awe-struck. "It's true."

But Mordred gathered credibility around him like a cloak. He raised a plaintive eyebrow at the dumbfounded King, and said, "Your suitor? My dear *cousin!*"

"You deny it?"

"What else can I do?" Mordred shook his head. "You mistake me for some other knight."

God help her, he was almost convincing. Even Perceval glanced at her with sudden doubt in his eyes. But there was a bittersweet joy jangling in her bones because the long-hidden foe was not Arthur of Britain. Blanchefleur stood her ground. "I have already said it is impossible. And if that were not enough, there is the word of your mother. Morgan showed to me the master who sent her to kill me. Her own son. *You.*"

There was a little stir, a little drawing of breath and wrinkling of brows in the pavilion. She felt some of Mordred's credibility falling away. Yet, if he heard now for the first time that his mother had betrayed him, Mordred hid it with delicate irony. "My mother is famed for her verity. When have you spoken with her?"

"Three times in the city of Sarras."

"In the city of Sarras?" Mordred laughed. "In the city of fancies and fables. Aye, and last night in a dream I spoke to the spirit of Achilles, and he told me I would be King of Britain."

His laughter fell dead in the pavilion's silence. Blanchefleur smiled, but it felt more like baring her teeth. "The spirits *you* converse with, deceiver and sorcerer, may indeed tell you what you wish to hear. But I, I am the last of the Grail Maidens of Carbonek Castle, and I walked the streets of Sarras. My blood yet stains those stones. I spoke to Morgan herself."

Mordred swung as if to appeal to the King. Arthur straightened in his chair and said, "Be assured the matter will be thoroughly sifted."

And his voice had the menace of a threat in it.

"Am I free to go?" Mordred asked. He did not look at her, but Blanchefleur felt malice beating oven-hot on her brow. She moved a little closer to Perceval.

"I counsel you," said the King, "to keep the company of the lord marshal for the present."

"Then let the lord marshal be advised that I go to make my disposi-tions," said Mordred, and wheeled and went out the door of the pavilion. As he went, Blanchefleur caught the gleam of his eye and nearly flinched.

"Bedivere," said the King, and one of the knights by his seat started after Mordred, who was already ten steps ahead, walking down the aisle between the King's men and Lancelot's. It was smoothly done, in an instant, before any of them were fully aware. As he came to the end of the line, Mordred broke into a run with a shout. A horse, saddled and bridled, came trotting at his call. Mordred flung his arms around the beast's neck, vaulted into the saddle, and quickened to a gallop.

Bedivere shouted, "After him! After him! Treachery! To horse!" But it was Perceval, still armed and within easy reach of Glaucus, who first took the trail.

BLANCHEFLEUR SPENT THAT NIGHT UNDER CANVAS. She lay awake for hours, straining her ears, before she felt rather than heard the slow thud of hooves and knew that Sir Perceval had returned. She rose, stepping carefully between the other sleepers in the tent, and stole out into the frosty moonlight.

"Perceval," she called.

He reined in and turned. Blanchefleur ran up to his knee, lifted his right hand from the rein, and kissed the glove. "Where is he? Did you lose him?"

"Yes, every trace." He slipped his hand out of the gauntlet. "You should not be out in the cold. We will speak tomorrow—" and with the sliding of his fingers through her hair he was gone.

The royal camp began to break up at dawn. By an hour before Terce, when a page was sent to bring Blanchefleur to breakfast, many of the pavilions had already vanished and Blanchefleur picked her way to the King's tent through mud stirred up by the passage of horses and oxen.

After Mordred's escape the evening before, Blanchefleur had given the King the summary of her acquaintance with Simon Corbin and her encounters with the Queen of Gore. Unfinished business of battle had prevented her telling more. The King had worked late on a grim matter, and when she slipped into his pavilion it was faintly jarring to see him sitting next to the Queen at a little table set for four, talking as if never a shadow had fallen between them.

Arthur was saying, "—told him he could have her, of course. He has proven himself in long service, and is the heir to a kingdom."

Blanchefleur hesitated in the doorway, but the Queen saw her at once and gestured silence to the King. "Come and sit, Blanchefleur," she called.

For the first time, Blanchefleur thought there was warmth in her voice. She slid into one of the empty chairs rather shyly. The King twinkled at her.

"What d'you make of this," he said. "Our lost daughter is restored to us not a day, and already I am asked for her hand."

For a moment Blanchefleur assumed he meant Perceval. Then, all in a flash, she remembered the words Simon Corbin had spoken, that night at the party, of the diplomatic marriage her parents no doubt intended for her. Why, could Perceval have had the time to ask for her hand between last night and this morning?

She swallowed. *What* heir to a kingdom had been told he could have her?

"He is well-known to you," the King reassured her, seeing the look on her face. Then a shadow darkened the entrance of the tent, and he turned to greet the fourth addition to their table.

The young knight came in, bending his head to avoid the low-slung doorway, and bowed to the King. "My lord, my lady." Then an affectionate gleam at Blanchefleur. "My love."

"Perceval!" And she remembered with a breathless laugh that King Pelles had made him his heir.

"Is he not to your liking?" asked the King.

"Oh! Yes! Yes, he is!"

"For he told me he has gained your consent. If he is lying, I'll have him scourged from Logres."

Blanchefleur opened her mouth to protest, but then saw the twinkle in his eye and had to laugh.

Sir Perceval sat down at the table next to her. "Why in such a pother, love?"

"It was—" Realisation stole her breath. "It was Mordred. It was something Mordred said to me, long ago." Even after all this time. Even knowing him to be a villain, his words still poisoned her thoughts.

The King tore a piece of venison from the bone, gave it to the hound Cavall, and said: "Ah yes, Mordred! His flight proves his villainy and argues in favour of Lancelot's story, that he has worked to Guinevere's undoing in all this strife." He glanced at the Queen and said, very gently, "That somewhat undoes the case against you, lady wife."

Guinevere bent her head in silent acknowledgement of his words. There was a wistful curve in the corner of her mouth, a sweetness of hope in the air. But if she was glad to be in the King's favour again, why did she duck her head as if to hide her face?

Perceval took a mouthful of wine and said, "Mordred's treachery explains much. For one thing, his alliance with that ruffian Saunce-Pité."

Blanchefleur nodded. "It also explains why, in Gloucestershire, Mr Corbin was able to guess all my secrets. Although if he wished to kill me, why did he ask me to marry him?"

Perceval said, "He saw the opportunity. Easy enough to deal with you as he liked once he had you. When you refused him, he sent the giant." He shook his head. "I never guessed Mordred was the man from Gloucestershire. In Logres he never spoke to me for more than five minutes together, never in clear daylight, never by his act but by mine. I told myself it was my imagination that he avoided me."

"You said he was Morgan's master," said the King to Blanchefleur. "Not her underling?"

"No." She traced the grain of the wooden table. "Morgan told me again and again that she was being used by someone. At first I did not believe her. But she acted so desperately… She gave me a vision to explain who that master was. I did not understand it at first."

She swallowed and picked her words carefully. "When I saw that Simon Corbin was Mordred, and that Mordred was Morgan's son, the vision made sense. The vision showed Morgan with a baby. Her son."

She looked at the King appealingly, not willing also to bring up the slander insinuated by Morgan and declared outright by Agravain—but wishing and hoping that he might tell her what to think of it.

The King either overlooked or did not see the question in her eyes. "Well?" he prompted.

"If Mordred was Simon Corbin, the man who dogged my tracks and tried to keep me in Gloucestershire," Blanchefleur argued, "then he must be Morgan's partner in crime, or more likely, given the purpose of the vision, her master."

"Certainly, he did not deny it."

The Queen said, "Rather, he fled, declaring himself without a doubt our enemy and sacrificing his strong position. This troubles me. He must have planned for such a possibility—he must have had his horse waiting. What will he do next?"

Perceval said, "We have men out looking for him. I have sent Caradoc north to watch the road to the land of the Silver Dragon. If Mordred travels that way, Caradoc will send word."

The King nodded. "Unless we take him soon, before he reaches safety." He wiped his moustache and stood up. "The sooner we return to Camelot, the better. I am uneasy away from my citadel, like a naked man in the snow." But he kissed his wife, called to his hound, and went out of the tent with none of the fatigue that had lain on his shoulders the previous day.

THAT AFTERNOON BLANCHEFLEUR CAME TO CAMELOT, riding with the King's vanguard. They took the few hours' ride from Joyeuse Gard quickly, not delayed by oxcart or siege engines. The ride was a pleasant one; winter sun flooded the floor of the leafless forest with light and warmth, so that beneath that golden eye it was easy to hope that all their troubles were over. And Camelot, which she had dimly sensed looming in the midnight sky a few nights ago, stood brightly unveiled now, its chaotic lines softened by the grey tracery of trees.

Camelot sprawled. Part of it had been built by the Romans, parts by other kings of other peoples, and now it was a rambling labyrinthine pile crowning the hill, sprouting turrets and stairways, little roads and tucked-away terraces, a haphazard heap of house, garden, city, and castle.

Blanchefleur and Branwen were given a roomy chamber on the south, where the sun sloped through big arched windows set with glass. From these the wall dropped sheer away into the castle garden, which at this time of the year was dead and bare. But Blanchefleur threw open the casement and called in delight, "Branwen, can you imagine how beautiful this would have been in summer? It must have looked like Sarras. What a shame it's all dead now!"

"It will come again." Branwen's voice was muffled. "Look what I found behind the tapestry! A whole room for storing clothes!"

Blanchefleur pulled the casement to and followed the sound of Branwen's voice to a little shelf-lined room. "For clothes? It looks more like a pantry to me."

"Well," Branwen giggled, "to be sure, let us keep some pork pies in here for when we are hungry in the night."

Blanchefleur shook her head. "No, you stick to nuts and plums. I don't care for pork-pie-scented dreams. I shall just have to get more clothes." She looked around the store-room. "*Many* more clothes."

Branwen laughed and darted out. When she came back, a saddle-bag hung from each hand. "Here are my things." She laid one bag on one shelf. "And here are your things." She opened the other, shook out Blanchefleur's spare tunic, and folded it neatly onto another shelf. The next thing she took from the bag was the little black knife in its leathern sheath.

"The obsidian knife," Branwen said, waving it at Blanchefleur. "You should wear this."

Blanchefleur took it gingerly. "Do you think so? For everyday use? Isn't it too fine?"

"Of course it is. I don't mean you should use it. But with that knife you defeated Morgan le Fay. It would be like carrying her head with you."

Blanchefleur laughed. "Ugh!"

"So that no one forgets who you are."

"If you say so." At that moment a knock sounded on the outer door, and Blanchefleur opened the door to Perceval.

"Come into the garden and talk," he said, gathering her into his arm. To Branwen he added, "You'll find Heilyn with Sir Culhwch in the hall. They want to see you when you are ready."

Branwen said, "Oo!" and looked at Blanchefleur with wide and eager eyes.

"Go, go," Blanchefleur told her, pulling her cloak around her shoulders. As Branwen darted down the corridor ahead of them, she said to Perceval, "She hopes they've set a wedding date."

Perceval looked wry. "It's a harder business than you might think. Especially when the marriage is an affair of state."

"So it won't be today for us?"

"It would be if I had a say in it. But the furthest your father will commit himself is to having his council approve a contract of betrothal by Sunday."

He pushed open a door and they went through into the icy garden. Blanchefleur sighed in disappointment and then said, "What a goose I am! Two days ago I was afraid you no longer cared for me. This afternoon it seems hard that I cannot marry you within the hour."

She slipped her arm through Perceval's and leaned her head on his shoulder as they went down a path with frosty leaves crackling underfoot. "I am so glad about the King—about Father and Mother. Will there be a retrial, do you know?"

"Your mother wants it. When Mordred is found."

"You don't think the new verdict would be in doubt?"

"I do not. With Mordred a fugitive, things that seemed certain a month ago are like daydreams today."

A hawk drifting in the sky to the south, above the forest, screamed. Blanchefleur smiled, lifted her face to the sun, and sniffed fresh cold air. "I am so glad! Yesterday, it seemed like everything had ended."

But Perceval shook his head. "Brothers of the Table have killed each other in battle, Blanchefleur. Perhaps you cannot feel it, but I can. A chill in the air. This peace is brittle as glass. One careless knock, and—" he made a scattering gesture. "All the King's work. All these years. His pride and joy—and it is no more. It has already gone."

Blanchefleur could not help shivering. Her mind went down gloomy paths; at last she said, "What is your father doing?"

"Sitting in the chapel by his kin." Perceval's voice froze. "He would not allow me to set foot over the threshold."

"Oh, Perceval."

"I went to speak to Lynet instead," he went on. "She yet barely comprehends what has happened. I have seen it before. There is a kind of elation in the first blow of grief. In three or four months she will begin to understand the meaning of *gone*. That will be harder."

"And you?"

He smiled wearily. "I continually forget what has happened. Remembering is like waking in the waste from dreams of food and warmth."

They walked on in silence for a few steps. Blanchefleur said, "And your father?"

"I cannot tell what good he thinks it does to be angry."

Blanchefleur picked her words carefully. "He was not the only angry man in the King's pavilion yesterday, dearest."

Perceval's jaw set. "One only has so much patience."

"I know, but…Didn't you hear what he said, about King Lot?"

"Grandfather has nothing to do with this."

Again she felt distance between them. And only the previous morning they had understood each other so perfectly.

But she had her own secrets, and she could not reproach him for his reserve if she kept hers. Blanchefleur said, "There's one thing I haven't told anyone, Perceval. About Sarras."

He nodded, but his voice came from far away, as though he was thinking of other things. "Yes?"

"I knew Mordred was Morgan's secret master because when I asked who, she showed me into her memories. Showed me that she had had a son."

Perceval nodded again. "You said so."

"Yes. But there was one other thing." Blanchefleur took a deep breath. "She told me, more or less, that—that the King was the child's father."

Perceval turned to her with a gesture of disbelief. "Of course she did! …What, exactly, did she show you?"

"Only the two of them walking together, years ago. And then Morgan leaving Camelot with her baby. And then she said that, if it comforted me at all, they did not know then that they were brother and sister."

"I will not believe it," Perceval said. "A brother and sister may walk together, surely."

"Yes, but that wasn't what she meant."

"I do not believe the King would do it."

"You didn't believe your father would be angry with you for fighting for Lancelot."

Perceval almost flinched. Blanchefleur said, "Oh, Perceval, forgive me. I just—need someone to tell me what to think about this. If it is true. You heard what Agravain said yesterday. Perceval, it's been preying on my mind for a whole year, and I haven't told a soul."

Their feet crunched through dead leaves. Blanchefleur shortened her step to match Perceval's limp. He said at last, "I know what you mean. If the *King*...if *he*..."

"...then it doesn't matter what Mother did. None of it matters. Logres is a lie."

Perceval's voice was husky. "No. Not a lie."

"There are times when I'm convinced she must have been telling the truth. Anything Morgan says is like a nut—you must crack the shell of falsehood to get at the kernel of truth. She has been a liar so long I don't believe she *could* give a straight warning to anyone, even when she so desperately wanted to warn me about Mordred. But what if there's a kernel of truth to what she says about the King?"

He didn't answer.

"And then there are times when I think it all impossible. Does it not seem impossible to you?"

"Of course." Perceval squeezed his eyes shut. At last he said, "Yet there is the resemblance."

"You saw it too."

"I could never tell who Mordred reminded me of," he said. "The King? Or someone else? It was, in the end, Simon Corbin. But Simon Corbin is the King's own image."

Crunch-crunch. Crunch-crunch.

Blanchefleur said, "He's trying to kill me so he can inherit Logres."

"Yes."

"That's *why*."

"But a bastard cannot inherit, and Logres split and weakened is no great patrimony." Perceval smiled down at her. "Let us hope! When Mordred is caught and questioned, the whole hard truth will come out."

Blanchefleur ducked her head and kept her eyes on the path. At last, almost in a whisper, she said: "Do we want it to?"

"Yes. Of course."

"Even if it's true? That Mordred is the King's son?" Blanchefleur pressed her lips together. "If it's true, he's been lying to us. Everything he's said or done for the last twenty-five years, a lie…" Her eyes were suddenly hot with tears. "Or even if we knew the truth, what could I do? How could I denounce him? Perceval, it's my *father.*"

He looked at her with a pain that mirrored her own. "God knows, Blanchefleur! If I knew, I would tell you!"

"But it isn't just me. He's been a father to all of Logres. Was it all for nothing? The Table? The Quest?"

"Never," he said, but his voice was ragged and weak. He cleared his throat. "Never. Logres is greater than one man. Greater than you or me, and greater than the King. Oh, Blanchefleur, I weep for the Table. There were a hundred of us on the Pentecost before the Quest. Now only sixty-two of the sieges have names on them, and a third of those are exiled to Wales with Lancelot. Even so there are enough of us left to keep Logres alight." He cast a glance over his shoulder, to the castle. "Or even if all of us perished…"

"Or even if all of us sinned as badly."

Perceval fell silent. "Yes," he said at last, and the words seemed to cost him some effort. "Even if all of us sinned. If we all turned aside and went astray. If we fell into ruin and the shadow of death together, Logres would go on, even if we were no more."

Blanchefleur said, very quietly, "Do you think that will happen?"

He passed his hand over his eyes. "Who can tell? But I have seen into your world, many years into the future, and I saw Logres there. It was wavering, perhaps even dying. But that is the pattern of the Kingdom. It will always be dying. But it will live forever. It was founded on another and greater King even than the High King of Britain."

A breeze picked at Blanchefleur's hair. She closed her eyes and breathed in. "You make me hope."

"That is why, in the end, it makes no difference how our fathers have sinned," he continued. "We know that the hearts of men are wicked. We have known it since the beginning. But shall Logres be utterly thwarted by the sins of man?"

Blanchefleur said: "Not forever; not when all is said and done. But in our time, perhaps…"

"Yes." Perceval stood stock-still, and Blanchefleur watched his struggle in anxious silence. "In our time…*Omnes enim peccaverunt*…" He drew his arm from her grasp. "Dear heart, I need to go."

"To speak to your father."

"Yes."

He turned his back on her and went without another word. But Blanchefleur no longer felt the distance lying between them like a wound.

34

I will weep for thee;
For this revolt of thine, methinks, is like
Another fall of man.

Shakespeare

erceval met Heilyn in the passage. "I came to find you," the
squire told him. "They are burying Gareth and Gaheris tonight. Did you know of it?"

"Lynet told me, but at first I thought it best to stay away."
Perceval turned and looked out the door into the garden,
where the slanting sunlight had already diminished, leaving the sky cold
and leaden. "So late," he murmured, and strode ahead of Heilyn toward
the chapel.

The little high-ribbed room was already full of people holding off the
dark with tapers. On the threshold Perceval turned to Heilyn. "Go in.
I'll wait here."

He sank back into the shadows in the corner of the door. Latecomers
passed by, apparently without noticing him. Perceval folded his arms,
let his chin sink upon his chest, and listened through the breathing and
shuffling of the crowd to the words of the funeral service. He knew the
words well; his lips moved with the prayer.

"Receive, O Lord, the souls of thy servants. Free them from the prin-
cipalities of darkness so that they be born into eternal blessing of quiet
and light, and deserve to be resuscitated among thy saints and elect in the
glory of the Resurrection, through our Lord Jesu Christ, thy son, who
with thee lives and reigns together with the Holy Spirit, through all ages
of ages. Amen."

A good prayer for the living, too, thought Perceval. In these days of confusion and strife, in these days of sin and foolishness, his soul longed for some assurance of eternal peace.

"Do not enter into judgement with thy servants, for before thee, no man is justified, unless all of his sins have been granted forgiveness by thee. Therefore we beseech thee, that they do not bear thy condemnation who are sustained by thy grace. May these be worthy to evade the condemnation of vengeance, who lived marked with the sign of the Trinity, through our Lord Jesu Christ, thy son, who with thee lives and reigns together with the Holy Spirit, through all ages of ages. Amen."

Life marked with the sign of the Trinity. What did it look like? How could he know a thing that nothing in the world could fully manifest? But already his lips were answering:

"Pour forth thy mercy on thy dead servants, O Lord, that they not receive the condemnation unto punishment because of their works. May thy mercy join them to the angelic chorus through our Lord Jesu Christ, thy son, who with thee lives and reigns together with the Holy Spirit, through all ages of ages. Amen."

Perceval waited. The coffins went down into the crypt; the flagstones grated within the chapel, covering two of the four brothers of Orkney. At last, one by one, the people began to leave: brothers-at-arms, lords, servants, merchant-men and craftsmen from the town. Only the King, with Sir Kay on his right hand and Sir Bedivere on his left, paused when he saw Perceval standing in the shadows.

He said nothing, only gripped Perceval by hand and by shoulder, smiling with pitying eyes. Then they moved on and Perceval stood looking after the King of Britain until his upright figure had vanished.

With a formless disbelief he remembered what he and Blanchefleur had discussed in the dead garden that afternoon. "It *can't* be," he told himself, and turned to see Heilyn in the doorway.

The squire nodded to Perceval, gesturing toward the chapel. Within, no more than two or three other men remained speaking to Gawain in low voices, and when Perceval's step sounded on the threshold, they left as if by some unspoken agreement, so that at last only the Knight of Orkney and his son remained.

Gawain, seeing Perceval, folded his arms and thrust out his jaw. "Well?"
Perceval went down on his knees on the threshold. "Sir, forgive me."
"For what?"
"For the angry words I spoke yesterday. For my insolent mood. For grieving you in taking part with Lancelot. I might have refrained from

the battle altogether…"

"Yes." The word was an accusation. Perceval gritted his teeth on a dragon's-breath of ire and said:

"Have I your forgiveness, sir?"

"Come and swear on your kinsmen's graves that you will avenge them," Gawain said, holding out his hand.

"Alas!" Perceval said, not moving. "This would be to disobey God and king."

Gawain laughed, short and sharp. "Then weary me no longer with your pretended remorse."

"You intend to fight Lancelot?" Perceval asked.

"You know I do."

"I beg you will not. Hear me. He has grieved you and greatly offended. But he is exiled for his crime, and can you desire any harsher punishment for a man of the Table and a brother? Sir, you have been the King's right hand and second only to Lancelot among the champions of Logres. I have borne your device and your name, and both have won me greater honour than I have gained myself. Do not blot your name nor your conscience with this deed. Do not spill Lancelot's blood, or it will be a grief and a shame to you in days to come that you have avenged yourself unlawfully, who have never borne blemish nor blame before."

Gawain was staring at the stones and the names on the chapel floor. At last he said, "No. The true dishonour would lie in failing to avenge the blood of my kin. Also I have sworn to ride out tonight, by oaths that I dare not break."

"And yet Lancelot was your friend, dear as a brother. Can you not forgive him?"

"Forgive him?" Gawain looked up at Perceval, and his eyes were dark with pain. "But he *was* a brother to me. That is what I cannot forgive. I have lost kinsmen before. I have lost friends before. But never at the hand of a brother."

Perceval waited.

Gawain began to pace the floor. "Lancelot! The best of us! Everyone said it. I *believed* it. I believed in him!…

"The best of us! If I were the only man he had wronged, I could forgive him! They say, 'Forgive'…They say…

"They do not understand. He did not only betray Gaheris, his brother-at-arms; he did not only betray Gareth, who loved him better than his own life. Not only me. Oh, God bear me witness, if I were the only one,

I could forgive him!…

"No, he betrayed all of us. *He* brought destruction to the Table. *He* took up arms against the gentlest King in the world. The best of us! And Logres is destroyed on his account!"

Gawain looked at Perceval despairingly. "Only his blood can wash out the reproach he has brought upon Logres. Logres, the kingdom of light, brought under darkness by his frailty."

Perceval said: "I understand…"

Gawain held out his hand, and his voice pled. "Join me."

Perceval rose to his feet. "I said I understand. But I cannot join you. Logres is not a kingdom of light, not yet. And Lancelot is not the only one of us who has sinned."

Father and son stood for a long moment looking at each other. Then Gawain dropped his outstretched hand, and it was as if icy doors slammed between them.

"Do as you like. You told me you intended to go your own way. Well. I will go mine."

He brushed past Perceval in the doorway and was gone.

PERCEVAL DID NOT SEE HIS FATHER again until the night of Heilyn and Branwen's wedding, at Christmas, two weeks later. When the feast was ended and the floor of the great hall cleared for dancing, Perceval went looking for Blanchefleur, whose seat at the high table in the gallery was, for the moment, empty.

These days she spent nearly all her time with the King, poring over books and chess-tables and case-law. Meanwhile Perceval was busy on his own errands. To him the King had given the pursuit of Mordred, and there were scouts to send out and reports to hear. And yesterday, although the hunt for Mordred took place of first importance, he had sent out another man to find Sir Caradoc, of whom no news had come since he had set out from Joyeuse Gard toward the land of the Silver Dragon.

"Take care," he had told Caradoc. "Watch and learn what you can, but do not attempt the chastisement of Sir Breunis alone. I would not risk you in this, but so many of the brothers of the Table are yet young and untried."

"In strength or in loyalty?" Caradoc's voice had been thoughtful.

"Both. Either."

And so Caradoc had gone. As Perceval went down the length of the hall, looking for the tawny gleam of Blanchefleur's head, he wondered if he should have gone himself. The bruised thigh he got from Sir Odiar had become swollen and inflamed after the hard fighting and riding he had done on the day of the battle of Joyeuse Gard, but the pain and the limp had faded within the last few days to an irking stiffness.

Maybe he could have gone. Caradoc was a married man and a father. With the Grail Quest toll and the battle of Joyeuse Gard, there were more than enough widows and orphans in Logres these days.

He found Blanchefleur standing against a wall, almost as if at bay, circled by a group of the younger knights and damsels whom Perceval still, as yet, hardly knew. None of them saw his approach, and the first words he heard, in Agravain's petulant voice, stopped him in his tracks.

"He appointed Sir *Perceval* as his successor? Why did I not hear of this?"

"It's no secret," Blanchefleur said, and Perceval could tell with what an effort she kept her voice so light and amiable. "There were three copies made of the contract; you might ask Father for the chance to read it any time."

"I don't see what better right Perceval has to Logres than anyone else," Agravain said.

"Well," said Blanchefleur, "he only inherits because he is marrying me. And the King thought it better to pass the inheritance to us jointly at our marriage. You see, if he passed it to me alone, if anything happened to Father, I might be at the mercy of anyone who chose to marry me for the sake of getting Logres."

"If it comes to that," Agravain said, "do you not think it rash of the King to accept you as his heir, so soon, without proof?"

Blanchefleur was silent a moment. Then she said, "Surely it lies within the King's discretion to so accept me. In any case, he has asked us not to marry until after the Queen's retrial."

Agravain looked triumphant. "So you admit that the King might be within his rights to disown you."

Perceval had listened long enough, and shouldered his way into the circle, which fell back with a nervous shuffle at his coming. Even Agravain recoiled a step or two. Blanchefleur looked up at him with relief and slipped her arm into his, and at that confiding touch his annoyance melted away and he spoke with the laughing insouciance that came so easily to him at awkward moments.

"By heaven, Agravain, are you jealous?"

"Only for the honour of Logres."

Perceval blinked. "A jealousy, then, that we all share. But one that is ill-served by such speech, in such a place, to such a lady."

Agravain glanced around to find that his silent ring of supporters had melted away. But his mouth set in a stubborn line. "When lofty kings and nobles show so little concern for truth and right, a simple gentleman must do what he can."

Blanchefleur stiffened at Perceval's side. "My father is not so great that he will not hear you out, if you go to him," she said. "If we take possession of this kingdom, it is from obedience to him, not our own ambition."

For the first time since Perceval came on the scene, Agravain looked both of them in the eye.

"Even so! I wish you showed less obedience and more ambition—more willingness to think your own thoughts and speak for the just rights of others."

Perceval grunted with disgust, and would have turned away if Blanchefleur had followed him. But her stiff arm tugged at his elbow while she stood looking at Agravain in puzzlement.

"Others?" Her voice was very low. "What others do you mean, cousin?"

Agravain looked at the floor.

"Sons have the prior right of inheritance. Not daughters."

"You mean Mordred."

Slowly, Agravain nodded.

Perceval said, "But Mordred is a traitor!"

"Why? Because he sought to defend his own? Because he fled, being wrongly accused?" Some of the old defensiveness crept into Agravain's voice. "Judge him when you know him."

Blanchefleur said, "I do know him," and Agravain stopped mid-breath and stared. She said, "Remember, he professed to be my friend. All the while plotting my death. I know how he spins fantasies with his words, Agravain. What has he been telling you? Why do you believe him?"

Agravain was silent for a long moment. "You're trying to turn me against him. Like you turned the King against him—on no proof but hearsay." There was a glassy sheen, like tears, in his eyes. "With your talk of honour, I almost imagined you might be willing to hear me—to go to the King and plead on his behalf—"

Blanchefleur caught a breath of surprise. "Plead on his behalf?"

"He would listen to the lady of the Grail." Agravain's mouth twisted. "But that is the trouble. He already has."

Blanchefleur opened her mouth, but Perceval interrupted.

"Come away, love."

She resisted him a moment longer. "Beware, Agravain. Mordred will make you into ten times the child of hell he is."

Perceval twitched her away, through the crowd, toward the music. Blanchefleur said, "I only wanted to warn him."

Perceval shook his head. "*Margaritas ante porcos.* After what we have heard tonight, crown me with cap and bells if I trust my fair uncle as far as I can spit."

He did not take her to join the dancers. Instead, he led a weaving path toward the door. A moment later they were hurrying across the courtyard.

"Where are we going?"

"Sir Odiar's companion," Perceval said. "What if that silent knight came from Camelot? I should have thought to look into it before. He carried an unmarked shield. Perhaps the blacksmith can tell us…"

"You think it was Agravain? Really?"

Perceval stopped. "Unless it was one of us, why should he disguise himself? And if one of us, who else would it be?"

"But he wasn't dissembling just now. He really believes Mordred is innocent—and how could he ride with Odiar to kill us if something like that still mattered to him?"

Perceval's forehead wrinkled. If Blanchefleur said that Agravain had faith in Mordred's innocence, then it had to be true; she was never wrong about such things.

"There is something sincere about him, Perceval, and I can't help but remember how *plausible* Mordred is."

"Or maybe Mordred has already twisted his mind into such a maze that he can no longer tell faith from treachery. In any case we should see the smith. Every trail has gone cold; perhaps the secret of Mordred's hiding-place is kept here, in Camelot."

Slow hoofbeats interrupted him. The horse that came in at the gate walked with drooping head and dull eyes beneath a shapeless burden, its sides streaked with a crusty darkness. Blanchefleur caught her breath.

Perceval said, "Gringolet?"

The beast came wearily to him and nuzzled his shoulder. The bundle on its back stirred and groaned and was Sir Gawain, lashed to his saddle with a thong that passed around his waist.

Moving through air that had suddenly become thick and heavy like molten glass, Perceval drew his knife and cut the strap. Gawain fell into his arms and Perceval clawed in vain for a handhold on mail grimed with blood and horse-sweat.

He was grateful that Blanchefleur said nothing. He was grateful that she only turned on her heel and left.

He sank down onto the courtyard stones with the dead weight of his father's head and shoulders in his arms. "You're bleeding, Father. Where? Where are you hurt?"

Gawain groaned and opened his eyes, focusing on him with drowsy labour.

"Not deep." He strained, trying to sit. "Help me stand."

"No, no, lie still." Perceval pulled him closer. "Help is coming—lie still."

Gawain sighed and slackened. Perceval felt his pulse—slow and sluggish.

He whispered, "Who did this?"

Gawain's eyes flickered open again. His lips moved, but no sound fell from them. Only his eyes and teeth gleamed, for a moment, with hatred. Then his eyelids fell and he breathed more softly and steadily.

Feet whispered on the stones around them. A hand fell on Perceval's shoulder, and he smelled Blanchefleur. "Is he—?"

"Swooned," Perceval said, and surrendered his burden to bearers and surgeons.

UNDER THE COVER OF MUSIC, BLANCHEFLEUR went back into the Great Hall to find the King. He was sitting with Sir Kay and Sir Bedivere at the top of the Table, and stood when he saw her coming with the vanguard of her news in her face.

"Sir Gawain is returned," she told him. "You'll find him with Perceval in the infirmary."

He understood at once; moreover there was a rattle of chairs as the other two knights found their feet. "I feared it would be so," the King said as they went down the hall to the door. "Is he much hurt?"

She shook her head. "I cannot tell. The surgeons are with him now."

"Blanchefleur." As they went past the side-door which led up to the ladies' gallery, the Queen stepped out of the shadows and called after her. Blanchefleur returned reluctantly.

"What's yon commotion?" the Queen asked.

"Gawain is back, and he's wounded."

"Dying?"

"I don't know. I think he has lost blood, but he said he is not deeply hurt."

"You can trust his word," said the Queen gently. "Gawain has seen more wounds than a college of surgeons. Come with me a moment."

She turned with a beckoning gesture toward the stair up to the women's gallery. Blanchefleur only hesitated a moment. The surgeons in Camelot were more skilled than she; in the infirmary, she would only be in the way. And the Queen wanted her. She went up the wooden steps wondering what Guinevere might have to say. She knew her mother well enough by now to know that she always kept some part of herself hidden, even with those she set most store upon.

Or perhaps especially with those she set most store upon.

The gallery, divided by intricate wooden screens, with its oak balusters and its eagle's-eye view of the hall—this was the citadel where the Queen of Logres ruled unchallenged. Blanchefleur followed her to a lonely corner above the feast, where the Queen paused and fingered the baluster like the frets of a lute and looked down on the merry-makers below. Branwen and Heilyn were dancing, crowned with ivy and winter roses. Agravain was dancing with the sister of Sir Pertisant, the young knight who had laughed in Joyeuse Gard when Lancelot swore the Queen innocent. Lines of people parted and met, swung and loosed hands—

One day, all this would be on her shoulders—hers and Perceval's.

The thought struck Blanchefleur, as it had once or twice in the last fortnight, with something akin to panic. If the Pendragon of Britain and the Table Round could so hardly defend this fleeting peace, what hope had she?

The Queen said, "I saw you speaking with Agravain, down there, before the dancing began. Tell me what he said."

Blanchefleur hesitated. The Queen cast her a sidelong glance. "Let me help you, my daughter."

Underneath her everlasting reserve there was a note of kindness in the Queen's voice that warmed Blanchefleur to the core. She said: "It was nothing serious. Agravain was chiding me for letting the King make Perceval and me his heirs."

"What did he want you to do?"

She laughed. "He wanted me to plead with the King on Mordred's behalf."

The Queen looked out on the festivity. "And?"

"I refused, of course."

"So would not I."

"You think something might be gained by it?"

"His trust. Perhaps, even, his loyalty."

"By helping him defend Mordred?"

The Queen's voice remained patient. "By *appearing* to help him defend Mordred. Thus you will persuade him that you are his friend, or at the least, his tool." She looked at Blanchefleur and smiled. "Bear it in mind, daughter. Others will come to you with petitions before long. Know how to turn such an occasion to advantage."

GAWAIN SPOKE TRULY—HIS WOUNDS WERE NOT deep. Lancelot had dealt with him as kindly as he might, and if Gawain had gone to have them tended, rather than leaving them to fester all the long way from Wales to Camelot, he would not have lain abed for the best part of a month.

"He means to ride again," Perceval told the King one afternoon in the solar where his father's friends had gathered.

"To Wales?"

"Yes." Perceval slumped forward and rubbed his forehead, straining after a solution. "Almost I could wish Lancelot had disabled him."

It was a terrible thought. He glanced at Blanchefleur, who met his eyes and shook her head. "He would only fret himself to death."

"He is going to die sooner or later." Perceval groaned, passing his hand through his hair. "He is no match for Lancelot! Not wounded as he is, and blind with rage!"

Sir Kay was using a knife to clean his fingernails. "Put him under lock and key. He is disobeying your express word, sire."

"Blanchefleur is right," Perceval said. "He would die more surely in confinement."

"Or perhaps he would come to his senses." Agravain, the last of Gawain's living brothers, lounged against the wall with his arms crossed.

The King said, "Have each of you pleaded with him?"

"Sir, all of us." It was Sir Bedivere who spoke, the King's marshal. "He refuses to hear."

"There must be something we can do," Perceval said.

The King looked at him with infinite pity. "Not always, fair son."

Perceval looked at his hands, clasped loosely before him. His had been Prince Alexander's key to all mortal woes: cut the knot of troubles with a blow of steel. But this knot was of adamant, and no steel would break it.

The King said: "I commanded him not to seek his revenge. I gave my word, and must enforce it."

Perceval shook his head. "What can you do? Fine him? He would laugh."

There was a knock on the door. Heilyn entered at the King's call and one look at the squire's face brought Perceval to his feet. Had Caradoc returned? He excused himself with a murmur and went out into the passage.

Heilyn waited for Perceval to pull the door closed and said: "Sir, be well."

"Out with it, man."

"We went to Lady Lynet to buy a horse."

Perceval saw Branwen also standing in the hallway, knotting her fingers together with an eager nervousness. Since her marriage, she had ceased to attend Blanchefleur, and Perceval had seen little of her. "*Salve*, mistress. Yes, I recall. I told you to go to Lynet first. She has Gareth's horses to dispose of."

Heilyn nodded. "Since the fight with Odiar, near Astolat, I have looked at every dun horse I see."

"And?"

"The Unknown was riding one of Gareth's horses."

"Are you—"

"It's the same horse," Branwen assured him eagerly. "We both agree. A rouncey, maybe six years old, with one white sock and leg bars. The mane has been cut, but it is the same beast."

"Are you saying that *Gareth*—"

Two heads shook in unison. Heilyn said, "Branwen thought to ask when the mane was cut."

"Lynet said it was after the King returned from Joyeuse Gard."

Heilyn cut in again. "Sir Agravain had it done. He told Lynet the mane was damaged and the horse would be more likely to sell without it."

"Agravain," Perceval whispered. The idea had occurred to him, but the fact struck him like a boot to the stomach. "Had Gareth loaned him the horse?"

"No one has ridden it for months, to Lynet's knowledge. But I asked in the stable, and one of the hands said it was missing just about the time of the Queen's trial. When the weather turned colder, the horses were brought in from pasture. The dun could not be found. It strayed in three or four days later."

Perceval pulled at his chin. "Agravain must have taken it, with the idea of throwing suspicion on Gareth if it was recognised. When Gareth died, the risk was of the horse being sold and identified. Therefore, the attempted disguise." Another thought struck him. "But this means that Agravain is more than Mordred's tool..."

He slapped Heilyn on the shoulder. "Well done," he gasped, and slipped back into the solar in time to catch the tail-end of Bedivere's words:

"—uphold the King's word of judgement in the matter."

Perceval wasted no time on speech. Drawing his poniard, he took Agravain by the elbow and set the blade at his throat.

"Agravain of Orkney, you are arrested for treason..."

Agravain said nothing. Only a dull flush spread across his face, and he looked at Perceval with something like reproach. Then he covered his eyes.

Others in the room rose to their feet. Blanchefleur lifted shocked hands to her mouth. But the Queen only smiled with thinly-pressed lips.

"Surely not," said Sir Bedivere.

Perceval said to Agravain, "Confess it, sir. We have the horse." He lowered his poniard and pressed it wearily into Bedivere's hand. "You are the King's marshal. I pass this man to you for examination. I have had my fill of hunting down my kin. I beg you'll let me leave, sire."

The King stopped him by a gesture. "Sir, we have determined to imprison your father if he tries to leave Camelot again."

Perceval stared at him for the space of five heartbeats before his unwilling mind made sense of the words.

"Any of us are prepared to meet him," Sir Kay said, and the jeering note was altogether gone from his voice. "But you have the right of refusal."

Perceval looked from one sombre face to another. "Meet him. You mean—fight him."

The King's head dropped in assent. "I doubt he will come willingly."

Even in the misery of that moment he knew why they asked him. Gawain would outmatch any of the other men here. It would be done by him, or not at all.

And yet— "Strike my father?"

The King's gaze did not falter. "Surely I may administer justice through you."

He stole a glance at Blanchefleur, but although she looked up at him with soft and pitying eyes, he read no answer there.

As fit. It was his own decision.

Perceval drew a long breath and closed his eyes. "I'll do it."

35

He that like a subtle beast
Lay couchant with his eyes upon the throne,
Ready to spring, waiting a chance.

Tennyson

 lanchefleur let a night pass before she went to the chambers on the north side of the castle where noble prisoners were kept in comfort under lock and key. It was in awe mingled with doubt that the guard unhitched the key from his belt at her command.

"Well, lady. But I'll come in there with you."

She had spent much of the night thinking it over. Should she bring Perceval?—Too great a show of force. Heilyn, then? But even the squire might put him on his guard, and she needed Agravain to trust her.

So she smiled blandly and said, "Good fellow, no. Hold the door and be ready to come if I should call."

For a moment she thought he would refuse. Blanchefleur lifted her chin and held his gaze. But at last he yielded the door, glowered at Agravain as he announced her, and closed it again behind her.

"Good morning," she said.

Agravain came bolting to his feet and then stood very still, watching her with narrowed eyes.

She said to him, "Sir, will you do me the honour of hearing me?"

He thrust his thumbs into his belt and said ungraciously, "If I must."

"I only come because I know that you love Logres."

He gave no reply. She went on.

"You know that you have provoked the King to wrath, and that he has the right to deal with you as a traitor."

"Have you come to gloat?" He took a step forward and his hands flexed by his sides. "I wonder you do not fear to come and taunt me thus, alone, to my face."

"Fear you?" She smiled. "No indeed, you are no Morgan of Gore," and she saw him recall who she was and come to his senses. "But I say only the truth, and I do not come to taunt. Last time the King sat in judgement on one of his own, there was war."

"As there will be if he attempts it again," Agravain muttered.

"Neither of us desires that, cousin. You know what it is like. Destruction of land and life, with every kind of evil and cruelty. There is much I would do to prevent it."

"Yet it may be the lesser evil."

"It may. And yet no king should readily spill the blood of his own subjects… You know that I have influence with the High King."

Under the glassy stubbornness of his eyes, she saw a flicker of interest.

"You know that he loves mercy better than bloodshed. If I can show him a way to pardon you, cousin, with no injury to his honour, he will take it."

He came forward another step, eagerly this time, and then caught himself. "Why? What does it profit you?"

"The peace of Logres profits all of us."

"And say we preserve this peace. Who sits on the throne?"

"Why, the King—"

"You know what I mean."

She lifted a hand. "The King's appointed heir, chosen in council. I. And Perceval."

Agravain's face darkened. "So. You think the people of Logres will stand by while the true heir is disowned—in favour of a cursed fraudulent *cuckoo?*"

She never heard the insult. The true heir. It occurred to her, with a force that took her breath away, that the prophecy made by Merlin at her birth referred to the Pendragon's *heir.*

Not to the Pendragon's daughter.

And if Mordred *was* the King's son?

She swallowed and looked back up to Agravain. "If Mordred is the true heir, then let him have Logres. I have no wish to set myself against the will of Heaven."

He blinked, taken aback for a moment by her evident earnestness. "Prove it."

"If I may, I will. Let it suffice for now that I prove my friendship to *you*."

"Well?" The sulky note was back in his voice.

"You can still save yourself, cousin. Show the King that you're willing to make amends." Blanchefleur came a pace closer to him. "My mother means to appeal the verdict that condemned her to the fire. By her account, she never spoke with Lancelot in the garden, and she never sent him her ring. She didn't, did she? You are the only one who can tell us what really happened."

He looked at the floor near her feet and opened his mouth. There was something so evasive in his face that she lifted a hand.

"Don't lie to me."

He closed his mouth again.

"Decide whether your life is dear enough to you that you'll tell us the truth in exchange for mercy."

Agravain chewed on his lower lip. At last he said, "Very well, I will. But tell the King I want to leave Camelot tonight. I want my horse and arms and food for five days."

According to her plan sketched out in the dark hours last night, Agravain would leave Camelot with watchers on his trail. But this was too good an opportunity to miss. Five days' journey? Could she narrow it down further? "Where do you mean to go? The King may ask."

"Orkney, I suppose."

He looked into her eyes unblinking, unmoving, and she knew it was a lie.

"I'm sure the King will have no objections." She went to the door, knocked for the guard, and turned with a smile. "Mind you, Agravain, if the King grants your petition and grants you parole, use your freedom wisely. Don't lose your wits, and run off to join Saunce-Pité."

A sudden panic, beating in the air. A fractional hesitation. A laugh.

"That's hardly likely, is it?"

That was a lie, too.

The door opened and she went down the passage with her blood drumming a victory march. No need now to send a spy with Agravain when he left. She knew where he was going.

More than that. She knew where to find Mordred.

PERCEVAL WAS STANDING IN HIS CHAMBER before breakfast, working the stiffness out of his hip with a series of lunges, when a sharp rap came on the door. He must have moved quickly to open it, but those few footsteps passed like an age.

Not already.

It was Heilyn. He said, "Sir, Sir Gawain has sent word to saddle his horse. I left word for them to prepare Glaucus, and came to help you arm."

"Well done," said Perceval, wishing for the first time that Heilyn was less meticulous in his duties. He went back into his chamber and took up the blood-red shield with the golden pentacle and the golden label. Near it was a leathern cover which he had taken from the armoury after the council in the King's solar yesterday.

Behind him, Heilyn was shaking out his hauberk and testing the straps on his spaulders. Then he heard the whisper of silk.

"Leave the surcoat," he said, tightening the cover around the shield and fitting it to his arm to try its heft.

Heilyn looked up. From the faint worried crease between his eyebrows Perceval knew the squire understood. But he explained it anyway, not just to Heilyn but also to any powers that stood by and watched what Sir Perceval of Wales, Knight of the Round Table, chose to do this day.

"I am going to take in my father, and I have not the nerve to do it wearing his device."

Perceval was ready and waiting on the Camelot bridge when Gawain rode down from the keep. His father spent no time on defiance, only laid his spear in rest and spurred his horse Gringolet to a gallop. Glaucus leaped forward, scenting war. But Perceval could not shake off a dazed, almost tipsy sense of unreality. The golden pentacle of Gawain filled all the field of his vision, reproaching him for what he meant to do. He seemed to be looking through the eyes of someone far away, and all his reflexes felt muffled by distance.

At the last confused moment his body remembered its old skill, and the wild boy of Wales flung himself headlong from the saddle of his horse as he had on the first day he fought a knight.

Gawain's lance swept through empty air. He yanked Gringolet around, dropping the spear-point, and his voice echoed in amazement within his helm.

"Perceval?"

Perceval climbed to his feet. "Sir, it is I."

"Why are you here?"

"The King sent me." Perceval wished he could see his father's face.

"He begs you to return."

Gawain sat unyielding and cold as stone. At last he said: "And if I refuse?"

"Sir, then I must compel you."

"You *dare?*" The words exploded out of Gawain, and his hand clenched on the lance. Perceval lifted appealing hands.

"What shall I tell my mother?"

The lance pointed. "Do not name her."

"I know she never ceased to love you," he went on desperately. "Shall I go to her in Avalon, and tell her that you killed yourself in pursuing this feud with Lancelot, and that I stood by and did nothing?"

"Your mother would be wise enough to know there are some things a man may not leave unpunished."

Perceval stared at the iron front of his father's helm. "But you are killing yourself by inches."

"I have heard it."

Perceval gripped his saddle-horn, pulled himself up, and drew back a little for the charge. "Will nothing move you?"

"I told you once before," Gawain said with dangerous calm, "that I am content to go my way and let you go yours. But do not think to stand in my path."

Perceval said: "Forgive me. The King sent me."

Gawain's spear crashed down like a gate. Gringolet surged into a gallop. Perceval couched his own spear, but weariness had sunk into his bones. There was a sickening jar as they met, and Perceval rolled in the dust of the road among the splinters of his lance.

He scrambled to his feet and saw that Gawain had already turned.

"Remount," said Gawain.

Perceval caught his horse and climbed back into the saddle, wincing from his bruises. At the other end of the bridge, Gawain looked for a moment as if he were about to forget the rules of war and use his spear on a knight who had none. Then he struck the lance headfirst into the ground and drew his sword.

This was Perceval's weapon, and for years he had been unbeaten with the blade. But it was a killing weapon, and he feared to wield it to his full strength. Instead, as they closed on the bridge, Perceval yanked his reins aside, forcing Gawain and Gringolet against the parapet. His left knee ground into Gringolet's shoulder, hooked against Gawain's knee, and thus wedged, held.

Gringolet snorted and tried to kick, but there was not room enough even for that. Perceval spoke. "In the name of the King, I am to commit you to—"

Gawain rose in his stirrups and his elbow lifted. Perceval realised what he was doing even as the steel-clad elbow smashed into the side of his helm. His teeth jarred together as he reeled sideways in the saddle; obeying the lurch, his horse stepped out, releasing Gringolet. The next moment Gawain caught him in the ribs with the pommel of his sword. Perceval tumbled onto the bridge with a crash of steel.

Sir Gawain snatched at one of Perceval's stirrups, worked it off the hook, and flung it into the river. Then he paused, looking down at his son lying on the road.

"Whelp," he said, and his breath was loud through the slit of his helm. "Since you have declared yourself an enemy and a traitor to your own kin, take this last counsel of me: See to it that your path never crosses mine again, for one of us must die if we meet. I swear it."

He spurred Gringolet into a gallop and was gone. Perceval rose to his feet and took off his helm, catching his breath as the icy winter air struck his face. Down below, Gawain dwindled on the forest road and at last vanished into the wood.

With one stirrup gone, there would be no following him.

A man trudging alongside an oxcart came up the same road and began to cross the bridge, stealing anxious and furtive glances at him. Perceval called, "Ho, fellow. Travelled far?"

The man nodded, ducking his head to look at the ground. When he spoke, it was with an accent Perceval dimly recognised—from somewhere in the north, Sorestan or Estrangore.

"This Camelot?"

"It is."

"The High King?"

"You have an errand to the King?" Perceval glanced at the cart. Within, under a blanket, lay something like a human body. Then he caught the smell, and his stomach clenched. "Who sends you to the High King, fellow?"

The man looked up. Fear clouded his eyes. "The Silver Dragon."

Perceval twitched the blanket back to reveal a headless body. From the crook of his own elbow, Sir Caradoc stared sightlessly at the sky.

Perceval gave a wordless cry. Not Caradoc. Not now. Not like this, stripped naked and spitefully used, with the blazon of Saunce-Pité scored into his chest.

"Sir knight?"

Perceval turned and saw two knights from the town, come to a standstill at the bridge's head. Was he blocking their way? For the moment their devices meant nothing to his numbed brain. "I do not know you," he said wearily. "What are your names?"

Perhaps the sight of the body in the cart warned them not to take offence at his tone. "Sir Pertisant and Sir Alisander le Orphelin."

That sounded familiar. "Knights of the Table?"

"Even so," said Sir Alisander, but the one named Pertisant said, "You must come from far away, not to know of us."

He had forgotten that his shield was covered. "I am Perceval of Wales."

Pertisant became all of a sudden very respectful. "Sir, we did not recognise you. May we pass?"

Perceval stared at him for a moment, then erupted into anger. "Go!" He set foot in his remaining stirrup and swung into the saddle. "Off into the forest, to play at being knights? Go! Go!"

Sir Pertisant moved forward uncertainly, but Alisander le Orphelin said, "Sir—?"

"Are you men?" Perceval roared. "Are you knights? Are you brothers of the Table? Can you look upon this murder without tears, without vows of justice? Back to Camelot, you brute beasts, and to arms! There will be deeds of honour to spare for all of us!"

PERCEVAL STALKED INTO THE KING'S SOLAR and laid the bloody bundle that was Caradoc's head on the King's chess-table.

"The Silver Dragon sends his greetings."

Only then did he see the other men in the room—the King's whole council—and the battle-fire dawning on their faces. Someone touched his arm, and he turned and pulled Blanchefleur close. Perhaps for the damsel's sake, the King did not reach out to unfold the napkin in which Perceval had wrapped the head. "Caradoc?"

Over the top of Blanchefleur's head, Perceval said, "Yes."

"I'll go and fetch Guimier," Blanchefleur murmured, pulling back.

"No. Send one of the women." The King rose; both his hands caressed the hilt of his sword. "Lynet, maybe." He swung around to Bedivere. "Send out the call for a muster. Kay, I need not counsel you how to provision a host. Lucan, have a clerk take down the confession of Agravain.

Saddle his horse, take his parole, and turn him loose."

"The muster?" Perceval blinked. "Agravain? What's this, sire?"

Lucan was already at the door and Blanchefleur had flung up a hand. "Father, if you'll have him in here to give his parole, I can guess if he means to break it or not."

"Let him break it. I'll punish no man before he has committed his crime."

"Sire," Perceval said again, as men and errands flowed past him to the door.

The King turned and gripped him by the shoulder. "Sir Perceval, ride with us to the land of the Silver Dragon. We go seeking Mordred."

NO ONE DOUBTED WHAT RESPONSE SHOULD be offered to Saunce-Pité's act of defiance. Not until the army of the Table arrived at last on the Silver Dragon's doorstep, looked about them, and doubted.

They met no resistance as they advanced—not even in the valley stronghold itself. In the village old men and women paused in open-mouthed surprise as they rode over the hill. Sir Breunis's castle stood closed, but no heads peered over the battlement; no defiance echoed from the walls. Without resistance, the gatekeeper admitted them to an empty and lifeless building.

"Where is your master?" the King asked the man. "Where did he go?"

The gatekeeper shrugged. Like the peasant who had delivered Sir Caradoc's body, he kept his eyes on the ground and mumbled when he spoke. "Don't know."

"Who in this valley does know?"

"Don't know."

The King looked at Perceval with a frown. "Saunce-Pité must have known we would come, and has already flown." He turned back to the gatekeeper. "Listen, fellow. There is a knight of about my height, black-haired, white-skinned, bearded and soldierly. His device is argent, a bend sable, and his name is Mordred. We know he is a friend of the Silver Dragon, and that he has been here before. Do you know the man?"

The gatekeeper licked his lips and darted a glance up at the King. "Maybe."

"Was he in this valley within the last two months?"

The fellow shifted. "No," he said at last.

"This is a lie," the King said. But the gatekeeper fixed his eyes on the ground and remained silent.

"It is plain that Mordred was here," said the King to Bedivere. "What do you counsel, old friend?"

"Track the Silver Dragon to his new lair, if possible," Bedivere said.

The King turned to Perceval. "And you?"

"I want justice for Caradoc, sire."

"So be it. Have the men lodged in this keep, Bedivere. Gatekeeper."

The miserable man began to tremble, but he did not look up.

"Your lord has left you unprotected. Shall I give this place to a lord who will defend you?"

The gatekeeper stole a glance at the King and moistened his lips again, but did not dare to speak.

"Say on, fellow."

"It is winter." The words came out slowly at first, then rushed to a torrent. "We have no medicines and no food and our houses are falling down. Our children shiver in the snow. Lord, give us a lord to mend our roofs and mill our grain."

The King's brow knitted. "Why do you not mend your own roofs and mill your own grain?"

The gatekeeper trembled again and his gaze fell to the ground. "Sir, the learned men have gone with our lord, and he has not given us leave to do these things."

The King stared at the man for a moment longer, and then turned to Perceval with a laugh. "*Quia et latrocinia quid sunt nisi parva regna?* But this robber is less a little king than a little god."

"A god?" Perceval flexed his hand around his lance, remembering a day that Breunis Saunce-Pité had lain with a poniard to the throat and begged for mercy. "And yet steel spills his blood as eagerly as any mortal's."

IT WAS DARK, AND PERCEVAL COULD hear an owl calling outside when a touch on the shoulder woke him.

"Sir. My lord."

He pushed back his blankets and sat up. Through the windows of Saunce-Pité's great hall, a little moonlight shone on the cocooned and sleeping forms of all the remaining brethren of the Table.

It was Heilyn's voice, Heilyn's hand on his shoulder. Perceval whispered, "Is it my turn to watch?"

The squire shook his head. "Someone is asking for you."

Perceval got up as softly as possible, buckled on his sword and fitted his shield to his arm. Outside in the courtyard, the cloudless February sky glittered with stars, and the puddles on the ground had the slick black stillness of ice.

A woman stood there by a horse, huddled into a cloak like a crow puffing its feathers against the cold. White breath drifted from each mouth. Heilyn murmured, "I will get the horses," and went to the stables.

At Perceval's coming, the woman pushed her hood back. "Sir Perceval, do you know me?"

Familiar words. "Lady Nimue. What brings you here?"

"Your father is asking for you," said the immortal Lady of the Lake, and Perceval felt the cold bite deep into his bones.

THEY RODE NORTH AND WEST UNTIL dawn brought them to a hut by the river called Deva. Inside, in the dark, a smouldering fire was burning. Perceval paused in the doorway and saw Sir Gawain lying on the floor with a cloak thrown over him, his head resting in a woman's lap. When the early light flooded into the hut, she looked up, and Perceval took a deep slow breath that was not entirely surprise. A little thin blade of pain lanced his chest as the last flicker of hope died. He said, "Mother..."

Ragnell the fay, wife of Gawain, put her finger to her lips. But Gawain opened his eyes and moved his head. "Perceval?" His voice sounded like stone grating against stone.

Perceval fell on his knees by his father's side. "Here, sir."

Gawain's eyes drifted shut. He seemed in little pain, but his breath was long and loud and laboured. At last he opened his eyes again. "Where is your shield?"

"Here. Close by."

Perceval lifted it up. It was still covered, as it had been since the fight on the bridge. Finding another device, or even equipping himself with a good blank shield that did not need a cover, had taken second place to preparing the invasion of the Silver Dragon.

Gawain lifted a hand, and his fingertips skimmed the black cover. "I cannot see it..." His hand fell, and he lay silent a little longer. At last he looked up at Perceval, and with an uncertain smile said: "You will have to remove the label, son."

Perceval softly drew his breath and glanced up at Ragnell. There was a sad curve to her mouth, but she smiled at him.

"You'll take it off?" Gawain asked again, and an anxious note was in his voice.

"I will, Father."

His eyes closed again, and his loud slow breathing continued. Perceval put his arm around his mother's shoulders, and they sat still, watching.

He said once: "Is there nothing we can do?"

She shook her head. "I dare not move him."

Gawain breathed slowly out. For five seconds there was silence in the hut, and then he breathed in again and Perceval found that he had been holding his own breath. But it was a thing he had heard and seen before, and he knew what was coming.

They were still sitting side-by-side on the ground when Gawain breathed out for the last time. The unmistakeable change of death crept over his face; what had been inhabited was now abandoned, and the oath sworn on the bridge of Camelot was kept.

Ragnell leaned her head on Perceval's shoulder. For a little longer, they sat with their dead.

OUTSIDE THE HUT, WHERE THE RIVER broadened into a quiet cove, in a little boat that had been pulled up on the sand, Perceval and Heilyn laid Gawain on a cloak and covered his face.

Ragnell took Perceval's hands and looked up at him hesitantly, as if loath to speed their parting. "I am going back to the Apple Isle, Perceval. Will you not come with me?"

"To Avalon?" It had been three years since he last saw her face in the grey of an early spring morning. Since then he had wandered the island of Britain from one end to the other, he had spoken with queens and ladies without peer, and he had escaped the snares of fiends spell-woven for his doom. And yet the ageless beauty of Ragnell the fay outshone all of them—all, he thought, with a little throb of loyalty, save one.

She said, "To Avalon—yes."

"Leave Logres?"

"Yes."

"In her hour of need? How can I?"

She said: "Logres is dying."

"This is no new thing, Mother."

"Dear son. Can you not see the signs?"

"What do the signs matter? There have been bad omens before."

Ragnell had not shed tears over Gawain's death, but pools glimmered in her eyes now. "In Avalon," she said very quietly, "even mortality may be cured. I will wait for you. Go and fetch your lady."

All at once, Perceval understood, and his heart leapt. Avalon, the Apple Isle! The undying realm would give him rest and ease and the thing he coveted above anything else in the world.

Time.

A hundred years of peace. A thousand years of peace. Peace until the world ended, with Blanchefleur at his side. They would grow old together, as he never before permitted himself to hope; and it would be age without feebleness, without death.

Ragnell had already watched a husband die. Why should she, being immortal, see her son follow the same dark path?

But even as all this passed through his mind, he remembered the city of Sarras, and the burden that had been laid upon him. Also, he remembered Nerys the fay, who desired to die because she prized Sarras even above Avalon.

"Mother, if I could, I would. But even if Logres does fall, there will be more work to do here. Not less. For he must reign until he has put all enemies under his feet. Would you have me a deserter from that service?"

There was pain in her voice, and something else, the high and haughty ring of steel. "Never, son of Gawain." She lifted her hand to his cheek. "He is proud of you, if he can see you now."

"Then we'll keep it so," he told her, and gathered her into his arms for the last time. Then he handed her into the little boat, and he and Heilyn pushed it with a complaint of stones across the shingle and into the current, and stood on the bank watching until it was lost in the distance.

Thus Perceval of Wales bade farewell to Sir Gawain and Ragnell the fay.

When the boat was gone out of sight, Perceval turned to where Heilyn and Nimue stood on the bank with their three horses. "Where is Gringolet?"

"Tethered behind," said Heilyn.

"Fetch him and let us be on our way."

"A moment," said Nimue.

In the pale winter sunlight, Perceval read some dire portent which she now permitted, for the first time, to show in her face. "What is it? Tell me—"

"Mordred has taken Camelot."

The words took a little while to sink in, while the water of the Deva murmured against her banks and a chill breath of wind stirred the naked winter branches. Perceval's first impulse was to ask if he had heard correctly. But if she spoke the truth—and Nimue always spoke the truth—there was no time for that. He blinked and shook his head, as if to clear his vision after an enemy's stroke, and said, "What do you advise?"

"Ride back to the King. Gather Lancelot and his men. Muster all the help you can. Mordred is in league with Saunce-Pité—"

"Even so, Camelot is defended—we left a garrison—"

"Young blades more nigh akin to Mordred than their own fathers."

Heilyn broke in. "But what about Branwen, what about Blanchefleur?"

Perceval turned on the fay. "Are they safe? Do you know?"

"No."

Perceval gathered up his reins and sprang to the saddle. "Lancelot is a few hours' ride west. I'll go to him. Heilyn, take word to the King, but linger not for me. I am riding to Camelot."

36

It is something to have wept as we have wept,
It is something to have done as we have done,
It is something to have watched when all men slept,
And seen the stars which never see the sun.

Chesterton

ime," Blanchefleur thought to herself in the bone-aching night cold, "is much too precious to spend like this."

Silence had fallen on Camelot long ago. Now the slow passage of hours was marked only by Branwen's soft breathing from the other side of the bed, where she had come in Heilyn's absence. In the midnight dark, Blanchefleur's lips moved over the words of the old enchanter in Broceliande.

"The Pendragon's heir…"

The King. Until he left a week ago, she had spent most of her time at Camelot in his company, receiving what he told her was the greatest gift he could give—knowledge. Statecraft, diplomacy, and the strategies of war. At every opportunity they stole minutes and hours from the King's day in a scrabbling attempt to fit years of instruction into however much time might remain to them. Every day she had followed him from council chamber to judgement seat, clutching a growing sheaf of parchment that held her notes. And every day he had spoken to her of justice, mercy, truth, and right.

She was sick of the sound of them.

What about Mordred? What did *he* have to do with truth and right? Was the King's love for mercy no more than the guiltiness of hidden shame, unable to condemn others because unwilling to condemn self? She wanted to trust the King; she knew his wisdom should come like rain on parched earth. But until she knew for certain that he had nothing to

339

do with Mordred's birth, he could say nothing to her that did not echo in her ears with mockery.

At times it had occurred to her to ask him outright. But she always shied away from the thought. How did one ask a question like that? Surely there was a law against falsely accusing the High King of Britain of a crime like incest? As subject and as daughter, was it right even to form such doubts, let alone voice them?

With a twinge of sorrow she remembered their meeting in Sarras, before ever Morgan and her crafty son came between them. One little taste of fresh water, then Morgan had poisoned the spring, and the bitter taste of that draught could not be cleaned from her throat.

Beside her, Branwen gave a little sigh and moved and went on breathing quietly. Blanchefleur got up on one elbow and turned her pillow over, in search of the feathers that had migrated away from her restless head. And what about Guinevere? With Agravain's confession signed and sealed in Camelot's records room, they now had good proof that he had accused the Queen falsely and stolen her ring to send to Lancelot. Though he had refused to admit Mordred's involvement, his evidence was enough to clear her mother's name.

But only of recent ill-doing. Blanchefleur remembered the earnestness in Lancelot's eyes when he had sworn the Queen was innocent. Thinking back on that night she supposed he must have told the truth, but was it not possible that he had spoken only to the present charges, and not to long-ago guilt?

Logres was shaking. Logres was sliding. Since the day Perceval came to fetch her from Carbonek there had been nothing but trouble. How much longer did she have—with Perceval, with the King, with the Queen, with any of them? Would the chance to know the truth pass unseized while she wavered and worried?

Perhaps Mordred *would* make a better heir of Logres.

SHE WOKE PERHAPS FIVE HOURS LATER to a soft pressure against mouth and nose, and to an urgent whispering voice that came from far away and long ago.

"Blanchefleur. Wake up. Wake up. We are already out of time."

Blanchefleur opened her eyes on the glow of a lamp. For a moment she wondered if she was back in her closet in Carbonek, with the Grail-light shining in the window. Then she felt the hand covering her mouth, and bolted upright with a kick of adrenaline.

"Hush!" the voice warned, and in the faint and flickering light Blanchefleur saw who stood by the bed.

"Nerys? *Nerys?* But…"

"Hush!" Nerys said again, reaching over to shake Branwen. "I am already too late. Mordred is here. Agravain has returned. And the men of the Silver Dragon are searching for you."

Branwen passed in a moment from sleep to full waking. "*Mordred? Here? How?*"

Blanchefleur's slumber-heavy mind began to work again, slowly and methodically. She pushed up a sleeve and pinched herself. When that did not shock her into a pleasanter waking, she slid out of the bed and fumbled for a tunic to pull over her smock.

Nerys said: "Save for Sir Kay and a handful of others, the garrison is already in Mordred's pay. They opened the gate to him. …How did the King leave Camelot so ill defended?"

Blanchefleur shrugged into her tunic. "I learned from Agravain that Mordred was with Sir Breunis Saunce-Pité. Then the Silver Dragon sent us Sir Caradoc's body. An insult we were eager to avenge."

Nerys only shook her head, rubbing her temples.

Branwen had not moved since waking; she sat like a tousled owl and said, "What are we going to do? Wait here for them to find us?"

Down the corridor, someone cried out and was abruptly silenced. The last sleepy cobwebs cleared from Blanchefleur's mind. This was no dream. This was real.

"Not if we have a choice," Nerys told Branwen. She glanced around the room, at the tapestries lining the wall. "Is there no other door?"

"There's no way out but the window." Blanchefleur fought to keep the edge of panic out of her voice.

"All I need is a door with a keyhole."

The elf-keys. Of course. Blanchefleur yanked aside the tapestry concealing the little door to the store-room where she and Branwen kept their clothes. "Here."

Nerys snatched a key from the pouch at her waist, thrust it into the lock, and opened the door on dark emptiness. Blanchefleur put her hand through and felt what lay beyond. Neither the rough surface of stone nor the nubby texture of tapestry greeted her fingers, but the silky cool touch of polished wood.

And the smell! Soap and camphor. Lavender and roses. Tea and roast beef. All the things she had forgotten about in the last two years, breathing benedictions upon her from the shadowed void.

"We're going back to Gloucestershire?"

Nerys said: "If you hide in here Mordred need never find you."

Branwen shuffled over and looked into the darkness. "We'll be safe?"

Something in the fay's words tugged on Blanchefleur's mind. "Nerys, what about you? Aren't you coming?"

Nerys looked away and said, "If Mordred takes hostages, he will be able to dictate terms. Most of all he will want the Queen."

Blanchefleur's conscience stabbed her. "Mother! Of course!" She glanced to the door. "I know where to find her."

"No. They know you. They will be looking for you. Go in and leave her to me." Nerys pushed the key into Blanchefleur's hand. "Hold the door ajar. Wait for me to return if you can. If not, close the door and lock it from the other side."

Blanchefleur nodded.

At the door, Nerys looked back.

"One last thing. If the worst happens. Know that if you lock this door and destroy the key, you will never find your way back to Logres. Logres will never find its way back to you."

Blanchefleur remembered the evening so long ago, when Sir Odiar first attacked, when she first told Nerys that she did not want to leave Gloucestershire for Logres.

That girl would have wanted the key, and the permission to destroy it.

That girl would never have been trusted with either.

Impulsively, she ran from the wardrobe door and flung her arms around the fay's neck. "I missed you," she whispered. "Come back safely."

"My darling, I missed you too. *Now hide.*"

BLANCHEFLEUR LET FALL THE TAPESTRY BEHIND her, and Branwen swung the wardrobe door nearly shut. For a moment they stood and listened, unmoving in the scented darkness.

Then Blanchefleur ran her hand over the silk-smooth panel on this side of the door until she found the keyhole, and pushed in the key. "Keep the door," she whispered to Branwen. "I am going to see where we are."

She navigated the room by touch, heart in mouth, envisioning every kind of glass-shattering blunder until her fingers brushed heavy curtains. When she pulled them open, moonlight flooded in and she looked out into a gracious silver world with a rolling skyline like an old familiar friend whose name is for a moment forgotten.

No gaslight spilled out of the windows on this side of the little house. Most likely the occupants were all asleep. They were safe, at least until the servants rose in the early pre-dawn.

Blanchefleur turned and saw in the moonlight the shrouded furniture of someone's best spare room. The door Branwen guarded on this side also belonged to a wardrobe, a tall-standing oak closet and not a tiny stone room. She saw a dressing-table and a basin and ewer, creamy wallpaper with delicate stripes, a big comfortable stuffed chair. How many of these pleasant things she had forgotten, and in so brief a time!

Following some instinct or long-ago memory, Blanchefleur crossed the bedroom and went out into the passage. A few steps further on, carpeted stairs led down to a little tiled entrance-hall with a front door, a hat-stand, and three spots of red on the white wall where the moon shone through stained glass.

One of the hats on the stand jogged a memory made unreliable by time, dislocation, and moonlight.

The Vicarage. Of course.

She knew, then, exactly where the back door would be, how to find a little gate in the garden wall, and paths through the hills for miles in any direction. That was comforting, and the choice, if Nerys had chosen the house, was a good one. On the other hand she did not know where she and Branwen would go if they had to, or how they would travel far on foot. But that could be considered later. This hiding-place need only shelter them until Mordred left Camelot, or relaxed his vigilance long enough for them to escape.

As Blanchefleur turned to go back upstairs, the cry of a baby drifted down from above.

She froze with one foot on the stair. There were no babies at the Vicarage! Another glance at the clerical black hat on the stand reassured her. This was the house she knew. Had Mr Felton been replaced by a younger man?

Blanchefleur stole back up the stairs. She had just reached the top landing when another door down the passage opened and Emmeline Felton—or Emmeline Pevensie, as she must be now—came out, trailing nightgown and peignoir. The baby had fallen silent and lay snuggled against her shoulder.

Blanchefleur recognised her at once in the moonlight streaming in through the window at the end of the passage, but Emmeline stopped dead and gasped. For a moment both of them stood motionless. Then Blanchefleur whispered, "Emmeline! Don't be alarmed! It's me—Blanche Pendragon."

Emmeline came a step closer. "You're not...dead?"

"No, Emmeline."

"I'm glad." Emmeline sounded rather dazed.

"Is he yours?" Blanchefleur asked.

"Yes. Small Arthur."

In a little corner of her anxious heart, hope flickered. Did Logres live on, even here? "He's beautiful."

"Yes." Emmeline refocused on Blanchefleur. "Blanche! Where have you been? Where did you come from? Why are you here?"

"I..." The question caught her unawares. "I can't tell you, Emmeline. Not just now. I'm sorry."

"But now that you're here, you'll stay? Dear, you know you can live with Arthur and me if you have nowhere else..."

There was carpet under Blanchefleur's feet and the scent of clean and delicate things in her nostrils—perfume, babies, soap and tea. Homesickness hit her like a clenched fist; this was worse than memory.

She smiled at Emmeline. "How I wish I could! But I can't. I'm engaged. And I have a family." For as long as it took Mordred to find them.

"You have? Goodness, Blanche, and all this time we thought you were—" Emmeline caught herself. "Let me put Small Arthur down and we'll get a cup of tea. Wait right there!"

Emmeline vanished into another of the bedrooms. The moment she was gone Blanchefleur opened the spare room door and passed in like a shadow, signalling to Branwen for silence.

She dared not close the door entirely, lest Emmeline hear the knob click. So she heard her come out of the baby's room and whisper, "Blanche? ...Blanche?"

Blanchefleur leaned her forehead against the lintel of the door and told herself that it was better like this. No goodbyes. No questions, either.

Emmeline hesitated, then went down the stairs. Her whisper, as it came floating up, was less sure of itself. "Blanche...?" With infinite care, Blanchefleur closed the door.

By the wardrobe, Branwen whispered, nervous. "I heard you speaking to someone."

Blanchefleur crossed to the wardrobe. "An old friend. She will think she's been dreaming. Has anything happened in Camelot?"

Branwen shook her head. "Not yet."

But then, on the heels of her words, she stiffened.

The voices inside the wardrobe were muffled by tapestry. Agravain said: "They have already gone."

Blanchefleur felt Branwen grab her arm.

"Not far," said another voice after an agonising silence. "The bed is warm. They're still in the castle."

She knew the voice, and hairs prickled on her neck. *Mordred.*

Blanchefleur eased the wardrobe door open another half-inch, reached two fingers through, and pulled on a loose thread at the back of the tapestry. The hanging moved just far enough to give them a slitted view of Blanchefleur's chamber at Camelot, now blazing with torchlight.

Mordred was saying: "Search the room. Beat the tapestries. Raise the alarm. She must have been warned—there's no need to tiptoe now."

Armed men clanked through their field of vision. In the spare room of the Vicarage in Gloucestershire, Blanchefleur eased the wardrobe door shut and turned the key.

For a little while they sat in the darkness while Blanchefleur counted slowly under her breath to keep track of time. She reached three hundred, turned the key in the lock, waited a moment longer with her ear against the crack, and then inched the door open again.

The torches were gone. Darkness and silence lay under the tapestry. When she pulled the thread again, she saw the walls and bed outlined in the first glimmer of dawn. As Blanchefleur's eyes adjusted, she thought she saw bedclothes tossed onto the floor and chests standing open and rummaged. Now that the room had been searched, maybe it would be safe to venture back in to wait for Nerys.

And maybe one of their enemies would blunder in at any moment, hunting for plunder or captives. Blanchefleur looked at Branwen, raised a finger to her lips, and kept watch in silence. In the Vicarage spare room, the moonlight shifted a little. In the Camelot bedchamber, the dawn imperceptibly strengthened.

At last Blanchefleur saw rather than heard the door to her room in Camelot open. Attended by the soft glow of her oil-lamp, Nerys slipped in and closed the door behind her. She was alone. What had become of the Queen?

Branwen, who had been sitting on the floor, went to rise to her feet. But Blanchefleur saw the look that suddenly froze Nerys's face, and gripped her shoulder in warning.

Inside the chamber the black-haired fay stood motionless for a moment. Then she said, "Mordred."

A shadow rose from one of the chairs by the dead fireplace, and moved into the light.

"I," said Mordred.

All at once Blanchefleur was drenched with sweat. He had been sitting there the whole time. Listening. Waiting for them to give themselves away with one rustling movement, one whispered word—and now he had caught Nerys—

"Why are you helping them? The Elves have little love for Logres, surely?"

"My people say our fate is sundered from the fate of men."

"Then why you?"

"Avalon will fall at last. Sarras never will."

"Sarras!" Mordred laughed. "You put your hope in a dream. The people of Logres need more than ideals and what-ifs. They need real solutions to real hardships."

"What could be more real than the City?"

"This." Mordred stretched out his hand. "Flesh. Time. And the power to do what needs to be done."

The warm glow of her lamp stained Nerys's white skin golden, and no look of fear or anger marred her brow. She said: "Flesh and time? What else is the King of Sarras King of?"

With a speed that made her gasp, Mordred caught her by the throat and snarled in her ear: "You are living in a dream-world. I tell you the Spiritual City has nothing to do with hours or minutes, blood or pain. Shall I teach you the taste of the truth? Will you still believe in the City when your last heartbeats echo in your ears?"

Nerys looked at him out of weary eyes. "You poor fool. I am immortal."

Mordred slipped his hand into a pouch. What he held, when he drew it out, was black as smoke and shadow.

"The Lady of Logres has flown," he said. "But she left this behind, too dangerous to be used like a plaything and thrown aside. Sharp enough even to part an immortal from life. Tell me where to find her."

Nerys yanked on his hand at her throat, but the strength seemed to have left her.

"Consider your answer," said Mordred. "I will not ask a second time."

Nerys spoke hardly above a whisper. "Go and ask them in Hell."

In the Vicarage, Blanchefleur's hand flew to her belt. To her pouch. She looked at Branwen in horror.

The obsidian knife...

Mordred struck. Three jabbing motions with the T-hilted knife. Three choking little coughs as Nerys slid to her knees. First the lamp thumped onto the rush-strewn floor, then Nerys followed.

Blanchefleur stared into her dying eyes. Nerys's bloody lips moved one last time. "*Naciens...*"

Nerys the Fay went into Sarras.

Mordred wiped the obsidian blade against his boot and tucked it back into his pouch. Then he reached down where Nerys's lamp lay licking the floor beside her, threw it onto the bed, and left, slamming the door.

Branwen gave a little high keening cry, put her arms around herself, and began to shake. Blanchefleur could not cry, not yet; she pushed up her tunic sleeve and pinched herself again. Again, the pain promised no waking from this nightmare.

She slumped down onto the floor beside Branwen, put her arm around her, and sat.

Again, the moonlight shifted. Somewhere out in the summer night of Gloucestershire, a blackbird woke and warbled and fell asleep again.

At last, Branwen stirred and sniffed. "Something's burning."

"Mordred set my bed on fire. Again." Well, the last time, it had been Perceval. But it was all Mordred's fault.

Branwen wiped tears from her eyes and then stared at her wet hands. "What happens if the door burns?" Her voice held little more than idle curiosity.

"I don't know. We get stranded here, I think."

There would be time for that cup of tea with Emmeline.

But Branwen turned to her in concern. "We have to go back. What about Heilyn? And Perceval?"

Perceval? "You're right," she gasped, scrambling to her feet. Through the wardrobe door, the flames had spread to the dry rushes on the floor. In a little time the room would be impassable. Blanchefleur stared in dismay. "Where will we go? What if Mordred is waiting for us outside, like he was for Nerys?"

Branwen dragged in a sniff and set her jaw defiantly. "I have a plan. If he means to burn Camelot, he won't stay inside till it falls on his head. He will wait outside until he is sure we're dead. So we will hide in here until he gets tired of waiting and goes away."

It sounded like a terrible plan to Blanchefleur. She said: "Where?"

"In one of the cellars."

"If the castle burns, we'll be crushed. If it doesn't burn, Mordred will keep looking until he finds us."

"Not in Sir Kay's secret cellar."

"Sir Kay's what?"

"The one he keeps the best wine in, in case it gets stolen. Only he and Sir Lucan know where it is. And me. And I told Heilyn, of course."

"Sir Kay told *you* about his secret cellar?"

"Well, he likes me! The cellar is quite safe. It lies under the garden, not under the castle. There is a hidden door in the big buttery."

"Branwen, you're a marvel. Let's go."

Branwen caught her elbow as she went to fling the tapestry back. "Yes, but let me go first. If Mordred is waiting outside, he won't catch both of us."

Branwen pulled a sleeve of her smock across her nose and mouth, slipped through into Camelot, and skirted the flames to the door of Blanchefleur's chamber. She was gone for as long as it took to count twenty before the door swung open again, and God be thanked, it was Branwen, beckoning with a smile. Blanchefleur took one final farewell look at the moonlit hills that had once been her home. Then she stepped into the smoke and heat and locked the wardrobe door behind her.

"Come on," Branwen was urging. Blanchefleur went gingerly through the smouldering rushes. Here by the bed Nerys lay where she had fallen, with her blood soaking the floor. Near her feet the fire licked the wool of her dress. Blanchefleur reached down, and touched the fading warmth of her cheek, and looked into her eyes.

Empty.

Alive, the fay's eyes had been bottomless wells of age and knowledge, into which no mortal could gaze for long without terror. Dead, they were like the broken windows of a house than has been plundered. Dead, they were just eyes.

Tears blurred Blanchefleur's vision. What could she do? What could she say? Nothing came. At last she wiped away her tears, and took the long wooden pin from Nerys's hair, and whispered, "Godspeed, oldest friend."

Branwen was standing at the door, and caught Blanchefleur's hand as she came. Outside, in the passage, no sound of voice or footstep ruffled the silent air. Branwen said, "No one is here. I went up and down the passage and looked."

They stole down back passages and stairways to the kitchen. This too was deserted; only a cauldron of hot water steamed pointlessly over a dying fire, waiting for the oats that would never come.

"Everyone's gone," Blanchefleur said with a swift premonition, hanging back.

"Good." Branwen took a firmer grip on her hand and marched her down into the buttery, a room sunk below ground and stocked with barrels, bottles, and wineskins.

And also with stranger store.

In the centre of the floor was heaped a great pile of boxes and bundles, but these had a sinister look, for one narrow black thread led from each of them to a thick black rope lying upon the ground, flame-tongued, sputtering and fizzing. All this was visible in the candlelight, for here at last they found another soul.

A woman in the sable robes of a nun, her shadow huge and gaunt in the flickering light, turned at the sound of their entry and smiled with thin red lips.

Blanchefleur saw her face, and all hope died.

"Morgan!"

The Queen of Gore smiled a little more broadly.

"So my errand is done before I begin," she said.

Though all lances split on you,
All swords be heaved in vain,
We have more lust again to lose
Than you to win again.
Chesterton

efore Blanchefleur could move, or speak, or think what to do next, Morgan glanced down at the sputtering fuse on the floor, and ground it out with her toe.

Blanchefleur lifted her gaze to Morgan's absurdly wimpled face, and quelled the urge to pinch herself again. "I warn you," she whispered. "Whatever it is you want from us, you will perhaps win harder than you can afford."

"I am not here to kill you."

"Really."

"Oh, for St Peter's sake…" Morgan gestured to the dead fuse. "If I wanted you dead, I would have stayed away and let this blow you to the other side of Sarras."

There was something strange in Morgan's manner, something new, and suddenly the hair rose on the back of Blanchefleur's neck, for she had the notion that a different soul now walked and spoke in Morgan's body. She took a wary step back. "True enough. What else do you want?"

A bitter smile curled half Morgan's mouth. She said: "I want you to trust me. Now, and without asking questions. I mean to bring you out of Camelot safely, but if we stand here much longer Mordred will come in looking for answers."

Blanchefleur stood speechless. Her first impulse was to laugh. Morgan lied the way other people breathed. Yet was this the best she could manage? Why no careful web of falsehood?

350

Did she count on them believing such a threadbare story?

And whether they believed her or not, what hope was there of escape? Not even Sir Kay's cellar would shield them from an explosion in the next room.

Blanchefleur looked at the stack of boxes and bundles and said, "What is it?"

"Dynamite," Morgan said, "and you saw it before in the spire of Sarras, for Mordred has the secret of its making, and by your leave I'll light the fuse and finish us all off before he comes in and finds us."

She swept the torch down toward the fuse.

"No!"

"Wait!"

Morgan looked up at them, and saw the surrender in their faces.

"Good," she said. "Now, here is the way of it: I came here when I knew what Mordred intended. In the north passage above the chapel I met Nerys the Fay. When I asked after you, she said you were safely hidden. Therefore she must have given you a key to the other world."

Blanchefleur made no sign of assent or dissent. Morgan shrugged and went on.

"Mordred suspects you are here. He thinks to destroy the castle and anyone hiding in it, and so he has had Camelot emptied and surrounded so that none can escape. There is only one chance. We must find a door that will weather the blast, and use the key to go through it. Between an apple-tree and a walnut, in the wall between the garden and the town, there is an iron gate. If I light the fuse, there will be time enough to run to the gate and use the elf-key…"

Morgan spoke almost too fast to be understood, but as the words tumbled out Blanchefleur took a step closer, and then another, studying the witch's face. Branwen dragged at her arm the whole way, speechless with terror.

That was it. Merciful heavens, that was it, that was the thing that was new in Morgan's manner.

She meant what she was saying, every word. No lies. No mockery.

Blanchefleur gathered her wits and spoke. "I have a key—Branwen, it's all right—and I know the gate you mean."

Relief flared in Morgan's eyes. "Then there is still a chance for us." She shifted her grip on her torch and looked at the fuse. "Run…"

Blanchefleur and Branwen fled. Branwen took the lead: "I know the quickest way." But at the door leading into the garden, Blanchefleur pulled her back and broke their stride just long enough to glance into the icy morning. In the drab winter garden, among the smoky blue-grey of naked trees, nothing moved.

They went out, running under the wall until they reached the place Morgan had spoken of—a beautiful gate, all scrolling iron-work, with a midsummer tree traced in the centre. But when Blanchefleur fumbled the key into the lock and flung it open its inner side was smooth oak and the Vicarage spare room loomed before them again.

They stepped down into the night and turned to see Morgan running through the trees behind them. Blanchefleur whipped the key from the lock of the gate and brought it inside, fitting it to the lock of the wardrobe. Then a thought struck both of them at once, for she and Branwen glanced from Morgan's flying figure, first to each other and then to the key.

She was still the Enemy of Logres. How much blood was on her hands? And all they had to do was lock the wardrobe door.

For a heartbeat or two they stared at each other, eyes wide, breathing fast. Then Branwen said: "No."

"No," Blanchefleur echoed.

Then Morgan was with them, gasping for breath, and Blanchefleur whisked the door shut and locked it.

For a moment there was no sound in the little room but their breathing and the slam of racing hearts in their ears. Then Blanchefleur said:

"Even if the gate is destroyed in the blast, we can use the key to open another door, can't we?"

Morgan settled herself cross-legged on the floor and shook her head. "From this side of the door only the Elves can do that."

"But you've done it without a key. With Sir Odiar."

"That was not Elvish skill," Morgan said. Her voice bristled, but after a little time she spoke again, more softly.

"In Sarras, you used the shadow knife to shear all my power away. Do you not remember? I can open no more gates; the rulers of the air come no more to my call."

Branwen was wide-eyed in the moonlight. "You have no magic any-more? Blanchefleur did that to you?"

"Yes."

Blanchefleur leaned her head back against the wardrobe door. How bitter a humiliation must that have been for one of Morgan's self-conceit? "I'm sorry. I didn't know I had done that."

Morgan shook her head in the darkness. "Why should you be sorry? The airy ones only desire the destruction of Sarras and the corruption of all mortal flesh. And after they abandoned me I was no more use to Mordred. I looked for a place of refuge, but no one was willing to shield me. Even my lover closed the door in my face, telling me to be grateful he did not turn me over to his new master."

"Sir Odiar? That must have been before Perceval killed him, of course."

"Odiar is dead? Then am I avenged." For a moment there was a fierce note of triumph in Morgan's voice. Then it faded. "No one would give me shelter, not even my true son, Ywain. Only the church gave me sanctuary."

Branwen stared. "You truly are a nun now?"

"I will be." Morgan paused, and went on almost shyly. "So be not sorry for what you did in Sarras. Nothing else could have woken me from those blasphemous dreams. When the light of day stripped away every illusion, what could I do but kiss the Son?"

A nun. It was dark in the Vicarage bedroom, for the moon had set. Blanchefleur stared at Morgan's dim outline and tried to stretch her mind around this notion. Morgan, erstwhile Witch of Gore and Enemy of Logres, now a penitent and an ally? Could it be true? Yet surely if there was a flutter of deceit in Morgan's voice she would have heard it?

"You said you met Nerys," Blanchefleur said.

"Yes. While I was looking for you. She told me you were safe. I have not seen her since."

"Mordred killed her."

"Surely not! One does not so easily cut the ties that bind an immortal to life."

"He used the same obsidian knife as—you remember."

Morgan drew in her breath. "The knife! Where is it?"

"Mordred has it."

In the dark, Blanchefleur heard the whisper of air and fabric as Morgan threw up both her hands. "Then how are we to kill him?"

"How? In battle, surely? Mordred isn't immortal, like Nerys."

"Not just like Nerys," Morgan said. She thrummed her fingers gently against the wardrobe. "Hear me: there is something you should know about my second son."

Blanchefleur felt her heart sink into her stomach. "He's my brother."

"Not in the way you mean. Mordred is..." Morgan's thrumming continued, as if collecting scattered or nervous thoughts. "...made, not conceived. I took a hair from the King's head."

In a flash Blanchefleur understood, and recoiled in horror. "The thing you intended to use the Grail for? *You already did it?*"

Morgan said, "Yes. Mordred is a *simulacrum*, an unnatural man made from a strand of hair. I made him to subvert his father's throne."

"And he knows this?"

"Mordred? Yes. He knows."

Blanchefleur's stomach twisted and she clamped one hand to her middle and another to her mouth, fighting back the angry words that threatened to pour out. Make a son to destroy Logres? How could she? How *dare* she?

And then all of the anger went out of her in a rush, and she gasped a breath of hope, scented and warm like the first day of spring. But this meant that Arthur her father was innocent in the matter. And all this time, she had suspected him wrongly.

She slid to the floor and sat down beside the others, suddenly weak. It occurred to her that this was the first real good news she had tasted in months.

Morgan went on: "Later, when he was grown, Mordred drove a bargain with certain of the rulers of the air. Under their protection, he cannot be killed. He remains in his body even when the wounds he receives are enough to kill a mortal. With my power gone, I cannot unmake him and steel cannot slay him. Our only hope is the shadow knife."

"Why," Branwen asked, "what will that do?"

"It shore all my power away," Morgan said. "It will do the same for Mordred: dissolve his pact with the airy ones and cut the ties that hold his unnatural body together."

"Kill him, you mean? But Mordred has the knife."

"Yes."

Blanchefleur saw it standing in front of her like a stone, just as the others did, but because she was the Pendragon's Heir and the Heir of Logres, she was the one who needed to say it.

"Someone is going to have to go and recover the knife and cut away the shadow."

"Yes," said Morgan.

"Have you any idea how?"

"Not just yet."

"Why is he destroying Camelot?" Blanchefleur asked. "Why is he not occupying it?"

Morgan said: "He is going to Trinovant to have himself crowned King of Logres. He means to move fast, to gather men and the crown before the King returns. So he dare not leave Camelot standing, nor the Heir of Logres for Arthur to regain."

"So," Blanchefleur said, thinking out loud, "he will destroy the castle, and perhaps search the grounds and the town one more time, and then he will ride for Trinovant, and he will take the knife with him. And we cannot know when the King will hear of it. Everyone else is captured, and we have no horses, and no one but us knows that Mordred cannot be killed."

"I have a horse, a palfrey, hidden outside," said Morgan. "And a brother came with me on another."

"Then we have a choice," Blanchefleur said. "We can send one of us north to warn the King. Or the three of us can follow Mordred to Trinovant, and try to get the knife from him to kill him."

Morgan said, "Arthur may already know. If Nerys knew of Mordred's plans, then Nimue also knew, and may have sent word to the King."

Blanchefleur nodded. "Then it's decided. We follow Mordred."

PERCEVAL COULD NOT REMEMBER HOW LONG it was since he had slept. Since leaving Lancelot's domain in Northern Wales he had pressed on with reckless speed; the horse he straddled now was the sixth he had worn out in three days. Sleep, he had told himself, was a luxury he could not afford—but at some point the night had stolen a march on him, for he remembered drifting from visions of danger and threat into waking dreams of trees and shadows.

Thus, when he rode down the last long hill early on the fourth morning, with pale dawn blushing in the sky, and passed beyond the trees and paused before the ford of Camelot, he thought for a long breathless moment that he must still be dreaming.

Camelot, the seat of the most blissful court in Christendom, decked in flags and banners, cooled and sweetened by tree and vine, was gone.

Where towers and walls had sprung toward heaven, and the high rafters of the great banqueting-hall had arched like the necks of war-horses, only a great blasted mass of rubble remained. Blackened stones littered the meadow like marbles hurled from a giant's hand. What destructive force could have so smashed and scattered the place? Perceval could not begin to imagine.

Nor had the little town clustered by the castle's foot escaped. Fire had raged through the whole place, consuming everything perishable to fine ash; here and there a stone wall or chimney stood above the wreck, but not even the massive oak ribs of the great merchant-houses remained.

For a few long heartbeats Perceval stared at Mordred's handiwork. He felt nothing: neither shock, nor sorrow, nor anger. Then, like the slow cold prick of a knife, he remembered that this place had been his home. Only then did it occur to him to fear what might have become of Blanchefleur, of Branwen and the others.

He forded the river and went up to the city gate. Much of the wall still stood, though blasted and blackened, and here, just within the gate, he found what remained of Camelot.

Makeshift shelters were pitched against the walls. Grey men and women sat hunched over cooking fires. Some sifted through the dust for anything that could be salvaged. Others worked on new shelters. Many lay huddled and hopeless on the ground.

At the sight of Perceval a shout and murmur went up. One ash-grey figure rose and came toward him, holding a child on her hip, and Perceval looked into a face smeared with soot and pinched with worry, which in blither days he had seen carefree and contented among the high ladies of Logres when they sat clustered in the great hall's gallery like the blossoms on an apple-tree.

"Lynet," he croaked, and a wave of dizzy tiredness washed over him as the plight of Logres settled a little more heavily on his shoulders. "Lynet, is she alive?"

"Yes, and at her liberty. But she went on ahead, and left you word to follow."

"Tell me."

ON THE EVENING OF THE SECOND day since Camelot, Perceval found Blanchefleur with Branwen and Morgan on a hill overlooking Mordred's encampment in a clearing of the trees by the River Tamesis. They had made themselves easy to track; they had ridden in the forest, not in the road, where he was able to pick their trail out of the soft ground of late winter.

Morgan saw him first, and snatched her knife from the sheath at her waist before he could lift a hand and say, "It is I. Perceval of Wales."

She lifted the knife. "Unhelm."

Blanchefleur turned from unbuckling a saddlebag from one of the horses, and when Perceval pulled his helm from his head she came running with a wordless welcome on her face. Perceval made three strides of it and swept her into a hug. "Dear love! All whole?"

She smiled up at him. "Whole, and something more. Mordred is no brother of mine."

Perceval glanced up at the black-haired woman with the knife. She said, "I made him from a strand of hair," in the blunt voice of one who speaks of detestable things.

Blanchefleur gestured to her. "Morgan of Gore, my father's sister. She saved us from the sack of Camelot."

"So Lynet told me." Although the Queen of Gore's ill name made the hair rise on the back of his neck, Perceval forced himself to bow over her hand with his best court manners. "Madam, I am in your debt."

Her eyes and teeth glinted. "For what? For not eating your damsel alive? Sir, it was a daily struggle."

"Blanchefleur." It was Branwen, who lay on a cloak at the crest of the hill, watching the camp through a gorse-bush. Blanchefleur crept to her side and Perceval followed her to squint through the glare of the setting sun.

"Where is she?" Blanchefleur asked.

"Walking near the trees."

They followed Branwen's pointing finger and saw the Queen on the edge of the camp near the foot of their hill, walking to and fro and rubbing her arms briskly against the cold.

"She walks like this every night," Blanchefleur whispered to Perceval.

"Is that why you came? To rescue the Queen?" He rubbed hot and sleepless eyes. All the way from Camelot, when he was not worrying about Blanchefleur wandering alone with the Witch of Gore, he had tried to imagine what could have possessed her to flee Camelot on Mordred's heels.

Blanchefleur shook her head. "Morgan says that Mordred can only be killed by one thing. The obsidian knife Galahad gave me in Sarras."

Perceval's eyebrows climbed. "You mean to use the shadow knife on Mordred?"

She looked up at him with a wry and wrinkled brow. "Yes. But Mordred has the knife. We have to get it off him, first."

"I thought we could steal up to the Queen and tell her about the shadow knife," Branwen suggested. "She could find it for us, and maybe even use it."

"We also thought that if you were here, Perceval, we could stage a rescue and use that as a diversion to search Mordred's tent. But Morgan said it would never work."

The Queen of Gore's voice spoke so unexpectedly close to his ear that Perceval jumped. "He will keep such a weapon in his own pocket. It is too powerful, and too dangerous, to leave in his tent."

Blanchefleur lay on the cloak beside Branwen with her knuckles pressed against her lips. Beyond the camp, the glare of the setting sun shone off the River Tamesis, forcing Perceval to squint. On this side, the Queen walked back and forth between the camp and the forest under the eye of a man-at-arms who leaned sleepily on a lance.

Blanchefleur said, "Mother isn't speaking to that guard tonight."

"Maybe Mordred replaced him," said Branwen.

"No, I believe it's the same man. That's rather short-sighted of him. If I was keeping my mother captive, I'd change the guards." She frowned and bit her knuckle. "I could show myself to Mordred. Ask for a meeting, alone. Think of some way to get the knife from him."

"Meet—? Out of the question," said Perceval.

Morgan said, "Have you taken leave of your wits?"

"You could be within a short distance, Perceval, in case anything went wrong. I can make him fear me too much to try anything. And once I convince him to give me the knife, he won't be *able* to try anything."

"The only way he will give you the knife of his own accord is between the ribs," Morgan muttered. Then she caught her breath: "Unless—"

Branwen murmured, "Look!"

At the foot of their hill, Guinevere put up her hands and unhooked the silver links of her necklace. She folded the great emerald-eyed medallion into the palm of one hand and went strolling back toward the camp, toward the guard.

The medallion and its chain dropped like a silver snake into the grass within two yards of his feet. Then she turned without looking at him and came back to the trees.

This time, she did not turn again. This time, she slipped beneath their shadow and they saw the grey glint of her dress moving through the forest.

"She's *escaping!*" Branwen went to start up, but Blanchefleur caught her shoulder and pulled her down again.

Perceval pointed in the direction the Queen was running. "Look. Smoke. A manor house. She is going that way."

Down below, the Queen's guard strolled over and pocketed the silver medallion. Then he gave a whistle and began to shout.

"Prisoner escaping! After her! After her!"

"Why, the two-faced—" Branwen sputtered into silence, unable to think of a name bad enough.

As the camp erupted into swarming life, Blanchefleur scrambled back on hands and knees and stood.

"Perceval, she needs help."

"A diversion." Perceval followed her back from the crest and, with the swift lift of her eyes to his, he knew what she wanted.

"You think there is a chance it will work?"

She was running her fingers through her hair, smoothing down her tunic. "We may never have a better chance."

She had done it before, too. With Agravain.

If this was the wrong decision, God help him.

"We'll do it." He turned to Morgan and Branwen. "Take your horses and find the Queen while we show ourselves to Mordred. Buy you some time." He pointed down the Tamesis valley. "Ride downriver toward Trinovant until you come to the wooded headland you see there, ahead. Wait three hours and then ride on to warn Sir Ector. Go!"

They climbed into their saddles and vanished among the trees. Blanchefleur smiled at Perceval. Sudden excitement whipped colour into her cheeks and a high gleam of danger into her eyes. Blinking in the unexpected radiance, Perceval caught his horse's reins and helped her into the saddle. She kneed the animal to the crest of the hill above the camp.

Perceval drew his sword and went to join her on foot. Down below, men were already moving through the trees in the Queen's wake. Behind, Morgan and Branwen crashed away through the trees.

Sudden doubt shook him. Was he mad to allow this?

He was about to find out.

"Mordred! Come out and speak with us, you dog of Gore! *Mordred!*"

Below in the camp, he saw the ripples his voice cut among the swarming men. He saw them turn; he saw some of them flinch and cross themselves as they recognised the lady of the Grail.

"Mordred! Come and face us, if you be not afraid!"

"I am here."

He came out in a little knot of his men. One of them, looming on his left hand, wore the sign of the Silver Dragon. Another bore the twy-headed eagle of Orkney. On the horse beside him, Blanchefleur stiffened, head to heel, and the horse moved restlessly.

"I wish to treat," Blanchefleur called. "Do you grant me heraldic protection?"

"You wear no heraldic colours. What authority have you to treat, Blanchefleur the Ill-Born?"

"Don't be a fool, Mordred!" It must be difficult to wring cold scorn from a shouting voice, but Blanchefleur achieved it. "I am the Pendragon's heir, chosen in council! And I tell you that a storm is coming from the North, you son of Hell! You have pulled the dragon's tail, and the dragon is awake! Your mother has told the secret of your birth, Mordred! Your hostage is gone, Mordred! You're a naked man in the storm, Mordred!"

Down below, the men around Mordred wavered like a field of wheat in the wind. Agravain stepped forward impulsively and Mordred thrust him back with a hand to his chest. There was a moment's sharp debate among them, which Perceval did not hear, and then Mordred turned again. "You have your wish," he called. "I'll speak with you, and on my oath you shall go free and unharmed from me."

Blanchefleur lifted her hand and pointed to the riverside meadow, where the sun streamed through withered brown grass. "Meet me by the river, and come alone."

BLANCHEFLEUR SAW THAT PERCEVAL KEPT A weather eye out for ambush as they skirted the camp, riding for the meadow. Her own heart jolted with each pheasant that rocketed skyward at their approach, but they saw nothing to suggest that Mordred had yet broken his word.

He was already waiting for her by the river, fifty paces from the edge of the camp. They approached from the east and at about the same distance Perceval reined in. She slid down from the saddle and smiled at him and said, "I won't be long."

He had taken her hand to help her down from the saddle, and he did not release it at once. "Beware," he told her. "Mordred wields many weapons."

"I will."

"Christ be with you, Christ within you," he muttered, and let go of her hand and left her to face the final few paces alone.

She stopped when Mordred's shadow ran across the grass and pooled at her feet. He stood with his arms folded and his chin tucked down, and she read no particular mood in him beyond a tightly-wound hostility. She smiled at him blithely and prayed that he could not hear her heart hammering in her ribs, for the sight of his pale and melancholy face had yanked her back into the Vicarage spare room where she had knelt and watched Nerys die.

"Are you surprised to see me?" she asked, and arched a brow.

"Exceedingly," he said, and bowed a little.

She folded her own arms. "You heard what I said before. You haven't a chance, Mordred. Your only hope was to use the Queen to drive a bargain, and by this time she's miles away." Please God it was true. "Arthur will cut you to pieces."

He smiled thinly. "Pray excuse me if I cherish higher hopes."

"There doesn't need to be another war. My father will be more than happy to drive a bargain, I'm sure."

"Is this like the bargain you made with Agravain?"

"It can be. Agravain got what he wanted. We got what we wanted. No one lost anything."

He cast a glance at the sun. "I have no pressing appointments. Make your offer."

"King Mark died childless a year ago. Cornwall has no lord. Perhaps the King would recommend you for the position."

His eyebrows flared up into laughter. "Cornwall."

"Why not? It's a richer land than Gore. Not bad for a second son."

"But I am no second son."

"Ah, I was forgetting. You're also a traitor and deserving of death."

"Oh, Blanche." A flicker of amusement crossed his face. "It's been too long. How far you've come."

She unclenched her teeth. "The offer. What do you say?"

"It is a good offer. Tell the King I will take it, on one further condition."

"What's that?"

"I want Britain after his death."

She knew what he wanted, of course. But when he said it to her face like that, with all that cool impudence, she felt her stomach twist.

"A plea to spare your life would be a wiser message to send, and one more likely to meet with favour."

He bowed. "Then you had best counsel the King for war."

"On your own head be it." She half-turned away, and then paused. "One more thing."

He waited.

"I believe you have a knife of mine."

"*Victori spolia.*"

"I'd like it back."

"Make me an offer."

She looked at him levelly and said, "An elf-key."

His eyebrows climbed and he made a soft exhalation of understanding. "Ah-h-h-h. You hid in a different world."

She knew she had him. She waited, half turned away from him.

"Done," he said, and took her obsidian knife out of his pouch.

"Lay it on the ground and step back," she told him. When he obeyed, she took the elf-key from her own pouch and went forward.

She kept her eyes on his face, willing herself not to show how suddenly dry her mouth was, or how badly her hands wanted to shake. He watched her calmly; no impulsive movement, no coiled and spitting treachery lurked in his eyes. She knelt down in his streaming shadow and closed her hand around the carven bone hilt. Then she laid the elf-key in its place.

And she flung herself forward and scored the shadow knife between flesh and shadow, deep into the ground at Mordred's feet.

With a sharp *crack* the blade broke. In the same moment Mordred's boot caught her in the chest and she toppled backward with a wail of pain. He was on her at once, dragging her to her feet by a double handful of her tunic.

"What *is* this?" He hissed through clenched teeth and shook her a little. Far away, through the sound of her gasping pain and the shock of failure, she thought she heard a rumble like thunder. He broke off and shouted toward the camp, "To me! Treachery! To me!" and then turned on her again with another shake. "Who told you to use the knife on me! Tell me! Who?"

"No one," she muttered through aching teeth. Morgan. Morgan had betrayed them again. What a fool she had been—

The rumble was louder now, resolving into the pounding tattoo of a horse's hooves. Perceval! Mordred drew his own poniard and dragged her against his chest with an arm like a bar across her throat, so that the blade of his knife dinted the skin of her ribs. She blinked and saw the knight coming down out of the Sun, out of the West, to run rapidly closing rings around them.

"Mordred! Coward! Let her go and fight me!"

He pulled her tighter.

Thwack.

Perceval's horse squealed and stumbled. An arrow sprouted from its flank. Even as it struggled to rise, another barb rooted in its neck.

Shouts. Footsteps. Reinforcements had reached them.

"Another time, perhaps," said Mordred, and from his voice Blanchefleur knew he was smiling.

Perceval yanked his horse around to face the oncoming tide and hefted his sword. "One last blow, love." She never knew if the murmur she heard was for the animal or for her. He spurred into the enemy with great crashing strokes. Blanchefleur twisted in Mordred's arms, and the knife nicked through the wool of her tunic and the linen of her shift, into her skin. She gasped and stilled.

Perceval's horse stumbled and went down, bearing him with it. The men-at-arms struggled over him, their blades flashing in the light of the setting sun. Blanchefleur moved again, and the knife tore through her a little further, but she whispered, "Mordred, please—"

"Enough!" Mordred rapped out, and they stood back and pulled Perceval to his feet. Mordred lowered his poniard, keeping a firm grip on Blanchefleur's arm, wiped the bloody point against her hip, and shot it into the sheath. "Bring them to my pavilion." He handed Blanchefleur to a man-at-arms, turned on his heel, and stalked back to the camp.

Blanchefleur glanced at Perceval. One of the men-at-arms had pulled off his helm and blacked his eye. He spat blood and grinned at her. Then suddenly, almost too fast to see, he tripped one of his captors into the others, drew a poniard from his boot, and strode after Mordred.

" 'Ware, traitor!" His voice rose over the warning shouts of Mordred's men. Mordred flinched around, almost comical in his surprise, but Perceval never had the chance to strike. He was too generous to his foe; he had waited too long and the men-at-arms were already on him. Perceval lashed out with elbows and blade, but then Mordred kicked him in the stomach and he doubled, gasping. Arms grappled his neck and he went down with the weight of five men on his back. Someone drew a fist back, there was a little muffled crack of bone against bone, and Perceval went limp.

Die rather, than do aught, that might dishonour yield.

Spenser

It took two men-at-arms to carry Perceval to Mordred's pavilion. When they dropped him onto the grass, Blanchefleur twisted from Mordred's grip by a trick of leverage Heilyn had once shown her and fell to her knees at Perceval's side. He lay bleeding from a split lip, and underneath the cuts and bruises on his face he looked more weary than she had ever seen him, but his pulse under her trembling fingers beat steadily.

Mordred slammed the elf-key onto the table, dragged a chair away from the board, and sat down. He motioned to the big black-bearded man who had come striding into the tent after Perceval. Ungentle hands gripped Blanchefleur's arms and plucked her from the grass. She looked up at the man and saw with another dull rush of fear that he wore the device of the Silver Dragon. Sir Breunis Saunce-Pité.

Others filed into the tent after him: men-at-arms and knights of the Table. Agravain came to her and wrenched the bone hilt of the shadow knife from her hand and gave it to Mordred. He would not look her in the eye.

Blanchefleur shook the hair back out of her face with all the dignity she could muster, ignoring the bitter taste of failure. "Listen to me, you servants of the traitor Mordred of Gore. You have violated the laws of Logres and taken up arms against your sovereign, Arthur, King of Britain. Do you yield yourselves to his justice?"

A hush fell on the tent. Mordred looked up at her, and the venom in his eyes beat on her like a hot wind. "Cease your bluster, damsel. How dare you take the high ground with my followers? You requested heraldic protection and I granted it, and you used it to attack me."

Blanchefleur opened her mouth and closed it again. God have mercy, he was right. She felt the colour climb in her face. Perceval would have known better. Perceval would have warned her.

"So much for the righteousness of your cause. I might hang you and no law of war would condemn me for it." He shook the bone hilt at her. "This knife. Used on flesh, it will part an immortal from life. Used on shadow, it will part the airy alliances. That's what this is, isn't it?"

Blanchefleur grasped for one thread of hope. "Then whatever your sorceries once were, they are lost to you now."

"Is that why you cut my shadow?" He barked a laugh. "You flatter my skill. It was my mother who leagued with the airy ones, and you have already rendered her useless to me. Long have I sought her since that day."

That last sentence agreed with Morgan's story. And yet Mordred sat laughing at her, for the knife had failed and she was betrayed into his hand.

By her own plan, which Morgan had warned against, and by a compact which she had broken and Mordred, apparently, had kept.

Blanchefleur lifted her chin. "She may yet do you some mischief. She gave me a strange account of your birth."

"My mother is full of strange accounts. You will not repeat them here." His voice was cool and contemptuous, but she felt his tension pulled as tight as a lute-string.

"Why not? Are you afraid of what I might say?"

Mordred pursed his lips and she saw that he was trapped, that he had to let her speak, or lose face before his men. "No," he said at last, and flung himself back in his chair with a half-smile.

Blanchefleur glanced around the pavilion. Agravain was still avoiding her eyes. By him stood Pertisant, Sadok, Alisander le Orphelin, and others whose faces she knew better than their names. She spoke directly to them:

"Did Mordred tell you he was a son of Arthur? He lied. Morgan says he was made by sorcery from a strand of the King's hair. A *simulacrum*. No son of his—or hers. Do you hear me, Agravain? Pertisant?"

Mordred did not speak, but his hand tightened on the broken hilt of the knife a little, and she was conscious again of those glaring eyes.

She pointed at him and laughed. "Look at him! He knows that it's true!"

"Silence her," Mordred grated.

"No one lay a hand on me!" Blanchefleur cried, and for one moment was obeyed. So they doubted him. In a flash she sensed her chance; the right words to the right man, and she would master them all, turn the tables, take Mordred prisoner. She cried out, "Agravain, this man has no right to Logres, and you know it. The true king is coming. Choose now whose side you will take."

All eyes in the pavilion fell upon Agravain, who paled and sweated under their pressure. Then he looked to Mordred.

"What do you say, cousin?"

"It is a lie. Naturally." Mordred wrenched his gaze away from Blanchefleur, and tossed the knife-hilt onto the maps and parchments littering the table. "Do you not know my mother?"

Agravain shuffled. "You hear," he said, presumably to Blanchefleur, but he went on staring at Mordred.

The air cleared. The knights of the Table moved like sleepers. Pertisant wiped a sleeve across his brow. Mordred looked at Blanchefleur and shrugged with false sympathy.

Blanchefleur raked the gathered knights with a look of scorn. "No doubt you mean to murder me among you all. How do you plan to justify that?"

Agravain still would not meet her eyes. "The just penalty for imposture—" he muttered.

"Enough, Agravain." Mordred turned to Blanchefleur, and gestured to a chair. In the aftermath of her failure, his voice was almost genial. "There need be no talk of penalties. Will you be seated? It is time for me to make an offer now."

Someone pulled the chair out for her and Blanchefleur sat, ramrod straight on the seat's edge. If Mordred was willing to talk, she was willing to listen. She had not expected to live so many minutes; she must be careful, and make the most of each breath, for each one might be her last. Again she remembered Nerys, and her stomach clenched a little tighter.

Mordred said, "I don't wish to kill you, Blanche. I had much rather arrive at an understanding."

Blanchefleur folded her hands in her lap with a little disbelieving laugh. "You have been trying to kill me for years."

Mordred shook his head. "Not always. Think back. I tried to win you to my side, not kill you. If you recall, I asked you to marry me."

"So that you could kill me at your leisure?" Perhaps, if she kept him talking, there would be time—but no, the King was still far away, and if Morgan was still on their side, she should have taken Branwen and the Queen far away from here.

No human aid could reach them now.

Mordred was talking. "Quite the contrary. As my rival for Logres, you stood in my way. To yield to you, out of the question. To destroy you, a waste. But to subvert you…" A predatory smile crept across his face. "Irresistible! You are, for some, the legacy of Logres and Arthur. All the influence and authority you wield could be thrown into the balance—on *my* side. Imagine if you had accepted my offer of marriage?"

Blanchefleur shuddered.

"Your guardians would have found you only when it was already too late. You would have been mine, and my claim on Logres, unassailable. Ah, and the satisfaction of wielding *you* as the instrument of my conquests!"

Blanchefleur felt the gooseflesh rising on her arms. For the first time she felt the force that compelled the loyalty of men like Agravain. There was a tremendous and titanic audacity in Mordred. For a moment she saw him as he saw himself, the masterly man whose contempt for petty rules unleashed him to ordain the fates of nations.

Something like a lightning-bolt shot through her and to her horror, she recognised it as a perverse kind of attraction. If he had spoken to her like this two years ago on the balcony at Kitty Walker's dance, might all things have happened differently?

"How you must hate Logres," she said in a dry mouth.

"Hate Logres?" He leaned back in his chair, shaking his head. "There is an anger that is deserved, Blanche. Tell me. Look me in the eye, if you can, and tell me—to my face—that Logres is without sin."

Blanchefleur looked up, timid of his commanding gaze, keenly aware now of how completely she was in his power. Her voice seemed to have shrunk. "Of course I can't. That would be foolish. Nothing on this earth is without sin."

"That's your excuse." Mordred's voice dripped contempt. "Let me show you a picture. Britain under Logres. Filled with injustice from one end to another. Ruled by a King without even the power to guarantee that his subjects will be free from oppression, invasion, or famine. Policed by a roaming, irresponsible gang of elite warriors whose whims and exactions are a harder burden upon the people than the monsters they claim to slay. Haunted by superstition. Enslaved by ignorance. Racked by disease."

"It's nothing like that."

Mordred fixed his eyes on the pavilion roof. "You are shivering, in part because it is a winter day and this tent, the best Britain has to offer, is a poor shelter even for a prince of the blood. Behind the arras in your own chamber in Camelot, my men found a dead rat, which argues the presence of live creatures. Three of the ladies of Camelot died in childbed within the last six months I was there. What must the number be among the poor? While half the Table recently disappeared on the quest for a magical relic, leaving these isles yet more defenceless."

"The Grail was real, and you know it!"

"Ask yourself," Mordred went on inexorably, "if Logres truly is the kingdom of light. This is a place, I remind you, where the king's steward strikes a perfectly harmless girl in the face for complimenting a young man, and goes unpunished. Where the penalty for adultery among the nobles is death by burning. Where the king and his champion go to war on a whim, and feuds follow manslaughter. Logres is rotten, root and branch. Riddled with hypocrisy upon hypocrisy—canting on about holiness, justice, truth, and brotherhood. Corrupt. Beyond saving."

Blanchefleur said: "I am not trying to save Logres as it is. I am—we are trying to mend it, on the pattern of the City, as it was always intended."

"Sarras!" Mordred barked with laughter. "Let me tell you the purpose of Sarras, Blanche. The purpose of Sarras is to persuade people of a better world after they die, to distract them from their pains in this one. Men and women so gulled are easily controlled. And the vision itself, if anyone takes the trouble to examine it, only strengthens the existing order."

"I see," she said. "You have no use for Logres, to save it or to better it. You want to destroy it entirely."

"Cleansed by fire," he breathed. "With a whole new world rising from the ashes."

Blanchefleur shivered. "Why, how can you speak of the hypocrisies of Logres? You set Lancelot against the King. You engineered my mother's trial. If she had burned, it would have been because of you!"

Mordred's teeth glinted. "I only did my best to hasten the end. That was surely my office. If Logres was without blame, could it have condemned any lady to such a death? Or gone to war over the question? As it was, Lancelot proved greater than his rivals, and by one act of submission saved the whole crumbling edifice a little longer. I am left to give the final push, but I did not undermine the foundations."

"You're mad." Blanchefleur cast a despairing glance around the tent. "Agravain, don't you hear him?"

Agravain's face twisted as if in pain. At last he lifted his eyes to her and said, "It's the only way, lady. God knows it grieves me, but it's the only way."

Blanchefleur stared at him. He flushed red under her eye and after a moment clapped Sir Pertisant on the shoulder. "I need to post sentries."

Pertisant glanced at Blanchefleur. "I meant to have my horse shod."

They left, followed silently by the other knights of the Table. The tent emptied, leaving Blanchefleur alone with Mordred, with Saunce-Pité, and with Saunce-Pité's men: scoundrelly-looking fellows, brutish and dull.

On the grass, Perceval lay motionless.

Mordred turned back to Blanchefleur with a thin smile. "It shocks you, Blanche. You have listened too long to the voices of priests and dreamers. They've brought you to heel. You were not always so easily led."

Blanchefleur thought, "I sit here defying you and all the peers of my age, and *I* am easily led?" But she knew that Mordred did not really object to her being led. After all, he had always tried to lead her down some path or another.

So she looked back at him in mute scorn, and waited for him to go on.

"You can be stronger than this," he urged. "Choose your own path. Join me. It's not too late."

"Why should I? You only wish to destroy everything I love."

He shook his head, more serious now, the mockery past. "No. No, Blanche. Burn out the rot, yes. But you believe in justice, don't you? In freedom? Knowledge? Progress?"

"Of course I do. All those things."

"Then join me. Make them happen," he pleaded. "You know that Logres can't go on as it is now. Can it?"

"No, I know, but—"

"Listen." Mordred reached out and took both her hands in his. "Haven't I been honest with you? I asked you once before to join me. I'm not the monster you think me. I don't want to kill you or use you; I want to show you the possible. Marry me, Blanche."

Blanchefleur shook her head. "My father made a deed. I won't inherit unless I marry Perceval. Otherwise, the throne of Logres is left vacant pending a decision by the Great Council."

He laughed. "Do you really think I would let a piece of parchment stand between us?"

He could do it, too, she thought, once again awed by his cool temerity. This time the jolt was stronger. She swallowed and whispered, "You mean you want to seize my father's throne."

"The mistakes of his generation resulted in feud and war. How many second chances should we allow men like Gawain?" He laughed, low.

"They need you to show them the way. I know you can do it. You've seen how high mankind can climb once the shackles of ignorance are broken. You and I have stood on the threshold of a new world. With your help, I can bring that new world to Logres."

It was all fraud, of course. But what else was there? Death?

He pulled her closer and dropped his head to her ear. "The old ideals don't work. You've tried them, haven't you? And look where they've left you."

If she married Mordred—her heart skittered like a mayfly—if she married Mordred, then at least he would no longer try to kill her. Might she have some influence over him? Could she temper his rule with mercy to those he conquered?

He seemed to guess what she was thinking, because he went on, even more softly. "I offer you no cold compact, Blanche. Since I first saw you I meant to have you, and have you I shall, or go mad. Don't tempt me too far—don't refuse me. Bend a little. See how far I might be willing to bend in return."

She was horribly conscious of his breath against her neck, of his hands gripping her arms above the elbow. Why not drive a bargain, she thought, to distract herself. After all, she would have given him Cornwall. What was that, if not a compromise? And what else could she do for Logres now that the shadow knife had failed them? When Mordred ruled Britain, would every woman and child of Logres who suffered under his hand rise to curse her for rejecting, or bless her for taking, this one last chance to speak for them?

The counsel of despair.

"Perceval." She croaked his name like an invocation.

"Forget him. I don't mean to share you, Blanche. Not with him. Not with anyone. Not after waiting this long."

"No," she objected, and her voice was a little stronger. It wasn't just that she was going to marry Perceval, it was something he had said—long ago, just on the boundary of memory—

Mordred ignored her. "Make your choice," he murmured, and bent his head and pressed his lips to her neck below the ear. At that touch, what remained of her willpower came loose and floated away and she watched it go without a great deal of concern.

For Logres. She did this for Logres. And yes, even for Perceval—that was a comfort, knowing that Mordred would spare him for her sake, even if she never saw him again. Not that he would understand. He would say—he would say—

He would say that a thing that could not be done without dishonour was not worth doing. That the citizens of heaven never had to choose between two evils.

But that meant he and she would die, now, in the usurper's camp, far from any help.

As Nerys had done.

She had no words. The thoughts in her mind were too tangled and too unsure of themselves. All that came to her was a sudden certainty that she had to refuse his offer, and at once, before she had the chance to straighten herself out again.

She lifted her eyes to Mordred's face. He was watching her with something like a smile on his lips, calm and confident and cruel. She sighed for sheer weariness, tugged a languid hand out of his grasp, and hit him across the face with her open palm.

The sound in the breathless quiet of the tent was like the crack of a whip, and Mordred flinched back, lifting a hand to his cheek. For a moment he blinked at her in blank amazement. "You refuse?"

She lifted her hand again and this time he caught her wrist and twisted it savagely. The pain cleared the last fogs from her mind and she cringed away from him. "I'll die before I join you!"

"You're mad."

"Like all the sons of Sarras."

"I don't want to kill you."

She laughed at him and began to feel the heat of his anger beating on her face again. "You'll find a way around it."

Over on the grass near the door, Perceval stirred and grunted and lay still again. Mordred glanced at him and laughed spitefully. "What a shame he missed that little comedy."

The jibe cut deeper still than her own self-reproach. Twice now since she entered the pavilion, Mordred had justly shamed her for breaking faith. Her cheeks flamed.

"God help me," she said, very quietly.

"Well," he said, watching her face as if enjoying her reaction, "I am a reasonable man. It might be amusing to try force, but I am too busy for such games, and I will be wanting a more tractable wife." He paused. "It's getting dark. Light the lamps, one of you."

One of Saunce-Pité's men moved to obey, and there was the grind and spark of steel and flint.

Mordred said, "I have said I prefer not to kill you. There is another way." He held up the elf-key from the table. "Take the swain—with my blessing!—and I'll send you both back to cosy little England in the reign of good Queen Victoria. That should suit your squeamish tastes nicely." His voice lost its mocking tone. "Only promise to stay there. I'll have it in writing. Logres is *mine*. Do you understand? All of Britain is mine. You will renounce every right you have. You will hail me undisputed king and lord. Then you can go, you can live in peace and you can never see Logres again."

Blanchefleur blinked at him, distracted for a moment from her resolve. He would let them go, just like that? So easily?

But—the price. God help her, the price!

She paused to remember the sweet smells of home, the silver hills slumbering in the moonlight. Perceval would like Gloucestershire. He might miss the trumpets, the clash of arms, the tourneys in sunlit meadows. But he had always spoken so longingly of peace and long life and an escape from the havoc of war and wounds.

She was sorry, for his sake, to refuse. But having refused Mordred's last offer, how could she accept this one?

"It won't do," she told Mordred.

"I'm not sure you understand—"

"No, I do," she interrupted gently. "I can't trade Logres to you in exchange for my life. It isn't mine to give away."

"I've—"

She interrupted him. "That's the difference between you and me, Mordred. I hold Logres of Heaven. You would hold it of yourself, vice-gerent of no higher authority. Fickle. Capricious. Pitiless. You would crush us all, small and great, on the wheel of your own notions, because you would not yield to the kind laws of Sarras."

"And those laws?"

"Tell us not to burn down a house before a better can be built. Tell us not to despise the day of small beginnings, or consider ourselves less fallible than our fathers."

For a moment they looked at each other in the most perfect enmity Blanchefleur had ever known. At last Mordred said, "I've given you two eminently reasonable choices. There are no more. I don't wish to be known throughout Britain as the man who slew the chosen heirs, but believe me, Blanche, that's what I will do if I must."

She smiled. "My name is Blanchefleur. And if that's my last poor revenge to you, Mordred, I'll die gladly."

He sat rubbing his chin, looking at her through narrowed and puzzled eyes. By the door, Perceval moved again and pushed himself up to his elbow. At that a smile once again curved Mordred's lips. He looked up at the fellow who had lit the lamps. "Bring one of those closer," he said, beckoning. "I want to see her face."

The man unhooked a lamp and lowered it to the table between them. Mordred was still smiling. Without taking his eyes from Blanchefleur's face, he said, "Breunis."

Saunce-Pité moved into the little circle of light. "Sire?"

"Take the Knight of Wales out. And remove his head."

"Sire."

Saunce-Pité turned away, gesturing to his men. Blanchefleur leapt to her feet with a strangled wail, then clapped her hand over her mouth.

Mordred lifted a finger. Stillness fell once again upon the pavilion. Mordred cocked his eyebrow at Blanchefleur.

She knew, as plainly as if he had said the words, that it lay in her power to save Perceval.

Abandon Logres and go back, into Gloucestershire? Escape Mordred—live at peace—die old, surrounded by children and grandchildren.

What could resistance profit them now? The kingdom was already lost, wasn't it? What dishonour lay in retreat?

But it wasn't just retreat. It was cession. It was an oath of submission to Mordred, and she had no business in giving him what he wanted without fighting for it.

Blanchefleur turned to Perceval. He was awake now, he had heard everything. While he was unconscious, someone had lashed his hands behind his back, and now they had pulled him to his feet, keeping a tight grip on his arms. He smiled at her in greeting, and he shook his head.

To protect Logres, Perceval had already abandoned the peace and comfort of his mother's home. And he had always been ready to die.

Blanchefleur dropped her hand from her mouth, turned a perfectly expressionless face to Mordred, and sank down into her chair, folding her hands in her lap.

Mordred looked at her for a long second. Then he shrugged and waved to Saunce-Pité.

Blanchefleur did not even turn her head to see him dragged out. When the sound of their feet had died away, she realised she was holding her breath. She forced herself to go on breathing soundlessly, counting each breath, straining to hear—something.

Mordred sat in front of her, fingers steepled, watching her. It was full dark in the pavilion now, and the light shone on his narrow pale face, so that it shone like a mad moon in some faraway sky. She avoided it, choosing instead to look at the darkness three inches to the right of his head.

Breathe in. Breathe out. Oh, Perceval!

It had only been a moment since she had last seen his face—but this choking panic was clouding her memory, as if years had already gone by. Suddenly she could not even remember the colour of his eyes.

"Sarras," she thought. Only a little longer, and the comradeship they had once shared would go on.

Breathe in. Breathe out. Easier now. Only a little longer.

Footsteps outside, coming nearer. Saunce-Pité entered, ducking for the flap of the tent. His shadow loomed huge on the pavilion wall.

Mordred said, "Is it done?"

Saunce-Pité nodded.

Mordred looked at Blanchefleur. "It is not yet too late—for you."

She stood up. "That makes no difference."

"Well," said Mordred, and pulled his chair to the table and took up a quill.

Sir Breunis took Blanchefleur by the elbow. She went without wasting a backward glance at Mordred, almost pulling the outlaw after her in her eagerness to escape, for she half feared that if she remained a moment longer, she would fling herself at Mordred's feet and beg to accept one or the other of his offers. Outside, the afterglow of sunset still hung in the eastern sky, giving them enough light to see. Blanchefleur remembered that there was no sun in Sarras. She would miss the familiar stars.

Sir Breunis led her out of the camp, toward the forest. Three men stood gathered there beneath the trees. One of them turned to her and took her other elbow.

She looked at the ground by their feet, searching for what must be lying there. Her lips stumbled over the words.

"Where is he? Where's Perceval?"

"Here, love."

She looked up at the man by her side with swift, speechless joy.

He passed his arm around her as her knees went weak for shock, and looked over her head at Saunce-Pité.

"How can we thank you?" asked Perceval.

"Drop a word in the King's ear for me," said the outlaw with an anxious kind of geniality. "Tell him I'm no murderer, nor thief neither if I could get the chance, except that Mordred has been sitting in my valley for two years carrying on his little war with the world under my banner. I'll be Mordred's dupe no longer, and now I've taken my chance to give the King a return on the favour he did me a while ago, it's off to Ireland for me tonight."

Blanchefleur stared at him wordlessly. At the edge of hearing, a horse shifted and gave a soft snort.

"Well, off with you," said Sir Breunis.

I knew
That some such tale would be
For all these years she grew more fair,
More sweet her low sweet speeches were,
More long and heavy grew her hair,
Not such as other women wear;
But ever as I looked on her
Her face seemed fierce and thin.

Swinburne

lanchefleur did not speak, or even think, for the first three miles of their journey. Perceval was there. She could smell him and could feel the steel rings on his shoulders chafing against her cheek. And Mordred was left behind somewhere, in the night, in the trees. That was enough.

Perceval, finding a road, had held their horse to a steady canter, but now he let it drop into a trot. Blanchefleur shifted to a more comfortable position, and said, "I'm not sorry."

Perceval's voice found its way to her through the dark. "For what?"

"He thought I would run away to save our lives. I'd do it again."

"Of course," Perceval said, his tone blank as if he did not quite understand her. Perhaps it had not even occurred to him that the choice could have been different.

She smiled in the dark. "Where are we going?"

"Trinovant. Only fifteen miles. We can make it by morning."

"We told Morgan and Branwen to wait for us."

"It is too late to find them now. Let them make their own way."

"I wonder if Mother is with them. I don't think Mordred recaptured her. If he did, he made no sign of it to me."

"Good. We will think of them all as safe."

The horse jogged on. Blanchefleur said conversationally, "Saunce-Pité."

"Yes."

For a little while they simply regarded the astonishing fact.

"Do you think he was telling the truth? About Mordred forcing him to do all those things against his will?"

Perceval stifled a yawn. "Does it matter?"

She laughed.

The road unwound before them, a pale skein in the moonlight. Blanchefleur slid in and out of full awareness; the only thing that kept her even partly awake was the fear of losing her balance and tumbling into the road. But the day's events had left her drained to the last drop. She let her mind slip into numb silence.

Meanwhile Perceval pushed the horse between canter and trot. She wondered during one brief moment of wakefulness if he was hurrying too much; they could not be left unmounted in this extremity, stranded between safety and danger. But Perceval was the better judge of horse-flesh. She resettled herself and closed her eyes.

Sometime in the night they reached the town of Trinovant and went to the great tower-fortress of the place, which at that time was held and governed by Sir Ector. She remembered torches, she remembered coming into warmth and seeing her old guardian blinking at them with the ruffled sleepiness of an owl. And then, for the first time in days—a roof over her head, and the softness of a real bed.

MORDRED'S VANGUARD APPEARED AT MID-AFTERNOON THE next day and began to pitch camp before the gates of the town. Blanchefleur passed the messengers in the passage as she went in to speak to Sir Ector.

"Blanchefleur," he cried, looking up from a table where he was seated amid parchments and quills, scratching at a ledger. "Come in, come in."

She hugged him and perched on the desk. "I woke late, and missed the excitement. What's afoot? Have Mother and Branwen come?"

Sir Ector threw down his quill and began folding parchments. "There's been no sign of them."

"Not yet? Could we not send someone to find them?"

"Not with an army on our lawn. Mordred is here with his vanguard. If not for the two of you, he would have caught us by surprise. Perceval tells me he has several thousand men on their way. There's nothing we can do for the Queen now."

Blanchefleur nodded, knitting her brows. "They'll take care of themselves, I'm sure, Mother and Morgan. Has anyone spoken to Mordred?"

"I sent a herald out to ask his business, making camp on our pastureland like that."

"What did he say?"

"Polite nothings. He did ask to see the Bishop of Ergyng."

"He came here to be crowned King of Britain," Blanchefleur recalled. "Perhaps he thinks the Bishop is more likely to do it if taken prisoner." And cold shudders went down her spine at the thought of the games Mordred played with his prisoners.

"Most like," Sir Ector agreed. "The Bishop is neither a traitor nor a fool, but I've sent for him to make sure."

"Does Mordred know Perceval and I are here?"

Laughter shone in Sir Ector's eye as he began to return books and parchments to their pigeonholes. "Sir Perceval thought it best to go out with the herald."

Blanchefleur put both hands to her mouth. "Perceval did that? Oh, how I'd have loved to see the look on Mordred's face."

"Perceval said it was a beautiful sight." Sir Ector unfolded a map of Trinovant on the table. Blanchefleur swung a leg and glanced around. The comfortable untidiness of this pigeon-holed room reminded her of the library in the old house in Gloucestershire, and also—for the memory was inextricably bound to the room—the day when Nerys and her guardian had first told her that she was not a child of that world.

Nerys. She took a breath, and then thought better of it, and said, "I can't call you Guardian anymore. What shall I call you now?"

Sir Ector looked at her with one eyebrow canted up above his spectacles. These were the only remnant of the things he had worn and used in that other world; instead of waistcoats and smoking-jackets he wore a furred gown, and he had grown a full beard to accompany his moustache. He said, "Did I ever tell you that I raised your father?"

"The King? Yes. Yes, you did."

"Times were dangerous for a baby heir then. I was only a humble young knight with a small son of my own. But for his own unspoken reasons, Merlin brought Arthur to me. Not until years later did I guess his true lineage." Sir Ector smiled at her. "Uther Pendragon died within two years. He was your grandfather by blood. But you might call me Grandfather, if you like."

"I'd love to." Blanchefleur twisted her hands together. "Well, Grandfather, I should tell you—Mordred almost captured us when he took Camelot. If Nerys hadn't got us to safety, I don't know what might have happened. But Nerys didn't make it." She paused, trying to give him time to prepare himself. "He killed her."

Sir Ector looked at her in unbelief. "How was that possible?"

"It was partly my fault. I left a knife of mine lying in my room, an obsidian blade. I got it in Sarras."

"Nerys!" whispered Sir Ector. "I thought she would outlive us all."

"Yes." Again, she blamed herself for leaving the shadow knife where Mordred could find it.

Again, she reminded herself that she could not have foreseen Mordred's crime.

Sir Ector pulled off his spectacles, slumped into his chair, and put a hand over his eyes. At length he said, "Yet it was her dearest wish. 'Think of it!' she said to me once. 'An end to the long war!'" He looked at Blanchefleur with a painful smile. "Some days I long for the same rest myself."

"The long war? Is that what she called it? But surely we can hope for some times of peace, even this side of Sarras?" Blanchefleur rubbed fingers against temples. "Do you remember the day you and she first told me about Logres? Do you remember what you told me then, about a prophecy?"

"About Arthur's heir being the life of Logres?"

"Yes. That one." Blanchefleur swallowed. "I've been thinking. I know the Ki—I know Father thought what I did in the Grail Quest fulfilled that prophecy, but what about Mordred? He's a worse enemy than Morgan, and I keep thinking that if Mordred is to be stopped, maybe the responsibility is mine to stop him. And I haven't stopped him yet."

Sir Ector looked at her in surprise. "The prophecy said Logres would go on because of the Pendragon's heir. Nothing about stopping Mordred."

"And to think that I lived in Gloucestershire and never thought…" She slid from the table and went and ran a finger along the shelves, setting tasseled seals swinging. "Did you know Mordred was going to do this? Did you never find one of those old books—did you never…" she glanced down at him nervously "…*read ahead?*"

He stuck his thumbs in his belt and tilted his chair back to look at her. "I thought about it," he admitted. "Every day for sixteen years, there in Gloucestershire, I thought about it. But in the end neither Nerys nor I thought it wise. I let her gather up the books—all the old romances that might hint how things would turn out—and take them away."

"I wonder if she knew…"

"If she did, she never told me, and it was against our agreement." He whistled softly between his teeth for a moment. "You see, the danger was that we could never trust the old romances. They were only memories of echoes, across the worlds, of the real thing that we are living. Who knows what might have been changed, or added, or forgotten? So we left them unread."

Blanchefleur puffed out the ghost of a laugh. "Perhaps it is just as well that I cannot find them and read them now."

Sir Ector said, so quietly that she almost failed to hear it: "I read the title of one of them as she took it away. It looked me in the face from her hands: I could not help it."

"And?"

"It said in Middle French, *The Death of Arthur*."

A cold hand settled around Blanchefleur's throat and squeezed. At last she said: "But death comes—"

"To us and all mortals. I know. It may be years in the future."

"Oh, Grandfather! There must be *something* I can do."

"Why, what are you thinking of?"

"I don't know. But if I really am the Heir of Logres, I ought to be able to do something to save it, oughtn't I?"

"And you will, if you're meant to. But serving Logres is not only about sitting in council with the wise, or outfacing sorcerers, or wandering the streets of Sarras in search of the Grail. There are also those who build houses, and plough the earth, and rear children."

"I suppose there are." She thought about that for a while and said, "But I need to know if I'm the Heir of Logres, don't I? And if I could only look back and say, yes, a thing I did preserved her, then I would *know* who I am."

Sir Ector laughed. "Oh, is that the trouble? If it concerns you so much, whether you're the Heir of Logres, why not ask?"

"Ask!" Blanchefleur stared at him. "Whom?"

"Your mother would know."

"Why, I couldn't."

This time, Sir Ector lifted both his eyebrows above his spectacles in incredulity. "Why not?"

"I…" But she had regretted her silence before, when it was too late, the night Camelot fell. Why, after all, not? "Perhaps I could." She slid off the edge of the desk. "If I see her again."

AT THAT, ONE OF SIR ECTOR's knights came in with the Bishop, and Blanchefleur, knowing she was not needed, slipped out and looked for Perceval. She found him in the armoury with his shield and a pot of red paint.

"Why," she said, "you're wearing your surcoat."

Perceval pulled her in for a brief hug. "Yes." He let go and picked up the little blunt knife with which he had been scraping flakes of paint off his shield. The three-pointed label across the gules and gold of Gawain was coming off, leaving a soft yellow cloud over the leather beneath. Blanchefleur took a second, closer look at his surcoat. Here, too, a darker red stripe showed where some appliquéd cloth had been torn away.

She understood. It was like swallowing a stone. "Oh, Perceval. When did it happen?"

He glanced back up to her. If there was any pain in him, it was so mixed with other griefs that she could not single it out from among them. "I do not remember how many days ago. The Lady of the Lake took me to him before the end came."

Again, Blanchefleur understood. "He spoke to you? I'm *so* glad."

"He did." Perceval blew the last of the yellow flakes off his shield and reached for the red paint. With careful strokes he smoothed over the yellow cloud; the label vanished. "In the end, he was given enough grace for that. It is hard to mourn."

Blanchefleur remembered what he had once said about the elation of first grief. She slid onto the bench next to him and leaned against his left shoulder. When the hard grief, the later grief came, she would be there.

Perceval said, "You have not told me what happened in the pavilion, with Mordred, before I woke."

Blanchefleur winced and laughed a little. "I hoped you wouldn't ask."

Perceval finished with the paint, and returned the lid to the pot. "I am asking."

"Well, he—he wanted to argue with me at first. He said a lot of nonsense, about Logres not being worth saving and the only purpose of Sarras being to distract people from what they can really do to help. He says Logres must be entirely destroyed."

"What, right there in front of everyone?"

"Yes! Agravain, Alisander, Pertisant—I thought perhaps one of them would come to his senses when Mordred said that. I begged them to hear what Mordred was saying. But in the end they agreed with him."

Perceval growled deep in his chest. "The shame of it! Even the Silver Dragon has some sense of honour, but not the brethren of the Table!"

"But they seemed so…" Blanchefleur searched for the right word. "So reluctant. So *torn.*"

He shook his head. "Have no unease on that account. There is a kind of flinty stubbornness that tricks itself out in the garb of pity. What happened after?"

"Well. Ah. Mordred asked me to marry him again. He said it would give him victory. So I refused. Then he said that he would let you and me go back to the other place, to Gloucestershire, you remember. Only we must sign away our title to Britain and Logres."

Perceval nodded. "So I heard when I woke. He asked you to marry him again? Why did he do that? He knows what you think of him."

"I don't know why." It was strictly true, but if she left it there, it would be like a lie. "But I nearly said yes. I am sorry."

Perceval looked confused. "What? *Why?*"

"Well, he said a lot of things."

Perceval went on staring at her. Blanchefleur felt herself becoming redder and redder. "It was only for a moment," she mumbled. "And just for that moment, it seemed like the best way to keep him from killing everyone. Please don't be vexed."

"Oh, I'm not vexed." She didn't tell him she could feel his displeasure weighing down the air like a storm. "It just surprises me. *Mordred!*" He shook his head and reached for a pot of water to begin washing the paint-brush.

Blanchefleur put her cool hands to her hot cheeks, resting her elbows on the table. Perceval swished the brush in and out of the water. Suddenly, irrationally, she was cross with him. After everything Mordred had said and done, was Perceval just going to wash his paintbrush and pretend not to care?

"Perceval?"

"Yes?"

"Would you…I mean, what would it be like, if we weren't able to marry for a very long time? How would you feel?"

Perceval's brows stitched together. "Very irked. Why do you ask? I intend to marry you as soon as we have a spare day for it."

"It's just something Mordred said. He said not to make him wait longer. He said he would go mad unless I said yes."

Perceval gaped for a moment. Then his shoulders heaved and his voice pealed out into laughter which cleared the air like thunder, until his face was red and tears streamed from his eyes and he was gasping for breath.

"Oh, Blanchefleur. I see it now. Do you not know the kind of thing a man says when he means to deceive?"

"No," said Blanchefleur, covering her face with her hands and wishing she had not spoken, for nothing could be worse than the lightning-lash of his laughter.

"Ohhh." Perceval tugged her hands away from her face. "Do understand me, dear love. I am *deeply* irked by each day that passes with this last barrier between us. Sometimes I do think I'll go daft. But I have lasted this long without you; what kind of chicken-livered weakling would I be if I couldn't last a little longer?"

He smiled at her, both amused and coaxing, and she gave in and melted against his shoulder. "Oh, Perceval! What a fool I've been."

He fended her off with an elbow. "Don't push me too far, woman. You might wake some of those raging passions of mine."

IN THE HALL THAT NIGHT FOR the evening meal, Blanchefleur recognised, with dreamlike surprise, the doom-laden air of a city under siege. She told herself that she was still in danger, but no answering ripple of fear broke the calm of her mind. After what had passed the previous night in Mordred's pavilion, it would take more than a siege to worry her.

They had finished the meal and were sitting with Ector at the high table, listening while he told them his arrangements for the defence of the town and fortress, when footsteps came on the pavement outside the hall and Blanchefleur looked up to see two women enter in the company of a man-at-arms.

She leaped to her feet. "Branwen! Mother!"

Even Branwen, huddled shivering under a cloak, seemed exhausted from wandering in the woods. But when she saw Blanchefleur, a smile broke like dawn across her face. She came running up to the table and flung cold, damp arms around her neck.

"Blanchefleur! Alive! And safe! I need to sit down."

She sagged into a chair and closed her eyes.

The Queen followed with more composure. "Blanchefleur. Now God be thanked. I mourned you as dead." As she kissed her mother's cheek, Blanchefleur thought she had never seen her so wet and draggled, even on the first morning in Joyeuse Gard. But if Guinevere felt the shame of her frightful condition, she betrayed it neither by word nor gesture, mistress of Logres still, despite the mud on her hem and the rain in her hair.

"How did you come here? Where is Morgan?" Blanchefleur asked.

Guinevere sank into a chair, smoothed her damp hair back, and said, "Do not ask me where Morgan is; we lost her, or she lost us, in the dark. We crossed the river, circled north, and came here. Did you find the knife?"

"The knife?"

"Branwen tells me you went to steal a knife from Mordred. This is all I know."

Sir Ector was speaking to the man-at-arms. "You say Mordred is leaving?"

"His camp fires have gone. We sent out a scout, but he came back almost at once with the ladies."

Blanchefleur said, "Oh, Mother. I got the knife from Mordred, but when I used it, nothing happened."

"Why, what did you expect?"

Blanchefleur waved her hands. "According to Morgan, Mordred was no natural child. She bore him like her own son, but he was made with a strand of the King's hair and the aid of hell."

To her surprise a whole tide of expressions passed across the Queen's face at this—some mixture of surprise, illumination, and relief followed by fierce triumph and something else that might have been disappointment or guilt. But all Guinevere said, in her soft high voice, was, "Indeed."

Far away, a trumpet sounded. Sir Perceval and Sir Ector looked at each other, and left the room.

"Morgan said that if we used the knife on his shadow, it would dissolve the unnatural bond that made his body. Victory at one stroke."

The Queen's mouth thinned. "Did she so? We were watching from the trees when he captured you. I had a mind to ride down and bring you help, but Morgan said there was nothing the three of us could do."

Blanchefleur opened her eyes in surprise and said, "It was a bold thought, but I'm sure Morgan was right."

The Queen cast her a sidelong look and said, "It was bold of you to face Mordred."

Once the dry tone would almost have injured her. But she knew Guinevere a little better now, and recognised her words as high praise. Blanchefleur flushed with pleasure and said, "And your escape. That was well carried out."

"I misjudged my guard." Her fingers touched her collarbone where the silver medallion once hung. "But once I was in the trees, it was child's play to get clear of the others. The sots!"

"Then Morgan and Branwen found you without trouble?"

"Yes." A serving-man had brought her food and wine and the Queen reached out, shaking the sleeve back from her wrist with a graceful gesture, to pick up the goblet. "That I never thought I should see: Morgan of Gore coming to my aid."

Blanchefleur sighed. "I believe she really meant to help us. Unless she was lying about the knife. Or did she really think it would work?"

"Which is more likely?" There was a sceptical twist in the Queen's mouth.

At the foot of the hall, the door flung open and Perceval came striding back in, grinning all over his face. "All's well," he called. "The King is here, and Mordred has fled."

In her chair, Branwen came back to life with a start. "Heilyn?"

"I'll find him for you," Perceval promised.

But Branwen was already on her feet. "Wait! I'm coming!"

She went down the hall to the door, leaving Blanchefleur alone at the table with her mother. Blanchefleur touched the Queen's elbow and murmured, "Mother? May I ask you something?"

Guinevere sipped her wine. "Surely."

She had had a whole long speech prepared, but now that the moment came, all the words had flown. So Blanchefleur lifted a palm and said, "Whose daughter am I?"

In the silence, the Queen tapped her fingers once or twice upon her cup, and as suddenly stilled them again. "What, do you not know?"

"I don't know who to believe. Elaine of Carbonek said I was Lancelot's daughter. Lancelot said I was the King's daughter, and his knights laughed behind his back."

The Queen set her cup down and took a bite of meat and did not speak again until she had swallowed. "We will talk of this another time," she said at last, and Blanchefleur did not dare to speak again until the King came.

NIGHT, HOURS DEEP, LAY ON TRINOVANT, but in Sir Ector's solar the candles went on burning. It had taken the King an hour or two to hear all their news, and a little longer to take reports from his rearguard scouts. When the King's men came upon Mordred's retreat, there had been fighting in the woods. Both sides escaped lightly, for the King, with a smaller force, had drawn his men off and continued to Trinovant. But in the skirmish they had freed more of the prisoners from Camelot, including Sir Kay.

Perceval crunched down a mouthful of apple and said, "Mordred seems nervous." The scouts and captains had gone, and only he, Blanchefleur, Sir Ector, Guinevere, and Arthur remained in the solar. "First he whips his men through a punishing fifteen-mile march to reach Trinovant, and then he runs at the first rumour of relief. What is frightening him?"

The King stroked his beard. "If we knew, perhaps we could use the knowledge to our advantage."

"What are we going to do next?" asked Blanchefleur.

The King said, "The scouts said he is going west. We'll follow and give battle when we can."

Perceval said, "With no footmen?"

Blanchefleur said, "And if we cannot kill him?"

"One man can be overwhelmed. Locked away."

Sir Ector said, "What about Lancelot?"

"Lancelot told me he would come as soon as he had mustered an army." Perceval tossed the core of his apple into the fire. "He said it would be a week at most before they set out."

The King nodded. "The longer Mordred continues to retreat, the closer he takes us to Lancelot. If all goes well, we may catch him between us, or join forces before Mordred stops to press battle upon us."

Sir Ector said, "Best of all, his men may resent the pace and fall away." He pulled his spectacles off his nose and folded up the map over which he had been brooding. "Mordred may have fled, but half the country has taken arms and gone with him. In the end it may take more than Lancelot to save us."

The King bent his head. "This is true."

There was a little silence. Then the Queen said: "Speaking of Sir Lancelot, you asked me a question a few hours ago, my daughter."

Startled, Blanchefleur glanced uneasily at the King. "I did."

"He told you you were no daughter of his. You should have believed him."

There was a note of blame in her voice, and Blanchefleur reddened. "I wanted to hear it from you. I wondered why you never said anything about the rumours. I wondered if, maybe, the reason was that they were true."

"No. No, Blanchefleur." Guinevere looked from daughter to husband.

"Arthur is your father. I swear it before both of you. Before every light of heaven."

The King did not look at her and his voice, when he spoke, was mildness itself. But he said, "You never made it so plain to me."

She shifted uncomfortably. "No?"

This time he looked her in the eye. "No."

"You mean you thought I—?"

"Not often. But I knew what you felt for him. It was always there in the back of my mind."

Guinevere drew back with a hiss of intaken breath as if she had touched hot steel. "You *saw* that?"

"Not until after the wedding, when it was too late to let him have you."

"You would have done that?"

"I like to think I could have."

There was a breathless silence. At last Guinevere said: "It was over within the same year it began, long before Blanchefleur. Hearts mend. You were patient. You taught me to love you in the end."

With a swift motion the King covered his eyes with his hand. When he spoke, his voice was ragged but no less quiet and gentle. "You never told me."

"That I love you?" Guinevere's eyes were bright and hard and her fingers were jumping on the arm of her chair. "You are right, I never did, just as I never told you Blanchefleur's true parentage. Let me tell you why. It was Morgan. There was a time when she delighted in hinting she had borne your son. I became angry with you then and I have been angry with you ever since. And now that I hear it was a lie, I do not know why I am angry with you still, except that I am the most thankless lady in Christendom."

The King looked up at her. Though his eyes were damp and his face had gone red, he spoke with as much authority as if he sat in his seat of judgement at Camelot. "It is a lie. And I do not swear it, not even by the lights of heaven, because you have never known me to speak a false word."

"It is true," and now the brightness in her eyes was more like tears.

He held out his hand to her. "Come. Forget it all. Twenty years is too long for lovers to live bitterly."

It was terrible to see the Queen, always so self-possessed, forget herself at last. That pale face had once seemed frozen into hauteur. Now it crumpled like the ice on a spring river. She fell to her knees, wound her arms around the King, and buried her face in his side.

At last she withdrew her head from the King's jerkin and put up her face to be kissed. Then she looked over her shoulder at the rest of them—her cheeks, for the first time since Blanchefleur had known her, flushed bright red—and laughed shamefacedly.

The King laughed too, heaving in a sobbing breath. He passed his hand across his eyes again and looked at Blanchefleur. "Have you more questions?"

She had once meant to ask about Mordred. But that was answered, and another question rose in its place.

She said: "It seems so dreadful to lose Camelot, and more than half the Table, in just a few months. Do you not wonder why this is happening to us? I thought the Grail Quest was meant to give Logres the grace to last forever."

"And it might have. But we failed," said Perceval.

Blanchefleur crooked an eyebrow at him. He said:

"Sire, do you remember what I told you about the Quest?"

"That the work is every man's." The King tightened his arm around the Queen. "That was what the Table forgot. Perhaps that is why we lost something stronger than cities. My army is full of old men. All the young knights, all the sons, have gone with Mordred. We never taught them the meaning of Logres. Now we will pass, and the work of our hands will go with us."

Perceval stiffened. "Sire! Some of us are left."

The King smiled, and they could feel the weight of his pride on their shoulders like robes. "Yes. There are always some left, some who feed on that heavenly food and drink of that heavenly cup. And therefore Logres will last forever."

40

Readily those rough men of the Round Table
With rich royal steel reave that mail;
Braided hauberks they burst and burnished helms,
Hew heathen men down, hearts in sunder;
Fight with fine steel, the fated blood runs:
The boldest of brow are feeble before them.

Morte Arthure

Because the King sent messengers to all the lords in the south of Britain to ask for knights and footmen to meet him at the ruined city of Camelot, and camped there two days waiting for them to arrive, Mordred was able to draw off to the other side of the Severn, crossing at Caer Glow and retreating toward the south. His army swelled as he travelled, slowing his progress. The King's army, because it was smaller, moved faster and crossed the river by boat at Lydaneg. Nine days after the skirmish outside Trinovant, Sir Perceval woke in the soft spring morning and received the report of a scout who told him that Mordred was not eight miles away to the north-west, drawn up on a bare ridge above the Wye, ready to give battle.

Perceval tucked his sword-belt under his arm and went to find Gringolet, whom Heilyn was already brushing and saddling for the day's business. In Perceval's race to reach Camelot, he had left the exhausted Glaucus with Lancelot in exchange for a fresh mount, and would not see the horse again until Lancelot came from the north. Meanwhile, his father's destrier was a beast he understood well, and trusted to carry him in battle.

He rubbed Gringolet's forehead in greeting. Heilyn glanced up at him and said, "A messenger has come from the King to bid you to council. I told him you were meeting with scouts from the west and would be with him anon."

"Good man." Perceval buckled his sword-belt and sniffed the deep warm air. A little of the old spring-fever quickened his blood. Was it really three years since he had left his mother's cot?

Heilyn asked, "What news from the north?"

"A fight, I hope."

The rhythm of brush-strokes went on and the squire said, "Sir, I much desire to win knighthood in this encounter."

Perceval hesitated. "I thought I would have you stay behind to guard the ladies."

Disappointment crowded the eagerness out of Heilyn's face.

"If the day goes badly they will need a protector," Perceval explained. "There is no one I trust as well as you, and you are a new-married man. Give your bride time to tire of you."

Heilyn only half-smiled.

"If we go to the Wye today, perhaps I may not return. Let me knight you now."

Heilyn slipped the bit into Gringolet's mouth. "Not if you love me. I had rather deserve it." He tightened the cheek-strap and looked up at Perceval pleadingly. "Will you not also need trustworthy men in the battle? And if the ladies require a champion, they will want someone stronger than I. Let me ride to war, and do you remain with the ladies."

Perceval fell back a step in blank astonishment. "What, send you to face battle while I lie snug in camp?"

"Even so."

Perceval looked into Heilyn's glum face and then, with a flash of understanding, he saw. "By the light of Logres, Heilyn, you may be no knight, but you have the soul and stomach of one." He drew his sword. "Kneel."

The squire still hesitated. "And the battle?"

"Not for anything." Perceval grasped him by the shoulder. "And not for any lack of love, my brother. But because all things pass away, and I would save you alive, if I could. I would send one thing out of the wrack and ruin of Logres, one soul to whom I might point in the end and say, 'I left a man to carry our hope,' that I might not be ashamed when I go to stand in my lot at the end of days… Let me knight you, and if you love me, consent to do this last duty for me."

Heilyn sighed. "As you will," he said, and he went to his knees.

THE ABBOT OF THE SETTLEMENT AT Lydaneg was an Irishman of a homely peasant sort, and it was in his low, warm house that Perceval found the King and his council gathered around a table which bore maps and messages and the remains of breakfast.

Perceval slid onto the end of the bench where Blanchefleur had kept a space for him. The King on his right, at the head of the table, had his hands loosely clasped on the board before him. Opposite Perceval, the Queen had reached out to put her hand on the King's forearm; it was another of the little soft gestures she seemed always to use these days. Next to her Sir Kay was sitting. Sir Bedivere held the foot of the table opposite the King, and Sir Lucan and Blanchefleur sat on Perceval's left.

On his right, Cavall the wolfhound rested his shaggy chin on the corner of the table by the King's elbow, and looked up at his master with liquid and adoring eyes.

It was, Perceval thought with his eyes smarting a little from woodsmoke, a far cry from the Round Table in the great hall of Camelot.

"The scouts tell me Mordred is drawn up for battle in the north-west," Perceval announced. He planted a finger on the map. "Here, above the Wye. What's your will, sire?"

"To take counsel on the matter." The King leaned back in his chair. "And to hear your thoughts on a thing I saw in the night visions."

Beside him, Perceval felt Blanchefleur straighten a little. Sir Kay lifted a perplexed hand and tugged his beard.

"A matter of songwarie? Surely the father abbot would give better counsel."

"That you may judge, when I have told." The King glanced around, and meeting the full attention of eight faces, he said, "I walked in a city, the fairest of any at this time standing, and there came to me a great train of ladies, and Sir Gawain at the head of them."

Perceval turned and saw Blanchefleur staring at the King with wide eyes and parted lips. Then she glanced at him and he knew that she too felt that pain of longing. It was hard, having once stood in the City, to return into exile.

"I said to him, 'Fair nephew, what are these?' And Gawain said to me, 'These are all the ladies I ever fought for in my life, and for the love of Logres they have begged leave to bring me where I might speak to you and counsel you.'"

Bedivere said, "And their counsel?"

"Not to fight today, but to ask for a truce and wait until Lancelot comes."

Perceval raised an eyebrow. "Father said that?"

"It seemed strange to me also," said the King. He unclasped his hands and laid the palms flat on the table-top. "What say you? Trust the dream?"

"It is good counsel," Bedivere said. He had taken the map and was frowning over the place Perceval had indicated. "Mordred holds a strong position. And Lancelot cannot be far off."

"I say we forget the dream," Kay said. "The Gawain I know would not have counselled you to delay a battle, or to seek help in the Knight of the Lake."

Perceval looked at Blanchefleur. She said, "Sire, the city in your dream. Was it golden-skied, on a great mountain that shadowed the whole earth?"

Remembrance stirred in the King's eyes. "Yes, with a spire at the peak. I could spend a year and a day in telling you all its beauty."

"It sounds to me as if you were in Sarras."

"So I thought in my dream, but hardly dared to hope when I woke."

She smiled, a little sadly, Perceval thought.

He cleared his throat. "Sire, before he died, my father sent for me." The memory was yet too raw for easy sharing, and he shied away from putting it into speech. "Had he given you counsel in his last moments, he might have said the same words."

The King nodded. "Then we will take his counsel. Let us go to the west and fall to bargaining while we wait for Lancelot."

"What shall we offer him?" Sir Lucan spoke for the first time.

"A month's truce to begin with," Sir Bedivere suggested.

The King rubbed his chin. "We will need to offer some bait, something to tempt him." He turned to Blanchefleur. "What might he accept?"

She looked up with a smile. "Less than the full dominion of Britain? I offered him Cornwall and he refused it."

"He refused Cornwall?"

"His counter-offer was Cornwall and the office of heir."

The King smiled at her. "To open with, I would have offered him something meaner. No matter." He rose from the table. "Send a messenger to find Lancelot, and pass the word to strike camp. Let us go to Mordred."

THE NEXT EVENING IN CAMP, SIR Bedivere came to the King's tent with news. "Mordred is willing to discuss a truce, sire. I have told him you will meet him in the morning at Terce to settle the thing. The terms are that each will bring fourteen knights."

"Fourteen knights? So many?" The King stroked his beard.

"Seven would have been better," Bedivere acknowledged. "But Mordred insisted on the larger number."

"Again," said Perceval, "as though he is afraid."

"We will take no chances," the King said. "If Mordred uses treachery, let us be ready for battle."

When Arthur went out to meet Mordred the next morning, Perceval stood behind the King on his left, sunlight warming his back, and smiled at Mordred, Agravain and the others as they advanced. It tickled him still to be alive after Mordred's order to kill him. He scanned the banners of the enemy host, looking for the standard of the Silver Dragon. There it was. According to Perceval's scouts, Sir Breunis and a few of his trusted men had indeed disappeared on that fateful night by the River Tamesis. After that, Mordred had invested one of Breunis's old lieutenants with the title that had once been his lord's, and Perceval idly wondered which of them—Mordred, Breunis, or Breunis's man—had really earned the name Saunce-Pité.

Mordred and the King discussed tribute payments, border disputes, and succession as if either meant the truce to last years rather than weeks. While he listened Perceval amused himself playing a game with Mordred's men. Each of these was a knight he knew, and some were men he had fought alongside at the battle of Joyeuse Gard. He looked into each of their eyes in turn, measuring how long it took them to glance away or transfer their attention to the sky above his head.

Sir Agravain, oddly, lasted longer than any of the others. For a while he tried to stare back, and with the effort a bead of sweat began to trickle down his forehead, but eventually he too dropped his gaze. What happened next was almost too sudden to see. Only Perceval saw him flinch away from something on the ground. There was a little ripple in the grass and Perceval saw the diamond-shaped head of an adder rise from the ground and strike at Agravain's booted foot. Then his uncle flashed his sword out: under the bright morning sun, it must have shone from the hillside like the flaming blade of Eden. The King broke off what he was saying mid-sentence.

"Treachery!" Sir Bedivere cried. He had only seen the sword.

Downhill, Sir Ector gestured to his trumpeter to sound the charge.

At the shouting and the trumpet-blast, Agravain looked up from the adder transfixed on his swordpoint. Other swords leapt from sheaths as both sides recoiled a few steps, and he stood suddenly abandoned in the space between two bristling forces. Sudden realisation of what he had done flashed across Agravain's face—then Perceval wheeled and ran with the others, back to where the squires held their horses. He shook his head. Agravain! God help the fool! Too soon, too soon!

Perceval reached Heilyn, whom he had permitted to come because there would be no battle, and snatched Gringolet's reins. He glanced up and down the hill. Trumpets blared, men yelled, Mordred and his knights were scrambling into the saddle to ride back up to their army, which crested the hill and poured down to meet them like a flood. Downhill, Sir Ector and the King's footmen—shadowed by banners of Trinovant, Camelot, and the southern fiefs—surged up the slope, a rising tide cut free of gravity.

There was no time to speak, hardly time to mount. Perceval got one foot into the stirrup before he shouted to Gringolet. The old warhorse wheeled and went trotting down the slope. Perceval pulled himself into the saddle, slid his other foot into the stirrup, and reached the safety of his own ranks, which opened to flow about him a moment before Sir Ector's trumpeter gave the signal to let fall the pikes.

Then the two bodies of foot met with a splintering of spears, and the shout of the charge blurred into the screams of the melée.

The King mustered his knights on the right flank. There were fewer than fifty of them all told, knights of the Table with other lords who had come to fight for the King.

In the commotion Sir Bedivere was pale and grinning. This must be the sound of the great wars of his youth, when barbarians from across the sea harried Britain and the King won his name on Badon Hill. He pulled on his helm and laced it shut, shouting, "What now, lord?"

The King turned to look up the hill where Mordred's knights stood waiting. Perceval had discussed the terrain with him last night. It was good smooth ground, but steep; a charge would tire and flag by the crest of it. If they waited for Mordred to charge down, on the other hand, the sheer weight and force given by the slope would work to his advantage even if he ordered the men to check their speed. Let Mordred's knights reach the main body of battle, which now straggled slowly down the slope in a swaying ribbon of steel and blood, and they would cut easily through the line. The best tactic would be to wait until Mordred's horse came downhill and then cut through their flank obliquely.

"We charge," said the King. "Now, before they move."

"Now?"

The King signalled to his trumpeter. "Mordred is bareheaded."

Perceval gripped his lance and tensed for the signal. Even so, the call of the trumpet caught him almost by surprise. With a heave like an earthquake, Gringolet bounded forward. Then they went flying up the hill, horses straining, lances in rest.

They caught Mordred unawares, as Arthur had guessed; his men were barely moving when the King's knights met them at the crest of the hill. Perceval saw and marked the golden eagle of Agravain, and wrestled Gringolet aside to strike him clear on the brow of his helm. So the last prince of Orkney was the easiest unhorsing of his life, though whether in the end Agravain was finished by lance or sword or snake-venom, Perceval never knew.

His spear splintered somewhere in that charge and he swept out his sword, but by now he had already broken through Mordred's ranks to the other side. Perceval pulled Gringolet into a trot and wheeled him almost straight into the gigantic blow of an axe swung by Sir Sadok, who had sat beside Sir Caradoc at the Table. Perceval warded the stroke, but it lit on Gringolet's neck, and the old horse went down.

Perceval rolled clear just in time and rose to his feet. Where were the others? Was he cut off, here behind Mordred's lines? But Sir Sadok was still trying to kill him and there was no time to look. Perceval ducked, lifting his shield against another buffet. The other knight circled him at a continuous tight canter, raining down blows from every direction. Perceval kept moving, catching the blows on his shield, feeling for the first time the panic of a foot soldier attacked by a cavalryman faster and bigger than himself. There was not a moment to stop, or to breathe, or to flail out at the horse's legs.

Perceval began to be dizzy.

Then another knight flashed past, sword swinging. Sadok caught the blow on his shield, but this gave Perceval the moment he needed to thrust his sword deep into the enemy's horse. Sadok slid from the beast's back, and then they were more evenly footed. But it was not for nothing that Perceval had once been called the greatest swordsman of Logres.

It was past midday when he struggled back from the rear of the line and found himself on the crest of the hill up which they had charged hours before. It was windy up here on the ridge, and there were clouds rolling across the sun. The cavalry charge had become a melée, and the melée had become a bitter killing match. Neither side yielded ground. There was little sound anymore but the wet thud of heavy blows. Downhill, the battle moved east a short way. Perceval strained his eyes at the crowd and saw Sir Ector's banner still flying.

He turned his attention back to the high ground. Many of the horses were dead now and the fighting was done on foot. Even at this hour it was impossible to say who was winning; the matter was still far too evenly matched.

And Sir Gawain, if it had been him, had warned them against fighting before Lancelot arrived. For the first time, Perceval began to worry.

He spotted Heilyn not far away, fighting some gigantic northern baron with a mace. Perceval shook off his weariness and went toward them. There was a brief fearful struggle in which he would have lost an arm if Heilyn had not been there by his side. Then at last the two knights of Logres laid the enemy twitching on the battlefield, and Perceval grasped the young knight's arm. "Heilyn. Leave us. You'll find horses at the camp. Go back to Lydaneg and tell them of the battle."

It was impossible to see Heilyn's face under his helm, of course. Nor did he make any reply; only turned and went away down the hill.

The wind sliced Perceval to the bone. Under his mail all his clothing was drenched with sweat so that if he stopped moving he was seized by teeth-chattering cold. He kept moving. There were ravens drifting overhead, black against purple sky, scenting a feast already. A little way uphill, two of them floated down and began to dig at one of the carcasses lying there.

There was something wrong with this battlefield, Perceval thought. By now, one or another of the sides should have fled, or should have been swallowed by the other. Today, some deep and stubborn enmity held men who had once been brothers to a grim and unyielding combat. Their numbers melted like snow, and still neither side gained the upper hand. Perceval ground his teeth in vexation. What about Mordred? If Mordred could be killed, surely his men would lose heart and flee. But the obsidian blade had broken upon the traitor's shadow.

He swallowed. What was about to happen here on Camlann ridge? Was this, then, the end of Logres?

He passed his sword to his left hand to flex his tired fingers. Then he closed them again on the hilt and went back into the fighting.

What passed in the next few hours blurred into one desperate, gasping struggle for life. But an end came even to this. He blocked a blow meant for Sir Ironside, and slew the man that was fighting him, but too late: the knight fell into the mud and died slowly of his many wounds. He saw Sir Kay's tall figure sink under the blades of three men at once, and avenged the gruff steward as he could. The sky blackened. Perceval found the last of the three knights who had killed Sir Kay, and beat him to the ground, and stood dizzily alone among dead men.

He lifted his head and blinked back his pain and weariness. Was no one else still standing? He went stumbling between the stiff bodies of men and horses until he found a man in battered armour leaning against the wind on a spear.

There was a dog lying with shallow whining pants at his feet.

"Who else is left?" asked the King through bloody lips. He had lost his helm; at some point it had been broken open and ripped off.

They turned and saw another. Mordred the traitor came limping toward them on dragging feet. His surcoat was stained in blood, every faithful knight of Logres had made him a target, but he was still standing, and now lifted shield and sword for one last charge.

"There he is," breathed the King, "the worker of this realm's grief."

And he gripped his spear, which still flaunted the Red Dragon of Britain, in a hand which trembled for weariness.

Perceval caught the King's arm. "Sire, if he cannot be killed…"

But his own hand was weak enough to be shaken off by a gesture, and the King looked at him with such wrath and grief in his eyes that Perceval was silenced.

"If this is the end of our fair fellowship, as Merlin told me when I was a youth, and the time of my departure from Logres, I go willingly. But first I will try if that traitor's carcase has lost its old virtue."

And he lifted his spear and charged. When Mordred saw the King coming he broke into a stumbling run. But all weariness had fallen from Arthur of Britain, and he struck the traitor with such force that his spear passed through shield, and armour, and body.

Mordred gasped and a gout of blood trickled out at his lips. The King kept his grip on the spear-haft, nigh fainting from his exertion. Then Mordred dropped his splintered shield, reached forward, gripped the ash, and with a dim straining grunt pulled himself closer to the King.

"Sire!" Perceval framed the warning with his mouth, but nightmarishly, his voice ceased to work.

Mordred's sword hung in the air. At the last moment the King lifted his shield, but his arm was too feeble. The blade bit into his skull. The King fell.

Then Mordred also crumbled to the ground, and when Perceval crept closer, he found the son of Morgan staring at the sky with empty eyes.

BY MIDDAY WHEN NO WORD HAD come from the north, Blanchefleur knew something must have gone wrong, and badly. That afternoon, as leaden clouds hid the sun and a cold wind blew from the West, the silence oppressed all of them more heavily. In the end, as the afternoon dragged toward evening, Guinevere put on her cloak and said, "Are you coming?"

"Wait for us."

They had their horses brought out and were climbing into the saddle when Sir Heilyn came riding up the hill into the courtyard, drooping upon a lonely horse.

Blanchefleur's heart stood still when she saw him. If Perceval were alive, surely he would have come to her, too?

"What news?" asked the Queen.

Heilyn said: "Battle, with no victory in sight."

"We will go," said Guinevere.

"Lady Queen, no. The battlefield is no place for you."

"Young knight, yes. When the fighting is done, then the battlefield becomes the place of women. I tell you we will go."

Heilyn looked from the Queen to Blanchefleur, and she knew he saw the same resolve in both of them. "Well." He turned to Branwen.

"If you are going back, please don't leave me here," she begged. "Am I to be the only one left in Logres?"

"We will go together," he said, and they rode west, into the wind.

It was near sunset when they came to the bare ridge called Camlann. In the valley on the eastern side, in the woods by the stream they found bodies and weapons littering the ground, but no sign of living men. The battle on foot must have fled away to north and east.

On the ridge itself, there was a heavy smell, like blood, on the air. Dead men, dead horses, and live birds covered the ground. At first Blanchefleur thought she would try not to look. But then she saw a shield that she recognised, and then faces swam into focus. There was Sir Kay. There was that amusing young traitor she had met at Joyeuse Gard, Pertisant. There was Agravain.

There was Cavall the wolf-hound, sleeping the endless sleep upon a headless body in silver and sable.

One thing was certain. Not a soul was left here alive.

Heilyn pointed south, where the ridge ran downhill into forest. "There is a chapel down there which may shelter our folk from the wind, if any are left."

They went down into the trees and found the place. Sir Lucan was lying by the doorstep in a pool of blood and entrails, dead. Inside the half-ruined stone building they found the King stretched out on the flagstones. Nearby, to Blanchefleur's inexpressible relief, she saw Perceval slumped against the wall, holding a torn scrap of surcoat to a gash on his leg and cradling something round and bloody under his other arm.

He looked up at them and croaked, "The King..."

Guinevere went down on her knees and took the Pendragon's hand. His head had been horribly wounded, and there was a scrap of silk tied around his head to keep the blood out of his eyes.

"Lady," breathed the King.

"Hush, be still," Guinevere begged him, her eyes filling with tears. Blanchefleur sat where she could hold the King's other hand and said to Perceval, "Is no one else left?"

"Only Bedivere."

"And Mordred?"

"The King killed him," said Perceval. He smiled sweetly, like a shaft of spring light. "See!" And he lifted up the severed head he had cradled under his arm.

There came a footstep on the threshold, and Sir Bedivere entered, moving stiffly, as if in pain. His eyes rose to the newcomers in greeting, and then he went down on his knees by the King. "My lord."

The King's eyelids flickered. "Bedivere? Tell me what you saw."

"I threw the sword Excalibur into the water, sire. And a hand and an arm came up, and caught the sword Excalibur, and took it into the water."

"Yes," the King breathed. "That is how it was when the sword came to me from the Lady of the Lake." He blinked and focused on the Queen. "What, lady, do you weep?"

"I do."

"Not for me," he began, but stumbled over the words. When he spoke again, his voice was stronger and more urgent. "I have waited too long, and time grows short. Help me."

"Where?" Guinevere asked.

"The river—down to the river."

With Bedivere supporting the King on one side and Heilyn on the other, they all straggled out of the chapel and down the western slope of the ridge. Fog shrouded their view on all sides. At last they came to the river, which with the mist hiding its further bank seemed like the shore of a pale sea. There in the water a black barge waited, with black-clad queens within. Nimue, the Lady of the Lake was there, and Queen Morgawse the mother of Gawain, and Morgan the Queen of Gore in the robes of a nun.

Perceval was walking with Blanchefleur, limping from his wound, still carrying Mordred's head. When he saw Morgan he hesitated, and then splashed out to the barge.

"Lady," he said, "this is rightfully yours. The shadow blade worked, but not as we thought. We are grateful."

He handed it over almost shyly, as if unsure how it would be received. But Morgan took it without a tremor, and if she felt grief at the sight of her son, she showed no sign. Only she turned in her seat, lifted the head in both her hands, and cast it out into the river. When she turned back to Perceval, she said, "I also am grateful."

He bowed to her and returned to the shore.

The Lady of the Lake spoke. "Sir King, are you ready?"

Guinevere looked at her uncomprehendingly, and turned to the King. "You are leaving us?"

"In Avalon there is a cure for this wound."

"A cure." Blanchefleur felt the taste of hope. "Then you'll come back to us one day."

"One day. There is yet work for me in Logres."

His voice faded into weakness. Heilyn said, "Quick," and the three knights lifted him into the barge, where a place was prepared for him to lie. To Blanchefleur's surprise, there were tears running down Morgan's cheeks as she received his head in her lap and helped the others cover him with blankets. "Alas, brother! Too long you have waited, and the wound in your head is grown cold."

Blanchefleur tried to stem her own tears, but as she splashed into the water and leaned over the gunwhale to grip the King's hand, they spilled over. "Father! Father!" she cried. "How long?"

A smile touched his lips. "Lady of Logres. Tarry not for me, dearheart. Farewell."

She lifted his hand and kissed it. "Farewell!" There was no time for more, Nimue was running up the sail, and the Queen had still to say her goodbyes. She turned to where her mother stood motionless on the riverbank.

Guinevere spoke in a grey and dreary voice. "My heart is a small and shrivelled thing, my lord, and it has never loved you as dearly as you deserve. But such as it is, all of it goes with you."

The King opened his mouth, but his strength was fading and only a whisper fell from his lips. Blanchefleur bent and caught it, and she laughed through her tears, and turned and ran to her mother. Then for the first time she dared to throw her arms around the Queen of Logres, and kiss her cheek, and whisper those words in her ear.

Guinevere's arms tightened around her with a sobbing laugh. "God-speed, my dear daughter, better than seven sons." And then she was gone, splashing through the shallows, climbing into the boat. The barge drew away on the river and went into the mist, and the High King of Britain departed.

Be glad thou sleeper and thy sorrow offcast.
I am the gate to all good adventure.

Lewis

I t was around noon the next day, and the sun was shining through the parchment-covered windows of Lydaneg's little guest-house with a dull-gold glow that reminded Blanchefleur of the sky in Sarras, when a knock came on the door. She pulled a tunic over her smock and cracked the door open far enough to see Branwen.

Branwen grinned knowingly, but all she said was, "Sir Ector is here to see you, and Sir Lancelot is with him."

"Oh, my. Give me a moment, Branwen, and we'll see them."

She shut the door and turned to Perceval, who was sitting before the fire finishing a breakfast of porridge and apple. "Did you hear?"

"I did." He half-rose from his chair, winced as the wound in his thigh caught him, and subsided. "Blanchefleur, I'm sorry—"

"I'll get it." After the battle his clothes had been so hopeless that one of the monks had loaned him a threadbare woollen tunic. Blanchefleur handed it to him together with a belt, pinned her hair up and then whisked around the room, hiding dirty dishes and bundling muddy clothes and boots into dim corners until Perceval complained, "Don't move so fast. You make my eyes tired."

She straightened the bedcovers with a snap and said, "Why not close them?"

"I had rather look at you. You might try wafting."

There was another knock, and at their call Sir Ector came in followed by Sir Lancelot and Sir Bors.

"Good morning," Blanchefleur said. "Grandfather! You're back!"

He paused inside the door with suddenly wide eyes. Perceval caught Blanchefleur's hand and bowed from the waist. "Sirs. My wife."

She kicked a foot back to curtsey. "The Abbot married us last night."

"Ah!"

"We thought of leaving it a day or two, but with so many gone in the battle, it seemed best to marry at once. Won't you sit down?" Blanchefleur gestured to the low bench by the fire. "I can send someone for wine."

Lancelot shook his head. "We'll not stay long. Only tell us what happened to the King. Some say he is dead. Bedivere tells us he went to Avalon, but we wondered if it was the fever speaking."

"It is the truth. The King was wounded killing Mordred," Perceval said. "We met Nimue on the river—I think it was foretold to the King once, long ago—we met Nimue on the river, and she took him to Avalon."

"Then Mordred is dead?"

"Yes."

Blanchefleur said: "We know now what Mordred was so afraid of. After I cut his shadow, he was furious. He hid it well, but he knew then that he could be killed."

Sir Ector said, "So the battle was won."

"But there is no Round Table left, no Camelot." Sir Bors spoke. "What next?"

"We haven't quite decided," said Blanchefleur.

Perceval grinned. "The marriage was the first thing."

Sir Lancelot said, "I would have come sooner, but word spread quickly that a usurper had taken Camelot. First a party of Saxons landed on the Deva, and then our way was blocked in Powys by the Knight of the Dolorous Tower. There are other tales of war in Cameliard and Listinoise."

Sir Ector looked at Perceval. "If you mean to take the throne of Britain, sir, there is no time to lose."

Perceval nodded. Blanchefleur saw the strain in his face and her throat tightened. It was too heavy a burden, she thought, so soon after a battle in which he had lost so much.

"Won't you tell us what happened in your part of the battle, Grandfather?"

"We fought until the afternoon," Sir Ector told her, "and then the man commanding them under the device of the Silver Dragon was slain. They turned and fled north. I gathered our foot and pursued them all the way into the arms of Lancelot's host."

Lancelot nodded. "The Silver Dragon will trouble us no longer, neither he nor his men."

Perceval glanced up at Blanchefleur and smiled. They would explain about the Silver Dragon another day, or leave it to Sir Ector to tell that strange story. He looked to Sir Ector. "Caerleon is the nearest stronghold. We will ride there and call Logres to council." He nodded to Lancelot and Bors. "Friends, are you with us?"

Lancelot bowed. "Sir, to the end."

"Bors?"

The quiet knight shook his head. "I am called to Brittany. King Ban my father is dying and I am chosen heir."

For a moment they stared at each other, the heir of Britain and the heir of Brittany, both Grail Knights. At last Perceval put out his hand. "We will lack your counsel, brother." He leaned back in his chair and closed his eyes for a moment. "Caerleon, then."

"Caerleon." Lancelot touched Sir Ector's arm. "We will leave you to rest." But at the door he paused and looked back and asked, "And the Queen?"

Blanchefleur felt an unexpected stab of pity. The waste of it, to give all that love and service, and to see it come to this. If he had never known the Queen, if he had loved Elaine and been content, how much heartache and destruction might have been avoided?

"She also went to Avalon."

"I see," he said, and closed the door behind him.

Blanchefleur retrieved an apple from the chest where she had tucked it, and sat cross-legged on the mat before the hearth. "Do you think he will find some happiness, now that Mother is gone?"

Perceval's words echoed her thoughts. "Certainly he would never have found it while she lived in Logres."

Blanchefleur tugged the silver moonstone ring from her third finger. They had exchanged rings again at the wedding, for the golden ring of Gawain had never fitted her terribly well, and after having worn it for so long on her forefinger, it felt a fitting piece of herself to give to Perceval.

"I can't think why I gave it up to you so readily, that morning in the pavilion," she said, holding the silver ring out to the light that filtered through the window. "I must have been in a fit of the sulks."

Perceval laughed.

"*Guinevera casta vera.* There it was, shouting at me all the time."

"And you never believed it."

She slid it back onto her finger. "No."

Perceval eased himself out of his chair and lowered himself to the floor beside her, where he tangled his hand into the hair at the nape of her neck, kissed her long and sleepily, and then lay down with his head settled in her lap. His eyes drifted shut.

"What do you think, Blanchefleur, of this kingdom we have inherited?"

"I like it. Do let's keep it."

His brow wrinkled. "In all earnest."

She tucked her hair behind her ear and said, "In all earnest, I feel I should be terrified. But I am not."

He laughed and cracked an eye open. "Why are you not terrified, Lady of Logres?"

She gave a little sigh. "Because…"

Because of a hundred things. Because Perceval had lived when all the chivalry of Logres went down in ruins. Because Sir Breunis had spared them at the end of every hope. Because an inexplicable impulse had held her back from agreeing when Simon Corbin first asked to marry her. Because although she had used the shadow knife amiss, the shadow knife had worked.

She smiled.

"How can I be afraid? All the awful mistakes we've made, and yet here we are. Still standing."

Perceval grinned and closed his eyes again. "And Logres also."

S.D.G.

The Great Houses of Britain

† - Knight of the Round Table

THE PENDRAGONS

Uther Pendragon (deceased): The first High King of Britain.
Igerne (deceased): Wife of (1) Gorlois, Duke of Tintagel, to whom she bore two daughters, Morgawse and Morgan, and (2) Uther Pendragon, to whom she bore a son, Arthur.

† *Arthur Pendragon*: The High King of Britain, son of Uther Pendragon and Igerne.
Guinevere: Daughter of King Leodigrance of Cameliard, wife of Arthur, mother of Blanchefleur.
Blanchefleur: Daughter of Guinevere and, at least officially, the heir of Arthur Pendragon.

THE HOUSE OF ORKNEY

King Lot of Orkney (deceased): The King of Orkney and husband of Morgawse.
Morgawse: Half-sister of Arthur. Wife of Lot, to whom she bore four sons. Queen-regent of the isles of Orkney.

† *Gawain*: The eldest son of Orkney, husband of Ragnell and father of Perceval.
Ragnell: A fay of Avalon, wife of Gawain.
† *Perceval*: Son of Gawain and Ragnell.

† *Gaheris*: The second son of Orkney, husband of Lyonesse.
Lyonesse: Wife of Gaheris and sister of Lynet.

† *Gareth*: The third son of Orkney, husband of Lynet.
Lynet: Wife of Gareth and sister of Lyonesse.

† *Agravain*: The fourth son of Orkney.

THE HOUSE OF GORE

King Uriens of Gore: The King of Gore and husband of Morgan.
Morgan, commonly surnamed le Fay: Half-sister of Arthur. Estranged wife of Uriens, to whom she bore two sons. Queen of Gore.
† *Ywain*: The elder son of Gore.
† *Mordred*: The younger son of Gore.

THE HOUSE OF BRITTANY

King Ban of Brittany: Father of Bors and Ector de Maris. Uncle of Lancelot, Blamor, and Bleoberis.
† *Lancelot of the Lake*: Foster son of Nimue. Champion of Guinevere. Father of Galahad.
† *Galahad*: Son of Lancelot and Elaine of Carbonek.

† *Bors*: Cousin of Lancelot.
† *Lionel, Blamor, Bleoberis, Ector de Maris*: Cousins of Lancelot.

Author's Note

DR GEORGE GRANT HAS SAID OF *The Song of Roland* that it is both entirely fictional, and more truthful than most history books filled with carefully verified facts. "Indeed, its true lies tell us much about ourselves, our world, and the shaping of Western Civilization that we might not otherwise know."

One might say the same of the body of legends known today as the Arthurian legendarium, or the Matter of Britain. Today scholars continue to debate the actual existence of the man whose adventures have come down to us in this form. Was there a real Arthur? Was he Roman in origin, or Celtic, or something else? What exactly did he do—unify feuding chieftains, build an army of warriors, or defeat Saxon invaders? About the only thing we *can* know for certain about the historical Arthur, if there was one, is that all the most well-known stories about him are certainly fictional. He cannot, in the fifth or sixth century, have known anything of the knightly code of chivalry, the technology, or the courtly love tradition that flourished from the twelfth to the fifteenth centuries, during which most of the great medieval Arthurian romances were penned.

My aim in *Pendragon's Heir* is not so much to use the Arthurian legends to construct something new, or to provide a faithful picture of any particular historical time, as it is to go back to the original Middle-English ballads and romances to demonstrate for my generation something of the purpose those original tales might have had for theirs. Accordingly, I have done precious little research into historical or any other kind of fact, for which I can give only a half-hearted apology. My focus has not been on fact and history, but on fiction, philosophy, and ideals; not on what the medievals *did*, but on what they *thought*, what they believed, and above anything else what they hoped to leave as a legacy to future generations. I hope that this story, however imperfect, has helped you to understand some of those dreams and ideals, partly because of their beauty, and partly because, to the medievals, those dreams and ideals were more important and more solid than anything else in the world.

IN THE TEN YEARS DURING WHICH I tweaked, refined, and occasionally wrote *Pendragon's Heir*, I received a great deal of help from a great many people. Thanks to Lorraine Black for lending me the story that started it all. Thanks to Rebekah White for critiquing Draft 1, to Alina White, Kate Saunders Britton, and Rosemary Williams for critiquing Drafts 2 and 3, to Schuyler McConkey and Christina Baehr for critiquing Draft 4, and to Elisabeth Grace Foley, David Noor, and Joshua Grubb for critiquing Draft 5. Thanks to my line editor, Sophia Field, and to my illustrator, Isaac Botkin, who also designed the drop caps, tweaked the cover design, and provided encouraging feedback. It has been a privilege to work with all of you.

I'm greatly indebted to Dr George Grant for the *Christendom* lecture series, Josephine Tey for *The Daughter of Time*, Roger Lancelyn Green for *King Arthur and His Knights of the Round Table*, Charles Williams for *All Hallows' Eve* and the *Arthurian Torso*, Christine de Pisan for *The Treasury of the City of Ladies*, Sir Thomas Malory for *Le Morte D'Arthur*, Saint Augustine for *The City of God*, and GK Chesterton for everything.

Dad and Mum and all my brothers and sisters, my debt to you is too great to be expressed on the back page of a sensational novel.

To all of you who gave me encouragement, friendship, help, and reproof over the years, I thank you. By investing in this author, you have invested in this book.

Let the words of my mouth, and the meditation of my heart, be acceptable in thy sight, O Lord, my strength, and my redeemer.

Suzannah Rowntree
February, 2015

About the Author

WHEN SUZANNAH ROWNTREE ISN'T TRAVELLING THE world to help out friends in need, she lives in a big house in rural Australia with her awesome parents and siblings, trying to beat her previous number-of-books-read-in-a-year record. She blogs the results at www.vintagenovels.com.

Suzannah is the author of non-fiction books including *The Epic of Reformation: A Guide to the Faerie Queene* and *War Games: Classic Fiction for the Christian Life*. In 2014 she published a novella titled *The Rakshasa's Bride*, a retelling of Beauty and the Beast. A second fairy tale retelling, *The Prince of Fishes*, is planned for release in 2015.

Pendragon's Heir is her debut novel.

10165606R00233

Printed in Great Britain
by Amazon.co.uk, Ltd.,
Marston Gate.